WEIRD THEOLOGY

Small Worlds Book 1

By Alex Raizman

For Laura. Without you, this never would have happened.

Table of Contents

Yesterday, upon the stair,
I met a man who wasn't there
He wasn't there again today
I wish, I wish he'd go away…
-From "Antagonish" by Hughes Mearns

Prologue

The Man in the Suit

"You have ruined my life," Ryan Smith said sourly.

The man in the suit didn't reply.

"Seriously," Ryan said, spinning his barstool around so he could look directly at the other man. "I know I haven't talked to you in a while, but I think that's the last thing I told you a few years back, and now I'm saying it again. You have ruined. My. Life."

The man in the suit didn't reply.

"Bartender," Ryan called over his shoulder. "How about one for my friend here?" He laughed and looked back at the man in the suit. "Wait, you don't drink, right? Guess I'll have to drink yours."

The man in the suit didn't reply.

"It's not about Karen, if that's what you're thinking. I didn't even like Karen that much. I mean, maybe I would have, if I'd gotten a chance to get past the worst second date ever."

"Hey, buddy," the bartender said. "I think you need to slow down."

Ryan turned back around. "I'm not drunk," he protested.

"You're definitely something," the bartender shot back.

"What? What did I do?"

The bartender rolled his eyes. "You've spent half an hour talking to your imaginary friend."

"Is the man in the suit here now?" Dr. Blankenship asked.

"Yes," twelve year old Ryan answered. "He's always here. What part of that is hard to understand? He was here

when you asked last time, too, and will be here if you ask again in five minutes."

"What is he doing?"

"He's taking notes. That's all he ever does."

Dr. Blankenship scribbled a note of his own, which was almost funny. Everyone in the room, it seemed, found Ryan fascinating.

"Does he ever talk to you?"

"No. I wish he would. I really wish he'd just disappear, but if he's going to stick around, he could at least say 'hello' or 'you doing all right'. You know?"

"And how long have you been seeing him?"

Ryan rolled his eyes. "You know you're like my fifth shrink, right? Isn't there like a file or something that gets passed to the next guy?"

"I need to hear what's going on from you directly, Ryan," Dr. Blankenship said soothingly.

"Fine. My whole life. He's been there every second of my entire life."

Ryan looked back at the man in the suit, who scribbled in his notebook and said nothing. "Right, there's no one there." He laughed again. "That's my fucking life, man…"

"Uh-huh," the bartender replied, scanning the room, probably wishing he could summon more customers.

"What's your name?" Ryan asked.

"Mike."

Ryan wasn't at all surprised that Mike hadn't asked for his name in return. *Don't talk to the crazies.* "Can I have another one?"

"I made it up," fifteen year old Ryan said quietly. He stared at the table, unable to meet his parents' eyes. "I'm sorry." He had practiced this dozens of times, but actually doing it was hard. "I think I was jealous of all the attention Isabel was getting, so I made up someone to pay attention to me. An imaginary friend, just like you thought. Then when I got older and kept talking about him, you started

paying attention to me, and...I liked that. For a while. Then I couldn't figure out how to tell you the truth."

Ryan forced himself to look up, taking in his mother's tears, his father's furious expression, and his sister's utter bewilderment. *There, he thought grimly.* I'm not crazy. I'm just a lying, attention starved asshole.

In the corner of the kitchen, the man in the suit wrote it all down.

"You know what's funny?" Ryan asked Mike. "People don't know something's weird until someone tells you it's weird. If we were all just smart enough to keep things to ourselves, we'd be able to ignore all the crazy shit that happens. That's my advice, man. If something strange is going on, just shut up about it. You'll be happier. Trust me."

"You should buckle up," Ryan said to his passenger. As always, the man in the suit did not respond except to write more notes. "Yeah, guess you don't have to," Ryan muttered, "you'd just float right through the dashboard, wouldn't you?"

The man in the suit didn't reply.

"What would happen if I ever beat you to the car? Can you run at seventy miles an hour? Would you just be waiting for me wherever I was going? What if the car was full? Would you, like, float on top of people?"

Ryan dropped his attempts at conversation-not that they ever mattered anyway. With his driver's license less than a year old, he didn't feel very comfortable with the slick roads and rapidly increasing snow. I should have left before it started, *he thought.* Well, too late now.

A few minutes later, the snow was blinding. Ryan gripped the wheel with both hands, leaning forward with his chest almost pressed into the steering column, like that would somehow improve his control, like it would somehow allow him to navigate the slick roads better.

It did not.

Ryan felt the wheel go wild in his hands as his car began to spin out of control. He forgot everything he'd learned in driver's ed and fought the skid.

Later, he wouldn't remember the accident clearly, but he would never forget what came next.

"Hey," he croaked. "Hey, man. I think I'm hurt pretty bad. Do you think I'm gonna die?"

The man in the suit didn't reply.

"Hey, could you say something? Anything? Please?"

The man in the suit scribbled busily in his notebook, and Ryan closed his eyes to wait for help. Or death. Or whatever came next.

"Have you ever had sex in front of somebody else?" Ryan blurted.

Mike sighed. "Seriously?"

"Oh, come on. That can't be the strangest question you've been asked in here."

"That doesn't mean it's a question I feel like answering."

"Got it," Ryan said. "So the answer's yes."

"No, it isn't. I'm not into that."

A flush had begun creeping up Mike's neck, so Ryan quickly handed him a twenty. "Here. That's for putting up with me. So we're cool, right?"

"Yeah, sure."

"I'm not into that either," Ryan said. "That's also been a problem for me."

"What did I do this time?" Jacqueline snapped.

Ryan winced. "You didn't do anything, I swear."

"Then what is it, Ryan? I try to be patient. I try to be understanding. But...honestly, if I didn't know better, I'd think you weren't into women."

"It's not that," Ryan protested.

"We're not in high school anymore, Ryan. We've been together for three years. I wouldn't care if you didn't want to, or you wanted to wait or something. But you

don't. You keep making moves and then freezing and I don't get why!"

Ryan looked at the man in the suit, standing in the corner of the bedroom and calmly taking notes. "I...can't."

Jacqueline had started to cry. "Why the hell not? What's the problem? And why aren't you looking at me?"

Ryan snapped his head back, but now Jacqueline was looking at the corner.

"You always do that, too," she said. "You stop, and then you look over there. Are you worried about hidden cameras? The government in your teeth? Just give me a reason."

Ryan took a deep breath. He couldn't bring himself to lie to her. I see a man in a suit, taking notes on everything I do. *But how do you say that? How do you tell someone you love that you're being haunted by someone no one else can see, and that you hid it from them for years? How do you make that seem anything but crazy?*

"I...can't."

Jacqueline looked at him, sighed, and stood up. "Then neither can I."

"You probably think I'm crazy."

"Yep," Mike said.

"I probably am. Doesn't matter," Ryan drained his beer and threw some more money on the bar, then turned back to the man in the suit. "Let's go."

Ryan could feel Mike watching him as he left the bar. He didn't care. He was used to being watched.

"You know," he said to the man in the suit, "people always talk about finding happiness. They want to know what the secret is. Funny thing is that I know. For me, it's simple. I would be happy if you just went away. Forever. Then my life would be normal."

Later, Ryan would remember that and laugh. Because when the man in the suit finally did walk away, that was when things really got weird.

Chapter 1

Ryan Smith was not a huge fan of souvenir shops. When he travelled - which was rare - he liked to *see* things and *do* things, and he liked to take pictures, but he had never understood people's compulsion to drag home shot glasses and snow globes and other random clutter. His sister Isabel, however, loved that kind of crap. When they were kids, even their thousandth trip to a local amusement park would inspire her to come home with a commemorative plate or tacky picture frame.

God, he missed her. He hadn't been surprised when Isabel had moved to California a few years back-she hated cold weather and considered rivers a miserable substitute for an ocean-but it had been a blow, especially coming so close to their parents' deaths. She had been a welcome constant in his life, unlike the decidedly unwelcome man in the suit.

The important thing was that Isabel was happy, and living the life she had always wanted...unlike Ryan who, at thirty, still wasn't sure what he wanted to be when he grew up.

He was in the middle of another mind-numbing morning of data entry when she texted "I miss Saint Louis". Glancing around to make sure his boss wasn't near his cube, he typed, "Yeah, the mosquitos miss you, too" and fired it back to her. She responded with a grossed out emoji.

She was in the land of beautiful beaches and year-round warmth and sun and pretty much everything she loved, but home was home. *I should send her a gift or something*, Ryan thought. *Something to remind her of home.*

That was all it took to encourage Ryan to stop taking work seriously. It really never took much-his job sucked, and if he actually gave it his full attention he'd blow his quota out of the water...and then his boss would probably increase it. By lunchtime, he claimed a stomach ache and headed out to go shopping.

Leaving the building, Ryan gave the man in the suit a sideways glance. After thirty years of being constantly followed by a silent, note-taking asshole that no one else could see, Ryan could actually forget about him every once in a while...but not for long. Every time Ryan heard someone complain about a hovering boss, spouse, parent, etc., he had to resist the urge to roll his eyes. They had no idea.

Tourist traps weren't common in Saint Louis - not the way they were in New York or Chicago or LA or other cities that had the kind of places that were big draws. Missouri, being in the middle of flyover country, had very little that was a major tourist haven. One exception was the Gateway Arch, a testimony to America's westward expansion. Knick-knack stores were able to survive close by, funneling tourists off the attraction so they could pick up miscellaneous items to remind them of their visit.

So Ryan found a suitably tacky store in the shadow of the huge monument and was soon wrist deep in a collection of random tat. He considered a marble with a model of the Arch in it, but it was too small, too easy to lose, and if he could find something flatter it would be cheaper to mail. The same went for the snow globes, although they were tempting because of Isabel's hatred of winter. *It might be worth the extra money,* he thought, but the decided against it. He didn't want to run the risk of it breaking in transit.

For a perverse moment, he considered asking his companion for his opinion. Sure, he'd say nothing, and just write it down in that damn notebook like he always did, but sometimes it amused Ryan to pretend the man in the suit would interact with him for once. *C'mon, Ryan, all you'll do is freak out everyone else in here.* For some reason, people got uncomfortable with someone talking to a person they couldn't see.

Imagine that.

Ryan had just about settled on a tacky key ring that said, "Show Me State" on it, but was still rummaging in the bin, when he heard a soft voice say, "Thank you."

Ryan turned, looking for the source of the voice, but there was no one near him. No one except the man in the suit, who was…

Who was *walking away.* He had his back to Ryan and was heading for the front of the store.

Ryan froze, looking at the man's back, which he had never actually seen. His silent companion had always been facing him, or right beside him, writing notes and refusing to give any answers.

And there will never be any answers if I just let him leave.

The man was already walking through the wall at the front of the store, and Ryan bolted after him.

"Wait, come back!"

A few people on the street turned to look, but Ryan ignored them and kept running. The man in the suit wasn't running away, just walking through the crowd at a relaxed pace that took him among and through every person who crossed his path. Literally through them - people passed through him without noticing he was there. Ryan, however, was a fully corporal human, and so he found himself shoving up against the crowd.

This man had put Ryan through thirty years of hell. People thought he was weird because he was always glancing at something none of them could see - cute when a cat did it, creepy when an adult did. Sleeping under that watchful gaze was a nightmare.

Ryan would be damned if the bastard was going to walk off after all of that without an explanation.

The man turned into an alley, and Ryan was grateful to duck out of the crowd, pushing past a pair of young women who shouted obscenities at him. Ryan felt a surge of relief. If the man in the suit had ducked through a wall, the chase would have been over in that instant. It had always seemed to Ryan that the man preferred to avoid walking through matter when he could, and this held true now.

"Stop! Just...stop! Please!"

The man...hesitated. He didn't turn around to look at Ryan, didn't speak, but he stopped walking and stared ahead at the brick wall.

"So you can hear me! Please, what's going on? Who are you? Why...why are you leaving?" Suddenly, the idea of the man *leaving* was every bit as bad as him staying. Now, Ryan could admit that there had actually been times when the man in the suit's presence had been a comfort. Ryan had never been alone in in his life, not in the way other people understood being alone. He'd had moments where he had no one to talk to, no one to interact with, but the man in the suit had been there, watching, writing. It was something.

When walking down a dark alley, heart pounding in fear that some murderer was going to hop out and stab him, he had at least known that someone would notice and write it down. When feeling alone and depressed, wondering if he even mattered and if anyone would notice if he was gone, the man in the suit had been there, letting him know that at least one person would.

On the whole it had been a nightmare, but nightmares still were dreams, and even though he had fervently wished to be alone, now that it might be happening the idea of losing his constant companion terrified him.

"I shouldn't be talking to you. I can't imagine how hard this has been." He paused and saw the fury in Ryan's face, and sighed. "Or...actually, I guess I can, I've seen it."

"Yeah, you have. Every day, for thirty years. I need something, man. You don't get to fuck up my life and then just walk away without saying anything! I have questions, damnit."

"You're going to have to be okay with not getting answers to most of these questions, Ryan. I'll give you this - one question, one answer. That's all you get."

9

"Only one question." Ryan made sure to keep his voice flat, so that last word couldn't be construed as a question, and to prevent himself from shrieking at the man. All this time, all this hell, and he only got one question? The first one that came to mind was asking him who the hell he thought he was.

"Yes," the man said. "More than most people get."

There was a finality to that tone, something that told Ryan it would be pointless to argue or vent his frustrations. So instead, question after question began to race through Ryan's mind. But he needed to ask the right question, if he was only going to get one. After a minute, maybe two, of standing there frowning in furious thought, it occurred to him. The question that would get him the most answers, and really, at this point, the only one that mattered.

"Why are you leaving?"

The man in the suit smiled. "Good question. And the answer is because my prediction was right - you were the one to find it." He saw Ryan's face, saw the confusion on it, and actually laughed. "Sorry for being vague. It's been awhile since I have spoken to anyone. You're one of over a thousand people who match some of our criteria as likely candidates. And...well, check your left pocket."

With a trembling hand, Ryan reached down into his pocket. His heart started pounding when he felt something in there. A couple somethings. He hadn't bought anything at the store...what was in his pocket? He fished it out.

One of them was the keychain that he had been intending to buy for Isabel, slipped into his pocket without thought when the man started running. *Gotta go back and pay for that.* The other object was a black marble flecked with glitter, something he vaguely remembered picking up to get to the "Show Me State" keychain. *Great,* he thought wildly, *more unconscious theft*. It didn't take any immense deduction to realize the keychain probably wasn't what the man in the suit meant.

"A marble?" It was a stupid thing to ask, and the man in the suit chuckled.

"Look closer."

So he did. He stared at the marble, and suddenly it seemed to expand, filling his entire field of vision. What he had thought were flecks of glitter in there were...stars. The swirl pattern in the center? A galaxy. It kept expanding, giving him an immense feeling of vertigo, like he was falling into the star field.

The man's voice seemed to come from far away. "You found a nanoverse. The last one of this Era, left behind by the Creator. We were watching to see who found it, to figure out who would be next. And now that it's been found...now that you're the one...my work is done."

Overwhelmed, Ryan squeezed his eyes shut and concentrated on his breathing. *This is too much. This can't be happening. I'm going crazy. Crazier.*

After a few seconds he opened his eyes and was relieved to see the alley instead of the impossible field of stars.

"What..." he gasped. "What was that?"

The man in the suit turned to walk away. "I told you, only one question. But I'll give you some free advice."

Ryan took another deep breath to steady himself. "Okay."

"Don't put it in a drawer and forget about it. You've got a pretty amazing thing there, Ryan. And in spite of the fact that I unintentionally turned you into a nervous wreck...I think you're going to do some pretty amazing things with it." The man in the suit smiled. "I've watched you your entire life, Ryan. I have faith you'll be able to pull this off."

Before Ryan could ask more questions that the man in the suit would not answer - what was a nanoverse, what he was supposed to do with it, what was he supposed to pull off, what the hell was going on - the man turned and walked through a wall. This time, there was no way around, no way for Ryan to follow. He was gone, and Ryan was, for the first time in his life, truly alone.

His mind was spinning. None of this made any sense, and Ryan felt like he needed a million years to process what was going on. Instead, he got seven seconds. Seven seconds where no one was looking at him, no one was writing down what he did, no one was watching him.

Then a gun cocked behind him, and a voice growled, "Put down the nanoverse, and you might get out of this alive."

***

Ryan Smith was the most boring human Enki had ever encountered. *And that's saying something for their kind*. Enki had spent most of his time watching interesting people. Warriors, conquerors, men and women who would shape history. Which Ryan Smith only had a tiny chance of ever managing. Hell, if things went the way Enki wanted them to, Ryan would only be a footnote in history. The man who'd found the nanoverse that had given Enki what he needed to escape the shackles of destiny.

The man who had given Enki what he needed to save the world.

The past year had been slow, dull work, following the Curator who was following the boring human. He couldn't risk being seen by either of them. No sane individual challenged a Curator directly, and one of the few things that could get them to act was trying to follow them.

But Enki had been sure that Nabu was worth following. This particular Curator had a great track record. Throughout the ages, he had consistently honed in on people who would find a nanoverse. With only one nanoverse left in this age, finding it before some dumbass human picked it up and stared into it was vital, so Enki had put his faith in Nabu, and he had been rewarded.

He'd waited almost ten thousand years for this.

This is it, Ishtar, he thought. *I know it is.*

Ishtar. Even after millennia, Enki's rage sometimes felt as hot as it had the day she had betrayed him. The lying traitor had been his friend, his ally, his trusted companion. He had forgiven her first lies, when she had claimed to be just like him, instead of admitting from the first that she'd hailed from a distant past, a time before humanity had even been a gleam in Earth's eye. When there were different continents, different lands.

She had told him of the death of her people, and his heart had broken for her. When she told him that it would happen again, he had believed her. One day, she had said, there will only be one nanoverse left, and when it is found, the end will be near. He had trusted her to know what to do when that time came. He had imagined that they would stand together.

Then had come Lamashtu, and the deluge needed to defeat her. Those horrors had opened Enki's eyes, and he had sworn he'd never let it get that bad again.

He had gone to Ishtar, and she'd betrayed him. They had all betrayed him.

Enki had accepted that he was alone, and that he was the only one who understood what needed to be done. He had made it his life's work to be the one to find that nanoverse. He would control destiny, and he would make the right choices.

His hands went down to his pocket, thumbing his own nanoverse. It was supposed to be impossible to command two of the things, but Enki had found a way. *And it's a hell of a lot easier if I beat this punk to claiming it.*

Loitering outside the souvenir shop, grimly reflecting on the past, Enki almost didn't notice Nabu strolling out through the wall. When Ryan bolted after the Curator, it took a second for Enki to process that Ryan was following Nabu, instead of the other way around.

He has the nanoverse! That was the only explanation for why the Curator would have left his subject. But if Ryan had looked into it, he would have been too shocked to chase. *He has it, but he hasn't claimed it. There's still time to get it before that fool ruins everything.*

Still time before I have to kill him.

Enki pulled out his gun and joined the chase. He was old fashioned and preferred swords and axes and weapons of a bygone age. But he'd brought a gun, because sometimes impressions mattered, and in this day and age people were more likely to respond to a gun than someone nutjob with an anachronistic armament. A guy with a sword was a lunatic, a guy with a gun was a threat. *And I sure as hell am not a damn lunatic,* thought the man who had spent a year following a boring bureaucrat following a human who might, only might, be able to get him what he wanted.

Enki began to draw on his power, preparing gusts of wind, storms, maybe even a fireball for effect. *No,* he thought. *That will spook him, and I don't want him to run. If he does, I'll probably be forced to kill him. If he gives me the nanoverse, I can spare him. If he doesn't, I can just take it from him.*

If he's claimed it, I'll definitely have to kill him. But no killing innocents unless you have to.

The only downside to a gun was that it wasn't part of Enki. Not like his clothes, or like a weapon he'd pulled out of the air. It was a physical object. It got stuck on things, on people. It slowed him down. It meant he missed whatever transpired between Ryan and the Curator in the alley.

But it also meant Ryan couldn't ignore it when Enki pressed it against the back of his skull.

Chapter 2

New Friends

Ryan's heart was pounding, and he turned around, every motion as careful as possible. The last thing he wanted to do was startle the brute into shooting him. To compare the man behind him to a gorilla would be an insult to the majestic apes. He was huge, the very definition of hulking, easily six and half feet and almost that broad at the shoulders. His brow jutted over his eyes, casting the little beads in a deep shadow. You couldn't compare tree trunks to his arms, because tree trunks weren't pale and bulging with muscle, and they didn't hold the largest handgun Ryan had ever seen, something so massive it looked like it had been drawn out of a cartoon or an over the top video game.

"Ohgodpleasedon'tkillme." Ryan's hands instinctively shot up in a "reach for the sky" gesture, and his knees threatened to buckle. Ryan had never seen a gun in person before, not a real one, much less found himself in a staring contest with the black pit of the barrel. This was a terror unlike anything Ryan could imagine.

The brute grunted at that. People passing the alley turned and gave odd looks at the exclamation, glancing at Ryan like he had lost his mind. He'd gotten such looks fairly often in his life, and as always, everyone was more than happy to ignore the obviously crazy man standing there. An unsettling realization built up in the small part of Ryan's brain not focused entirely on the gun.

"They can't see you, can they? I'm...I'm holding my hands up in an empty alley, as far as they can see."

"Yup."

"So...you'll pass through matter, too? If you shoot me, the bullet...it'll just pass right through me?"

Again, a grunt of "Yup." For a moment, Ryan felt a wave of relief, then noticed the evil gleam in the man's eyes.

He gulped, his mouth once again going bone dry as he realized that there were multiple ways to interpret that last question. "It'll just pass harmlessly through me?" Ryan asked, knowing a hopeful note was creeping into his voice, a note that didn't belong there with a man pointing a gun at his face.

That gleam in the man's eyes brightened, and Ryan began to recognize that in spite of his caveman appearance, there was intelligence in those eyes. "Nope."

"I...okay, you can have it."

"Good lad. Most of your kind isn't so reasonable. Just give it over here, nice and slow like, yeah?"

Ryan reached out, his hand clutching the nanoverse so hard his knuckles were turning white. The brutish man took one of his hands off the gun and held it out...and some perverse urge overtook Ryan. He was going to give it over, he really was...but then the last thirty years would have been for nothing. He'd probably be shot anyway, but even if he wasn't, he'd never know what it was all about.

So he took a gamble, and while the man was still reaching out, Ryan darted forward, straight at the brute. The best case was unlikely. The worse case was to smack into a small mountain of flesh and go tumbling to the ground. The *worst* case was for that horrible gun to go off, which would also send Ryan tumbling to the ground, but not in a way he would be getting up from.

Instead, as he hoped, he passed right through his mugger. The brute roared in anger and turned around. The whirling motion brought his hand in contact with the wall. He seemed startled when the gun clanged against the brick. It wasn't much, but it gave Ryan a chance to get a bit more distance between them before gunfire rang out.

Something tugged at Ryan's collar, and he knew with absolute certainty that he'd find a perfect hole inches from his neck. He ducked right after the tug, an entirely instinctive reaction that saved his life as another bullet parted his hair.

Adrenaline kicked in, and Ryan ran further into the crowd with a speed he didn't know he had. People were starting to scream and scatter as well - even if nothing else about the brute could be seen or heard by anyone else, the sound of gunshots was very real.

For a terrible moment, Ryan wondered if he was about to get some innocent people killed. He'd be relieved to learn later the first bullet had buried itself in a street light, and the second had in fact blown the head off of a mannequin in a store window across the street. Once he was fully into the crowd, however, the gunshots stopped. It seemed his attacker wasn't interested in collateral, and he was able to escape into the crowd.

***

Several blocks later, Ryan was in another alley, panting with fear. Without a direct threat, the panic of earlier was starting to fade, replaced by a bone deep fear and the gradual swell of the sea of questions.

He pushed them down. He was very strongly getting the feeling that, no matter what happened, he'd never get all the answers. And right now, only one mattered - had he been followed?

It didn't seem that way. Either the brute couldn't move all that fast, or hadn't known which way Ryan had gone. Glancing around again, and taking a deep breath, Ryan pulled out the nanoverse and held it up to his face again.

It was hypnotic. An entire galaxy spinning in a black sphere the size of a golf ball. It was much easier to see clearly than it had been earlier.

It's the size of a golf ball.

It had been a marble when he'd found it, right? He kicked his jumbled brain into going over the last few minutes. Yes, when he'd been talking to the man in the suit, it had been a marble. The fact that it was growing somehow was one more bit of unreality, just one more oddity in a day full of them.

Another realization followed that first one, this one slower but more inexorable. The man in the suit was gone. No one was watching Ryan. For the first time in his life, he

17

had privacy. He'd realized it in the first alley, sure, but that thought had been interrupted by the sudden threat. No one was watching him right now, something he'd wanted his entire life, even as he dreaded it.

And he'd never wanted it less. He slipped the nanoverse into his pocket and got back onto the street, joining the crowd, drawing strength in numbers. His attacker wasn't looking to kill bystanders, and if he decided to follow Ryan, Ryan wanted a chance to survive.

But the questions still burned at him, and the brute had given him another clue. He pulled out his phone and did a search for "nanoverse". The first couple results were some toy line, then some links to something from comics, then a company working on nanomachines. It wasn't until the second page of Google results, the home of the truly desperate, that he found something that looked relevant.

What Is the Nanoverse?

He tapped the link. The page it brought up did not inspire confidence. It looked like something that had been slapped together by a high schooler back in the Geocities days, and the last update to the page had been in 2006. He was about to hit the back arrow and check other pages when a photo loaded.

It was Egyptian, or something like it. The man it depicted evoked the brute from earlier. Ryan couldn't put his finger on it at first, since this man looked proud and regal, not like some sort of borderline ape-like killer. It was a very impressionistic work, like most early art. It wasn't until he looked at it for a bit longer that it started to make sense. The shape of the nose, the gleam in the eyes, the overall impression of the art just echoed that man. The caption labelled it as being from ancient Sumeria, and the figure as Enki, one of the chief deities of the region. The idea, crazy as it seemed, that he'd been attacked by someone who looked like an ancient drawing of a god would have been the focus of Ryan's attention in any other picture. However, one detail managed to outshine even that and fully captivate his attention.

The man was holding a small sphere, carved with smaller, starlike dots.

The crowd faded into the background. Ryan began reading.

The article was long, rambling, and poorly edited. It referred to Curators, mythological monsters, the Labyrinth, and Pantheons, and connected all of that to the Hollow Earth, Illuminati, chemtrails, Lemuria, the Bermuda triangle...it was a mess of random crap, but Ryan read it all, hoping for a nugget of truth in there. It took almost a half hour to read, and Ryan was all but done with the page.

And then he got to the last line.

"Of course, the only way someone could stand to read all that rubbish was if they actually found something. Click HERE to contact the website's admin."

He pressed it, out of desperation more than anything else. Instead of bringing up an email form like he expected, it gave him a phone number. More modern than the page seemed.

Hoping against hope that this would mean *something,* he hit call.

After a few rings, a voice on the other end answered. A woman's voice, sounding like she had just dashed across the room. "'ello?"

"Uh...hi. I'm calling about...the nanoverse?"

There was a pause on the other end. "Oh hell. Now? Of all times, *now*?" The broad sound to her vowels sounded to Ryan's American ears like a British accent.

The sheer irritation in her voice shocked Ryan. "Uh...sorry."

"I was just getting settled into this country. Fine, fine, it's not your fault love."

"Uhhh...what?"

Another pause, then a swear. "You're a local, aren't you?"

Ryan cut off yet another "Uh" from his response. "I think so?"

"Got the number off that bloody website, didn't you?"

"Yes." This one, at least, he could say with confidence.

"Scared half out of your mind and on the run from forces you can't understand?"

"Oh God, yes. Can you make sense of all of this for me?"

"Oh, oh dear. I can maybe help some." A pause during which he heard some tapping sounds, someone with long nails typing at a touchscreen. "Have you gazed into it yet? Rushing sensation, nanoverse filled your entire vision?"

"Yeah!" Relief. Finally, someone who could help him.

"Great, great." Her tone didn't sound like she thought it was all that great, but Ryan was still just ecstatic to have someone who was talking to him. "Turn left into the store, there's a dear."

He did. The door he stepped into belonged to some upscale clothing boutique.

The room, however, looked like a planetarium on steroids, a platform that was surrounded by open, starry sky. A tall woman, dark hair falling almost to her waist, stood in front of a bank of keyboards and monitors. She turned, and Ryan saw that despite the accent she didn't look British-not that British people all look alike, but her skin tone and bone structure suggested a Middle Eastern ancestry.

Then she glanced up at him through a few wisps of stray hairs that hung in front of her forehead, and Ryan saw her eyes. They were the oldest eyes he had ever seen, eyes that seemed to stare right through him and to the stars beyond. He didn't even register that she was frowning. "Do me a favor, love? When the view overwhelms you and you need to puke, stick your head out the door, yeah?"

Reeling from the shock of what he was seeing, Ryan did exactly that.

People tend to shy away from someone throwing up in the street, but he was still drawing stares. He pulled his head back into the door - and back into the strange room that seemed to stretch into infinity. It still made his head spin looking at it, but he fought back the nausea this time. He glanced out into the door behind him again, still seeing the normal city, before turning his eyes back into the room and seeing a field of stars and galaxies further than his eyes could process.

"There now, feel better?" The woman asked, her voice overly chipper.

"Ugh." Not the wittiest response in history, but everything was happening so fast that Ryan had not really had a chance to process everything. His brain was running a thousand miles a minute and he was holding on for dear life.

"Right, fair enough I suppose." The woman gave him a knowing smile, and Ryan wondered how many other people she had seen get sick at the sight of another universe inside a building. "What's your name?"

"Ryan Smith." He felt a bit bad for giving such short responses, but right now he felt proud he could manage to speak at all. His anxiety began to worm its way up his spine to settle into his brain. *You can't handle this. No one can handle this, but especially not you,* it whispered to him.

She gave him an encouraging nod, and if his brusque replies bothered her, it didn't show on her face. "Ryan Smith. Doesn't get much more generic than that, does it, love? Well, Ryan, your world's gone straight to bollocks today, hasn't it? You can call me Crystal, that's what I go by these days." The accent was starting to sound more and more like a bad impersonation. It was like something out of a film set in England but with American actors who had never actually spoken to a British person. A caricature, a fake.

And in the grand scheme of things, a totally irrelevant detail.

Even with the affectation, getting a name for one of these people was a huge relief. It made things real, made things anchored. She was not the mysterious woman with the British accent anymore, she was Crystal, a person with a name. The growing anxiety attack slunk away to crouch in the back of Ryan's mind. Without the bracing effect of the fear, he started to sink down to the floor.

Or at least, he would have, but the floor rose up to meet him, silvery liquid ooze that formed a chair under him. It might have been the most comfortable chair he'd ever sat in, perfectly molded to fit him. For a moment the anxiety tried to claw its way back in, but he was able to push it aside. When your day included talking to a mysterious man who had followed you your entire life, someone trying to shoot you to steal the pocket universe you were holding, and stepping into another universe in a storefront...the floor becoming a chair seemed much more manageable.

"Crystal." He clutched the name like every remaining bit of his sanity depended on it. "Thank you."

"I haven't done anything yet. At least let me help before you thank me." She flashed another quick smile and tapped on the computer screens a few more times. "There. That should give us at least a bit of time without interruption." She motioned, and the chair he was sitting on slid across the floor to where a table and another chair were forming. She took a seat in the new chair, practically flopping into it. "So...you, love, look like you've been having a hell of a day. Probably a hell of a life. Why don't you tell me about it, yeah?"

Despite his own questions building at the back of his mind, words came spilling out of Ryan's mouth. The man in the suit. The strange conversation. The nanoverse. The brute. Running. All of it, up until…

"So I googled nanoverse and I found your site and I clicked the link and a phone number came up, so I gave it a call and then you answered and you said-"

Crystal, who had been quiet throughout the entire thing, finally interrupted him with a soft and concerned tone, "Yeah, yeah, I remember that bit, was there for it."

Gentle tone or not, Ryan snapped his mouth shut, and felt himself blushing. "Right, of course. Sorry."

"No worries. Honestly, I'm shocked that looking into the nanoverse didn't completely fry your brain. As little as you understand..." She shrugged.

"Can I ask some questions?"

She nodded. "I'm sure you're just full to the brim with them. But before you do...a lot of the answers involve words your language doesn't even have concepts for. I'll do my best to explain, but I'll need to - no offense - dumb it down for you."

"No offense taken." Ryan had never felt dumber in his life, which after all the confusion of today was saying something. His life had been a steady barrage of weirdness, which helped some with accepting what was going on, but Ryan had never felt more lost. The one thing he was sure of was that he had almost been killed earlier today, and a smart man put survival in front of erecting a veneer of intelligence. He decided to start with one of the questions that was pressing on his mind the most. "What is a nanoverse?"

She smiled. "Exactly what it says on the tin. An entire universe, but in a little bubble you can stick in your pocket and carry around."

Ryan instinctively reached out to touch his pocket. The nanoverse was there, and as near as he could tell was bigger now, about the size of a pool ball.

"What...what do you do with it?"

For some reason that seemed to be the funniest thing Crystal had heard in quite some time. She laughed so hard she snorted. "Sorry, sorry, I shouldn't laugh, but...oh God, you humans! Found an entire universe big enough to fit in your pocket, and first thing you ask is 'what do you do with it?' Completely brilliant. I love you lot."

"You're not human?"

"Oh, no, of course not. 'What do you do with it?' Priceless!"

He frowned. "Why's that so funny?"

She let out a few more laughs, followed by a long, amused sigh. "Because it's just so...practical. Skips over the hows and the whys and the whos and just straight to the 'what do I do with it?'"

Ryan shrugged, looking at the floor. "Well...I don't mean to be rude, but you said we only had a bit of time?"

"Too right, sorry. You become a god is what you do. Ryan Smith, not the most divine name ever conceived, but give it a couple thousand years and it'll be up there."

"I'm sorry, become a what?"

"A god. Same as me, and that brute. That was likely Enki, by the way. Nasty piece of work, that one. You can even get some friends together, form a pantheon...and that nanoverse, that'll form the seat of your power. Your divine spark."

Ryan leaned forward, resting his head on his hands. It was good to have confirmation for the name of that trigger-happy bastard that had tried to steal his nanoverse. It made him seem less monstrous, more human, and therefore less oppressive.

Of course, it was marred by the idea that he literally was holding another universe in his pocket. The idea was several orders of magnitude more outlandish than being followed by an incorporeal notetaker. "I'm sorry, it's an entire universe? That...how is that even possible?"

Crystal shrugged. "How is it possible gravity curves both space and time, love? Roll with it, yeah?"

"I don't know if I can just roll with that."

"Look," Crystal sighed. "You've had someone no one else could see following you around your entire life, yeah? So, you already had a choice to make: you had to believe you were mad, or accept that there was magic in the world. Great news, love: I'm telling you it's the second."

That hit home. The relief rolled over him like a wave, almost bringing him to tears. He wasn't crazy.

When he was able to think about anything besides that, it finally sunk in that Crystal had also said there was a ticking clock over this whole affair. "Okay, fine. There's a universe in my pocket. So I...what, shape it, somehow? Get worshippers?"

Crystal was shaking her head. "Language is really difficult here. No worshippers, not anymore. We don't get power from that - most people are too bloody scientific these days for it to be much good anyway - but you do shape the nanoverse. Give it life."

"How?"

"You already are. Which is kind of bad, since you're full of panic and fear and confusion, so that's gonna be pouring into it." She gave him a concerned look. "Look, all of this is a metaphor for what's really going on. It'd be equally accurate to say you becoming an alien force working in the shadows, or a number of other things."

Ryan took a deep breath. "Crystal? Not helping."

"Right." Crystal shook her head. "Saying you're a god is what pretty much what everyone does these days anyway, so it should be fine. Take a bit to catch your breath. But, and not to put pressure on you, you don't have a lot of time to sort this out."

Ryan groaned into his hands. "Why not?"

"Most of us? We got centuries to work through all of it. Hell, I wasn't even human - my people predated you lot by a good million years. But that thing you got there?" She motioned towards his pocket. "It's the last nanoverse. This means that whatever else you are, and you could become, you're the Eschaton. Which means as you go through your personal apotheosis, you're also going to need to manage the end of the world."

"I'll need...what?" The anxiety came back now, stronger than ever. "You want me to end the world?"

"Oh, no, love. I don't *want* you to end the world." Crystal waved her hands as if she was trying to brush the thought away. "I'm just saying you *are* going to end the world, no matter what you want."

"I..." Ryan took a few deep breaths, but his heart was pounding. Despite being in a room the size of a universe, it felt like the walls were closing in.

The human brain is an interesting thing. It was designed for apes that wandered the beach and picked up food, did some hunting, maybe managed some interesting vocalizations. It was an adaptable tool, to be sure, one that was able to navigate cars far faster than the little apes could have ever imagined going, it could process all the information of the modern age, and it could even take the apes beyond the atmosphere and to the nearest space rock.

But sometimes, it was over capacity. Sometimes, events were too much, too weird, too mind blowing for it to keep running the way it was supposed to. In such cases, it had a number of defense mechanisms available to it. Ryan's brain flipped through the available options like they were a flipbook of possible breakdowns. In an instant it considered tears, denial, turning into a complete nervous wreck, and ultimately decided it would be best served by just shutting down for a bit.

As Ryan fainted, the chair shifted so he wouldn't land too hard on the floor.

Chapter 3

When Ryan came to, he was in a bed. For one sweet, blissful moment, he thought it was his bed, in his apartment. He'd roll over and open his eyes and the silent man in the suit would be taking notes and none of this would have ever happened.

When he opened his eyes, there wasn't any such luck. He was in a strange bed in a strange room, and the ceiling above him was an open sky of galaxies, and instead of the man in the suit there was Crystal in a dress.

"Oh, good, you're awake." She looked up from the tablet she was tip-tapping away on. "You'll probably be doing that a few more times."

He groaned as he sat up. "There's that many more Earth shattering revelations?"

"Well, yes, I suppose that's true too. But mostly it's your brain reconfiguring to fit your new role. Tends to lead to fainting." Her tone was matter of fact, and she tapped away at the pad.

"My...what?"

She sighed and took off her glasses, giving him a bored look. "Ryan, love. You're a perfectly intelligent individual for the limitations of your species. You know exactly what I said. Your little nap used up much of our completely safe time, and I could give you an entire textbook to try and explain it all and by the time you got done reading it, you'd understand only a tenth of what it was saying. Try to just roll with things, yeah?"

Ryan took a deep breath. "Okay. But I need to ask a couple more questions, at least." She motioned for him to go along. "First, who was the man in the suit?"

She shrugged. "Exactly who, I don't know. There's lots of those buggers running around. Gone by different names throughout history, but they go by 'Curators' in our circles. They make sure things don't go too out of sorts."

Ryan felt more follow up questions building but reminded himself of what Crystal had said. "Okay. I'll roll with it."

She smiled. "Good, you can learn! And the other?"

"What does Enki want with me?"

Crystal sucked in air between her teeth. "Ah. Good question. You're bound to the nanoverse now, yeah? Well, none of us has ever managed to hold on to two of the things. He gets that, he'd be the most powerful, without question. So he wants your nanoverse, and he wants you dead so he can claim it."

"So...just giving it to him isn't an option?"

"Not while you're alive." She cocked her head a bit as he got the rest of the way out of the bed. It was silver, like the chair had been, formed out of the floor. As he stood up, the bed flowed away like it had never been there. She gestured, and a chair formed for him to sit in. "And I'd prefer it if even if you decide you'd rather not be alive, you don't give it to him. Enki is a right bastard."

"Okay. But I'm good. Want to stay alive for now."

She chuckled again. "For now? Love, you're immortal now. Staying alive is going to be easy, especially once you learn to master your new powers."

"I have powers? Like...flying and lightning?"

"Maybe. It varies for everyone, depending on your personality and your nanoverse. You can selectively filter the perceptions of lesser minds, ignore things like walls and crowds, and if your nanoverse is intact and hasn't been compromised by another god, you'll come back from pretty much anything. Eventually. It'll take a while for you to sync up to it fully enough, yeah? You're still undergoing Apotheosis, what we call a Nascent. You're vulnerable right now."

"Wait, Apotheosis? What do you mean-"

Crystal wasn't interested in waiting for Ryan to finish the question. "Apotheosis. The act of fully becoming a god. It's a subtle change, but once you're done you'll have the full powers you're capable of. Nowhere near as dramatic as being Nascent - becoming a baby god. Which, love, you are."

Ryan blinked a few times to process that. He was a long way from accepting it as gospel, but saying 'that's impossible' felt like a waste of breath. "Okay. How long..."

"Nope!" She interrupted, her voice full of false cheer. "Question time is over, Ryan Smith, the dullest named god in history. For starters, roll with it, remember? Second of all, we're here."

"We're...here? Where's here? We didn't go anywhere."

"Sure we did, love. You think this is just for show? We're in my..." She tilted her head and tapped her chin. "Let's call it a ship."

"A planetarium ship?" Ryan asked with a frown.

"Sure, yeah. Why not, that's a fine name." The door appeared against the wall. "Why don't you go ahead and look? It'll be awhile before Enki thinks to look here. Try not to faint or vomit again, love."

He opened the door and peered out. He hadn't felt any movement, any motion, but there was no question that they weren't at the same storefront they had gone through before. Or the same city. *Or the same sky,* Ryan thought, his eyes drawn upwards. The sky above him wasn't like anything he'd ever seen. It was full of planets that hovered close to the ground, dozens of them, the smallest one twice the size of the moon and easily as bright.

Some had rings circling them, others seemed to have their own shattered moons. They didn't appear stationary either, but danced across the sky in an impossibly intricate ballet, dancers ducking and weaving amongst each other in ways that gravity would never have allowed. As he watched, the planets got larger and smaller whenever they passed into a new section of the stained-glass sky. The whole tableau would have been nauseating if it wasn't so fascinating.

From behind him, Crystal said, "Welcome to Cipher Nullity. It's not a wretched hive of scum and villainy - it's where you go where you're trying to hide from one of those hives."

Ryan registered her words and filed them in the back of his mind to process when he could stop gaping at the landscape. That sky drew his eye, and it was an effort to force himself to look away and at the ground. The earth - or rather, the surface of Cipher Nullity - was a collection of dust that looked black, except where the wind whipped it up into a cloud to show that it was actually made of tiny particles of every color that shimmered into a rainbow when they caught the planetary light from above.

This field of iridescent dust led to a city, an old one. *No,* Ryan corrected himself, *not an old one, an ancient one.* Many of the structures showed serious signs of erosion from age and the multicolored dust. Even so, what was left were still massive ruins of golden stone, forming pillars and pyramids. In spite of the beauty, there was an empty sadness to it - it screamed that it was once grand and glorious.

Ryan had encountered a word, shared in some useless social media list that flitted about the internet, something like "20 Words We Should Use but Don't! (You'll Want to Use #7 Right Now!!)". The word had stuck with him, one he'd never thought he'd use but perfectly summed up what he felt watching the dust storms weave though pathways that hadn't known footsteps in millennia: kenospia. It was the feeling that you get when something is empty and shouldn't be. When you could sense the life and energy that had filled a place that was now desolate, and couldn't help but feel sad that it was gone.

Staring at this grand, glorious, and abandoned city, Ryan was overwhelmed with kenopsia down to his bones. He felt his vision grow dark again, but Crystal was there in a flash, a hand on his arm, gentle and reassuring. Real. "We'll be safe here for a while, love. Not because Enki can't get to us here - he can - but he won't think to look."

Ryan took a deep breath. "What is it? Another world?"

She smiled at him, and if Ryan was floating in a lake of kenopsia, Crystal's smile was an ocean of it, a sea of loss. "Something like that. It's a long-abandoned afterlife. No one's been here for at least a hundred millennia, and all the souls that were here have faded away." Ryan focused on her eyes, which was a mistake. There was pain in them, pain and wonder and sadness and bliss and more emotions than Ryan thought he'd ever feel in a normal lifetime.

She continued, "The gods of Lemuria - yeah, it was real - built it for their worshippers. It was a heaven." She pointed at the central pyramid. Time had worn away a huge chunk of it, leaving it bare and exposed, like a wound. "That was Mount Olympus for them. Where they ran an entire continent *like* gods and incidentally protected the little universes where they actually *were* gods."

He felt goosebumps rising on his arm. "What happened to them?"

She didn't look at him, instead casting her gaze over the abandoned city. "The last Eschaton did. Lemuria, Atlantis, Mu, Hyperborea, Leng...the five continents of the last world, making the seabed of the new one. One of the greatest eras this world has ever had, the people that came after the Saurids and before humanity. Ten billion people - and six different species, the only era this world ever had with multiple sapiens - walked the world. They were about to leave, about to go into space...and then it ended. But still...you should have seen it."

He gulped. "I know you said not to...to just roll with it, but...is that what I'm going to do? Will someone be standing in...I don't know, Hades or something, talking about the Americas and Europe and Asia and Africa and Australia and all of it, and how I destroyed it?"

She turned back to him, putting a hand on his cheek. Every one of those millions of emotions he had seen in her eyes before crystallized into a single one, into a determination so hot and fierce he thought for a moment he would be incinerated in it. The kind of determination that was only born of loss and pain. "Not if I have anything to say about it, love. Let me show you around."

And keeping a firm grip on his arm, she led him into the wasteland of a Lemurian afterlife.

Chapter 4

Ryan spent the next couple hours following Crystal through the ruins of Cipher Nullity. She talked almost without breath about what they were seeing – "This was the Palace of Lost Souls, where children who didn't outlive their parents were cared for until the parents arrived and got to be reunited. Heartbreaking every time we got a new arrival, but just melted your heart every time we got a reunion. I remember this one time..."

He studied the building as she spoke. It reminded him somewhat of the Parthenon in Greece, in that it was a shadow of its former splendor. Instead of columns the pillars were shaped like elongated beehives, honeycombed with tiny hex shapes that contained statues. Even sheltered from the wind as they were, the ages had worn them down to indistinct blobs. He was going to ask a question, but like a tour guide on coke, Crystal was already dragging him to the next building without pause.

"So this was Reliquary of Squandered Dreams. One of the punishments the Lemurians had for those who sinned in life was a particularly nasty piece of work – you got to watch, over and over, what your life would have been like if you had actually followed your dreams. Never had anyone make it to the last bit – most people bloody begged for some other punishment after getting to early adulthood. I wouldn't go in there, love, it might still work, and we wouldn't want you getting all depressed..."

This building stood on top of four columns that were wider at the base and the top than the center. The area in the center of the structure was arranged like a theater, and the seats circled a central dais where Ryan supposed their occupants would see their failures in life played out for their torment.

Ryan heard the warning, but curiosity was strong. *What* would *life have been like if I'd taken more chances?* When Crystal turned to the next bit of architecture, Ryan stepped inside.

Ryan blinked.

"I see a man in a suit, Jacqueline, okay? There's some guy in a suit that follows me around everywhere I go, and no matter what I do, I can't not see him. Everywhere, for as long as I can remember! Therapists couldn't help me. I finally told my parents I made it up. That's what I'm always looking at, and every time things get close, he's right there and I'm uncomfortable."

Jacqueline stared at him, and as Ryan watched, the anger melted away. She reached over and pull him close. "Why didn't you tell me?"

Ryan blinked.

"...so I'm giving up on making him go away. It's about coping skills. I already have some, and I'm going to get better at it. Learn to live with it, you know?" He smiled at Jacqueline. "I can't believe you're still with me. I mean, now that you know I'm crazy."

Jacqueline gave him a kiss. "It's an ok kind of crazy," she said.

Ryan laughed.

"I'm serious," she told him. "It is...strange, but it doesn't change your personality, or make you dangerous. And you're coping. You're like the guy in that Russell Crowe movie."

"A Nobel Prize winning genius?" Ryan grinned.

"Dream on." Jacqueline paused for a moment, eyes narrowed in thought. "Hey, I've been thinking...the man in a suit? Is he wearing night vision goggles?"

Frowning, Ryan shook his head. "No, why do you ask?"

Jacqueline reached across him and hit the light switch, plunging the room into darkness. "Can you see him right now?" she whispered, directly into his ear.

"No," Ryan said, his voice low.

"Then...do you think he can see you?"

Ryan felt his eyes widen, his heart rate speed up. "No, I guess he can't."

Jacqueline kissed him again. "Then let's turn on some music so he can't hear what comes next."

Ryan gasped, trying to move, but the vision kept going, speeding up-

Blink.

Ryan was in a restaurant, down on one knee, looking up at Jacqueline's stunned face. "Will you marry me?"

Tears in her eyes. "Yes! Yes!"

Blink.

Jacqueline in a wedding gown, so amazingly beautiful.

"You may kiss the bride."

Blink.

A baby in Jacqueline's arms, wrapped in a pink blanket.

Make it stop…

Blink.

A four or five year old girl running towards him, leaping into his arms.

Blink.

Ryan could feel tears streaming down his face, his hands shaking. He tried to tear himself away from the vision, but-

Blink.

"Oh, you stubborn wanker." There was someone there, a woman he didn't know, and she was grabbing him, pulling him away from his family...

Ryan tumbled back to reality with Crystal's arm crossed over his chest like she was dragging him from a burning building. He fell on his back and laid on the ground, shuddering.

"I told you not to look. Bloody hell, was it worth it?"

"I…" Ryan took a deep breath. "I screwed up. Oh goddamn did I screw up."

Crystal sighed and reached out to pat him on the shoulder. "We'd all have lived a better life if we had perfect foresight. That's why it's a punishment and not a reward, love. Now dust yourself off, yeah?"

Ryan took a deep, ragged breath and got to his feet, doing his best not to look back at that damned echo of could have been.

Crystal nudged him when she caught him looking over his shoulder. "Stop it. The past is in the past, and those are for the dead, not the living. C'mon, you should see this."

As they walked away, Ryan decided this was the cruelest punishment he could imagine. *I'm still alive. I can start taking chances.* For the dead, though? Every person - and that included Lemurians, he supposed - was full of regrets and doubts. To see that your life would have been, without doubt, better if you had pushed yourself was a special punishment. *Then again, if you know this awaits you in the afterlife, probably a good motivator to take more risks in life.* That thought was a nice distraction from his grief at what he'd never even known he'd lost. He wondered what that would do to a society, having something like that as a central part of their mythology. He would have asked Crystal, but she didn't seem to be interested in questions, instead telling him every story, every fact she could think of.

Ryan wondered how long she had been waiting to show this to someone.

Her voice and her stories washed over Ryan in a calming tide. Having an excitable woman who was also a long-lost goddess explain the ruins you were walking through wasn't anything close to "normal", but for Ryan, it was at least grounding. Sure, the buildings were weird and empty and kind of sad, and that impossible sky made his head spin, but the more she talked, the more things made sense, and the more he felt like maybe he'd be able to make sense of all of this before he died of old age. *Except you won't anymore, you've got thousands of years, don't you?* Ryan let Crystal's voice wash away that thought.

"What did those pillars do?" he asked, staring at a trio of pillars that were interwoven with obsidian lines that branched out like a spider web to form a gaping mouth at their base.

"Oh! Those were amazing. They held a Soul Forge, churning out new ones. Some people elected to get reincarnated, so they could also just step in, get broken down into a new soul, and sent back up to get a second shot at life. Always a gamble, sure, but it paid off – especially if you went into the Reliquary of Squandered Dreams first. Souls that knew what you could do if you didn't quit, they were hungry when they got topside, and their second go-around really produced some amazing art and science, yeah? Wish some of the afterlives of this era had kept the combo around. You could also-"

Sudden panic gripped Ryan as he noticed something, and he clamped a hand over Crystal's mouth. She let out a "mmmfh," looking at him in angry confusion.

"I saw something move," he half whispered, his heart pounding. She reached up and gently moved his hand away.

"Okay. Where?"

He pointed down a side street. "Over there, by the giant statue." Nothing was moving there right now. The statue was a strange sight, to be sure – a man, legs missing any connection above the knees, so the body hovered over where the thighs would be. His head was likewise not connected to his shoulders, and the face was just a giant, open mouth. On either side of his body, three or four dozen hands floated – if they had been connected to arms, they would have overlapped terribly, but without arms they were free to move about like they were attached to the shoulder. Ryan was wondering how they hung there when Crystal's face went white.

"That's not a statue. Ryan, bloody get behind me."

A small, Neolithic part of Ryan balked at the idea of getting behind a woman for protection, but his rational brain and survival instinct teamed up to kick that thought in the gut and throw it down some stairs, and his feet carried him behind her. She was a goddess. "What is it?" he asked, ducking his head just enough so her slight frame would cover more of his body.

"It's a Hecatoncheires. And it's probably getting ready to-" Whatever Crystal thought it was getting ready to

36

do didn't matter, because it started to act – and that act was to charge. That open mouth was screaming now, and it was not the deep bellow of rage Ryan expected from such a giant, but a high wail of grief and sorrow. When it got near it swung at Crystal with fifty fists, and Ryan realized he was going to die.

Crystal, however, drew a sword out of the air, and her hand moved so fast it was just a pale blur. Every single one of the oncoming hands was blocked in less time than Ryan needed to blink, and the giant recoiled, letting out another one of those wails. Red lines erupted on the knuckles of every fist – she hadn't just parried them, but cut them.

It moved again, bring both sets of hands to bear. The palms were open this time, and Ryan realized that it intended to clap her to death.

He turned his head away before he heard the impact. The sound was like a fatal applause, one of those group single claps they have you do at award ceremonies to prevent every single name from taking forever. It was not, however, the wet squish he would have expected.

Trembling, he looked. Crystal was standing atop the pile of hands, balanced on her toes. The hands began reaching for her, grasping and clutching, but she danced along them, leaping and bounding from hand to hand and then flicking away before they could close on her feet. Each step took her higher, and then everything changed. Ryan saw more than her movements. He saw equations. He recognized force = mass x acceleration as the simplest of the math whirling around the fight, and there were others full of Greek letters and cos() and symbols you didn't learn until more advanced mathematics. They resonated with Ryan – it was a mathematical map of her movements, and a graph of the likelihood the hands would catch her. It was the most beautiful thing Ryan had ever seen.

Ryan stared at the graph, in awe at the shifting equations, the stunningly fast calculations. It was like he was able to see the primal beauty of the universe laid out in numbers and letters and it almost brought him to tears.

It was also a representation of a monster try to rip his new friend apart.

The equations fled from his vision. She had, as the equations had predicted, danced her way up to where the Hecatoncheires was reaching straight up for her, and finally pushed off those tallest hands in a graceful arc. She did a lazy half-flip as she reached her leap's apex, and then pushed off something Ryan couldn't see. It was a jump that flung her downwards far quicker than gravity would allow. It caught the Hecatoncheires off guard, and although it brought its hands together to grab her, it was too slow. She slipped through an instant before the hands closed around her and brought the sword down straight into its open mouth.

Instead of gurgling or gasping or even visibly dying, it just exploded. Chunks of ink-black flesh were flung away from it – many of them headed right for Ryan. He had an instant to wonder. *Is this going to just coat me with goo? Or am I about to have every bone in my body broken before I dissolve from whatever is in that - why the hell am I not moving?* But as Ryan braced himself for the impact, the chunks passed through him like they were made of shadow.

Ryan stared at his chest, wondering if he should be expecting to see some trace, some residue, perhaps even his own mangled body. Instead he was completely untouched, and no trace of them existed anywhere he could see. *So standing still and doing nothing is a viable strategy? That's...that's awesome. That's probably my best skill. I am the world champion of inaction. If there was an Olympic medal for inertia, I'd take home the gold.*

In a daze, Ryan looked to where the creature had been standing. Crystal was there, crouched in a perfect three-point landing, her sword arm parallel to the ground. She smiled at Ryan. "Oh, good!" she said, like she hadn't just impaled a giant in the mouth. "You figured out how to phase, so we don't need to clean the bloody goo off you."

"Ah." His head was pounding. "Uh..." His vision began to darken, a collapsing tunnel around his eyes.

"Oh bloody hell you're about to fa-"

Crystal likely finished the word, but Ryan didn't know. His vision completed its darkening, and he fell to the ground. The last thing he saw as he did so was an incredibly complex equation that he knew governed how that stained-glass sky stayed in place.

**

This time, Ryan wasn't out long enough to be put into a bed. When he came to, Crystal was crouched over him in the sand.

"I saw math," he croaked at her.

She blinked. "Damn. That's a terrible thing to have to see."

"I don't see anything wrong with it." Crystal blinked at him, and Ryan shrugged. "I thought it was amazing." She put the back of her hand to his forehead and made a tutting sound.

"What's wrong?"

"Well, besides the fact that you enjoy the maths?" Ryan scowled, and Crystal grinned. "Oh, I have no idea what that's supposed to do. Just saw it on the telly." She grinned and offered him a hand. He took it. "But likely nothing. Your brain is still adapting to its new capabilities. Seeing maths is probably just a way of processing it. Hopefully it passes and your brain doesn't decide that is the absolute best way to see the universe."

"I don't want it to pass!" Ryan blurted. "It's the best thing about this mess so far."

Crystal shook her head. "And I'm the odd one?" She gave him another smile. "It won't pass, not really. But you might get sick of it after a few thousand years, love. I know I bloody did."

He was on his feet, and his head was pounding. She glanced downwards. "Oh god, please tell me that's your bloody nanoverse in your pocket."

He looked at the bulge and blushed. At some point in the passing out the pants had gotten twisted, and the lump created by the nanoverse was awkwardly placed. He shifted his pants around and pulled the nanoverse out. It was about the size of a baseball, maybe slightly larger.

"It's so big," she said, wonderingly, and his blush deepened. She gave him a grin. "Teasing you, love. But you should probably soak some of that power out before it gets too big to carry easily, yeah?"

"I...sure? So how do I do that?"

"Remember what we said about rolling with it?" He nodded, and she continued. "So, roll with it love. You have a bloody universe of power in a little ball in your pocket. What do *you* think you should do to get power out of it?"

After a moment's hesitation he took the nanoverse and cupped both his hands around it, so they were almost completely covering it. Feeling silly and wondering what Crystal would do when this failed, he squeezed.

The sensation was difficult to describe. It was like someone had stuck an IV in each arm and in one was pumping ice cold water, in the other boiling tomato soup. It was like being smacked in the face with a sock full of gold-plated dandelions. It was like being shot to death with down feathers freshly plucked off a duckling. With every nanosecond, it was like increasingly unlikely similes, until it was finally like having your cheeks sliced open with the first rays of a dawn while chugging molten lightning.

He didn't pass out again, but he did scream. Crystal took a step back, smiling. "Oooh, yeah, should have warned you. First time is a bloody bugger of a rush, innit?"

Again he noticed that her accent was forced. He didn't think any British person would call something a bloody bugger, although he wasn't sure. He wasn't sure of anything, he was light, he was sound, he was...feeling pretty dizzy.

"I'm gonna..." Before he could say, he sat back down hard.

"Oh, please don't pass out again."

"I won't. Just...give me a moment."

She did, giving him some time to gasp until he was back into the realm of normal sensations and sensible analogies, where it just felt like the time in college he had downed way too much caffeine after pulling three straight all-nighters, and not because he had a paper to finish. This time, it had been on a camping trip with friends, and it had been the highlight of his college career. Drinking, telling stories, spending time with people - and best of all, the thick brush meant that for most of the time, the man in the suit had been partially obscured so Ryan could almost forget he was there.

"Okay. I'm good. Wow." He stood up on his own again, then gave a bit of a shiver.

"Right? It's a good look on you, too."

He glanced down. His arms were thicker and the musculature was more defined, and his gut was pulled back under his shirt. He hadn't been in terrible shape, just the general pudginess you get when your metabolism slows down but you don't change your diet or exercise at all. *Holy shit. All those fad diets, all those unused gym memberships, and all of a sudden I look like...this?* He looked up at Crystal with eyes wide and full of wonder. "Squeezing a universe made me ripped?"

She laughed at that for a couple moments, wiping her eyes after she did so. "Not exactly. You're getting the ability to impose your will on reality. And most beings, first thing they do - subconsciously - is turn themselves into an idealized version of what they look like. Later on you'll have more control over it. For now..." Her eyes sparkled. "Squeezing a universe made you ripped."

"Oh." A thought crossed his mind as he pulled himself back together from regaining awareness and then the rush of squeezing the nanoverse. "Wait. Hang on. What the hell was that thing?"

"I told you, it was a Hecatoncheires." Crystal said, if that explained...well, as if that explained *anything.*

"Pretend I don't know what that means," Ryan said, feeling a slight annoyance at yet another non-answer from his companion.

"It's a giant bloody beasty with a hundred hands. The Greeks thought they were as dangerous a bloody titan, but they were wrong."

"So on top of gods, monsters are real?" Ryan asked, wondering if he was ever going to run out of bad news to receive.

"Oh, of course. The details don't matter, love, not really. Roll with it for now?"

Ryan's nostrils flared at the catchphrase, but he pushed it aside. "Fine. If there was a Hecatoncheires here, couldn't we still be in danger?"

She shook her head. "Was wondering how long it would take you to think of that. No worries, love, I checked while you were having your nap. We're clear."

The tension that had sprung up faded away. "That's...thanks."

She cocked her head at him. "Ryan. You're on another world, just watched me kill a giant, and got your first taste of the rest of your life and seemed to like it. Why the bloody hell are you all frowns and brooding all of a sudden?"

"It's just..." He chewed his lip for a moment. "I felt powerful, when I got that energy. Powerful enough to do anything. Leap a tall building, run a marathon, and slay a dragon – all at the same time," She kept her head cocked and quirked an eyebrow. "Powerful enough to end the world," he finished.

"Oh." She nodded and put a hand on his shoulder. "Try not to let it get to you, yeah?"

"The fact that I'm going to end the world? How the hell do you not let *that* get to you?" Images had been flashing through his mind. Some were big and terrifying. His sister, burning in some kind of nuclear fire. His friends from college running screaming from a tidal wave that had swept miles inland. Scenes drawn straight from one of Roland Emmerich's fever dreams, nightmares of crowds of people fleeing a disaster that they could never escape. Bruce Willis wouldn't take the drill to space; Will Smith wouldn't fly Jeff Goldblum into the alien mothership. On top of that, little things. Never knowing how the Marvel movies ended. Not getting to find out what successor to Dark Souls came out. Not getting to see how A Song of Ice and Fire finished.

Granted, that last one might not happen either way, but *still.*

"You roll with it. All you can do."

"I know you said that, but Crystal...can I avoid it?"

She sighed. "Way to ruin the moment, Ryan." There wasn't any actual anger in her tone. "Technically, you can, but I wouldn't recommend it. Things get ugly if you do."

"How?"

"This is one of those things where I can't explain how. You won't understand enough. But short version? And you won't ask any more questions about it for now?" He nodded. "If you don't end the world, my little Eschaton, then the world dies."

He felt himself blink, opened his mouth, remembered he had agreed not to ask any more questions, and closed it. Then he opened it anyway. "That's not a fair answer, that doesn't make any damn sense. If I don't end the world than it dies? How is that an okay answer to that question?"

Crystal took a deep breath. Not a sigh, more like she was bracing herself. "You know what, love, you might be right. Might. But our time isn't infinite, and right now I'm the only friend you have. So can you *please* accept that for now and give me a sodding inch of trust?"

Ryan felt he'd been fairly trusting so far but raised his hands in submission. "Okay. I guess that'll make more sense when I understand more."

"Yeah, too right it will. Glad to see you're catching on." She forced a smile back on her face, and Ryan acknowledged the olive branch with a grin of his own. "So instead of focusing on that, why don't we head to Earth? It's been long enough Enki has got to be thrown off your trail, yeah? Let's see what you can do, now that you've seen the math."

Ryan considered for a moment. The idea of putting himself back in Enki's line of sight was enough to make him start to breath heavier, to start feeling his heart rate accelerate. On other other hand, he'd have Crystal with him. He'd seen her take out the Hecatoncheires like it was nothing. *Surely, she could take on Enki if he pops up.* "If you're sure it's safe."

"Of course I am," she said brightly, grabbing his hand. "Time flows funny; it's been a week back in the Core world, so he's probably buggered off to do something else. Come on, let's go."

And before he could try to ask any more questions – and get told to roll with it, he was sure – he was getting dragged back to the doorway to the planetarium ship.

Chapter 5

A Storm Gathers

When Ryan stepped out of the door again, it wasn't into a city at all. The door now lead out the back of a highway gas station, a run-down one near a sign saying Kansas City - 180 mi. The gas station was old and run down - not the complete run-down that comes from being abandoned, but the one that comes from low business, minimal visibility, and an absolute lack of shits being given.

He glanced up, and instead of the stained-glass sky of Cipher Nullity, there were clouds that loomed over the landscape, trying their best to hug the terrain. He glanced back to the planetarium ship. "You take me to the nicest places."

Crystal gave him a kind smile that was offset by an extended middle finger. The gesture reminded Ryan of his sister so much that he felt disconnected from reality for a moment, wondering how she was doing. *I never did send her that keychain.* Crystal shattered the recollection with a word, snapping him back to the present. "Look," she said, lowering her hand. She'd been pointing at something, and Ryan had missed what it was. "We need to help you harness your power, yeah? Well, this was the best place to do that right now." She pointed at the clouds. "What do you see?"

He stared at them as Crystal exited the doorway as well. "Clouds. They're cumolulus, I think."

"Cumolulus? It's cumulus, love."

Ryan shrugged, rubbing the back of his neck. "I...I only know the one word for clouds." She raised her eyebrow at him. "Fine. I only *kinda* know the one word."

"Look again. Harder this time."

"What does that even mean? Just stare longer?"

Crystal shook her head. "No. Focus more on what you're seeing."

So he did. At first he just felt silly, staring at the clouds, like a kid trying to find shapes in them. One was a bunny, that was a duck, that one looked horribly like one of the hands that had tried to crush Crystal earlier, and that one looked like a series of symbols and Greek letters because it wasn't a cloud, it was an equation being imposed on top of the clouds.

It took a moment for the equation to become clear. He watched, mesmerized as it took shape. *The fluid density of the air being multiplied by its velocity and volume as a starting point, then branching out to factor in the exchange of hot air and cold in an upward rush. I'm seeing vortex formation in real time! Fluid dynamics playing out in the sky! It's amazing, it's incredible* - Ryan blinked a couple of times as reality pushed away math.

"Uh, Crystal? A tornado is forming," he said, his throat horse with the effort of just seeing and understanding the math in the sky. She nodded beside him.

"Don't worry, love, that's why I brought you here."

"You brought me to watch a tornado form?" Ryan asked, his voice cracking. Multi-handed monsters were one thing, but this was something else. Ryan had grown up in Tornado Alley. The destruction they could unleash was something tangible and real, something he'd seen yearly on the news. The fact that he was now standing right under one as it formed was something he'd never wanted to imagine, let alone experience.

"Relax, love. You're more than just a bag of meat and bones now, yeah? You're a god. Take a deep breath and think about the sodding maths."

Ryan did as she instructed. At least the math was calming as he tried to force himself back into that mindset. "Okay," he said after a moment, "I see it again."

"It'll take some time, but eventually you'll be able to do that with just a glance. But right now, the fact that you see it is enough, yeah?"

"Enough for what?"

"Enough for you to stop it."

That broke his concentration and he looked at her, his eyes wide and round. "You want me to stop a tornado?"

She chuckled at his expression. "Pretty much, yeah. It's a good starting point - natural forces bow most easily to us."

"Okay. And...how do I stop it?"

"How do you move your arm, love?" She shrugged. "It's just like that. There's a science behind it, but that'll just get in the way of things, and…"

"...and my brain isn't ready to understand it, right?"

She beamed at him. "Glad you're paying attention. So...go ahead. Focus, and try and stop it."

Ryan looked at her, back to the clouds, and then back to her. She motioned for him to go ahead. "You've got another minute before it really gets going, so I suggest you get a bloody move on."

He turned back to the sky, pinpointing what would be the heart of the vortex. He extended his hand - it felt right - and spread his fingers in a claw gesture, like something from a movie. His heart was pounding in his chest. *I'm trying to stop a tornado, a goddamn tornado, by throwing math at it?* The equations started to slip away, and Ryan began to feel like none of the past day had happened. That he was alone and frightened and out of his depth, followed by a man in a suit, a borderline nervous wreck. Right before the anxiety consumed him, he felt a glimmer of that power again. *Get it together, Ryan,* he chided himself. *Get your shit together, or people are going to die. One of them will probably be you.*

For a few moments, nothing happened...but then he began to feel a tingle in his fingertips. Like they had fallen asleep, but even more aggressive. That feeling started to grow further out of his fingers, like a phantom limb, but racing up to the sky.

Those phantom fingers began to plunge into the clouds. They weren't touching the clouds, although it seemed like they should be. Instead, he could feel them contacting the numbers, like the equations were physical things he could shape like clay. *I need to change...no, I can't just change the variable, and I can't just decrease the mass. Mass is a constant, I don't think I can just make it go away.* He made a mental note to ask Crystal if he could at some point, but for now he needed to do something to reduce the forces involved. Then it struck him. *Don't remove numbers, add them.* He began sticking fractions in front of the velocity, halving it at first - it was all he could manage - but then reducing it by a third, a fourth, a fifth. Ryan felt a thrill run through him. He was actually doing it! He was actually manipulating a forming tornado.

"See, love? Not hard at all."

Crystal really had a gift for understatement, possibly born of her fake British stiff upper lip. Sure, it was as natural as moving his arms, but it was as easy as moving them with half ton weights strapped to them. He could feel beads of sweat forming on his forehead, and his knees trembling. Every time he changed a variable, the natural order started pushing it back into place, like reality knew what was supposed to happen here and didn't like being told differently.

"Keep pushing. It's like any other muscle - the harder you work it, the stronger it gets." She put a hand on his shoulder. "And when you pass out, don't worry, it's expected."

Oh goody, I have that to look forward to. It almost managed to sour the joy of manipulating a literal tornado. The constant passing out was becoming a bore he was getting utterly sick of, but he did he best to push those concerns aside. He would pass out, fine. But not until after he beat one of the deadliest weather events known to man into submission by manipulating math in the sky. *That's something to be proud of. Focus on that.*

It was a back and forth, but with every second he got quicker, and the numbers were changing under his manipulation slower than they were for reality. Inch by inch, variable by variable, the natural forces began to obey him, the pocket of heat that was shooting upwards dispersing before it began to twist. "I got it! I've got it!"

Crystal clapped her hands in excitement. "Good show! Keep at-"

Without warning, the variables started to change faster than he could manipulate them again, faster than he could even follow. "I don't got it!" The forces were pushing back against him. They were acting - and that word send a lance of panic coursing through him. Because they were acting. They had agency. Crystal frowned beside him.

"Ryan, stop! It's not natural, someone is pushing back." She raised her own hand as she said it, twisting against the aggressive forces. Variables he had been struggling with started to ripple under her fingers, warping to obey her will, but still the changes came quicker and quicker, until Crystal was actively struggling against the brute force pushing the tornado into place.

"Guess that's my cue," a voice said. A low, dull voice. From around the corner of the gas station stepped a huge brute of a man, one massive arm raised towards the sky. Tiny eyes peered out from beneath a jutting brow.

"Enki," Crystal hissed, as Ryan felt his vision began to grow black.

"Ishtar," Enki responded, his voice low and angry. A small part of Ryan's brain, the part that wasn't fighting exhaustion or terror, wondered why Enki was calling Crystal by a different name. He would have to ask her if they survived this. "Thought you learned your lesson back during the Crusades. Thought you were going to stay the out of my way." In a single, swift motion he lowered his hand, no longer attempting to strengthen the tornado. The lack of resistance on Crystal caused her to overcorrect, like they'd been playing tug of war and he'd let go of his end, but instead of a rope whipping to lash at the people who had been tugging on them, the variables did. The vortex was dispersed with a clap of thunder that radiated outwards, forming a mile-long ring of clear sky in the middle of the storm clouds.

Crystal cried out and clutched her head in pain from the backlash. Ryan sank to one knee, still trying to fight away the clouds of darkness that tickled the edges of his vision. He thought that the raw terror would cut through that, but it wasn't enough to overcome his need to pass out. Enki continued talking. "Thought you were going neutral, like the damn Swiss. You should have. I'm going to kill this Eschaton, then I'm going to rip you apart every time you reform for the next hundred years, you obnoxious whore. But for now…"

And he gestured. Equations that moved so fast Ryan couldn't comprehend them leapt across his swirling vision. Their effect was immediate: massive iron chains shot up from the parking lot, forged from the pipes that ran under the gas station. They stabbed into Crystal's forearms and legs, and she screamed again in a combination of anger and pain as they burrowed in.

Ryan doubled over, realizing he needed his hands on the ground to stay upright. He could feel tears forming in his eyes from the effort of keeping them open. He certainly didn't feel the strength needed to fight off the slowly advancing brute. Enki reached down and grabbed the back of Ryan's hair, pulling him to his feet. Enki still focused on Crystal, like Ryan was some trash Crystal had dropped.

"For now, I'm going to make you watch while I beat him to death."

Before Ryan could react, Enki was already there.

***

The punch didn't toss Ryan into the air. It lobbed him, sending him a twisting arc that tumbled him end over end floating through the air with the grace of a drunken chicken. This flight took him up and away until his motion was arrested by a brief but solid interruption in the form of the gas station wall.

Ryan's everything hurt. The wall of the gas station wasn't drywall but solid concrete, and Ryan had felt it break behind him. He was certain down to his core that if he had still been fully human, that blow would have killed him, as opposed to just scrambling his brains.

The shock should have at least cleared his vision, but instead the clouds at the edge grew stronger, thicker. Tendrils of darkness started creeping further into his line of sight.

"No. Not now. I won't-"

"You won't do shit." Enki had crossed the distance and again had Ryan by the hair. "You won't do any damn thing, you hear me?"

He tossed Ryan upwards. The sensation of being thrown by the hair with enough force to launch him thirty feet was immensely painful, a pulling sensation that ran down his scalp and face all the way to his neck. Through the fog of pain, Ryan found himself wondering if Enki could have pulled his face off like that. That thought sent a fresh wave of fear through him that helped clear the pain, but not fast enough to prevent gravity from reestablishing its dominance over Ryan and sending him falling back to the ground. His reunion with the Earth was cut short, however, by Enki's foot - a kick which sent Ryan tumbling across the pavement until he skidded to a stop at Crystal's feet.

Ryan felt nothing but pain and terror. Judging from Crystal's expression, though, what she felt was rage. Ryan found himself looking forward to what she was about to do.

Unfortunately, before she could do it, Ryan was sliding along the ground, pulled towards Enki by an invisible force. He scrabbled at the ground with his fingers, which was as effective as if he was falling out of a window and trying to grab onto the side of a skyscraper.

Think, Ryan, damnit. Enki was toying with him, dragging him at a lazy pace. Once he got ahold of Ryan again, he'd toss him or punch him again and Ryan didn't know how much longer he could hold back that darkness in his eyes. He needed an edge, he needed to...

One hand stopped scrabbling at the ground. *This has to work.* If it didn't, he was dead, Crystal was dead, and Enki would do...whatever it was he wanted to do. If Crystal could have done something, she would have by now. It was up to him. He stretched out his hand to try and twist reality before he reached Enki. He called up the same certainty that he would die if he failed to stop this that had allowed him to overcome the tornado. This time, though, it wasn't an attempt to manipulate a rapidly changing system like a forming tornado. It was a relatively static manipulation - weakening the laws of electromagnetism holding together molecules. *Simple, really,* Ryan thought sarcastically.

It was still almost more than he could stand, and for a moment he blacked out. He came to a good foot closer to Enki, almost within the brute's grasp, and readied himself for what he had to do as soon as he got in range.

"I'm gonna slap your face in, son. I'm going to rip your throat oooooOOOF - " and it was Enki's turn to get an unexpected one-way trip into the air. Ryan lowered his foot from where it had connected with Enki's gut. Enki's eyes widened from either shock or just the impact, and he was lifted off the ground and sent careening away what had to be at least twenty feet, slamming into the parking lot's sole lamp post. The post bent in half from the impact. *I did that?* Ryan thought to himself, blinking stupidly at this own foot as the tendrils resumed their worming path across his vision. *I...holy crap I just kicked him across a parking lot?*

Enki wasn't wasting time extracting himself from the ruins of the lamppost. He took time to brush himself off, tilting his head back and forth. Even from here, Ryan could hear his neck crack. Enki flashed him a grin full of more spite than a thousand invectives, and Ryan realized all he had accomplished with the kick was pissing his opponent off. "Whoo boy. You got a spark there. Some of that good old-fashioned gumption. Course, you're still Nascent. Can't have a whole lot of juice left. Gotta be running on empty, really. So go ahead, boy. Hit me with your best shot."

Ryan rose to his feet and extended his hand. The storm still roiled above, building with potential. He began to twist his hands, the right one modifying variables, adjusting positive and negative charges until -

With everything that would come later, if he survived, Ryan would do some amazing things, see some incredible things. But nothing would ever compare to the rush of the first time he hurled a lightning bolt from the heavens and struck Enki with five hundred of mother nature's very best megajoules of electricity.

The light seared his retinas, the thunderclap obliterated his hearing. Enki vanished behind that flash and that rumble as the world exploded. If he screamed, Ryan

52

couldn't hear it, the sound completely drowned out by the detonation of lightning so close to Ryan's face.

Before Ryan's vision could recover, Enki came bursting out of the light, slamming a fist into Ryan that sent him flying back into the gas station.

"Damn, boy, you've got a bit of a punch." Enki approached slow and heavy. His skin and hair were singed, but otherwise he was unharmed. He cracked his neck as he approached. "I felt that, I really did. But it doesn't change a single thing. Not one single damn thing. I've been drawing power off my nanoverse since humans first crawled out of the mud. I was one of the first." He was right next to Ryan, and crouched down, nearly spitting in his face. "Do you really, honestly, think you could fight me, could outlast me?"

Ryan let out a pained chuckle. It wasn't a defiant chuckle, or an arrogant chuckle. It was the kind of laughter that slips out of your lips when everything is falling apart, and the world is collapsing, and at the last possible instant you notice a ray of hope so faint you could almost miss it. "I didn't...need to outlast you. You're the one...without backup."

Enki's beady eyes suddenly contained a glimmer of something besides the murderous rage. Just a glimmer, but seeing fear in those tiny eyes was the most satisfying thing Ryan had seen since this whole thing started.

It was even more satisfying seeing that fear turn to shock as a foot connected with the side of Enki's head, driving it into the wall.

Crystal reached down with a blood-soaked arm, grabbing Ryan and helping him to his feet. "Good bloody show, love. I just knocked him senseless, though. We gotta move before he wakes up, yeah?" Ryan nodded, and they rushed back to the door. Crystal was limping from the wounds in her legs, and Ryan was gasping with pain. Behind them Enki bellowed with rage, pulling his head out of the wall with immense, groaning effort.

The door was still open, and the pair dove through. It slammed behind them and began to vanish.

"We made it. Bloody hell, we made it...oh no, not again."

Ryan heard Crystal's voice, but it didn't matter. The irrefutable fact of their safety sung like a song in Ryan's thoughts, and the effort to hold back those black tendrils was finally overwhelming. For the third time, he passed out.

Chapter 6

Red Tape

Ryan awoke to a faint buzzing sound. While godly resilience had kept him alive, it did not prevent every single muscle in his body from being in pain. He supposed he should be grateful - after being rag dolled around a parking lot, even if he wasn't dead he probably should have broken every bone in his body. But at the moment, any feelings of gratitude were washed away by agony.

Groaning, he rolled over on his side in the silver bed. Across the room, Crystal lay in another bed.

Some people were just angelic when they slept. Hair perfectly falling around their faces, small smiles playing upon their lips, cuddled under the blankets.

Crystal was not one of those people. She was sprawled out on the bed, one hand flopped over the side. Her hair was a messy halo and her mouth hung open. That faint buzzing sound had been her breathing, not quite loud enough to qualify for a full snore but far too loud to qualify for any word more dignified.

There was a paper laying on the bed next to her, with a note on it. The ink had been smudged by what was probably spittle flying from her lips as they droned out a snore.

If you're up before me, check my arms. If the wounds are gone, wake me. If not, bloody let me sleep and get yourself some food from the fridge.

Ryan did check her arms, and the wounds were mostly gone. The flesh was still pink and puffy, scarred from where the chains had punched through flesh and bone. Ryan decided to let her sleep for a bit longer just to make things were fully healed up, and walked over to a silver box that definitely hadn't been there before.

In the box was a variety of sandwiches in individually wrapped bags, each one labeled. *Salami. Pastrami. Roast Beef (Don't Eat This One You Wanker). Turkey.* Ryan grabbed the pastrami and took a few bites. It occurred to him that this was the first time in his life that he'd ever been alone and could really bask in it. Sure, Crystal was there, as the gentle buzz saw reminded him, but she was asleep. No one was looking at him, no one was watching him.

It was a terrifying relief. On the one hand, the idea of being fully alone had always fascinated him. It had sounded wonderful in theory, but in practice he'd always had the ability to make eye contact with a silent watcher. Not having that comfort was like walking a tightrope when safety net was gone and had been replaced with a tank of boiling acid full of sharks that could survive acid and heat. And he didn't have a gas mask.

The constant buzzing provided a degree of comfort, a reminder that there was another person there. He decided it still didn't count as being alone, not really. Just unwatched. And unwatched was...comfortable.

Ryan reached in and grabbed another sandwich. He took a moment after grabbing to make sure it wasn't the Roast Beef (Don't Eat This One You Wanker), and, realizing he had grabbed that sandwich, put it down carefully apart from the others so he wouldn't make that mistake again. *I do not want to find out what Crystal would do if I ate her roast beef.* Probably nothing, but why risk it? Trying to clear the sleep from his eyes, he grabbed another one, and this was definitely wasn't the sandwich calling him a wanker. It occurred to him that, aside from passing out a few times, he hadn't need to sleep, eat, or use the restroom since he'd stared into the nanoverse, and hadn't seen Crystal do any of those either. *Do I not need to anymore? Or I just need to do it less frequently?* Now that he was eating, it felt good - felt great, really - but there hadn't been any hunger or weakness before the fight.

Crystal stirred on the bed, looking up at him. Her hair had somehow gotten even messier in the process of getting up. "That better not be my bloody roast beef, you wanker" she said.

He smiled. "No, it's not. How're you feeling?"

"Like I got stabbed in the arms and legs by some prick. Oh, wait, that's what happened." She got out of bed and walked over to the fridge, grabbing the sandwich. "Clever play, breaking me free like that. So, that was your first taste of gods clashing. What'd you think?"

Ryan rubbed his face, realizing how clammy his hands felt as soon as he started thinking about it again. "It hurt. But it didn't feel very divine. Aside from the chains and the dragging and a lightning bolt, it was mostly just...punching."

She took a bite out of the sandwich and let out a happy little moan. "That's the way it usually goes, love. We save the power for the big plays or the drama. Most fights between us really comes down to who tires out first, yeah?"

After a moment's thought, Ryan nodded. "That's why Enki waited till I was stopping the tornado to attack."

A nod from Crystal as she took another bite. "Pretty much. Even with you being nascent, two on one aren't great odds, even for a powerhouse like Enki. Same reason he forced me to hold back the tornado, even as he pushed it down. Much more effort on my part."

He bit his cheek in thought. He saw what Crystal was doing, walking him through everything step by step to calm him down, and it was not unappreciated. "No, don't tell me. Because..." he finished his own sandwich to give himself time to think. "The storm wanted to form a tornado. That was where it was headed. So it's harder to make it go against that because you're not just pushing against Enki, but pushing against what the storm was already doing."

She beamed at him. "Hole in one, love. You've almost gotten a first-grade understanding of how we work." The tone was teasing, but Ryan still felt his ego deflate. She patted him on the cheek. "Don't worry, we'll get you there."

"In time to end the world?"

The patting stopped, but she kept her hand on his cheek. "Yeah. That's about the long and short of it." Her voice was sad. "But don't worry - we're not gonna kill everyone. We'll figure out another option."

He stared at her a moment. "Why? What happens if the world doesn't end?"

She pulled her hand away with some hesitation, like now she didn't want to break contact with him. She didn't seem to want to meet his eyes anymore. "I told you, Ryan. The world dies."

Ryan was insistent, "How?"

"Roll with-"

"Crystal." His voice was hoarse. "Please, I need more than that."

She looked up at him, and he saw the same look in her eyes he had seen in Cipher Nullity. Pain from wounds a million years old, cut with determination that could burn a man alive. "If you don't, the sun expands into a red giant. The end of the world is a sacrifice that resets the sun's life."

He blinked at her. "But...that's what the sun's going to do in five billion years anyway."

That at least got a dark chuckle out of her. "True. And the sun going red giant has been five billion years away for about eight billion years now. Which means if we don't do it, those five billion years come due plus three billion years of interest. It'll probably go supernova right away." She looked into his eyes and let out a small, sad laugh. "Told you it was best to roll with it, love."

"I don't...I don't understand. What about the rest of the stars? Wouldn't we be able to tell?"

"No. Earth isn't all that special. Happens on other worlds across the universe all the damn time, keeping the whole thing young. Can you leave it at that?"

"I...okay, yeah." He could feel a headache coming on. "But how can you be sure?"

She finally looked away from him, but he didn't take her hand off his chest "Because it almost happened. Last time. We...thought we could break the rules. It didn't work. Barely did the reset before the world exploded."

"You were *there* last time?"

Crystal nodded. "I saw it all happen. Maybe I'll tell you the full story some time later on love."

"Crystal...you're talking about the end of the world. I need something more to go on than that." Ryan hated pushing her right now. She looked almost fragile. But...*Ryan, she wants you to end the world. You can't just 'roll with it.'*

She sighed. "I don't know how I can prove it to you. I'd love to, I really would, but it happened a million years ago. There's no trace of it left."

"Surely there's something. In the fossil record or-"

Crystal was shaking her head. "Ryan, love, your science is great. Your people have gotten pretty damn far with it. But we're talking about things that were designed to escape mortal eyes. The Creator, whoever they are, apparently didn't want people to spend their time worrying about the end of the world. Whatever has to happen to hide this from people happens. So please, don't make the mistake we did. Don't think you can beat this."

There was that plural again. "We?"

She nodded, and when she turned back to him, her eyes were firm. "That's the thing, love. I wasted my time trying to stop it, and so the only way to save the bloody world was to go fast, brutal. We couldn't save anyone. But we have more time, you and I, and I'm not...I'm not going to let you repeat my mistake, yeah? We're going to find a better way. I know it has to end. I saw it, I lived it. But there's rules. And rules can be broken, rules have loopholes. We're going to find those loopholes and we're going to find a way to end the world while saving every single one of the wankers on it. I don't want to end lives, Ryan. I want to save them."

Ryan nodded. Ending the world was a terrible thing to contemplate, but this...this was something he could get behind. *I mean, it's still bugnuts crazy. But at least she doesn't seem like a psychopath.* "Okay, so...what are the rules then?"

"That's the thing, love. I don't know all of them - if I had, I would have found the loopholes and used them.

Here's what I know for sure: no one god is powerful enough to end the world, *except* you're the Eschaton. You get one shot at it. The ability to exert your power on a global scale. When you do, it's a sacrifice of...not the people. There's power in human sacrifice, but that's not...not the same that you'll find in *this.* You're sacrificing an entire era, an epoch. The power from that is enough to stop the bloody sun from exploding." Crystal tried to force a smile and failed miserably. "So, that's a plus right there, love. If you can't end the world, I'm lying to begin with, right?"

"Sure, but-"

"No. Ryan. No buts." The moisture in her eyes was beginning to spill over and out. "I *was* the bloody Eschaton. I know how badly buts go. So please, *please,* don't try and not end it. Find a better way."

Ryan took a deep breath. "Okay. Crystal, I promise." *Assuming what you're saying bears out.* The promise was made more to comfort the woman in front of him, not anything else.

She sighed with relief and finally stepped away from him. "I must look a right mess, yeah? Let me freshen up." She walked, and a curtain of silver rose around her.

"One problem," he said, unintentionally adopting the raised voice used to speak to someone in the shower. "We're not going to get a damn thing done with Enki breathing down our neck like that."

"I was thinking about that while I was trying to get to sleep. We need to call up the other gods. Enki won't take long to get back up to full strength. He took less of a beating than we did." Her voice echoed on the silver curtain. "And you've got some tricks, but you're still Nascent, and I don't like my odds one on one against him."

"There's more out there?" As soon as the words were out of his mouth, Ryan realized how stupid they were. Of *course* there were other gods out there. Every culture had their own religions, their own belief systems. Why hadn't it occurred to him that there would be more? *In my defense, I've been a bit busy.*

Ryan was relieved Crystal was giving the question an actual answer. "Oh, of course. Where do you think all the bloody myths and legends come from? I'm done back here, you want a go?" She stepped out. Her hair was impeccable, her clothing new and fresh, and she was even wearing makeup.

"Uh...sure." He stepped behind the curtain. Light began to play over his body. "But..." Ryan sighed. "Crystal, we're not exactly the good guys here, are we?"

"How do you figure?"

"Well, you said we're going to be the ones ending the world, right? I mean, I don't know much about this whole thing, but don't we sound like the bad guys? 'Brave hero ends the world' isn't exactly the kind of story that's easy for people to swallow." *Hell, I'm having trouble swallowing it.* Ryan knew he was supposed to just 'roll with it', but the idea of ending the world wasn't the kind of thing that could sink in over the course of a few days and a couple of battles. Right now, the only thing keeping him going was the idea that if Crystal was lying to him, he didn't *have* to end the world.

"I won't lie, love, a lot of people are going to see it that way. Most of them will sit on their hands and wait to see how things shake out. But if we don't get allies, we're completely hosed. So we've got to at least make the effort, yeah? Otherwise, best find Enki and let him kill you this time."

Ryan shuddered at the thought. "Fine, I guess. So how do we call them up? Do you guys have phone numbers or something?"

She laughed outside the curtain. "Hardly. Only one group can contact them all in time: the Curators." Crystal paused, then sighed. "Technically I suppose the angels could, but they're a stubborn bunch. Plus, there's a bit of a...ruckus going on for them with Hell right now, so they're kind of busy, yeah?"

"I'm sorry, what? A ruckus in Hell?"

Crystal nodded. "Long story. Lucifer got tired of billions of years on the throne. Gave it to the next bloke that stumbled into the pit. It got messy."

"Wait, Hell is real? Lucifer is real? And he did...what?"

"Ryan, love," Crystal said with a small smile, "the universe spins on without us. Other gods have other things going on, same with angels and all that. If you try to keep track of it all, you'll be too distracted to worry about the problems in front of us. So why don't you just-"

Ryan cut her off. He didn't think he could stand to be told to roll with it again. *She has to be pulling my leg, anyway.* Instead, he focused on the bit about the Curators. "Don't suppose we can get the Curators on our side?"

"Nope. They're neutral as all else. Nice thought though."

He stepped out from behind the curtain. He felt cleaner and neater. He ran his hand through his hair and found it untangled. It didn't ache anymore from when Enki had tossed him by it, but the memory of the pain lingered. *Everything else was painful. That part right there was downright embarrassing.* "Hey, any chance this thing can cut my hair off? After what happened last time, I think I'd like to drop from six inches to a nice buzz cut or something."

She nodded, touching a few buttons. "Step back there, I've got you."

Ryan felt a buzzing sensation against his scalp and his hair fell to the floor, now down to a nice smooth cut. "Wow. Thanks. How does that even work anyway? I just step in here and...poof, I'm clean?"

"Something we had back in old Lemuria," Crystal said with a trace of pride. "I can't remember the bloody name for the thing, but it uses concentrated soundwaves. Creates a counterwave to not burst your bloody eardrums."

Ryan frowned. "Two things. You can't remember the name of a machine you own?"

"I'm a million years old. You forget things."

Or that's just a fancy way to say I should roll with it. Ryan decided not to press the issue. There were plenty of things he wanted to know, that he didn't understand, but the name of Crystal's sound machine wasn't high enough on that list. "Fair. But soundwaves did your hair and put on you makeup?"

"Oh, no, love, not at all. Being a bloody goddess did that." Crystal's face shifted, and in an instant, she looked as unkempt as she had when she'd gotten out of bed. A moment later she shifted back. "You'll learn the trick love. Unless you're a Protean, shapeshifting like that takes a bit to learn. You won't need a haircut again once you do though!"

Ryan almost asked how it cut his hair, but he was able to answer his own question before the words were out of his mouth. *I can buy soundwaves slicing it short, I guess.* Besides, she'd used a new term there, and Ryan was finding it hard to keep up. "A Protean?"

"Someone who picks up shapeshifting before they do twisting reality. They're pretty bloody rare, though." Crystal gave him a smile. "And that's enough, love. Back to the business at hand. The Curators, yeah?"

Ryan knew that tone of voice. To avoid getting told to roll with it, he shifted the conversation back to where it had been. "Okay, so what, we contact the Curators and see what allies we can get for this?"

"That's the plan, at least. I'll set a course for their home base, yeah? We'll be there in a couple hours."

Ryan nodded. "So why did Enki call you Ishtar?"

Crystal gave a nonchalant shrug, undoing her hair to let it fall around her shoulders. "It was a name I used, long ago. Back in Sumeria, and again in Babylon. I've changed names a few times throughout the centuries, love, but Ishtar's what I'm best known by. I prefer Crystal, though. It's probably the closest to the English version of my real name.

"Speaking of English, I've been wondering something..." Ryan said hesitantly, hoping he wouldn't get shot down again.

"Oh, bloody hell." Crystal forced a smile. "Yeah?"

"Sorry, it's just...why the fake British accent?"

Crystal blinked at him. "Beg your pardon? What do you mean, fake British accent?"

"You sound like someone faking a British accent."

"I'll have you know, I have an excellent British accent," Crystal said, her voice growing heated.

Ryan's eyebrows furrowed. "No, you don't."

"I bloody well do. I've been working on it for centuries!"

"It needs more work." Ryan said dryly, and Crystal pursed her lips. "Look, we can agree to disagree on that. But...why even fake a British accent?"

"What should I have been doing in the 1800's? An American accent? That meant sod all back then, the Brits still ran half the bloody globe. If I wanted to blend in, it was best to learn the accent everyone was used to, yeah? Couldn't go around speaking like I didn't know the language. Then it was too much of an effort to learn to mangle the language the way you Americans do, so I stuck with it."

Ryan held up a hand. "Makes sense." *It really doesn't,* Ryan thought, but from the way she was glowering at him, the sharp edge to her tone, Ryan decided the last thing he wanted to do was stumble upon the one thing that could offend Crystal, which was apparently her British accent. *Also, it's getting worse as the conversation goes on. I should **not** try to push her into saying "pip pip".* The thought made him grin. "So, if we've got a couple hours, any idea what we should do?"

Before he could finish the sentence, Crystal stepped forward, surprising him as her hand went up to his cheek, and she went on her toes so that her lips met his. It was an intense kiss, a passionate kiss. There was a hunger in that kiss, a need, and Ryan's shock was obliterated like a bomb had gone off underneath his brain as he responded to it, wrapping his arms around her waist and drawing her closer until their bodies were molded together.

"I think we can find a way to pass the time, yeah?" She said, breaking the kiss with a smile.

Desire and confusion warred within Ryan, and the confusion managed to get control of his mouth. "I...but Crystal, wh-"

Crystal's hands hadn't left the back of his head, and she pulled him in again, their lips locking with that smoldering hunger that set his heart racing, not with panic, but with excitement and anticipation. When she broke the kiss again, she was grinning even wider. "Ryan, love? Why ask questions? Unless you're not interested - and say so if you're not." The grin turned impish. "Although I'll be surprised if you do."

For a moment Ryan considered it. He couldn't help it. His heart was pounding, he felt his hands begin to tremble. His eyes flitted about the room, and it was empty, just a field of stars and galaxies. One of Crystal's hands slid from his back to cup his cheek. "We're alone. You're safe, and no one's watching. Take a deep breath and just roll with it, love."

That was enough. He leaned down to be the one to kiss her this time and, for once, without reservation, he rolled with it.

***

Ryan rolled over to look at Crystal as she was getting dressed. "So…what was that?"

"That, love, was sex. Are you not familiar with the concept?" She gave him an impish grin, and he blushed.

"No, I know what sex is, but...why? I mean, you seemed pretty pissed at me, and there was no indication that..." Ryan shrugged. "I didn't think you were interested?"

She laughed, pulling her pants the rest of the way up. "I wasn't, and then I was. We were both Hungry, of course."

Ryan blinked at that. "What...what do you mean?" *Please don't eat me,* Ryan thought in a moment of insane panic.

She sighed, though she still had a smile. "Better band aid this, then. Ryan, look at me." Half-dressed, she put her hands on her waist and cocked her hips just enough to be enticing. She hadn't gotten around to putting on a shirt yet. "Do you want to go for another round?"

"I mean-"

"Shush. Wait. Really think about it. Don't go with your first reaction, yeah? Really, really think about it. Do you want to go again?"

He thought carefully, looking at her. She was beautiful. *Of course she is,* Ryan thought. He had been schlubby and out of shape not long ago. As soon as he squeezed his nanoverse, he'd become an ideal version of himself. Crystal'd had millenia to be a human, why wouldn't she have been as beautiful as she could? *I know I'm going to be doing the same...*His mind wandered at the forms he could adopt. *And you're getting distracted while looking at a beautiful, half naked woman.* That snapped the realization into place. He had as much desire for her as he would for the Venus de Milo. Only that wasn't quite right. He wouldn't want to sleep with a statue, but there was still a physical attraction there. If he walked over there right now and kissed her, and she responded, he had no doubt they'd enjoy going back to bed together. But there wasn't an urge to do it.

"I...no, I don't."

She nodded and turned around to finish dressing "And while that was some very nice sex, I don't want you either. Any more than I want another sandwich, or to sleep some more. We're gods, love. We don't have mortal hungers anymore."

He felt his brow furrow. "Mortal hungers?"

She looked up at the starscape above them as she finished buttoning her shirt. Her frown had a playful edge to it, mock frustration in every line. "Can't you just roll with it?"

He let out a slight chuckle. "I did earlier."

That got a laugh at least. "Cheeky bugger. Fine. Get dressed and I'll give you a version you'll understand."

He got out of bed, looking for the clothes that they had, in their haste, scattered around the planetarium. The idea should have excited him...but didn't.

"So," Crystal said, walking over to the control panel that had risen back out of the ground while he searched for his shirt. "Mortals are defined by five Hungers that separate them from us. Food, Drink, Air, Rest, and Company - the last of which includes sex. Every mortal hungers in one fashion or another for all of those."

Ryan nodded thoughtfully. "I mean, the first four are biology. But not everyone wants Company - loners do exist."

"Oh, of course. But they still get it, yeah?" Seeing the confusion on his face, she adopted what he was beginning to think of as her "patient voice." "What do loners usually do?"

He scratched his chin. "Uh...read, watch tv, play video games-"

The tone she used to interrupt him was still encouraging. "Art. It's a passive interaction, sure, but they are getting that Hunger filled with the art of other humans. And when they don't, they get it from nature, or pets, or from whatever. Everyone has something or someone or some idea or cause they bond with, yeah?"

"Okay," he said, biting his cheek in thought as he did. "I'll accept that. So we...don't?"

"Not unless we burn a lot of power, become more mortal. Like we did against Enki. Then those desires come flooding back, and it's best to fill them. Take a few deep breaths, have a bite or six, down a bottle of water, take a nap, and get some time with people - and the quickest way to satisfy that last one is a good old-fashioned boffing, yeah?" She grinned at him with the last line. "Always make sure once you burn through everything to that degree that you fill each Hunger somehow. Otherwise it'll fester and grow, and you'll end up like Zeus, as a best-case scenario. It gets even worse if you can't fill them in time."

Ryan knew enough myths to shudder at the thought. If those were even half-true... "Okay, point taken. But...I'll never again enjoy a good meal unless I burn through power? Or enjoy sex?"

"See, this is why I don't like explaining things. You keep going to the worst possible conclusion. You can still enjoy a good meal, a good drink, a good shag You just don't feel a *need* to." She finished working the control panel. "Curators are coming up soon, and I'm bored with lesson time. That at least satisfy you?"

"Oh hell yes," he said, grinning. She laughed, but he noticed with even the innuendo, he didn't feel any stirring, any desire to take her back to bed. Academically it sounded fun, sure, and from what she said it would still feel good - but he didn't feel an urge to do it. "One last question." Crystal rolled her eyes good naturedly as Ryan continued, "So you're saying every time I burn through that much power, I'll need to get laid?"

She shook her head. "Or go to a party, or have a good conversation, or read a book, love. Last one's my favorite. Sex is just best when time is short, yeah?"

"Yeah," he said, nodding. "I understand."

"Good. One more thing because I know you, and you're going to think to ask this at some point soon." He gave her a raised eyebrow and she continued, "Love and sex are different things, yeah? Nothing's going to stop you from falling in love, having romance, all that good stuff. Just keep in mind we live for thousands of years, so those relationships tend to end in breakups."

"Oh yeah?" Ryan gave her a grin, although he was glad she had answered that question before he had thought of it. "Don't suppose you have any good stories there."

Crystal shook her head and chuckled. "Oh, I do. Don't hold your breath on getting them anytime soon, especially because we've arrived. Officium Mundi, their home plane." She began walking towards the door that appeared.

"Wait, what should I expect out there?"

She looked back over her shoulder, and didn't stop walking as she did so. "What do you think I'm going to say, love?"

He sighed as she opened the door, rushing a bit to follow her. "Yeah, yeah. Roll with it."

"Good lad." They stepped out the door. The world outside...well, an initial glance made it clear this wasn't Earth, and it wasn't the blasted wasteland and stained-glass sky of Cipher Nullity. First of all, they were in a building - a building so large, the ceiling had clouds. Lining his vision were rows and rows of shelves that stretched so far he couldn't see the end of them. On those shelves were books, and between them walked people. Men and women, all of them wearing suits. Sometimes they climbed ladders that stretched impossibly high, sometimes they walked along the shelves hand over hand or crossed bridges that had been built between them. Filing cabinets floated among them.

Ryan stared at it, knowing his mouth was hanging open but unable to care. *After Cypher Nullity, you'd think I'd be out of wonder.* He wasn't, though. Part of it was in one key difference - this place was alive. The suited denizens of this realm were bustling about in a controlled whirlwind of paperwork in this impossibly large office. Ryan wondered how far it stretched. Was it actual miles? Was it the size of a country, a continent, a planet? Had he stumbled into the heaven of bureaucrats, where souls that had spent their entire lives fighting the madness of systems with weaponized TPS forms got their eternal reward?

As he watched, a woman in a suit strode by, a file tucked under her arm. She reached one of the floating filing cabinets and snapped at it. Like a well-trained dog getting a command from its favorite human, it whirled to face her and floated down to the ground, and Ryan half expected it to start quivering eagerly for her command. Instead, she opened it and put a file in one of the drawers. Then she gave it a quick pat on the top and said, "Records of the Last Era of Gillespie-B," and the cabinet took off.

It was wonderful, but in a dry, mechanical way. A paradise of numbers and forms and efficiency. Part of Ryan found it immensely comforting.

"Welcome," said Crystal, "to the place where the universe makes its red tape. Try not to look too hard, love - I think it would give you a bloody terrible headache and probably cause another faint, and we're on the clock, yeah?"

He didn't answer directly, just followed her as she walked towards a door in the side of one of the shelves. Before they could open it, a man in a suit stepped out.

Ryan looked at him a second time, and his eyes widened. It wasn't just any man in a suit. It was *his* man in a suit, his constant companion for most of his life.

"Ryan," the man said, his voice still hoarse, "and Crystal. I don't suppose you're here to catch up on old times."

It wasn't a question, but a statement. Ryan clenched his fists near his pockets. *Catch up on old times? You mean the last thirty years of my life? You mean you watching me every day?* The urge rose like bile to reach out and throttle this man, to kick him as hard as he had Enki at the gas station. He didn't want to use his powers on this man, he wanted to beat him with his bare hands. He also wanted to ask him how he'd been, reach out and give him a...well, not a hug, but a manly handshake. It was a confusing torrent of emotions and Ryan did his best to squash them. "We need help," he managed to growl as he glanced sideways at Crystal. Those three words had been for the man in the suit, but they were also a reminder to Ryan why they were here. Crystal gave him a slight nod of approval and Ryan continued. "Your help, apparently. We need to contact the other gods before-"

"Not out here," Crystal interrupted, and the man in the suit nodded.

"Agreed. Call me Nabu, Ryan. And please, step into my office."

Trying not to think too hard about how good it was to see the man in the suit again, trying to push back his desire to smack the sense out of his lifelong antagonist, and desperately trying to not let it show how good it was to finally have a name for him, Ryan followed the other two inside

The man in the suit - *Nabu,* Ryan reminded himself - sat in the chair on the other side of the desk. Ryan took a moment to gape around the office.

He wasn't sure what he expected in the office of the man who had followed him his entire life, but if pressed, he wouldn't have expected the answer to be "a giant, unholy mess." Nabu had always seemed so neat, so tidy, so put together. Ryan was almost offended at how messy the office was. Nabu was an omniscient presence that had hovered in Ryan's life for thirty years. *Where the hell does he get off having a messy office?* But that's what he had - a

70

desk covered with papers, a haphazard look to the placement of every object, a dead houseplant in the corner - and along one walls, hundreds upon hundreds of notebooks, stacked so high they almost brushed against the ceiling.

Ryan felt his heart stop as he stared at them, because he recognized those notebooks.

Nabu followed his gaze as Crystal took her chair. "Yes. Every moment of your life is recorded in those."

Ryan walked over, then glanced back at Nabu, who gave him a wave of the hand.

Feeling unaccountably nervous, like a student called to principal's office after breaking so many rules he couldn't be sure what he had been caught doing, he pulled off one of the top notebooks.

Day 3578

Subject has become aware of my presence as something abnormal and begun avoiding speaking of me, and for thirty-three days now has ceased all attempts to communicate. I do think he is more than just a finder. Perhaps he has some divine blood in his ancestry, although I can't imagine how Home Office would have missed that.

He's awake and brushing his teeth. He's glancing towards the shower as he does so, again, and I think subject has become uncomfortable with the idea of being seen unclothed. This will be the third day he elects not to bathe if he chooses that path, and I think there is a real risk he will gain a reputation for uncleanliness. I should give him space, perhaps, but-

Ryan closed the notebook, his cheeks burning. He remembered that, and remembered a couple years of being the weird smelly kid. It had been humiliating, one of the worst periods of Ryan's childhood, and he'd eventually overcome his aversion to showering with Nabu there, but still...

"Not a pleasant trip down memory lane?" Nabu did sound like he was honestly wasn't sure, like he wanted a serious answer, like he hadn't been there and caused it.

We need his help, Ryan, he reminded himself. *Like the lady says: roll with it.* "No, it wasn't, and you damn well know it," Ryan snapped. *So much for rolling with it.*

"Ryan," Crystal said, a warning note in her voice, but Ryan barely registered it. "I dealt with this too. Believe me, love, I know what having a Curator follow you can be like. But you have to-" Ryan cut her off.

"You were there, you bastard. Every second of it, you were there. You were watching, and waiting, and writing down every single thing I ever did. Do you have any idea what that's like? Knowing your every moment is being watched, knowing your every deed is being recorded?" Ryan leaned on the desk, his face as close to Nabu's as it would get. "No, you don't. You were the one doing the watching, doing the recording. I thought I was crazy! Do you remember the therapy sessions? You should, you were there for them. Do you remember the therapists that thought I was faking because it didn't fit into any known diagnosis? Or how much money I burned through on MRI's? The side effects of the drugs I tried because I just wanted you to *go away*? Did you ever care what you were doing to me?"

Nabu waited to see if Ryan was finished before speaking. "Yes, I did. And I know I can never give that back to you. I owe you an immense debt and will do what I can to repay it." His eyes locked with Ryan's, and Ryan couldn't find a single trace of a lie in them.

Ryan slumped back into the chair, his energy spent. He still wanted to throttle Nabu, but he also didn't. It wouldn't do anything. It wouldn't change anything. It wouldn't fix anything. Getting it off his chest didn't even make him feel better, just like he was yelling at a brick wall that had kept him from going where he'd wanted. The wall had been there, and yelling at it wasn't going to get it to move.

Crystal put a hand on his shoulder and spoke up, "Nabu, we need to file a request for a mass message to every god or goddess the Curators have locations for."

He nodded. "Two mass messages in a single day, virtually unheard of these days."

"What?" said Ryan, hearing his voice spike with panic. "Who else did?"

"Oh dear, I shouldn't have said that. Terribly sorry." Nabu's tone did not match his words – he didn't sound apologetic, but like he was simply informing Ryan and Crystal of the weather. He glanced at Crystal. "Have you told him it is expressly forbidden for a Curator to interfere with the Eschaton or those who would oppose the End Cycle?"

She shrugged. "I would gotten around to it, yeah? He knows now." She caught Ryan's look. "Don't panic that we don't know who it is, love. It was Enki, it had to be. No one else has reason to right now."

A moment passed as Ryan waited for Crystal to elaborate. When she didn't, he asked, "What do you mean? Why isn't that reason to panic?"

"Oh, it is. It absolutely is. But now there's no reason to panic over the fact that it *might* be Enki, yeah? If you're going to panic, might as well have good reason to."

Both Nabu and Crystal watched as Ryan took a deep breath. "Okay. So Nabu, can we do our own message?"

"Of course. But...do either of you have the paperwork done?" Ryan looked at Crystal, who shook her head. Nabu sighed. "When the last individual who sent a message came, he had the forms pre-filled out. In triplicate. You'll need to do so as well." He motioned. A monstrous stack of paper appeared in front of Ryan. Another one appeared in front of Crystal.

Ryan gulped. "Well...at least we have the triplicate part covered."

Nabu raised an eyebrow. "Ryan...what do you mean?"

"Well, that stack's so big, it's got to have three copies of the forms already in there, right?" Nabu looked at him blankly as Crystal rummaged around for a pen. "I mean...that can't all be one copy." Nabu looked at Crystal, who was still looking for something to write with, then back at Ryan. "Nabu? Am I right?"

Nabu shook his head mournfully. "I suggest you get started."

Ryan had to fight back the urge to scream. "Do you have pens we could borrow?"

Nabu handed them each a pen, as well as a "Temporary Pen Reallocation Form – 17B" to fill out.

In triplicate.

* * *

The good news was that, free of mortal Hungers, neither Ryan nor Crystal needed to take a break to eat or sleep or even have a drink. That didn't make the endless paperwork any less mind numbing – "Permission to Speak for Divine Personage 3240-G," "Request for Messenger 9354-X-84I," "Nature of Message 8-23-TY," "Text of Message 666-Sigma-D," and so on and so forth, every possible layer of what they were going to do.

They did get a break when they paused to discuss the message. They kept it short, which would end up sparing them much of the paperwork – "End times beginning. Trying to save humanity. Eschaton found. Contact Ishtar if willing to help." About as subtle as a boot to the nose, but it got the essential points across. Like a tweet with divine tags.

The whole process took them about six hours. Six long, tedious hours. By the end, Ryan was almost wishing mortal hungers had interrupted them a few times to make the process less boring. It was like watching paint dry during Chinese water torture while elevator music played.

"All done?"

Ryan nodded, looking despondent. "I guess we'll need to do that two more times?"

Nabu looked at them without saying a word, and the stacks jumped in height. Ryan leapt back with a start as they did, as if the stacks of paperwork were a beast that would bore him to death if he wasn't careful.

"As far as I can tell, you did." Nabu smiled.

"Wait, what?" Crystal was the one to object this time, and Ryan felt a great thrill at seeing her baffled for once, while also hoping that she wouldn't somehow talk them into more paperwork. "Not that I mind, I bloody well don't, but isn't this a neutrality violation?"

"But teacher, didn't we have homework?" Ryan muttered, and Crystal gave him an annoyed flap of her hand to silence him.

Nabu faintly shook his head. "I spent thirty years ruining a young man's life, Ms. Crystal. The Eschaton is, no offense, a semi neurotic wreck because of me."

Crystal frowned. "That's never bothered you lot before, Nabu. That's usually how this goes. Are you trying to tell me, love, that this is something you'd do for anyone if they'd just asked? Or is Ryan special somehow?"

Nabu's head shake was more emphatic this time. "I've watched hundreds like you before," he said, indicating Ryan, "and I've seen what we do to you. We like to complain about how distant gods are from mortals, here in this office, but we ignore the fact that we're destroying your mortal years. It means so many gods enter their godhood with minimal connections. It means so often we end up with Eschatons unprepared to deal with the immense burden placed upon them. I've decided that, as far as I interpret it, is a violation of my neutrality." He turned his focus back to Crystal. "Doing this is a small way to redress the imbalance, wouldn't you agree?"

Ryan could practically hear the gears turning in her head. "I would..." said Crystal, glancing at Ryan, "But I think it would be best for the Eschaton to decide, as the wronged party."

Nabu made a show of widening his eyes, and Ryan realized that once again, Crystal knew what was going on and he was the baffled one. "That is an excellent point, Ms. Crystal. Ryan, would you consider my debt to you discharged?"

"Um, I mean-" he saw Crystal out of the corner of her eyes, drawing a sideways hand across her throat and shaking her head with such exaggerated gestures that Ryan was afraid she'd pull something. "No?"

"Oh dear." Nabu smiled slightly. "Then please, when you think of something that could be done to eliminate that debt – or wish to transfer the debt to another," and those words were said with exaggerated weight, glancing at Crystal as he did so, "then please, let me know."

"Weeeeell…" Ryan drew it out, thinking carefully to make sure he was following the dance. He glanced at Crystal, who was nodding and pointing at herself with the same exaggeration as earlier, "I suppose I can let you know…that I wish," another encouraging nod from Crystal. "To transfer the debt to Crystal?"

"Ah." They both relaxed some. "Very well. Then, Ms. Crystal, how may I pay this debt?"

Crystal grinned, leaning forward. "I need the exact message Enki sent out, and to know which gods if any responded in the affirmative."

Nabu went over to one of the piles and pulled out a paper. He handed it over, and Ryan leaned over Crystal's shoulder to read.

Fellow Beings of Higher Power,

An Eschaton has awoken. This Eschaton is being guided by Ishtar – and she, when she was Eschaton, slaughtered every single other deity before destroying the world in sea and flame. If you wish to save humanity, we must put aside old grudges and make common cause.

-Enki.

Crystal swore in several languages, and Ryan gave her a sympathetic pat on the shoulder. "C'mon, Crystal. Roll with it."

She glared at him, and Ryan gave her an impish grin before continuing. "Seriously though, c'mon, right? That's the most obvious manipulation ever attempted, even I caught it. So any god who falls for it we probably didn't want on our side anyway, right?"

She looked at him for a long moment, then started laughing. "Too bloody right. I'm rubbing off on you. Alright. Any response yet, Nabu?"

He shook his head. "But to satisfy my debt, I will inform you if there are any."

"You're a peach. We should be going." She motioned for Ryan to get up, and he followed. "Been lovely Nabu, really has been. Ciao!"

With that, they left. Ryan had so many questions to ask Nabu, but right now, he was legitimately glad to be on his way. On the one hand, getting a chance to really talk to Nabu, getting a chance to sit across from him like that was nice. *It also felt wrong, like...his name's Nabu? He talks? He has opinions, feelings?* It had in some ways been easier when Nabu had still been the man in the suit, this silent presence in Ryan's life. Sitting in an office with him humanized Nabu, and Ryan didn't know when he'd be able to endure something that made Nabu seem more *human*. "So we wait for responses. What do we do until we start hearing from people?"

Crystal smiled. "Well, we stay away from Earth, that's for bloody sure. Unless you want round two with Enki?"

Ryan groaned at the thought. "No, I'm good."

"Thought so." She grinned. "Well, then, how about we do some more training, but let's try somewhere different." She headed to the door they had opened earlier, and motioned for him to come through. "I hear Mars is lovely this time of year, yeah?"

It took Ryan just a bit to process what she said, but once he did he all but bowled her over in an attempt to rush them both into the staging area. "Oh, yes please."

She smiled and went over to the control panel. "Then setting course for the red planet. Let's see how you do with that."

Throwing a lightning bolt for the first time had been the most incredible feeling, but Cipher Nullity had been almost too alien, and Officium Mundi had been too bureaucratic. To set foot on Mars...that was real, that might make it all worth it.

"Yeah, let's...let's go."

And once again the planetarium ship moved without momentum through reality.

Chapter 7

The door appeared, and Ryan glanced at Crystal. "Wait. Every other time we've gone somewhere, we've appeared in the door of some other structure. What are we about to walk out of on Mars? Don't we need a door?"

Crystal shrugged, changing her shoes to work boots as she did. "Two things. First of all, no, we don't. We can just make one out of thin air. But I like using an actual existing door - it's a bit less bending of reality, and I just like the drama of walking out of an actual doorway as opposed to a magical door in the air, yeah?"

"Makes sense," Ryan said after a moment. "And the second thing?"

"We're on Mars, love. We can just use one of the doors already here. You ready?"

She didn't wait for an answer, walking over to the door and opening it. Outside was the red dust of the Martian soil. He'd expected it to be whipping abound in a massive sandstorm - that's how it always looked in movies - but in reality, the air looked still. He followed, unable to stop himself from running to leap out into the red dust that covered this world.

It wasn't much to look at, if he was being honest, but that didn't matter. Christmas had come early, and Santa had brought him a Nintendo, a puppy that his parents would take care of but would still love him more, every Lego set ever made, and a heaping pile of chocolate. *I am on Mars.* That thought sent an electric thrill through him. Like three quarters of all the little boys in America, he'd once dreamed of being an astronaut, and of being the first person to set foot on Mars. Now, he was here!

And didn't have a spacesuit, or enough air. The thin air on Earth's celestial neighbor made him feel like every breath was being sucked through a straw. He gasped a few times, and he started to feel lightheaded, like he might faint.

"Ryan," Crystal said, her voice rendered tinny in the thin air, like it was coming from far away. "Stop. You don't *need* it, remember?"

Crystal's voice was an anchor, something he could grab onto. He clenched and unclenched his fists to steady himself. *She's not breathing, and she's as real as you are. You're not just a guy anymore, Ryan. You can do this.* It wasn't easy. For thirty years, Ryan had been in the habit of breathing in and out. Stopping - in a way that wasn't holding his breath - was as easy as blinking your ears. Crystal watched with amusement as he practiced. He noticed that her chest was completely still, undisturbed by the usual rush of air.

Finally, after what was probably fifteen minutes of gasping and holding his breath, but felt like a full day, he was able to overcome the idea he needed to inhale. Another ten get him used to not thinking he needed to exhale. Finally, he stood back on his feet. "Gonna take a while to get used to this," he muttered. Crystal nodded in sympathy.

"I spent a month on the moon to finally overcome the feeling that I *needed* air. It's a tough one - it'll feel weird for a while."

"Wait, if we aren't breathing, how are we talking?" He saw Crystal's face and raised his hands in surrender. "Okay, okay, rolling with it. But here's a question that doesn't require a special god-brain to understand, I hope. Why isn't Mars windy? I thought it was always windy, but I'm just feeling a gentle breeze"

She did grin at that one. "Oh, that's easy. Air up here is super thin, so that 'gentle breeze' is going at almost fifty kilometers an hour. If it picks up much more, it'll start whipping up the dust since that's so light, but we aren't going to get blown around."

"Nice to get an answer, at least," Ryan said. "So…" he turned around and saw what the doorway was built into. It was the side of a cliff, but the entrance was square, and dozens of other square holes dotted the cliff-face. "What the hell?"

Crystal smiled. "Remnants of the Martians, a couple cycles ago. Most of what they built has completely eroded long ago, but these cliffs are pretty resilient."

"There was life on Mars?"

"Oh, yeah. Tons of it, actually. Definitely ran a lot colder than life on Earth, but they were some beautiful creatures, from what I've heard. Before my time of course, but from what I was told, there were two different species of Martians back then."

"What happened?"

She shrugged. "The Eschaton before me didn't like life on Mars and Venus, so he or she turned Mars into a barren wasteland, and ran temperatures on Venus to a few hundred degrees above 'the ninth circle of hell.' And when it was my turn at it, I was kinda in a rush. Had to make sure the sun didn't explode, yeah? So no time to make it possible again."

"Oh."

She smiled then. "If we get done with this whole Enki business, love, and time allows, we could totally get the ball rolling on that. Let there be life on three of the worlds in our little corner of the universe, maybe even Titan and Europa."

He felt a bit overwhelmed at that and had to sit back down in the dust of Mars. "But...is there other life, out there?"

"Of course, love." She gave him a big smile. "Why do you think the other stars haven't gone supernova? Only time it happens is when some Eschaton doesn't do their job right. Shame that the Eschaton always happens before contact between stars can be made, though."

He could feel the anxiety creeping up and held up a hand. "Too much, Crystal. I'm overloading."

"Not surprised. You'll keep learning, but for now, love, let's get some practice. Let's see if you can start a rainstorm on Mars."

It wasn't easy. He had to find the traces of water in the atmosphere, then begin copying it by splitting apart other molecules. The equations that danced in front of his vision were complicated beyond belief, but instinct told him which variables to change, and after a bit...

After a bit, for the first time in the memory of every single living being currently in the cosmos, water fell on Mars.

Crystal laughed in delight, clapping her hands in the rain. "That's it, love, that's it. Have you ever seen anything like this?!"

He had to laugh with her. The Martian rain reflected the dimmer sun oddly, catching dust particles so every ray was turned into a stream of shimmering rubies.

They spent the next few hours playing with the storm, creating tornados of thin but wet air, watching the dust turn to mud. Crystal began to use that soup to teach him how to shape matter directly, manipulating the systems that governed what shape it was in - the same kind of tricks Enki had used to make chains from pipes. It wasn't long before a mudball fight broke out, each of them launching the globs back and forth with divine power as opposed to their hands.

For a moment, Ryan was able to forget about the impending doom that waited. For now, he just had fun.

***

While Crystal and Ryan were playing in the mud of Mars, Enki was getting responses to his missive. *It's nice to see how much people sit up and take notice when you say "save the world."* Enki had set the meeting in an old temple hidden in the deserts where his people had once resided. A temple that had been untouched by humanity for millennia, owing to it having been buried in the Deluge.

The interior had been cleaned out, a project Enki had completed around the time Columbus was introducing the Americas to the wonders of European expansionism and smallpox. The lights in here were electric, which had been a later project, but everything else retained vestiges of its former splendor. Seven frescos adorned the walls, depicting seven gods. Well, depicting most of them. Enki had scratched off the face of one of them.

Your sacrifice wasn't in vain, my friends. I'm going to finish what I started. He ignored the scarred fresco. Ishtar had defied him. *Continued* to defy him.

Well, history would show who had chosen the winning side, and it sure as hell wouldn't be Ishtar.

Thinking about the Americas made Enki wonder if any of the deities from there would turn up, and if so, which side they would be on. Quetzalcoatl was always a wildcard, being a pretty benevolent guy aside from the whole human sacrifice thing. Coyote, like all the tricksters - Anansi, Loki, Kitsune, the whole lot of them - was also unpredictable. The others? Enki frowned. *The Mayans love their cycles. They might go with Ishtar. Aztecs? Damn, I dunno. They never liked either of us. What about-*

Enki's thoughts were interrupted by a doorway opening in one of the empty archways of his home. *You know, you're going to have to abandon this place after this one meeting. Too many hurt feelings after you're done.*

Enki put on a smile for the god that stepped out. Týr. He gleamed. His hair was long and a sandy-brown, his chin perfectly cleft, his armor shining in the light...even his teeth were perfectly clean by god standards. Týr cut a dashing figure.

"Týr!" Enki boomed and walked over to him, clapping him on the back. "So good of you to show up. Surprised you're still going with armor - figured you would have moved on to spandex by now."

Týr laughed. Most gods chose one face to wear as their main visage throughout the millennia, but Týr changed his constantly to keep up with the current image of "heroism" wherever he went. "Superheroes are a fad, Enki. They've only been around for what, seventy years? I'm sticking with the knight in shining armor. If I'm wrong about the costumed folk, if they're still popular in another century, then I'll consider taking up the cape and spandex."

"And if you do, I'll never stop calling you a ponce." That voice was from the woman behind Týr, walking out of his nanoverse. Them arriving together was a detail that caught Enki off guard. It didn't matter, not really, but if they were together, were they *together*? *It could be a complication.* Enki pushed the thought aside. It might be a complication, but it wouldn't be a problem for the overall plan.

"Never," the woman repeated as she stepped the rest of the way out and into the light. Athena, goddess of wisdom and war. She had the long, dark hair of the Mediterranean, but her most striking feature were her eyes. She'd kept them gray, and they were so noticeable she'd even been called by poets "Gray Eyed Athena." Enki had wondered a time or two how she managed to make them so prominent. He'd tried a few times but he always came across as bug eyed.

Not that Enki looked like he normally did. The more bestial appearance he favored these days was entirely practical - longer arms for greater reach when fighting, slightly shorter legs to reduce how vulnerable he was down there, small eyes to minimize those weak spots. He could even travel on all fours if needed while still appearing fairly human. But that's not how he appeared for this meeting. He looked more like the god he had been, back in Sumeria. *Once I'm done, I'll be able to look like this all the time. After all, who could possibly oppose me?* "Athena!" He offered his hand to her as well, and she took it with a smirk. "So glad you're here too. With you two, it won't take much more to crush this lunatic."

Athena shrugged. "I'd rather not underestimate an enemy before we've taken a measure of his worth."

"Still," Týr interjected, smiling at both of them, "it's good that we'll be able to rely upon each other. I must admit, Enki, I was glad to get your missive. Rumor had spread you were...not quite on our side anymore."

Enki's grin didn't waiver in the slightest. "I did lose my way, Týr. But I've gotten it back. It's good to be on the side of the angels again." Enki paused and laughed, "Of course, not the literal angels. That's a damn mess, everything with Heaven and Hell right now."

"We stay out of those fights, Enki," Athena said. Her eyes were narrowing slightly. *Reel it in, Enki.* He cautioned himself. *The ham might work on Týr, but you're rubbing Athena the wrong way.*

"Don't worry, Athena, this doesn't involve them."

Another doorway opened. The woman who stepped out of this one was of a slightly smaller build than Athena, with her hair jet black. She'd done it up carefully to give it the appearance of cat ears, and her eyes were emerald.

"Bast!" Enki shouted, going over to her to shake her hand, doing his best to seem pleasantly surprised she'd actually shown, as he had for Týr and Athena.

Of course, unlike the other two, there had been no doubt Bast would arrive. She took the proffered hand and clasped it firmly. "Enki, it's been too long," she lied, glancing past him to the other two. "Týr! Athena! How have you been?"

Athena snorted. "Last I saw you, Bast, you were ready to murder Marc Antony for what happened with your favorite queen. Now you're happy to see me?"

Bast shrugged. "That was over two thousand years ago. I'm not Hera, Athena. I don't hold grudges that long."

Mentioning Hera seemed to have the effect Enki suspected Bast was going for. Instead of being focused on her millennia old grudge with Bast, Athena was now occupied with an entirely different millennia old grudge. *Nicely done,* Enki thought. Anything to distract Athena was worth it right now.

Týr put an arm around Athena's shoulder. Enki watched it carefully. It wasn't a lover's embrace. It was friendly, reassuring. *Better,* Enki thought. Lovers were more complicated. "Enki," Týr said, trying to change the topic so blatantly he should have just cleared his throat, "you said you had a plan?"

Enki nodded and gestured, summoning a table and chairs. "Have a seat, Týr. Trust me on this one - we're going to get him with no problem." The other gods joined Enki at the table. As Týr and Athena sat, Enki met Bast's eyes and gave her the barest of nods.

Regardless of what they discussed here, the real plan was on.

Chapter 8

"Oh, I've gotten word from Nabu."

Crystal's voice startled Ryan enough that he almost dropped his book on his face. After training, he had some Hungers, so he'd taken care of most of them and was now reading to fill the need for Company. Crystal hadn't been up for any kind of socializing - instead, she'd gone to sleep, saying she hadn't burned quite enough power to be worth a proper recharge but some rest would do well enough. He'd hadn't realized she'd woken from her trance, let alone gone over to the panels.

"Great, what's it say?" He didn't want to let her know how he'd jumped, but from the grin on her face he knew she already did.

"Enki's getting some responses. Týr, Bast, and Athena. Good news is we've got at least one interested party - Moloch's in."

Ryan bit his cheek for a moment in thought. "Uh...I'm not exactly a mythology nerd, but isn't Athena a good goddess?"

Crystal nodded. "Oh, yeah. Just and wise. Týr you'd probably also call good, he's all about heroism. And Bast too, yeah? She's big into protecting people, from back when she was guarding the Lower Kingdom."

"Right. Okay." Ryan furrowed his brow. "And Moloch...wasn't he a demon?"

"Yup! But don't worry about that, love. That's just Judeo-Christian propaganda - when they got big, they started calling tons of us demons, yeah?"

Ryan let out a sigh of relief. "Oh, good, because I was worried-"

"Of course, he was big on human sacrifice, so he's not exactly hugs and cuddles, yeah? But he's mellowed on that in the last millennia."

"Oh."

She looked up at Ryan and pursed her lips. "You're not happy with that one, are you? And don't bother, love, I know that look - you can't just roll with it."

Ryan nodded, frowning. "It's just...Enki's getting a lot more response than we are. Three to one, and it doesn't sound like our one response is a particularly nice god."

"He's not." Crystal shook her head, not in negation, just brushing away an errant thought. "I mean, he's better than he used to be, but...yeah, his nanoverse is a nasty place. He's been trying to reform it some, though."

"Wait, what do you mean?"

"He's...look, love, a lot of the old morality is gonna go out the window right now. Every god or goddess that wants to protect humanity, no matter what? They're gonna go with Enki, yeah?" Her brow furrowed at that. "I'm the only one who remembers how badly that worked last time, love." The forehead smoothed. "Of course, on the other hand there will be all the gods or goddesses that are just terrified you're gonna hit the reset button like I did. So you'll have selfish and good reasons for being over there."

"Well, okay, but-"

Crystal was relentless, "and in our corner, we're gonna get two types, too. Those that know there's nothing else to do, that this is the way it's gotta be - and then ones like Moloch, who is probably hoping you're gonna go big. Ice age, plague, meteor impact - major slaughter event. So good reasons and psycho ones on our side, yeah?"

"Okay, Crystal, I get it."

She smiled, with a hint of mischief in her eye. "Good. Any more questions?"

"Yeah, but you're asking so you can tell me to roll with it."

That got a genuine laugh out of Crystal. "Hole in one, love."

Ryan noticed at that moment that his nanoverse was getting big and gave it a squeeze. He savored the barrage of sensation, and a small part of his mind wondered if he was getting addicted to it. It was still the most phenomenal feeling he could have ever imagined. For a moment he wallowed in feeling like he had taken a sip of liquid thunder that had been strained through solid gold and cut with chunks carved out of a rainbow. "Does that ever become less of a rush?"

"Not really. But you'll start doing it less often - it's rare you drain yourself all the way down to no power. Your body stores a little bit each time, and that builds up. I haven't done it in years."

Ryan wanted to ask about life in his nanoverse, but the look in Crystal's eyes told him that he knew the answer. "Okay. But...Crystal, what do we do next? I mean, are we just going to gather up a bunch of gods and goddesses, have a big old punch-up with Enki, then end the world?"

"I've been thinking about that. We need to get back to Earth, find out what Enki's up to. He's a crafty wanker, and if we're not careful he'll sucker-punch us right when we don't notice it."

He nodded. "But how do we avoid him finding us right away? Hell, how did he find us last time?"

"It's easy to detect when a door opens somewhere, if you know to look. But right now lots of deities are popping in and out of their doors, chatting about the upcoming dust-up. Makes it impossible to know who is opening what door, so we should be able to sneak in without him knowing it's us, yeah?"

"That...makes a ton of sense, actually. Then let's go." Ryan settled back, grabbing his book to wait for the ride to Earth.

***

"Well, I didn't expect it to be *this* bloody easy," Crystal commented, rolling her eyes. They'd stepped out into an alley, and the first thing that happened had been Ryan's phone going insane. Apparently, cell reception in Crystal's planetarium ship - or, you know, on Mars - wasn't the best. He'd checked his alerts - friends were all sharing the latest viral video and tagging him in it. His sister had also sent him about a dozen messages on every social platform, demanding to know what the hell was going on, but he got distracted by the video.

It showed the fight from that derelict gas station. Ryan thought back to it and was pretty damn sure there wasn't anyone with a camera present, which raised the question of how Enki had gotten the video. He also was sure Enki didn't look like that. Sure, the man in the video had echoes of Enki in his features, but only if you assume the fight had knocked all the ugly out of Enki with so much force it had disrupted space-time and made him retroactively handsome. *He...looks more like the photo of that bas-relief,* Ryan realized with a start. This must be the man the people of ancient Sumeria saw. Not the brute Ryan had faced before, but a man of refinement and dignity with an air of somber gravitas.

To make matters worse, newer and prettier Enki was currently doing a live interview with the American News Channel.

"Oh, bloody hell, this is so much absolute bullshit," Crystal muttered.

Enki in the interview was not the Enki Crystal and Ryan knew. He was smooth, handsome, and articulate.

"So you see, Gail," Enki was remarking to the younger woman sitting across the desk from him, while a still of the lightning bolt coming out of the sky sat in the background. "We have decided that we were tired of hiding, tired of protecting humanity from the shadows." He gave a smile that was so perfect, Ryan half expected his teeth to make a little *ting* with a lens flare effect. "Myself, Athena, Týr, and Bast are the first to step forward."

"I see. And you are all actually the mythological figures?" The reporter, to her credit, didn't sound like she was swallowing the story hook line and sinker, but wasn't dismissing the whole thing out of hand like Ryan wished she would. *The problem,* Ryan thought with his lips curling into a sour frown, *is that Enki has just enough truth on his side to make his story seem plausible.*

"Of course." His smile managed to somehow widen, even though it seemed it was already stretched to its maximum. "And don't worry, we aren't expecting to be worshipped like we were in times of old. We just want to help."

"And you've demonstrated some impressive powers so far. But tell me, Enki, why wait until now?"

Enki motioned, somehow, to exactly where the box was on the screen. "Because of reactionary elements like these two. Cruel beings who want nothing more than to destroy the entire world and watch humanity suffer."

"Hey!" Ryan interjected, unable to stop himself from shouting at the tiny screen, "I don't want people to suffer! Just...the first one." Ryan paused at this, frowning. It was hard to argue with Enki right now. There were two sides to this conflict. One that wanted to end the world, and one that didn't. Granted, he and Crystal were trying to save the people on the world in the process, but most people would miss the nuance there. "I mean, I don't *want* to end the world, I just...kind of have to?"

Ryan's head was starting to hurt.

Crystal made a shushing noise at Ryan. Ryan frowned. *Are you the bad guy?* That question seemed to be the more relevant one. Ryan knew his own motives. He knew he wanted to save the world. But...how could he trust Crystal? *If Crystal was lying, Enki would have used that during the fight.* It wasn't much to pin faith on, but it was something. Something concrete, a real reason to trust Crystal over Enki. Besides, only one of them had tried to kill Ryan, and it sure wasn't Crystal.

Enki was still speaking, "...calls herself Crystal now, but in the old days she was Ishtar, goddess of wanton fornication and murder." Ryan risked a glance at Crystal, and noticed a vein was throbbing in her forehead.

"I was a fertility goddess, you *git,*" she hissed to herself.

Enki continued, "The man, on the other hand, isn't old like most of us. He's new, probably about thirty. Ryan Smith. But your people have been warned about him, and know him by another name."

Oh no please don't go where I think you're going with that.

Gail was leaning forward, caught up in Enki's charisma.

"And who is he?"

"I believe your bible refers to him as the Antichrist."

Ryan's jaw dropped open. *Okay, at least now I know he's full of shit.* Calling Ryan the Antichrist wasn't the kind of move someone with the right argument made. It was what you did when you wanted to rile people up, whip them into a fury. It was what you did when you needed people to react with emotion, not reason. It was the domain of slick TV Evangelicals, of grasping politicians. Ryan knew damn well he wasn't the Antichrist. *And man does it suck to be called that.* How many people would believe Enki? He had powers, he was something extra normal. It was easier to believe it when Enki said Antichrist than when some random guy did.

On the screen, professionalism had flown out the window as Gail let out an audible gasp, and Ryan wondered if Enki was manipulating her somehow. She seemed to realize how over the top that had been and took a moment to compose herself. "So, if that's true...I mean, you're trying to imply that..."

Enki nodded somberly. "Yes. Armageddon is here, and this man will bring it about." He turned to the camera. "If you know this man, we've set up a hotline for any information about him. Please, if you see him, call us, but do not engage - he has the power of a god, and will kill you."

"Well, thank you for that." The camera zoomed in on Gail's face. "Right now, Enki's companions - this 'New Pantheon,' are currently at labs across the country, providing additional verification of their abilities. We go now to Chad in Atlanta, where Bast is-"

"Turn it off," Crystal said. Her voice was an angry growl that Ryan didn't expect to hear from her. "Turn the bloody thing off."

Ryan did. "How bad is this?"

"It's pretty bad, love. He's just turned the entire sodding planet into his spies against us. And when he finds out we're working with Moloch..."

90

"I doubt he'll hold back on mentioning the whole 'used to kill children' thing." Ryan could feel a headache building.

"Right." Crystal leaned against the wall and rubbed her own temples.

"Crystal, are you sure we should be working with Moloch? I mean, I know we're hard up for help, but...literal murderer?"

Crystal shrugged. "I'm sure we don't have anyone else, Ryan. I've never worked with him before - only his own pantheon, the old gods of Canaan really did - but..." Crystal trailed off and shrugged. "He's better than not having any help, yeah?"

Ryan rubbed the back of his neck. "Is he, though? I mean, really."

"Look, we're meeting with him soon. After that's all done, love, if you're not convinced, we're done. Okay?"

Ryan nodded. It wasn't ideal, but he could live with it. "Okay, sure."

Crystal turned back to the phone, where the talking heads were starting to discuss Enki's interview. "Okay. How do we deal with this?"

Ryan almost recoiled from the question. "You're asking me?"

"Yeah. Love, this is a media thing, yeah? I had to hire someone to build me a website; you know more about viral videos and all that than I do."

Ryan looked at the ground, thinking hard. Enki had backed them into a corner here - if they wanted to be able to move on Earth, they'd have to deal with tons of eyes looking out for them. At first the situation seemed absolutely hopeless, like they were trying to wrestle the entire planet at once, but bit by bit an idea began to occur to him.

"He gave my name, and they have my face," he said, every word carefully chosen to try not to break the fragile idea as it formed.

"Right. And?"

Ryan began scrolling through his phone. Tons of missed calls and voicemails, some from friends, but others from numbers across the country Ryan didn't know.

"And that means some of these calls are from reporters. I think, Crystal, our best bet is to play his game." He smiled and held up the phone.

Crystal groaned. "If you're going where I think you're going with this, love, I'm going to regret giving you the lead here."

"I don't like it any more than you do, Crystal. Honestly." Ryan shrugged. "But it's the game Enki's playing, and it's the only way to keep up. Everyone's going to be looking to us as well since he fed the media his line of bullshit - only thing to do is get some of those people on our side. Unless you want to be hunted by most of the damn planet?"

"Damnit, damnit. Fine," Crystal sighed. "Find us a reporter, love."

Ryan started scrolling through his phone. It didn't take long to find a reporter wanting to do an interview. In fact, the hardest part was sifting through the voicemails looking for the one in particular he was hoping to get - and after a bit, he found it, listening to the voicemail with a wide grin.

"Found it. Give me just one moment."

Crystal nodded. Ryan still hadn't mastered - or practiced, or even thought of in days - the skill that both Nabu and Enki had used to be invisible and intangible to normal people, so she kept a lookout while using that trick.

Ryan dialed the number.

"Mr. Smith?" The voice on the other end sounded excited, the same upbeat tones he'd heard coming out of his voicemail. Gail. There was a nice "screw you" in using the same reporter Enki had, and for the plan to work, it needed to be easy for Enki to find them.

"Speaking. Did I reach Gail Pittman?"

"Yes. Mr. Smith, millions have heard Enki's side of things, but I'm sure you have your own story."

Ryan nodded, then realized she couldn't see him, but kept nodding anyway for a moment because he'd already started so might as well keep at it. "That's why I'm calling. But we - that is to say, Crystal and I - we don't want to do it at your studio. Too exposed."

There was a moment of silence as Gail thought the implication of his statement. Ryan didn't do anything to interrupt that thought process or to try and nudge it in the direction he wanted to go, instead waiting for her to come to the right conclusion on her own. "You're worried Enki will attack the studio?"

"Exactly. Not the most heroic choice on his part, but he has a pretty bad hate-on for us. Honestly, I think I'd be flattered if it wasn't so murderous."

Gail let out a huff of air that might have been amusement. "I'd still need to have my cameraman present."

Ryan glanced at Crystal, who was still scanning the street. "That would be fine with us. There's an abandoned warehouse I'm going to give you the address to."

This actually got a laugh. "Mr. Smith, you want to meet at an abandoned warehouse? Slightly cliché, don't you think?"

"Well...how do you usually interview people being hunted by a cabal of gods and with a chunk of the planet thinking they're evil?"

A moment's hesitation. "Conference room in a hotel. I have one I use for interviewees in town who don't want to come into the station. I'll give you the location."

"Give me a moment?" Without waiting for a response, Ryan put his phone on mute, turning to Crystal, "She wants us to go to a hotel, instead of a warehouse."

Crystal cocked her head, then nodded. "Warehouse was just the first idea I had, yeah? As long as Enki doesn't know where we are right away - and the studio is too bloody obvious, he'll have watchers - we should be safe."

Ryan unmuted the phone. "Sure, we can do that. Tell us where."

Gail provided the location and told them she'd be there in two hours. Plenty of time to get there and scout for possible threats before they went on TV.

Crystal frowned at the news. "Okay, I guess that's alright then."

"Everything okay? You don't seem particularly thrilled at this."

She shrugged, then shook her head. "I'm not. I've stayed out of the public eye since the days of Sumeria, love. The idea of appearing on camera? Bloody terrifying, I won't lie. On top of that, I don't like that we're still reacting to Enki, yeah?"

"I hear you, really. But look at the bright side - we're gonna end the world after we deal with Enki, so it's not like being on camera will matter for long, right?"

That got a laugh out of Crystal, one of those short, shocked ones you make at jokes you weren't supposed to laugh at because they weren't appropriate, but still found funny. Ryan was glad it went over well with her - joking about the end of the world made his stomach churn, but she'd needed it.

"Thanks for that. C'mon, then. Let's meet Moloch, then I'm ready for my bloody prime time debut."

***

Ryan had tried to go into the meeting with Moloch with an open mind. They connected in Detroit, in an abandoned apartment building that was housing a variety of squatters and other people society did its level best to forget existed. If any of them claimed to see this meeting, they'd be disbelieved. The logic made sense, but given what Moloch had done in the past, the idea of meeting him surrounded by people who could just vanish without a fuss put Ryan's teeth on edge. *Steady now, Ryan. Crystal said he's better now.* Ryan thought back over Crystal's words. *Or...did she ever say he stopped it altogether?*

He couldn't remember. To Ryan, it seemed that *no longer a murderer* is the kind of detail you'd want to make explicitly clear.

The apartment Moloch was waiting in for them was about as terrible as the hallway outside suggested. Moldy rugs, yellowing, flaking wallpaper, a half-trashed card table with crusty stains on its surface that Ryan tried not think about. Instead, he did his best to focus on their new ally. Moloch at least fit the room, and his appearance did nothing to ease Ryan's misgivings. Moloch wore a suit, but it looked like it had seen better days. *Probably in the 1800's,* Ryan thought with a sour twist to his lips. The man wearing it didn't inspire much more confidence. He was tall and thin, with stringy hair and rotted teeth. His fingers looked almost skeletal, they were so thin, and they twitched spasmodically when Crystal entered behind Ryan. He glanced at them with eyes sunken deep into his head. "Were you followed?"

Damnit, even his voice is grating. It was sickeningly wet, like it two slabs of beef sliding against each other. "Of course not, love, we just popped out of our nanoverses," Crystal answered as Ryan groped for his words.

For her part, Crystal seemed perfectly at ease. Ryan reminded himself that there was no reason to be on edge. Moloch was offering to help them. There was no need to judge him for how he looked.

Moloch met his gaze, and Ryan flushed. *You're being a dick, Ryan,* he chided himself. "Thanks for answering our letter, Moloch."

"Of course, of course. Enki is...problematic. I'd rather not see him have power any more than either of you would."

"Too bloody right," Crystal said, grabbing one of the chairs near the card table. Hesitantly, Ryan did the same.

"I have a plan," Ryan said. "We're going to meet with a reporter. The same one that interviewed Enki."

Moloch frowned in thought. "You mean to lure him out?"

"Bingo," Ryan said with a forced smile. "Him, Bast, Athena, Týr. The whole bunch. As far as Enki knows, it's a four on two fight. That's where you come in."

Moloch nodded slowly as he considered. "I arrive at an opportune moment and...correct the odds."

"Absolutely," Crystal said. "I know you don't do much physical engagement, Moloch."

Ryan blinked at that. It was news to him. "Why not?" he asked, drawing both of their attention.

"Well…" Moloch let out a phlegmatic cough. *Can we even get sick? Is this all a show?* "to be perfectly honest? I detest it. I feel such scuffling should be beneath us. We have for so many millennia slaughtered people who got in our way, or even as bystanders in our conflicts. We are...we should be better than that. Example for humanity to follow, no?"

Ryan blinked a few more times. "You...you used to demand human sacrifice."

"Ryan!" Crystal said, like he'd just broken wind at a fancy dinner.

"No, no, Crystal - it's Crystal now, right? - he's correct. I understand his misgivings." Moloch leaned forward and focused his attention on Ryan. "I did used to butcher mankind. By the thousands, if I'm being honest. I liked the extra power I could draw from their souls, and a part of me...enjoyed it." His lips twitched in a faint grin, and Ryan wondered if Moloch was smiling at his discomfort, or if it was some memory of a past atrocity. *Stop it, Ryan. Listen. Don't be so damn shallow.* "That's why I keep my shape so twisted. A reminder of the weight of past sins. That's why I am here now - I am using my powers to help these sick, damned beings. I can never undo what was done, but I can be better in the future."

Crystal gave Ryan a firm look. *You satisfied?* the glance seemed to ask.

Ryan nodded. "Okay. Thank you for explaining." He gave Moloch a smile that felt a bit more genuine. The other god still made him uncomfortable, but at least he'd given Ryan answers, and they were good answers. "So, here's how it's going to go down." They spent a good hour discussing the plan, killing most of the free time they had before meeting Gail. Moloch didn't like how violent the plan was, but agreed "risk of collateral is better than extinction."

"I see one minor flaw to the plan." Moloch pointed at Ryan. "He's still Nascent. How does he intend to defend himself against swords?"

Ryan frowned, looking at Crystal. "Swords?"

"Oh yeah, love, we use them all the bloody time." Crystal grinned. "At least, usually. You just have to grab one out of your nanoverse, yeah?"

Moloch chuckled wetly at Ryan's confusion. "I think you need to explain a bit better, Crystal."

Crystal sighed. "Right then." She turned towards Ryan. "We can grab simple tools out of our multiverses. The more complex, the less likely it is to work over here. Swords, axes, bows, arrows, all of the old classics - iron is iron, steel is steel. They work just fine. So most of us favor them."

Ryan's frown deepened. "So, wait, what about creating or destroying matter? Doesn't that add new matter to our universe?"

Moloch answered after another chuckle. "Our nanoverses are part of this universe. The only difference is scale. When you pull it out..." He shrugged. "It scales up."

"Okay." Honestly, as far as strange things went, this one didn't make Ryan's rapidly revised personal top ten. *I mean, it's completely bugnuts bonkers, but I guess it's really not that much odder than having a pocket universe in the first place.* "So...how do I do it?"

Crystal reached into the air and pulled out a beautiful silver sword. "Like that?"

Ryan did the same thing and pulled out...nothing. "Uh...maybe there's a bit more to it?"

Moloch got up and walked behind Ryan, putting his hand on Ryan's shoulders. Ryan fought back an urge to shudder. Moloch leaned down and whispered in Ryan's ear, making Ryan's skin crawl. "Eschaton. Everything we do is a matter of will. We exert our will upon reality. We bend it, we break it, we do what we need to it. You are treating your nanoverse like it is a child. It is not. It is a *battery.* It is the source of your power. It is yours to do with what you *will.* Do not gently hope your nanoverse will give you what you need. When you need something from it, you reach out and *take it.*"

Ryan took a deep breath. "Okay." He focused on his need, on his desire. He was not asking, he was taking. He plunged his hand out into the air again, and this time he felt...something. Something solid and real under his fingertips. It brushed the edges and then it was gone. "I...I almost had it."

Moloch walked away, grinning. Ryan relaxed some. It felt real. He could do this! He noticed Crystal's frown, but assumed it was because Moloch was being so damn creepy.

If it was something else, Crystal decided not to clarify. Instead, she said, "Try again."

It took a bit more time, and Ryan was starting to sweat by the end of it. Just when he was ready to give up, worried about burning too much power before the battle with Enki, his fingers were able to close on something.

It wasn't a sword he pulled out. It looked like a flat wooden club, almost a thin paddle, with blades of obsidian stuck into its side. Crystal clapped her hands in excitement. "Oooh, your people haven't gotten swords yet, love. That's a...what'd the Aztecs call it, Moloch?"

"A macahuitl," Moloch said with a nod.

"A...mak…" Ryan glanced helplessly at them. "I'm never going to be able to pronounce that," he muttered.

"Don't sweat it, love." Crystal grinned. "You don't need to name it to pull it."

Moloch chuckled, and Ryan rolled his eyes. "But I was reaching for a sword. Why'd I pull out...this?"

Moloch answered for her. "It's likely the people of your nanoverse have not yet discovered metallurgy. When you reach in, you pull out...the best version of what you were looking for. If you reached for an arming sword but they don't have one yet, you'll get a gladius if they have those. If they lack swords altogether, you'll get the closest weapon your nanoverse has." Moloch indicated the macahuitl. "The Aztecs favored those weapons. Don't underestimate them - obsidian is scalpel sharp. I'd avoid trying to parry, you'll shatter the blades, but…" Moloch shrugged.

He does that a lot. I wonder why. Some people just had ticks, but Ryan felt like there was some mockery he was missing with every shrug. He gave the weapon a few experimental swings. At least it was balanced well. With his own shrug, Ryan reached out and shoved it back into the nanoverse. That, at least, was easier than reaching in to pull out a weapon. "That's...really cool, actually." Ryan smiled. He'd just pulled a weapon out of *nothing.* It wasn't the same as manipulating the math that underpinned reality, but it was definitely something he liked. *It's like being a video game character, but my inventory is bottomless.* The thought made him grin.

"Something funny?" Crystal asked.

"Long story. I'll tell it to you later, but..." he glanced at his phone, "We have to head out to make it in time. Moloch, you good on the plan?"

"Oh, yes," Moloch said with a thin smile.

Ryan nodded, and he and Crystal got up to give an interview. And, if things went well, finally get a leg up on Enki.

***

It didn't take them long to get set up. Gail was a professional, at least, although she did seem somewhat flustered by their presence.

"Okay, we're live in three, two..." the cameraman held up a single index finger for the last number.

"Good evening, this is Gail Pittman with ANC. As a follow up to our interview with Enki earlier today, I'm here right now with Ryan Smith and Crystal - the two individuals that Enki alleges are his adversaries, for an exclusive interview. Ryan, Crystal, thank you for talking with me."

Ryan put on his best smile. It felt like it was being forced lengthways through a sieve. Crystal's looked more natural, but Ryan was beginning to suspect Crystal wouldn't be phased by a hungry T-Rex wearing a sombrero.

"We're happy to be here, Gail. Want a chance to clear the air," Ryan said as Crystal nodded in agreement.

"So, let's start with the big one - Enki claims that you two are gods, like him. Is that true?"

Crystal spoke up here, her smile not wavering, "I wouldn't exactly say like him, not in the details, but in the broad strokes, we're gods too."

"Details? What details are those?" Gail leaned forward, a hungry motion, the wolf that had spotted its prey. In this case, the prey was the chance to break new information about what was undoubtedly the story of the century.

"Well, Ryan here, he's only been a god for...two weeks, that sound right love?"

Ryan nodded. "Yeah, two weeks."

"Enki's been a god for about ten thousand years, so that's a difference right there."

After giving that statement a dramatic pause to hang in the air, Gail turned towards Crystal. "And you, Crystal? How long have you been a goddess?"

"A little over a million years."

That got Gail to lean back, giving her time to process that. "That would make you...about as old as the earliest humans?"

Crystal nodded. "I remember when you lot started figuring out tools. But, Gail, most of that isn't relevant to the current situation, yeah? I can talk about millions of years of old news later on...if that's alright."

Gail nodded. "And in that case, Ryan. Enki also alleged you were the Christian Antichrist. Is that true?"

Ryan shook his head. "Of course not. But don't ask me to prove that, Gail."

"Why not? Surely people at home would be relieved if they knew you weren't."

"Oh, believe me, Gail, I'd love to." He could feel himself sweating under the lights and hoped it didn't show on camera. "But...well, it's a HUAC thing, from the 50's? 'Prove you're not a communist.'"

Gail gave a polite smile. "So you're saying it's impossible to prove?"

Ryan nodded again. "I mean, I can assure you I'm not having anyone put a mark on their hand or forehead - or anywhere else, for that matter - so I should get some points for that." He scratched his chin, "Plus, last Crystal heard, Hell is a bit too much of a mess right now to organize a proper Apocalypse, isn't it?"

"It is," Crystal said, "and I know you're going to want more information about that Gail, but only have so long, yeah? So I'm gonna ask that you just roll with it, so we can focus on what Enki is claiming."

Gail blinked at that, and Ryan thought he was starting to get a feel for the woman. Gail was a good reporter and always opened to new ideas, but she had the sort of perfectly practical mind that was doing its best to cope with the perfectly impractical reality of gods walking the Earth and doing interviews. "I see. Then...why were you fighting Enki in that video?"

"Two things there, love." Crystal regained control of the conversation - they had both agreed that she was the more charismatic of the two. "First of all, it's because Enki is an absolute tosser. What you'd call a tool. But the two of us went off to help Ryan acclimate to his changes, yeah?" Gail nodded along, her forehead wrinkled with intense concentration. Ryan realized exactly how tightly wound she was and felt a perverse urge to lean forward and shout "Boo," as loud as he could. Even though Gail was maintaining a professional demeanor, her eyes screamed that she was terrified of the two of them. "When we got back, he ambushed us. Probably because he sees us as a threat."

Gail played along, not realizing there was a script Ryan and Crystal had come up with in the two hours they had to wait, and so far, she was playing her role with all the skill of a master thespian. "You two did do a number on him in that fight. But what is he afraid you'll do?"

"Stop him." Ryan took back over, leaning forward for the camera's benefit.

"From doing what?"

"He's going to blow up the sun." Ryan delivered the half-truth with the absolute certainty of a preacher that's been dipping into the donation plate to line his own pockets, and with about as much honesty. "That's what he wants to do."

As well as Gail's composure had been maintained throughout the interview, it cracked a bit here and she blinked slowly, giving herself just a quarter second to process that. Ryan was now certain her gasp earlier when interviewing Enki had been some manipulation of his. "He wants to...blow up the sun?"

Crystal took back over. "I noticed he left that out of the interview he did with you, which seemed like exactly the kind of underhanded move that git would pull. He's also the type dumb enough to think that would work, that we wouldn't tell you the truth."

"Wait," Gail was starting to realize that she was losing control of the conversation. "You're saying he's dumb based on-"

"-on knowing him for multiple thousands of years, love. Back in the day of Sumeria, he was pretty clever. Since then, he's devolved into a nasty brute who can put on a good show, sure, but at the end of the day, he's a common bloody bully. The god of being a common bloody bully, really."

Gail opened her mouth, but another voice spoke up, coming through the door that should have been locked. The door to the adjacent room, which was also the door Ryan had very carefully suggested Crystal *didn't* block with her ship's door.

"You've got quite a mouth on you." Enki wasn't bothering to control his voice, although the weirdly handsome face he'd worn for the news was still the visage he was presenting. "But you made a mistake, going on live like this." His grin didn't fit that handsome face - it was like halfway through a cartoon about musical princesses, the handsome prince started to beat the villain to death with a severed arm wrapped in barbed-wire. Ugly and twisted and just wrong.

Behind Enki, two other figures walked out of the doorway. Both of them women. One had a wicked smile and hair that was curled up in a pair of buns. They looked almost like the points of a cat's ears. *Cat ears, huh? Guess that makes you Bast.* He glanced at the other. She had strong, Mediterranean features and eyes that were as warm and welcoming as garrote wires. *And that must make that charming lady Athena.* A fourth figure was coming through the doorway, though Ryan couldn't make it out yet.

"Yessiree Bob, you made a big mistake. Because this time...the two on one odds favor me."

And for a moment, the only sound was Gail scooting her chair out of the line of fire.

Chapter 9

Out of Hand

If Enki had hoped his little speech and pointing out the odds would frighten Ryan, he had another thing coming. Oh, sure, it terrified Ryan to his core, which wasn't the same as frightened. *It's okay, Ryan,* he reminded himself, doing his best to not let the panic show. Instead, he made a show of shrugging, and looking at Gail as Týr emerged.

"Seems a bit less heroic when he's gloating, doesn't he?"

"Heh." That, at least, got a chuckle of Enki. Not quite the reaction Ryan was hoping for. He knew it was a long shot, but he was hoping Enki would slip up here, say something stupid, something that made him the obvious villain. Anything other than coming across as a cocky hero. "He's playing you all."

Athena sighed and rolled her eyes. "Enki, this a waste of time. We have the Eschaton here; can we just *end* him already?" Her voice was dripping with annoyance. *Dissention in the ranks? Or just not one to mince words?* Ryan wasn't sure, but had a feeling it wouldn't matter for long. "You know," she continued, "before he ends the world?"

Bast nodded in agreement, and Týr...struck a pose. Hands on hips, chest jutting out. Like some kind of nineteen-forties superhero. It was so ridiculous that Crystal started to giggle, which drew Enki's attention to her. "You think something's funny, you evil bitch? You think the end of the world is a joke?"

Crystal chortled for another couple moments. "No...no I swear, I'm not laughing at the end of the," and the laughter overtook her again for a moment, "end of the world. I swear. I'm laughing at you all...oh damn it all," and she all but doubled over with laughter as another fit hit her.

Enki's face was twisting in a scowl, and in his case, that was more literal. His heroic visage beginning to run like a wax figure shoved under a heat lamp, fading back into his more familiar paleolithic features, eyes shrinking into tiny little beads of spite. "I'm going to rip your head off."

"To save the world," Týr interjected.

"Of course." Enki glanced at Bast, then at Gail, who had stayed silent, and the cameraman, who was still broadcasting to the world. Ryan could see Enki's brain churning, rusty gears clunking into place with metallic clanks. "Bast, you know why you're here. Keep the humans safe."

Ryan let out a breath he hadn't realized he'd been holding. If Enki had been willing to throw aside his pretense, Ryan and Crystal would have had terrible odds, and would have had to protect the innocent people *they* had dragged into this. The entire plan had hinged on that point, on Enki's ego - which Crystal had said "was like betting on the sun coming up, love. Not a sure-fire thing, but you're pretty unlikely to be wrong, yeah?"

Now if only we can pull off the rest of this, we might have - fist. Granted, the word Ryan had been about to think hadn't been "fist," but when a fist as large as Enki's filled your field of vision it also tended to dominate your thoughts.

And then said fist fully occupied Ryan's mind by sending lances of pain through his nose and face. The blow picked him up out of the chair and sent him crashing through the wall and into the adjacent room. A naked woman screamed as she hopped off some man. She clutched the sheet around herself as the man's hands went to cover his lap and he started to roll over the side of the bed.

For some reason Ryan's divine senses decided to note atoms of gold encircling one of her fingers, but none on any of the man's. Before he could take any time to figure out why his divine senses decided to focus on the importance of some random woman's infidelity, he impacted the opposite wall. It barely gave him any resistance as he passed through that one too.

Enki followed, blocking Ryan's view of Crystal's fight with Týr and Athena. A small part of Ryan's brain tried to remind him of the plan, but the majority of it was focused on the fact that Enki was bringing a foot down on Ryan's gut.

The blow punched Ryan through the floor, and then the one below that, and then a third. "I'm going to feed you your own entrails, you little shit!" Enki was coming down the hole after him.

Ryan threw out his hand and grabbed the equation for gravity. It had been the first equation from physics to ever really click with him, and he could recite it in his sleep. Those numbers needed to obey him. He slapped a minus sign in front of the vector of gravity, turning it around to pull Enki in the opposite direction. Enki's downward progress slowed, coming to a stop inches from impacting Ryan, hovering for just a second like a basketball player getting perfect hang time. They were almost face to face, and Ryan got to enjoy the look of realization grow in Enki's beady eyes.

"Oh, *fuck* you," Enki nearly whispered as gravity began to reverse, and then he went rocketing away as Ryan quickly slapped a ^{3} onto the gravitational constant.

"Antigravity cubed, bitch," he said to the retreating form. He could still hear the sounds of fighting above and shook his head to clear it. Crystal needed his help.

It took a few quick leaps to carry him up between floors. At the top was a gaping hole where Enki had punched through the ceiling, and Ryan knew it was too much to hope for that he'd keep sailing all the way to space. He raced past the naked woman and man - who were midway through rushing out of the room. Neither had bothered to get dressed. The man was still wearing only the clothes he had been born in, and the woman was clutching the bedsheet across herself as she ran. He ignored them both, dashing through to where the battle raged.

Crystal was moving in the same graceful dance she had used against the Hecatoncheires, flitting between their blades. Athena's came at her low as Ryan approached, and Týr's was moving in a high arc, but she dove between the two swords. Her weapon snuck like a snake to nick Týr's arm.

But she was also bleeding from a dozen small cuts herself, and Athena and Týr only had five total between them. Hundreds of millennia of experience, it seemed, only counted for so much.

Ryan rushed in, like they'd practiced, and reached out to draw a macahuitl out of thin air.

He brought the primitive weapon down towards Týr's back in a wild swing.

A small part of Ryan noted that Bast was watching the fight and hadn't moved during his charge. She could have tried to give Týr a warning, but instead had just let Ryan get in the surprise attack. Ryan wasn't sure why, but was glad for the opportunity. Say what you will about obsidian as an alternative to metal, but it was razor sharp. Týr howled and whirled around, but instead of striking at the sword, he curled his fingers.

Shit. He could see what Týr was doing, although it was difficult to understand - the math was wrong. Whatever it was, it wasn't a simple twist. Ryan tried to grab the equations Týr was manipulating, force some order onto the chaos. As natural as tampering with the fundamental equations of reality was starting to feel, Týr had centuries of practice on Ryan. He pushed back against Ryan's manipulation with a deft ease. Ryan was still fumbling when the equations fell into place, and Týr selectively changed the coefficient of friction of Ryan's clothes and, simultaneously, the density of air.

Those two factors' new values caused Ryan to burst into flame. With no other option, he dove out the window. The small part of him that wasn't focused on the fact that he was on fire was glad to note that Týr leapt out after him.

Hardened steel met solid wood a couple times in the air, and then both of them impacted the street below. Týr was on top, and Ryan, for the third time in under a minute, found himself slamming into an object that should have shattered his body. In this case, the ground. Concrete cracked in a spiderweb around their impact.

The pain was incredible, but through it all Ryan was sure of one thing. He might not have been able to prevent his impending impact with the ground, but he could at least not burn to death in the process. He twisted reality to force all the air away from himself, and the flames went out. Týr didn't seem interested in trying to incinerate Ryan completely, and let the normal laws of friction and air density around Ryan resume. *Allowed. I couldn't even break it, Týr just stopped maintaining it.* In some ways, Týr was more dangerous than Enki had been. Less brutal. He was the scalpel to Enki's claymore. And now that Týr was on top of him, Ryan had no idea how he was going to survive.

He didn't have to answer that question, because Týr stepped back. It was a stark contrast to the relentless assault Enki had dished out. Týr was actually giving Ryan a chance to stand up as opposed to pressing his advantage. *Is he stupid?* Ryan thought, trying to get to his feet, *or is he just that good a guy?* Thankfully, this gave people on the ground time to scatter. Unfortunately, the people on the ground were...people, and only backed up some. A few had run - at least, Ryan hoped they had - but for the most part people were reaching into their pockets and pulling out cellphones to record. Men and women in business suits going about their day. Teenagers holding skateboards. One group in particular drew Ryan's eyes, a man and a woman standing there, with the woman holding a small child who was staring at them in wonder. *Seriously? You have a damn baby, run you idiots!*

Ryan realized how the two of them looked. Týr was still spotless, his hair blond and his smile gleaming, his sword shimmering in the sun, while Ryan had skin covered with dark soot that still smoldered in places and a primitive weapon with black glass and skulls. *Skulls? Seriously? I should learn to shapeshift so I could sprout horns,* Ryan thought through the pain. *Might as well go all in.*

Ryan noticed how carefully Týr's posture was constructed. Chest out, sword extended, a firm yet confident gleam in his eyes mixed with a half smug grin. It looked, to the people surrounding them and to the camera phones like an angel fighting a demon. Exactly what Týr wanted. *He's not stupid. He's mugging for the damn cameras.*

Before Týr could take maximum advantage of the mixed poses, a window shattered, and Crystal and Athena repeated Ryan and Týr's descent - with Team "End the World" getting similar results this time around. Crystal got buried in the concrete as well, but Athena backed off. For a moment Ryan thought Athena was going for the same effect as Týr. Then he noticed Crystal still had her sword up and was already rolling out of the pit. Athena hadn't moved to try for the dramatic effect. She just didn't want to get impaled.

"It's over, you foul abominations!" Týr shouted as Athena stepped next to him. "Your plan to destroy the world ends here, once Enki returns from whatever you did to him! Your reign of terror is over."

"Seriously?" Crystal spoke up here, giving Ryan time to catch his breath and push away the pains of his burns. "What kind of wanker talks like that?"

The ghost of a smile crossed even Athena's eyes with that. Týr scowled. "Fine. You're both badly hurt. Surrender now and we'll show you mercy."

"Any time now!" Ryan said, his voice as loud as he could make it through the pain. "Can we hurry it up?"

"Hurry it up? So you wish to surrender?" Týr and Athena shared a confused glance.

"I wasn't...ah, damn, that hurts...I wasn't talking to *you.*"

Athena whirled around while Týr kept his blade pointed at Crystal and Ryan. The door to the front of the hotel opened, and out walked Moloch. "Terribly sorry about the delay," he said, "Horrible traffic around the Void Nebula, you know how it is."

"Moloch," Athena hissed. That one word carried more actual emotion than every earlier statement combined. "So you're the backup."

Moloch smiled. His mouth was a rotten graveyard overgrown with black moss and yellow, crooked headstones. "No, my dear. You know I detest physical confrontation or utilizing my divine powers in so crass a matter." His voice was thin and airy, like the breeze through a mausoleum. From the doorway behind Moloch came a high, plaintive wail, the inhuman agony that Crystal and Ryan had heard on Cipher Nullity. Moloch's rotting grin widened with Ryan's eyes. *What is he doing? What the hell is he doing? This isn't what we talked about.*

Hands began to emerge from the doorway, pitch black hands that did not attach to any arms. The Hecatoncheires, almost half again as tall as of the one they had encountered before, pulled itself through the narrow doorway like ooze sliding through a pipe. "That, my dear, is the backup."

***

Ryan's mouth fell open. *This isn't the plan. That's not the plan at all. No part of the plan called for a damn Hecatoncheires! What the hell is Moloch thinking?* The monster let out another long, mournful wail, and Ryan subconsciously edged closer to Crystal. *Not behind her, definitely not wanting to get behind her again...* he glanced around at the crowd.

Logic would dictate that the sight of an abomination against biology, physics, and several known religions (and at least two unknown cults) would have more people running in the kind of screaming terror that later on necessitates a change of undergarments. Apparently, however, the fight or flight instinct had a third partner in the modern age of camera phones - fight, flight or photograph. Most of the crowd was, distressingly, choosing the latter.

"Can't be that bad, right?" Ryan half whispered to Crystal, watching Athena and Týr get ready to square off against the monster. "You smote the one we faced earlier pretty quick."

Crystal let out a choking sound that Ryan could only call a rage laugh. For the first time since Moloch's betrayal, Ryan saw Crystal's face. If looks could kill, Moloch would have been completely removed from reality from the sheer force of Crystal's glare. "Love, that was a half-starved Hecatoncheires, and we were in a realm where I was queen for a few thousand years. This is Earth, and that one is nice and healthy."

Týr and Athena didn't wait for Moloch's brute to make the first move. They charged in, each of them taking a different side in half arcs. The Hecatoncheires' hands moved, but it was different from what Ryan had seen before. The hands were all moving independently - not two giant masses, but swatting and grasping like a swarm of bees with fingers.

"We should...we should go." Crystal's voice still tight with anger. "This was the plan if we were losing, yeah? Get Moloch here, let him distract, we get out."

"Right." Neither of them moved as Týr got swatted aside on the left, ramming headfirst into a stoplight post so hard that it was bent in half, and a dozen hands latched on to Athena on the right. They began to tug on her arms, and she started to scream in agony as it tried to tear her apart. But that wasn't what Athena and Tyr were focused on. Both of them watched as Moloch headed back into his ship, the hotel doors closing behind them.

You played us, Moloch. The realization hit Ryan with a sudden flash of rage. *You set us up. If we help Athena and Týr, we'll be too tired to fight Enki and Bast. If we don't...*Much as he might wish he could, Ryan couldn't escape the reality that that Hecatoncheires was going to go on a rampage after it killed Athena and Týr. They would get better, but the random innocent people? Not so much. *I knew we couldn't trust you. I just hope I get to pay you back for that.* Crystal and Ryan didn't need to share a look. She drew her sword, he his obsidian weapon, and they ran in.

They both began twisting equations as they ran. Ryan dropped the coefficient of friction of Athena's skin to nearly zero, a reversal of the trick Týr had tried on him. The hands trying to tug her apart slipped off and went flying wide. Crystal did something far more complex than just changing an equation. Instead, she twisted the atomic number of the nitrogen in the air around the horrible lamprey head of the giant. Seven changed to nineteen, and the nitrogen changed to potassium, as every molecule of water in the air for a full block was sucked in towards the monster. Before it could move far from the head, the temperature jumped up several hundred degrees and the potassium reacted with the water, as potassium is prone to doing.

All that science meant that Ryan learned how to create a fireball.

The sudden explosion was deafening, and the shockwave startled Týr into consciousness, in defiance of what explosions typically do to states of awareness. Athena brushed her hair out of her face and glanced at the giant, then back at Ryan, her eyes narrowed. "Why did you help me?"

"Because giant monster! Rampage! Question later, we have to stop it!"

She gave a single curt nod, then rolled away as the Hecatoncheires slapped at the ground where she had been. She threw her sword at it, but she changed the acceleration of the tip as it flew instead of letting it tumble end over end, and the sword punched through the giant at hypersonic speeds. Glass shattered nearby from the sonic boom.

Ryan couldn't help but wonder why he could follow the complex changes Crystal made, but couldn't see how Athena sped up a sword.

The Hecatoncheires seemed to dislike being stabbed by a supersonic sword, as anyone would, but was not as inconvenienced as Ryan had hoped. Two of its free hands slapped over the entry and exit wound, stemming the tide of ichor flowing from the holes.

"Bast! We need your help!" Týr shouted, and he did his own twisting of reality. He wasn't pointing his hand at the monster before them. His hand pointed upwards. When no response came from above, he snarled and turned towards Crystal and Ryan. "If you be not villains, keep it busy, and jump away when I say!"

"Crystal?" Ryan asked.

"Roll with it!" She dashed in, and Ryan followed. Three on one, and they were still getting beat. This monster was clearly annoyed by them, but they were wasps stinging it, and they could only keep stinging until they got swatted.

The Hecatoncheires could do more than sting. Ryan got slapped away like a naughty puppy, bouncing across the concrete and slamming into some poor bastard's car. That would have been worse, but Týr chose that exact second to shout "Jump!"

Crystal and Athena broke free as Týr's manipulations took effect. A small part of Ryan wondered what Týr was seeing, if not math. Lenses of air, maybe? Nordic runes? Something stranger? Maybe when this was done, he'd get to ask Týr.

No matter what Týr saw, fifty kilometers up, the atmosphere warped. A circle of darkness five kilometers wide formed as every single photon coming from the sun was shocked to find it had been squeezed into a point one meter across. Dusting themselves off in confusion, the photons then continued their journey to the Earth, but now packed together. The result? A beam of golden light shot from the center of the dark spot in the sky like it had been fired from an alien spaceship and for a few seconds, almost half a billion watts of solar energy found itself meeting the top of the Hecatoncheires' head.

It may have been an unholy monster, anathema to the normal laws of physics, but normal physics didn't allow for that much sunlight to come into a single point under typical circumstances. Two cases of abnormal physics met, got confused, and decided that they should let plain old ordinary physics decide this.

Ryan shielded his eyes as those physical laws looked at the situation and decided that the Hecatoncheires didn't get to be anything anymore. As the Hecatoncheires was vaporized, the beam cut a hole into the ground for another three hundred feet before the energy was expended.

Fortunately, Týr had accounted for energy radiating outwards, and the four gods and dozens of stupidly watching onlookers were not fried alongside the giant. The final touch was a deafening clap of thunder as air rushed back into the column of sky the photons had vaporized.

Ryan stared as he realized he'd watched a man command even a small portion of the sun's power. *I don't think anyone could blame me for staring at it like a moron. I'm sure everyone else is.* He couldn't completely savor the moment, however. In the back of his mind, a small niggling doubt jumped up and down for attention. *Where the hell is Enki?* He should have rejoined the fight by now, surely. So why wasn't he? *Maybe he realizes he's beat. Týr and Athena have to be questioning him right about now, too.*

After a few more moments, someone in the crowd cheered. That man was, in fact, Bob Robertson. He'd come to this hotel in the hopes of finally catching his wife in the affair he was certain was going on. He was right - the affair had been interrupted by Ryan flying through a wall. His wife would confess the entire affair later that day after the near-death experience of two gods battling through her lover's nest. Bob's cheer started a round of applause and shaking the four gods out of their stunned stupor.

Bast jumped out of the hotel finally, landing next to the hole Týr had cut in the Earth. *Shit,* Ryan thought. He and Crystal were both drained. Týr and Athena weren't in great shape either, but Bast hadn't done a single thing the entire fight. Her power was unspent, and she was grinning like the proverbial cat that had gotten that damn canary.

"Bast, wait," Athena gasped "they tried to protect people - why would they do that if they were going to end the-"

Athena's protest was interrupted as Bast shot Týr in the head.

Her gun - which Ryan noted was made of some strange metal and had some odd design that he couldn't place - tracked over and, before anyone could react, her next bullet punched through Crystal's skull.

Ryan was still trying to stand. The shock of seeing Týr die had frozen him, and he was not ready for the way Crystal's head snapped back at the impact. It was almost like she'd noticed something above her head. The gesture was so natural that, even as the blood began to run down her forehead from the impact, Ryan was half tempted to look up himself. What wasn't natural was the way her body crumpled, all tension gone out of her bones. Crystal was gone - this was just the body she had inhabited, and without her to animate it anymore it was collapsing into a pile on the ground.

Ryan screamed wordlessly in rage and fear and hatred. He tried to move towards Bast, but he couldn't find the strength to do anything but slump back to his knees. Crystal was dead. The first person to show him any kindness in ages, the person who had been there to help him through this, the first woman he'd actually been intimate with - seeing her die was more painful than Ryan could have imagined. The gun began to track over to Ryan, but he didn't care. He was weak, he was helpless, he could barely rise to his feet, and the first friend he'd had in years was dead on the street in front of him.

While Ryan grieved and Bast got ready to shoot him in the head, Athena let out a scream of her own, a surge of emotion that almost cut through Ryan's own despair. Her scream held depths of anguish Ryan couldn't match. Athena must had twisted reality the moment Bast had taken the shoot at Týr. The sword she had thrown through the Hecatoncheires earlier finally got back to her hand - passing through Bast's elbow in the process, disarming her of both armament and arm.

Bast stared at the bleeding stump in confusion. Athena made a step like she was going to follow up the attack, then caught herself and turned to Ryan. She looked as drained as Ryan felt. *Even one armed, can we take*

Bast? The cat goddess's gaze was already clearing, and she was summoning fire to cauterize the wound.

Seeing Bast injured spurred Ryan to action. He reached out his hand to twist reality and felt...nothing. No math appeared, no power came to his hand.

He could feel his Hungers gnawing at him. *I'm out of juice. I ran out of power.*

Athena, it seemed, was in the same predicament. "Eschaton!" She shouted, her voice tight with restrained emotion. "We must go! She'll recover quickly!"

"What about-"

Athena was moving. She grabbed Crystal's corpse as she ran, throwing it over her shoulder. "Now, Eschaton. Live to fight another day."

Hating himself but knowing she was right - Bast's arm was already reforming bone and muscle - Ryan pulled himself to his feet and, giving his nanoverse a squeeze for the energy, ran after Athena.

Chapter 10

"Eschaton, take us back to your door!" Athena was limping with every step, unable to keep up the pace they needed. The dead weight of Crystal's corpse did nothing to help her move. On his end, Ryan felt a few cracked ribs slowing him down, although he couldn't find the energy to care even as lances of pain radiated out from every step. He could barely think.

"My door?"

"Yes." She looked at his face and he saw a glimmer of emotion. Was it pity? Sympathy? Annoyance? Stomach pain? Ryan couldn't tell. "You haven't learned. Fine. Then where is her door?"

Ryan bit his cheek, trying to fight back the hopeless feeling. *Crystal is dead. You're not. You have to keep moving.* "Follow me," he said, turning to walk down the street. People turned to stare. Athena was a beautiful woman, both of them were injured and battle scarred, and Athena was carrying a corpse.

Phones were coming out. "We're going to have police soon," Ryan muttered.

"Then we should hurry." They picked up the pace, and a couple blocks later - around the time they were hearing sirens approaching - they got to the exit point Crystal and Ryan had established. *I wonder what happens to her ship now. I guess I can use it? At least until this is all over.*

The door opened, and they stepped into the planetarium. Athena unceremoniously dumped Crystal's body on the floor.

"Hey! Be careful with her!" Ryan almost reached for what little power he had left to lash out at Athena. *How dare she? Crystal was dead and if it weren't for Athena,*

---

she'd be alive still! That wasn't entirely fair - Moloch and Bast and Enki bore the brunt of responsibility - but Ryan didn't care at the moment. He needed someone to take blame for Crystal's death, and Athena was the closest person he could reasonably cast in that role.

Athena scowled at him like he'd just gotten mad at her for throwing away a tattered rag. "Why? It's empty. Just a load of meat."

That was it. Ryan took a step forward, clenching his fists. They shook from the tension. It didn't matter that he was almost too weak to stand, it didn't matter that Athena had thousands of years of fighting experience on him. Right now, Ryan wanted to punch her in the face until she felt something other than disrespect. "Just a load of...she was my friend! And now she's dead! Because of you! Show some damn respect!"

That got a reaction out of her. Athena stepped forward and shoved Ryan in the chest with a single hand, using her free hand to slap his pathetic attempt at a punch aside. As he stumbled back, she was the one clenching her fists, and her lips twisted in bitter fury. "Respect? *Respect?* I left Týr behind to save her. And you were too Hungry to carry him, which is why I had to make that choice. So forgive me if I don't show respect for her meat!" The last words came out in a sarcastic snarl, tinged with bits of indignation.

Ryan stepped closer, anger dulling the pain. He was ready to throw down, right here and right now. *How dare you act like I owe you something!* "If it wasn't for you, she'd still be alive! You were helping Enki!"

"And it's because of me she'll get to fight another day!" Athena spat, her eyes narrowed in fury to match his own.

"Well...wait, what?" Ryan felt himself deflate. It suddenly was an effort to stand again as confusion and hope obliterated rage in an instant. "What do you...fight another day?"

Athena stared at him, then let out a long breath. "Oh, you're not a callous prick. You didn't know. Ishtar didn't tell you? As long as her nanoverse is secure, she'll reform."

Relief washed over Ryan, followed by his old friend embarrassment. "Oh. Uh...Crystal did tell me that, but..."

Athena sighed, and there was a bitter edge to it. "I guess forgetting is understandable. You've never seen someone die before, right?" Ryan shook his head. He'd seen people after they died, but it was something entirely different to actually watch the life go out of someone. "Well, time to get used to it. It sure as hell won't be the last time you see it."

"Wait..." Ryan's brow furrowed. "Leaving him behind means Týr-"

"Bast will likely destroy his nanoverse, yes. He will not reform." Athena clenched her hands again. "I had to make a choice, Eschaton. All I know about what's really going on was based on what Enki fed us, which seems less reliable now. Ishtar might know the truth. She's also one of the most powerful of the gods. If we want to fight back, we're going to need her. There wasn't time to search for Týr's nanoverse. So I let my friend die to save our best hope. Please, yell at me again for not treating Ishtar's meat with kindness."

Ryan winced "I'm sorry. I didn't-"

"-no, you did not. Why did you act to protect us?"

Ryan blinked at the abrupt change of topic. He hadn't even had time to process his relief that Crystal was alive, let alone that Athena seemed to be switching sides. "Well, we couldn't let those people just get torn apart after you and Týr were dead."

"Why not? You're going to end the world, Eschaton. What does it matter when and how they die?"

"We were - are, I guess - trying to find a way to end the world without resorting to mass murder. If we don't, everyone dies. At least, that's what Crystal said. But we might be able to find a better option. Something where not everyone dies, or no one dies, or...anything other than total annihilation."

Athena bit her lip in thought, and Ryan took time to really take stock of his new companion. She looked like the

119

goddess she was, reminding Ryan of the women sculped in ancient Greece. He'd seen statues of Athena in history books, and while they weren't perfect, he could definitely believe that she'd modelled for at least some of them. But she was...sharper. More defined. Those statues had always had a softness to them, a trait Athena lacked in person. "And how would one end the world without killing everyone?"

Ryan shrugged. "We hadn't gotten there yet. We've been too busy trying to teach me how to be a god, and trying to keep you all from letting the sun blow up and scorch the world barren."

Athena frowned. "I'm sorry, but the sun blowing up?"

Hah. I know something you don't. "Why do you think we're going to end the world? Crystal can explain it better than me. But...apparently the only way to save the sun from going supernova on us is to end the world. If we do, the energy from that can...it can reset the ticking clock on the sun. Crystal never mentioned it?"

Athena's frown deepened. "No, she did not."

"I guess she thought I needed to know what was going to happen." *You pestered her until she told you, but no need for Athena to know that little detail.* Ryan smiled. "I don't understand it. Hell, I'm not even sure I believe it. But apparently, I won't be able to end the world if it isn't true, so...I'm doing my best to roll with it."

Athena rolled her eyes. "I'm surprised you're not sick of that phrase. Ishtar's always been one for her catchphrases. They grew tiresome even back when I liked her."

I am, but no way am I going to tell you that. "Well, someone's got to say it without her around."

"No. No, no one needs to." Athena sighed. "It's not important. I'll have her explain it when she resurrects." Ryan wondered if she really thought it was unimportant, or if she was just saying it to get him to stop talking about it. *Probably the latter.*

"Fine. At this point I'm just kind of hoping you have some idea what Enki is planning to do next - we have been kind of fumbling blind."

"No," Athena said, with a shake of her head for emphasis. "And even if I had been given that information, we could not trust it. It's apparent that Enki intended to sacrifice Týr and me this entire time. That means I'm as blind as you are."

Ryan really wanted to get off the topical roller coaster talking to Athena was becoming. "Wait, back up. How is that apparent? It was Bast who shot Týr and Crystal, and Moloch was obviously working with her."

"The anti-gravity trick. Clever, but Enki should have been able to undo that in less than thirty seconds. The only reason he wouldn't have come back to the fight..." She deliberately trailed off, looking at him expectantly.

"Was if he knew what was coming. To keep up appearances, he would have had to join us against the creature, and put himself in danger."

"Good, you're not a complete imbecile. I was beginning to worry."

It was Ryan's turn to purse his lips. "Gee, thanks for that."

Athena shrugged. "I'm not Ishtar. I don't have time to coddle you, and I'm not here to worry about your feelings. We have to survive until Ishtar revives, and since I did have a hand in her death, it falls on me to teach you how to not die. I won't tell you not to mouth off to me - I just want you to understand I won't care if you do."

Ryan sighed. *I suddenly miss being told to roll with it.* "Are you always this pleasant?"

Athena's nostrils flared. "I lost a friend today. Again. *Please,* forgive me for not worrying about *your* feelings."

Ryan winced, knowing better to pry at that 'again'. "No, I get it. I'm sorry for your loss." She nodded, a simple acknowledgement of what he had said. Ryan continued. "Can I ask...I mean, I'm not ungrateful, but...why? I mean, besides the tactical reason you mentioned."

"Why did I choose her instead of Týr? You really want to go into that now?" Athena pursed her lips and answered before Ryan could. "No, you're right. The more you know about how we think; the better things will go for you. A few factors...is there anything to eat here?"

Ryan nodded, walking over to the banks of touchscreens. "I'll see if I can figure out how to call the food."

Athena nodded and moved to sit down. A chair appeared as she did so - that, at least, seemed to still be automatic. "For starters, it was what Týr would have wanted. He always loved that sort of thing." Here Athena did give a ghostly smile, a small gesture that didn't seem to be tinged with any kind of bitter edge. "I don't think he ever would have forgiven me had I let a 'maiden' die to save him."

Ryan returned the grin. Knowing Crystal was going to be alright put him at ease. *Damn, imagine what this must be like for Athena*. "He seemed like that type of guy." The buttons were all in a language Ryan recognized vaguely from inscriptions in Cipher Nullity.

"He was." She sighed, and the bitter edge returned. "But there were also other practical considerations, aside from what we've already covered. Unless you need a repeat of that?" Ryan didn't think he'd be likely to need a recap, and shook his head. She continued, "Enki seemed particularly concerned with one or both of you. You pose a threat to him in some fashion. But even more importantly, the monster that would have born of her permanent death would be far, far worse than what will come from Týr."

Ryan blinked a few times, as if fluttering his eyes would make his ears relay information that they had missed the first time around. It did not help. "I'm sorry, what's that last one?"

"Endless void, did Ishtar tell you anything?"

"Uh..." Ryan rubbed the back of his neck. "When I asked too many questions, she usually told me to just roll with it. That I wasn't able to process the information because I was Nascent." Realizing how that made Crystal sound, he continued. "Of course, we were also focused on things that were pressing, y'know? Like the end of the world and Enki and all that."

Athena took a moment to process that. "I guess that was the best course of action. But this you should know. Hecatoncheires and their ilk, all sort of abominations, form from when a nanoverse is destroyed and its god is dead. The older the god, the more potent the abomination. I can't imagine what would have formed from one as old as her."

Ryan swallowed hard. "I think this one is for food." He pushed the button, and the refrigerator appeared. "Huh. That worked."

"Why wouldn't it have?" Athena walked over and grabbed a sandwich out. She tossed one to Ryan as well.

"Well, they weren't written in a language I know."

"And that was a barrier for you?" Athena took a bite of her sandwich. She swallowed before Ryan could respond and continued, "Your lack of knowledge could easily get you - and us - killed. Slake your hungers, Eschaton, and then once you've rested I'll take up your education until Ishtar revives. And before you ask - I can't be certain how long that will take. It varies."

"Okay. Uh, about the need for Comp-"

"No." The flatness to the word stopped Ryan short, and his ears reddened at even making the implication.

"Okay, yeah, that makes sense." Ryan took another bite of his sandwich. "I'm going to...figure some way to keep her body safe."

"As you wish." Athena leaned back in her chair, eating. "Once you've taken care of the Hungers, we'll start with the basics."

"What's the basics?"

"You don't know how to make your door. We're going to go to your nanoverse. You're a god now, Eschaton - you should learn how to actually be one."

Chapter 11

Into the Nanoverse

The rest of the day was filled with making sure their Hungers were satiated with books and food and sleep. It wasn't until the next day that they sat down to open Ryan's nanoverse.

"So Ishtar didn't speak with you on how to open it? At all?" Athena frowned.

"Nope. Like I said, we had more pressing matters. And she prefers Crystal."

"She can address that with me when she revives, if she wishes to," Athena said dismissively. "And yet she brought you to her own. Fascinating."

Ryan blinked at that. "Uh, no, she didn't."

Athena cocked her head just a fraction. "Eschaton," she said, and here Athena made no effort not to let her tone how condescending she felt. It was the same way you'd talk to a child that had just said something both adorable and stupid. "Where do you think we are?"

"Well, I've been thinking of it as her planetarium ship. Because of...the stars."

Ryan hadn't ever thought what being patiently condescended to would sound like, but Athena was giving him a lesson. "Planetarium ship...first of all, it's a staging area. And now, please, try to think. A field of stars and galaxies. And when you look into your nanoverse, what do you see?"

Ryan felt his cheeks flush as he glanced around. It never even occurred to him - but the celestial field that surrounded them did look a *lot* like what he saw when he stared into his nanoverse.

"So, this is the interior of a nanoverse?"

Athena nodded. Then paused and closed her eyes, taking a deep breath. "I guess I shouldn't expect you to know these things instinctively," she allowed. "I just cannot believe how little Ishtar told you. You...really have no idea about anything."

"I mean, she did say it could fry my brain if she told me too much."

Athena just stared at him for a long moment, then burst out into peals of mocking laughter. "She said it would...oh stars of Olympus, she told you it would fry your brain?"

Ryan frowned. "What's so funny about that?" He had a sinking feeling he knew the answer but was hoping he was wrong.

"I just can't believe you fell for that. I suppose that would be a good way to get you to stop asking questions." Athena had gotten the laughter under control, but still looked amused.

For his part, Ryan was in full on blush. "How was I supposed to know any better? I get told I'm a god, that I'm going to end the world or everyone dies, and I'm the moron for thinking that takes it too far?"

Athena studied him for a moment, the smirk fading. "I guess when you put it that way...I shouldn't judge. Let me make it up to you."

"I thought you didn't have time to worry about my feelings."

"Don't push it, Eschaton." Athena's eyes flashed with a bit of sardonic humor.

Ryan smiled. "Well, how about you call me Ryan instead?"

"Very well." By the look on her face, he'd just asked her to pull out her fingernails. Apparently, the moment was over, and she was back to tolerating him. "I'll...attempt. It's accurate to say this is inside her nanoverse. The first area - a staging area, as I said. All nanoverses have it, and can be used to control where doors open outside by aligning the nanoverse with the core universe."

"Okay, that kind of makes sense." Ryan chewed his cheek for a moment. "Only, wait. She has her nanoverse on her as well."

"Yes." Athena thought for a moment. "Oh. I now understand why Ishtar often asked you to just - what did you say it was?"

"Roll with it," Ryan said.

Athena nodded. "Yes, that was it. You can take a nanoverse within another nanoverse, and you can even take a nanoverse within a copy of itself. Don't try to think too hard about it, Ryan. The nanoverse is the physical object in the universe we all share, but it's also a separate place. When you take it inside itself...well, the mechanics can be explained later. For now, I'd appreciate it if you could let that pass."

"I've gotten used to rolling with it. So I'll have an area like this?"

"Since this is what you saw at first, yes, it'll be like this. Over time it will change to suit your individual tastes. Now, opening a door - for starters, it's best to have your Nanoverse in hand. Later on you won't need it."

Ryan nodded. "Okay. So then I...do what?"

"You open it. Try whatever makes the most sense - it's not something your higher brain needs to be involved with."

Ryan felt stupid, but remembered squeezing the nanoverse the first time and how silly that had felt. *Okay, it's too small to try to fold a hole out of, so what if I...* Feeling too absurd to even finish the thought, with nanoverse in hand, he reached out to about waist height and twisted, like he was turning a doorknob.

As he did, he heard the click of a latch, and a door opened. "Oh holy shit."

Athena almost smiled. "You do have a knack for it, it seems. Go through - I'll be right behind you."

The room beyond did look a lot like Crystal's, although a few differences jumped out at him right away, before he even could even really take them in. The touchscreens, for example, all had text written in English. There was already a bed, chair, and lamp present. Ryan noted that their arrangement, relative to each other, was almost exactly the same as his old bedroom at his parents' house. *Why isn't it my apartment?* Ryan wondered as he began to walk among the relics of his childhood.

Over there were the colored blocks he'd spent endless hours building with, making starships and castles and undersea bases before leaving them out to be stepped on later. The lamp he'd broken in high school was still intact, apparently drawn from before the time he'd chucked it through Nabu's head in a fit of pique. Here was the book of dinosaurs he'd read until the pages started falling out, and underneath it...underneath it was a battered and worn copy of *"Why Does My Cat Meow?"* Ryan ran his fingers over it. "I thought it would be more like Crystal's," he muttered.

"It will, in time. It responds to you, Ryan. It is your reflection, your echo. It always starts looking like what you think of when you want to go home."

"Oh," was all Ryan said aloud. *So that's why it's my old bedroom. Has it really be this long since I had a home?*

Then his eyes wandered upward, and introspection was obliterated. Instead of the ceiling of his bedroom he saw a field of stars and galaxies that spread out into infinity. It was far too real to be like something out of a movie. He'd seen the effect in Crystal's nanoverse, but something about seeing them in his bedroom really brought home how vast it all was. It was also completely different from Crystal's nanoverse. The stars were brighter and the galaxies were packed much closer together, like the entire universe was scrunched into a smaller space. *Maybe it is. My nanoverse is younger, after all.*

Athena followed after him. "You can tell how much younger your nanoverse is," she commented, looking at the galaxies that swirled around them.

Ryan felt a surge of pride for getting it right. "Because of the star field?"

Athena nodded. "Most are much brighter than Ishtar's, but she is very old. Your nanoverse, when you first look into it, undergoes a Big Bang. Time runs extremely rapidly in it at first, right up to the point where the first sentient life emerges - then it still runs faster than normal time, but not so rapidly that millions of years pass in an hour."

"Gotcha." He took a moment to just stare at the "sky", his heart pounding as he did. "Uh...is there some way I can make this not my childhood bedroom? I mean, it's a bit...much."

"You're a god here, Ryan. This is your staging area. You can make it into a theme park if you want."

"Okay, fair. But...how?"

Athena sighed. "This will be good practice for when you go into your nanoverse fully. You can impose your will on this. Picture what you want and *will* it to be so."

Ryan decided to start by picturing the interior of Crystal's nanoverse, hoping a mental model would make it easier. He focused on the image as hard as he could, but when he opened his eyes it was still his childhood bedroom.

"If you can't even manage this, you'll find your nanoverse is impossible. *Focus,* Eschaton. Like you do on the sword when you draw it from your nanoverse. Like you do on whatever you see when you manipulate reality. This is no different."

Ryan took a deep breath. Having the mental model of drawing his sword helped. He clung to that feeling and reached out, trying to apply it to the room around him.

Like wax put out in the sun, it melted away into the shape he desired. "Okay. Got it."

"I hadn't noticed," Athena said, but she didn't look annoyed. Ryan wanted to believe she looked impressed but couldn't force himself to believe something so at odds with reality.

Besides, it didn't matter if she was impressed. He had questions. "So from here, I can open a door anywhere in the universe?"

"Not right now. Your door was opened from Ishtar's nanoverse, so you can currently open a door anywhere in *her* nanoverse, or travel to anywhere in your own. To get anywhere in the universe, you'd have to head back out to the universe, then open a door to here from there."

Ryan took a couple moments to process that. "I...don't blame Crystal for waiting to tell me all this. It's a lot to take in." He could feel the need to faint begin to form again, for the first time in a while. Only not awhile, it had only been yesterday, hadn't it? Spending time under a constant field of stars, not needing to sleep unless pushed too far, and bouncing between universes and worlds has taken his sense of time for a wild ride and passionate night without even buying it dinner or calling the next day.

Athena regarded him with what looked like it had some relationship to sympathy. Maybe its distant cousin. Or she had a shoulder cramp. It was hard to tell with her. "It takes time, Escha- apologies. It takes time, Ryan. But time is short, and you should know what you have here."

"Okay." He took a few more breaths, fighting back the urge to faint. His vision started to clear. *Holy crap, I held off a fainting spell!* That realization hit him with a jolt. He was sure he wasn't lucky enough to be done with them completely, but it was a nice chance of pace. "Go on."

She motioned to the touchscreens. "It seems that's what you use to command this platform. Take a look."

So he did. They were covered with icons and text. "Okay. Some of these - Refrigerator, Bed, Lights, and Temperature - those refer to this platform, right?" Athena nodded for him to go on. "Then there's a bunch of greyed out ones, like prophecy and endow - I'm guessing those are after I finish Apotheosis?" Another nod, this one with a hint of approval. Ryan was sure of it this time. *See? I'm not totally incompetent!* "And then…" Ryan read what was on the screen. Three little faces were on the monitors, with English labels pointing out each one's name. "So Batherians, Graphids, and Shal'nath. These are sentients, I'm guessing?"

"Very well done," she said, although her tone only carried a hint of the praise. *It's better than being made fun of,* Ryan thought, deciding to take the victory. "And three already? Shocking. Later on that will be filled with hundreds, maybe thousands of sentient species. Or you could make it all one species. Whatever you wish. So which would you like to visit first?"

Ryan gaped at her. "I'm sorry, visit?"

"Yes. As interesting as it can be to play on dead worlds, I think it would be more educational to pick a species and meet them. They'll all be human-like for now, so don't worry about that too much."

"Uhh...then the Graphids, I suppose?" They looked the most like humans, and unlike the other two their name didn't twist his tongue into knots.

Athena motioned for him to go ahead, so he pushed the tablet. The moment he did, the field of stars around them began to move, and Ryan had to sit down as they raced by. It felt like when you're sitting in a parked car and the car next to you backs up in the corner of your eye – you're not moving, but your brain thinks it is, because your brain was designed for a hairless beach monkey and 'cars' weren't a factor in that equation. It's really doing the best it can, bless its heart. And Ryan's brain was still designed for a human, not fully adapted for a god, and it just was doing the best it could to handle the stars rushing by.

It was an immense relief when they stopped to hover over a planet. The star it orbited was bright, younger and more energetic than the Sun, and the planet itself was covered with vast oceans a few patches of green. Clouds swirled around the globe.

There was a button Ryan couldn't resist pressing. "Orbit."

As soon as he did, an almost transparent dome rose form the sides of the platform and extended over the top. As soon as it closed, the platform shuddered. The planet beneath them slowed its rotation, until it looked like they were actually in a space station orbiting the world instead of watching it spin with artificial speed. It felt more real than what he had been seeing before. *It's not like we're watching a world. It's like we're over a world.*

Ryan grinned at it, then started laughing. *Holy crap, that's not what it's like, that's what it is.* Athena gave him a raised eyebrow. "What is so funny?"

"It's not...it's not humor. Goddamn, Athena, how long has it been since something was just so amazing you had to laugh?"

She didn't answer, just favored him with a small, sad smile. "Point taken, Ryan. Did you want to savor the moment? We're operating on your nanoverse's time now that you've dropped into orbit – into what we call realspace, since you're not a real part of the nanoverse - so you can wait as long as you want to. It'll be hundreds of years before even a minute passes in the Core Universe."

He turned towards her, feeling his eyes widen. "Wait...then can we bring Crystal here? So almost no time passes in the core world while she revives? And why don't we spend like a year training here?"

"Two problems. Training you here is useless because you are nearly omnipotent here, and Ishtar's nanoverse – and mine – will not function here. We get treated the same as any other sentient being. And-" Ryan started to open his mouth, and she cut him off "-since Ishtar is not part of your nanoverse, you cannot return her soul to her body here. You cannot reach beyond your own nanoverse."

Ryan let out a deep breath. "Should have known it wouldn't be that easy. Nearly omnipotent, eh? So I can...create a new world if I wanted to?"

"Of course."

"But...not out of nothing, right? I mean it's a basic law of physics – matter cannot be created or destroyed, right?"

Athena bit her lip, trying to find the best way to explain it. "This is your nanoverse. In the Core Universe, you can modify the laws of physics, cheat and manipulate them. Here, you *are* the laws of physics."

"Oh."

"Don't overthink it. You can change the rules later – but for now, stick to what you know."

Ryan felt the urge to faint building up again. "Yeah. Probably for the best."

"Do you need to rest?"

If it had been Crystal, he would have said yes in a heartbeat. Because Crystal knew him, he knew her, and he trusted her. Athena was...well, still an unknown. She was on their side, Ryan believed that, and was an ally – but only because they shared an enemy. She wasn't a friend, because the popular wisdom that the enemy of your enemy is your friend wasn't true, at least most of the time. More often, the enemy of your enemy was just someone who had a shared interest in seeing your enemy's ass kicked.

"Nah, I'm good. Let's go meet the natives."

The trip down to the surface was as exciting as Ryan had always hoped. Watching as their entry caused the air to compress, forming a giant wall of flame to form in front of them, was everything ten-year-old-Ryan had always wanted it to be.

As they got closer, a joystick emerged from the floor. Something he could steer with. That was appreciated. It felt more like he was actually flying a spaceship instead of on a ride. *Is this thing responding to my subconscious desires?* He pushed the thought down and instead grabbed the joystick to fly over the planet.

From the air, the part they were over looked like a jungle, although the plants didn't match anything Ryan had seen before. Which made sense – they were a product of his unique nanoverse. Spotting a clearing, Ryan moved in to take the vessel into a landing.

As soon as they touched down, the plants began shooting thorns at them, a hail of razor sharp wood. Each of the thorns was attached to long vines, allowing the plants to coil them back in. Ryan could spot barbs in them as they bounced harmlessly off the ship's dome and shuddered at the thought of what they would do to a living creature. *Carnivorous plants. Awesome. Should have gone with the Batherians.*

Athena didn't flinch. "I'm assuming Ishtar didn't tell you how your emotional state impacts the nanoverse?"

Ryan shot her a glower. "Actually, she did. So that means that life is going to evolve to be dangerous? Since it's been a rough few days."

"That is a common side effect, yes. Especially during its infancy. I'll be staying here."

"What?"

"I don't have any of my divine power here. Without knowing the dangers of your nanoverse, I could easily be killed."

"But what about me?"

Athena managed to avoid the frustrated tone this time, which Ryan felt she probably deserved credit for. "You're nearly omnipotent here, remember? If something manages to kill you – which should be unlikely – you'll be able to reform."

"Oh." Ryan looked at the thorns, which continued to bounce off the glass. "Okay. Can I still feel pain?"

She nodded. "So do be careful. Your wrath could destroy this world and the platform with it, which would also kill me. I'll reform back in the core world, but it'll take days, same as Ishtar."

"Noted." *Okay, so I'm omnipotent.* That was too much to take in, and the need to faint began to crowd his vision. *So…let's try something more manageable.*

If he controlled the rules here, he could probably do some minor changes to himself. Like, say, giving his skin a near indestructible coat. He focused on the idea, trying to will it into reality. Unlike grabbing the sword or making his bedroom vanish, this was simple. A thin sheen covered him, like he'd been shrink-wrapped. Athena actually smiled. "Clever. I'll see you when you're done, Eschaton."

Nodding, and not bothering to correct his name, Ryan stepped out a door and into the grass. He could hear it crunch beneath his feet, and the thorn-shooting trees continued to pelt his skin, but at least it didn't hurt.

I just wish they'd stop.

The exact instant the thought crossed his mind, they stopped, the thorn pods curling up to wait for actual prey. *Oh. I suppose I could have tried that first.*

When they had been coming down, Ryan had spotted smoke on the horizon. Now that he was on the ground he could barely see it through the thick tree lines. The trees might not be firing their thorns at him anymore, but they still loomed. It wasn't menacing like a haunted forest in a fairy tale, but held a different, more primal menace. The part of Ryan's brain that had evolved leaping through trees like these screamed that there was danger all around. Ryan took a deep breath to calm that thought. *Remember, Ryan. Nothing here can hurt you. You made yourself invulnerable. You can do whatever you want. You are literally the scariest thing in this universe.* It didn't help much - primal instinct was not so easily sated - but it gave him enough courage to begin walking into the jungle.

A few things started to resolve as he did. There were massive flowers at various intervals, iridescent with shades of purple near the base and blossoming along the color spectrum to gold at the tips. Among them buzzed insects that looked like bees but were nearly as big as Ryan's hands and had elongated tails that ended in flexible stingers. Sometimes the insects got too close to the center of the flower, and it sprayed them with a sticky substance that caused them to fall into the center. *Even the flowers are murderous.* That disturbed Ryan more than the killer trees.

Then he heard a roar, and his first pair of large fauna burst out of the undergrowth.

The first animal was about the size of a squirrel and covered in a bright red fur. It froze when it saw Ryan, looking up at him with a single central eye that wrapped almost halfway around its head. It reared up, preparing to turn away, and Ryan could see its front legs ended in long, boney spikes.

Then a tongue burst out of the foliage and latched onto the cyclops squirrel. The creature had a moment to look like it knew its fate, and then the tongue retreated with the creature. A moment later Ryan heard a sickening crunch.

What loped out of the underbrush still had a bit of tail sticking out of its jaws. It was built like a tiger with a low-slung body but was covered in black and green feathers that blended into the jungle. Its head was broad and flat, the eyes on the edge of protrusions like a hammerhead shark's. It regarded Ryan carefully. *I'm not food, I'm not food, I'm not food* Ryan thought frantically, not daring to move.

Apparently, the thought worked. It turned and slunk away, twin tails lashing behind it.

Ryan's heart was pounding. It was a short hike to the fire, about two kilometers. He'd barely managed fifty meters without giving himself a heart attack. If he kept this up, he'd be screaming by the time he reached the Graphids. *So why walk?*

Taking a few deep breaths to steady himself, he held out his hands, palms facing the ground, and imagined a force pushing him into the air. Inch by inch and then foot by foot as he accelerated, he rose until he was above the treetops. "I can fly!" he shouted aloud, exalting in the moment. Twisting his palms, he propelled himself towards the smoke.

When he got close, he heard voices. The smoke was rising from a cluster of simple huts, and people were running between them. Like Athena had indicated, they looked pretty much like normal humans, although their hair colors were bright reds and greens and blues – like the flowers of the jungle that surrounded them. They were pointing at him, and many of them were gathering obsidian weapons of a design that Ryan had seen before. *Oh, that's where that came from.*

He landed among them, giving them his biggest grin. "Hi. Don't be afraid – I mean you no harm."

"What are you?" It was a woman speaking, and people moved to give her space. She was about Ryan's height, with grey skin and thick, broad shoulders. She had sparse hair across her head, although calling it hair might be a bit much. The strands were too thick for that word, looking more like solid tendrils. Beads had been placed along them. She wore armor that looked like scale but had the dull white color of bone in between the elaborate paint that covered the armor. As Ryan looked at the others, he saw they were attired similarly, although none of them had as many beads or as much paint on their bone scale.

"I'm Ryan. And...well, I'm your God." Ryan cringed as soon as the words were out of his mouth. *Seriously, that's your opening line? Could you be any more arrogant?*

She pursed her lips. "Our god? Our god is Xapheda, She-Who-Brings-Storms. Our god is Raedalis, The-Beast-That-Hunts. Our god is-"

"Oh, I'm sure they're impressive, really, but...well, have you ever met them?"

Her lips thinned. "No."

"Right, because they're false gods. I'm the real deal here."

Her knuckles whitened on her weapon. "Prove your divinity, then, Sky-Man. Prove that you are not just a trick of the Grass Walkers, or some other mischief."

Ryan thought for a moment. "Okay. Go get all your sick and injured."

She laughed at that, throwing back her head in a mockery of mirth. "And why should I show you our weakest? So you might slay them?"

"No," Ryan's voice was quiet, and he kept his grin showing even though it wanted to waiver. "What's your name?"

She spat. "I am Saphyn. Daughter of Ruphari. Chief of the Fire Masters."

"Well, Saphyn, nice to meet you. I want you to get them, so you can see they're healed. You don't even need to bring them here – just go check on them."

Saphyn motioned for some of the men, who ran off. A few minutes later they started trickling back out of the huts. "The Sky Man speaks truth. They are healed." Their eyes were wide.

Fear filling her eyes, Saphyn dropped to one knee. Seeing their leader kneeling before this strange man, the others began to follow. "Ryan, please forgive our ignorance."

Ryan coughed, suddenly feeling hot. "No...it's...rise, please." They did, slowly and cautiously and looking at him with a wonder that was both thrilling and embarrassing.

"A feast! A feast for Ryan, the Sky God!" Saphyn shouted, and immediately men and women began to scurry about.

"That's really not..." *Why not, Ryan? You've been running scared for weeks, freaking out constantly – why not have a feast in your honor?* "I'll double your food stores so this causes no hardship."

Her eyes grew even wider at that. "You are a merciful God, Ryan. Please, come, sit with us."

***

It was a great time, Ryan had to admit. The Fire Masters knew how to party. They had a huge bonfire going in the center of the camp. Drummers provided a primal beat, and the Graphids danced to the rhythm. Some animal was roasting over the flame on a spit, a massive beast that required full logs to support its weight. They carved chunks off at intervals and dunked them in a pot containing some variety of spice. The spice was sharp and had real heat to it, and Ryan was glad there was plenty for seconds. *Don't eat too much, Ryan,* he reminded himself. *These people need to survive, you just want it because it tastes amazing.* Even with the doubled food stores, he didn't want to be greedy.

Although it would be hard to manage greed the way they kept shoving food in his face.

The meat was served in edible bowls, something like a pepper that was roasting alongside the meat. As Ryan watched, he picked up that the correct way to eat it was to put the meat into it, then squeeze the bowl around it so it absorbed the juices and spices. When eaten that way, it was delicious. Without the absorption, it had a bitter aftertaste Ryan wasn't fond of.

Drinks were passed around as well. These people hadn't discovered fermentation yet, but they had discovered something sweet, and whatever he was drinking - they called it Xan Milk, but when Ryan had asked said it came from plants, not animals - was thick and creamy. It was almost like a root beer float, although not quite that level of cloying, and it complimented the heat of the spiced meat well.

He ate and drank while watching the festivities. A few of the Graphids asked him to join the dance, but he declined. As complex as the movements were, he'd absolutely make an idiot out of himself. *Even more than you normally do when dancing.* Instead, he spent a great deal of time talking with Saphyn.

"...so Bast betrayed her allies, Moloch betrayed us, and Enki was behind it. We are waiting for Crystal to rise from the dead, and then we're going to go on the offensive."

The story had drawn crowds around the fire. He'd left out the fact that it was Earth, instead framing it as a battle for Heaven, casting himself as the leader of the group and Enki as basically the Devil. *So this is what drunk on power means.* It was intoxicating, to be sure, the way they drank in every word. After he'd endured days of being confused and lost and needing to ask for help with every little thing, it was a much-needed respite. *These people are awesome. And I don't just think that because they're actually treating me like a god.*

Although that's definitely part of it.

Ryan couldn't remember the last time that he'd been the center of positive attention. Certainly hadn't happened since finding his Nanoverse. But here, these people liked him, they respected him. *Hell, why shouldn't they?* He'd just cured their sick, all of them. Sure, he'd done it to prove his claims, but at the same time he could have done the same thing with something flashy or dangerous.

Why does anyone ever leave their nanoverse? I could spend a year here, be back on Earth before anyone knows I'm gone. Why not come here every single day for a year local time?

There had to be a reason, although Ryan couldn't see it. So he started thinking about what he could do to make these people's lives better. He considered making them immune to disease of all kinds, but a small part of him worried it would cause overpopulation and starvation down the line. *I'll be doing the next best thing before I leave, though.*

Ryan frowned for a moment. *Here I am making plans, and I've spent the whole time talking about myself.* He turned to Saphyn, "Enough about me, though. Tell me more about yourself, your people?"

"And what would you like to know?"

Ryan shrugged. "Why are your people called the Fire Masters?" he asked.

Saphyn frowned. "You do not know the story?"

"I want to hear the story," Ryan lied. From the way Saphyn's eyes lit up, he'd given the right lie.

"In the Dark Times, fire was untamed. It came with the lightning, or from the Mountains that Burn. All the people gathered fire when they could and kept it burning. When fire went dark, we would have to send people to the Mountains that Burn to breathe their poison air or wait for Xapheda to send her storms to gift us some."

Ryan sat back. Saphyn had a voice made for storytelling, or perhaps it was a skill she had honed over the years. Rich and textured, each word carefully inflected for maximum impact. Either way, it was a pleasure to listen to her. The rest of the Fire Masters gathered around.

"One day, a great rain came. Our fire had not been fed properly. Golma, the Fire Keeper, had failed in his duties. The people demanded that Golma be the one to go to the Mountains that Burn. That he be the one to breathe the poison air. That he should return with fire or perish in the attempt. Golma refused the people, so my ancestor," and Ryan couldn't help but noticed the fierce pride in her voice, "he demanded that Golma pay the price for his failure.

"With him went Nansti, a great warrior. Nansti was sent to make sure he did not flee or cower, that he did not shirk his duties. That he would reach the Mountains that Burn or die in the attempt. Golma left. He set out across the Deep Jungle to reach the Mountains that Burn to breathe their poison air and get the fire that he has lost.

"And Golma tried to flee. He feared the Mountains that Burn, he feared their poison air. Nansti hurled her spear at Golma. It did not strike the coward, because she did not wish him dead. She threw her spear so it hit just in front of Golma's face, hit the rocks so that he might see what awaited him if he fled. So that he might know he should fear Nansti more than he feared the Mountains that Burn.

"Sparks flew from the rock when it struck. Sparks that caught Golma's beard alight! He died, as was fitting for his failure. And Nansti returned with these magic rocks, these rocks that produce sparks when struck with a spear. We keep the rocks secret, we keep them safe. Now, when other peoples lose their fire, they need not go to the

Mountains that Burn, they need not breathe the poison air. They trade us for our fire, and we have grown wealthy off their need."

Ryan nodded, trying to look wise. The idea that fire could be a good that was traded had never occurred to him, and he wondered how much longer it could last on this world. *Maybe, if I do what I'm thinking, it'll be recorded and I can find out later.* "What happened to Nansti?"

Saphyn's fierce pride returned. "She wed my ancestor. I am her descendant, and her blood flows in my veins."

Ryan smiled at her pride. "I wish I could stay longer," he said. *If not for Athena, I would. But she's waiting for me, and literally can't go anywhere until I get back.*

Saphyn returned the smile. "You honor us by saying so. But…you must go. Enki awaits."

He nodded, somberly. "But before I do…I need something from you, Saphyn."

"Anything, my god. Anything."

Good thing you took care of Company before you came out here. It was more of an idle thought than anything else. Ryan grinned, then touched her forehead. Her eyes widened in shock. "I just taught you how to read and write. A way of turning words into symbols, so they can be passed from person to person." He gestured into the air and pulled out a book. A huge, thick book, just labeled "Science."

"What is…what is this?"

"Everything my world knows of science. I need you to teach it to the rest of the Fire Masters, and to the Grass People, and the Tree Walkers. To everyone. It will teach you medicine, so you may fight off disease and cure injuries. It will teach you mathematics, so you might understand the universe better. It will teach you engineering, so you might build great things to keep your people safe from the woods and the animals. It will teach you ecology, so you might stay safe without destroying your own habitat. And it will teach you technology, which will be used to entertain, to build, to create...and to destroy." Ryan leaned forwards. "Because when I need a weapon, I draw it from you – and Saphyn?"

She met his eyes. She didn't seemed overwhelmed anymore. She seemed to be acutely aware of the enormity of what was happening.

"I need the best weapons you can make."

She nodded. "We will make weapons for you, Ryan, the Sky God."

Ryan smiled. "Then I will return, and look forward to seeing what you have created." With that, he pressed his hands down again and took off into the sky, heading back towards where he had left Athena. *It's a win-win. I just saved them thousands of years of plagues and crap.*

It was amazing, this feeling. Incredibly heady. And given how time flowed, by the time he fought Enki next, he'd hopefully have some major firepower to bring to bear.

He was even to push down a small part of him that insisted he was using these people. In fact, Ryan was feeling so great that he didn't even notice the urge to faint start to creep back in. Emboldened by his lack of awareness, the feeling crept closer and closer until, like a thief, it stole away his consciousness and plummeted him into darkness, the exhaustion of several days of throwing divine powers finally catching up with him.

He didn't wake up when he landed on top of his ship. Athena did look up in surprise at the thud, and slowly tracked him with her eyes as he slid down the side to land in the jungle. She considered getting him, she really did – but the risk was too great.

Athena turned back to her book to wait for Ryan to wake up, wondering how exactly she was supposed to defeat Enki working with *that.*

Chapter 12

Moloch stared out over the lost city of Ys, a small smile playing over his lips. *I love this view.* Before him stretched hundreds of people, petrified and dried by salt, their hands held up in eternal gestures of protection. Others were bowed low, laying with their faces into the dirt. Still others had their faces covered or were cowering to protect others. A few were pointing to some central point. That was where the catastrophe had originated - in ages long past, the citizens of Ys had angered some god. Or perhaps a pantheon of them. For their crime, the god had sucked all the moisture out of their bodies, turning them into salt mummies. *I would have loved to see it.*

Moloch had made the central castle of this place his home, so he could watch them in their eternal torment and fear whenever he wanted. It was a reminder of what gods were capable of if they were unshackled from expectations, from these stupid, arbitrary rules they had made for themselves. *It's also a reminder of what awaits this entire world. Forgotten by all but me. Just as it will be with Ishtar.*

Unfortunately, he could not enjoy the view as much as he wanted, the way he usually did. There were visitors. Bast at least was a polite guest, being relatively quiet. However, Enki was screaming at them, and with a sigh Moloch turned to face his 'leader.'

"You had one task, one simple job!" Enki's neck bulged out, and a vein in his forehead pulsed over his eye. His hands were shaking. He'd returned to his more brutish appearance, ditching the one he'd worn for the cameras, and his eyes were practically glowing as spittle flecked from his lips. *It had been perfect.* Enki thought. He liked the thought so much he repeated it. *It had been perfect! And then...we were so close!*

Bast glanced at Moloch, who could only shrug. Enki had been yelling for some time now and was beginning to repeat himself.

"I served the Eschaton up to you on a platter, and what do you do?" He leaned into Bast's face, close enough that the goddess had to lean back from him. "You shot Týr and Ishtar first! Then you got your hand cut off!"

Bast's eyes flashed with rage. "I work with you, Enki. Not for you. Watch your tone."

He raised one brutish fist, his neck pulsing with the beat of his heart. "Don't you *dare* try to give me commands, you catty little bitch, I should-"

His tirade was interrupted by a dry chuckle from Moloch. Both Bast and Enki turned to the rasping sound. "Hmmm?" Moloch intoned. "Oh. You called her catty. Bast. Catty." He glanced back at them and sighed. "Surely I can't be the only one that finds that humorous?" Their scowls deepened, but at least Enki was lowering his fist.

You still need them, Enki reminded himself. *As painful as it is, you aren't strong enough to go it alone.*

Yet. He continued his rant, "We had a plan. We had a plan, and it was a good one. I set up the fight, let the four stuck-up prigs slug it out, Moloch shows up and drops the giant, and then Bast mops up the survivors." His scowl deepened. "But you," he pointed one fat finger at Moloch, "you decided to vamoose, to amscray, before making sure the job was done, and then you," shifting that meaty digit to Bast, "ooooh, you. You decided that Týr and Ishtar were more important! Ishtar will be back on her feet in days!"

"And you completely forgot your role in the finale, dear Enki," Moloch hissed, the false joviality gone. He leaned forward. "You were meant to be the failsafe, to pick off any who fled. Yet they did so unopposed. Why was that, hmmm?"

Enki directed the full force of his wrath at Moloch. *I tolerated you, you damn psychopath. I made you a part of my plan. And this is how you repay me, you reject god?* The idea was galling, and Enki found himself wondering if

Moloch was even worth the effort. "The Eschaton is stronger than we thought, okay? Took me a bit to undo the twist he did on me."

"The Eschaton," Bast countered, her voice full of the lazy grace of a hunting tiger, "is a Nascent, Enki. How did a Nascent manage to twist you so hard, you couldn't return to the battle in time?"

Enki slammed his giant fist into the table. "I. Don't. Know!" Each word was punctuated by a slam until the table cracked, and Enki took a few deep breaths, staring at the destruction he had wrought upon it. *It's Ishtar, it has to be,* a small voice in the back of his mind chimed in. *She was always a dangerous bitch, and with her teaching the Esch-*

"Tantrums will avail us nothing," Moloch said, interrupting Enki's thought process. "We still won the day. Týr will make a fine addition to my collection, and every god and goddess that saw our battle will know we are the winning side. Can you not, my dears, revel in the victory?"

Bast gave Moloch an indulgent smile, and Enki took a breath. "You're not always right, Moloch, but when you are you're very right." *Toss the prick a bone. You can salvage this, you can make this work. It's not all lost. You're not going to lose the world.*

"I agree," Bast said, "and as such I'm willing to put the threats behind me, Enki, if you will do the same for my...failure." The last word was plucked out with verbal tongs, as if it were something slimy and disgusting.

"Fine." Enki nodded. "Moloch, how long till you can make something deadly out of Týr?"

"Likely done before Ishtar revives," Moloch responded as he picked some invisible dirt out of his yellowed nails. Enki's neck bulged at the insolence, and he had to take a deep breath to avoid throttling Moloch. *You're useful, Moloch, but I can't believe I have to tolerate you right now.* "I'm more concerned about Athena. Ishtar may have been a war goddess, but she was never much of a strategist. Athena, for her part..."

Bast had to nod, reluctantly. "I was going to shoot her next. The Nascent should have been easy pickings without them." Pausing for a moment, she gave a small smile before continuing. "We can hope, however, that her personality prevents them from heeding her council?"

Enki let out a snort of frustration. "Not likely. We have to assume they're going to be all hugs and kisses from here on out."

Moloch returned to the window, pursing his lips as he did.

"Something you want to share, Moloch?" Moloch could feel Bast's eyes on his back. *You're curious, Bast. Very curious. And you know what they say about curiosity and cats.*

"Yes." Moloch didn't turn away from the window. "The very first day he obtained his nanoverse, when he was still just a mere Finder, you could have killed him. Stopped all this then, with a bullet to the back of the skull. Why not?"

Now Moloch turned, slowly, to see that Bast had also focused her attention on Enki.

"What kind of question is that?"

"You've been working on this plan for centuries. Updating as needed, but always the same core plan. Why did you not kill the Eschaton before he could begin to come into his powers, you short-sighted oaf?"

Enki bristled at the tone, but Bast spoke up. "I've been wondering that too, if we're being blunt. Why did you spare him?"

"Because I didn't know he was the Eschaton then. He might have still been an innocent person, who just found the Eschaton's nanoverse."

"And?"

"We're not killing innocent people unless we have to, Moloch. I told you that from the beginning. If you have a problem with it, you can take a long walk off a short dick." Enki slammed his left fist into his right palm to release some of the frustration that was welling up within him. "I know you get your jollies off letting people sacrifice each other to you, but that's not how we do things." *I'm not a monster.* Enki clenched and unclenched his fists. *I sure as hell want to do something monstrous to Moloch, though.*

Moloch sighed. "Enki, our plan was to unleash a Hecatoncheires in the middle of a busy city. Did you really think there wouldn't be civilians caught in the crossfire?"

"Crossfire happens, Moloch. Casualties happen. A casualty is different than murdering someone for what they might be, you hear me?"

"Oh, I hear you Enki. I'm just not sure I follow your reasoning."

Enki sneered. "You don't have to understand my reasoning. I know why you're here. You'll get your wish, I've got no sympathy for the bitch. She's enabling the end of the world. But to get that, you're going to play by my rules, or you can go fly a kite made of go fuck yourself."

Moloch and Bast's eyes met again, and Bast shook her head. *You might be better than Enki, Moloch, but you're still not the* **good** *option. Then again, I work with what I have.*

"Well, at least it's a reason." Moloch said aloud. "But I wish to confirm we are still going ahead with your plan."

Enki clutched his hands into fists again. *Of course we are, you idiot. I've waited thousands of years for this. Do you think a setback is going to stop me?* He took a deep breath. "Damn right we still are." Enki shook his head. "We've got Týr's nanoverse. I have shit to take care of. I need you two to distract the Eschaton for a bit. I can't risk interruption. Think you could manage *that?*"

Bast stood up, sauntering over to the window with Moloch. She looked over the ruined city, and a smile crept across her face, inch by inch, until she was grinning a Cheshire grin. "I do."

Enki grunted. "Finally, some efficiency. Care to share with the rest of the class?"

"No, Enki. I'd like to work with Moloch on this alone." She saw Enki's blood begin to rise and held up a hand to placate him before he could explode again. *I want to do this without you screwing us over,* she thought as she said, "I want to make up for my mistake, free you to work on other angles."

The little hateful dots that were Enki's eyes lit up. "Too clever, Bast. I'll let you two do it, then."

"One thing, Enki," Bast said before the brutish god could turn to leave. "I want my prize. Tell me where it is. You got outplayed by the Eschaton already once. I am not going to risk losing it because you got yourself killed."

Enki laughed. "Tell you what, Bast? You finish this task, and I'll tell you where your little toy is. That shouldn't be a problem - if the Eschaton's distracted, he can hardly bother me, now can he?"

Bast fumed. "Fine."

With a grin, Enki turned and walked through the doorway that lead back to his nanoverse.

Moloch grinned. "Black void, he's a thick little jackass, isn't he?"

Bast laughed to hide the seething hatred she felt. "Yes. But I do have a plan. Not that I'm upset Enki left us alone to deal with things."

"Oh?"

"Oh yes, Moloch. Ryan gave us his weakness earlier; it just took me a moment to figure out."

She cast her eyes over the ruined city of petrified corpses, and it took a bit for Moloch to follow her gaze. When he saw what she saw, he started to laugh that hacking laugh again as she nodded in confirmation.

There was a saying of the modern era. You can't make an omelet without breaking any eggs. And when you were a god, sometimes the eggs you broke were massive. She'd tried to contain the fight before, but now...breaking eggs was the best option. *Or really, the only option. You forced me into this, Eschaton.*

Aloud, what she said was, "Like Enki, our Eschaton thinks himself a hero. Can you do it?"

Moloch's laughter slowed to a diseased chuckle. "Oh, absolutely, my dear. It will be a pleasure. Just tell me...where should I raise hell?"

***

There had been a battle on United States soil. Not a terrorist attack, not a foreign power. Men and women claiming to be gods had brought a monster into the United States and fought in an urban area. They'd somehow set of a WMD that had harnessed solar power into a concentrated

147

strike. Casualties had been miraculously nonexistent, but with the kind of power these beings wielded, no one expected such miracles to endure. A response had to be issued.

Rear Admiral Dale Bridges was going to make sure it was.

He had not been prepared for this. No one had. No existing branch of military or law enforcement was equipped to handle this situation. The Navy was chosen because these beings could hop around the world as they wished, so a global response was needed, and because only Bridges had wanted the duty.

Cowards. That was his verdict on the lot of them. The fact was that whoever lead the response would be the one who was blamed if things went sideways. Given that they were dealing with an entirely new type of threat, no one had been willing to leap at the command.

And no one else had a plan. Bridges turned to face the group he had assembled. "Now, ladies and gentlemen. We do not have experience with this type of threat. We do not have plans for this type of threat. This requires outside the box thinking, and your respective fields mean that you are now experts in exactly what the military needs." *And to hell with anyone who thinks differently.* "I want to thank you again for joining us – what do you have for me?"

The Rear Admiral took a seat as he stared at his assembled think tank. Representatives from the Air Force, the Army, DARPA, and the rest of alphabet soup were present. But that wasn't who Bridges was talking to, and they weren't the people he expected to have the answers.

The first group of consultants were the best mythologists the Navy could snatch up. Academics who knew more about the myths surrounding figures like Enki and Bast and Ishtar and Athena than anyone else on the planet, people who might know their myths better than the beings claiming to be gods. That had not attracted any controversy – he'd been praised for bringing them in.

Then there was the second group. Many of them hadn't even bothered to dress up. They were not especially clean cut, they were not very disciplined, and many of them were in terrible physical shape. If they were new military enlistees, Bridges would despair. In this situation, however, the Rear Admiral was going to give them the same respect he gave the Joint Chiefs of Staff, because unlike the Joint Chiefs, they had the expertise he needed.

This group of people wrote comic books.

"The problem," said Lazzario Littleton, who had been writing for one of the major comic companies for nigh on twenty years, "is that they've demonstrated an extremely wide powerset. We're not talking energy controllers, we're not talking paragons, we're not talking bricks. The closest archetype in the genre is Reality Warpers, which," and here he gave a small nod to the Mythologists, "makes sense given what they're claiming to be, your admiralship."

"And how, then, does one beat a Reality Warper?" Bridges liked that term better than gods. It fit more into reality, and it was not sacrilege. *They're demons, I'm sure of it, but there's no need to argue the fine details.*

"They're some of the toughest villains we have," Lazzario replied. "I mean, when a Reality Warper is in a story? It's a full comic event, you know? Every story we write that year ties into it, and we use our entire cast of characters to take them down."

"Sadly, we have a dearth of superheroes, Mr. Littleton. Up until recently, such things were believed to be impossible."

Lazzario nodded. "Which is why you need to fight fire with fire. You need your own gods."

Bridges frowned. "I thought we were going to be discussing a conventional response to this threat, Mr. Littleton."

"That's the problem, though!" Lazzario exclaimed. "Conventional doesn't work here. That's the thesis of pretty much all superhero fiction – normal responses don't work against superhuman threats. We're all suddenly cavemen armed with clubs trying to figure out how to take down a B-52. We're not going to manage it because we can't touch it."

The Rear Admiral felt his frown deepen. *I do not want to have to admit this was a waste of time. More importantly, I don't want it to be a waste of time. We need creative thinking here, and when life starts to imitate fiction, then the fiction writers should be able to come up with the solution.*

"He's right, Rear Admiral, sir," said Carmen Durden, a professor from Harvard. In contrast to the hefty Lazzario, she was built like a collection of sticks, with hair that poofed around her head and glasses that looked ready to fall off her nose. "The tales of mortals besting gods almost always involve one of three things – another god, trickery, or some kind of enchanted item. We don't know if conventional weapons will even harm them, let alone kill them."

And the academics are proving equally useless…just like military intelligence already has. Rear Admiral Bridges reached up and pinched the bridge of his nose. "So you're telling me you have nothing?"

Carmen nodded to Lazzario. "Well," the man said, leaning forward. "We're fully outside the realm of realistic here, but…"

"Out with it, man." Dale Bridges didn't mean to snap, but he couldn't help it. He was used to people speaking and acting with the efficiency born of endless discipline.

"They bled all over the battlefield. In both the comics and the myths-" a glance at Carmen, who nodded, "-divine blood can have special properties. The scene's been quarantined, right? Why not collect some of their blood and see what your research guys can make with it?"

"Ichor," Carmen clarified, "divine blood was called Ichor by the Greeks, sir."

Dale Bridges scratched his chin. *It's not the worst idea I've heard so far.* "Don't you mean make of it, not with it? We should have our research team analyze this blood and try and figure out-"

Lazzario wasn't so rude as to cut him off, but he was shaking his head. The Rear Admiral stopped and motioned for him to continue. "I mean, that's good too, but I meant make *with* it. Smear it on some bullets. Stick it in an engine and light it on fire. Mix it with chemicals and see what it does later."

"There's precedent," Carmen added. "Arrows dipped in the blood of Lanerean Hydra ultimately slew Heracles. Talos, an automaton, was only beaten when it was drained of Ichor – like it had its fuel line ruptured."

"There's also a scientific reason to pursue this line of inquiry."

Bridges turned his attention to Doctor Shivani Pivarti, an Indian woman in her thirties, with long hair done up in an elaborate style. A bioengineer, she had been among the first in the scientific community to publicly state that Enki and the others could have powers that "some would consider supernatural". Her discussions with the media, as well as her well-reasoned posts on her blog, had quickly put her on his radar.

He also liked that she called them "things". He'd prefer if someone else agreed with him on their demonic nature, but anything was better than "gods".

"We don't know anything about their physiology," Doctor Pivarti continued. "They could be an evolutionary mutation, or a new subspecies. At this point we can't even rule out the possibility that they're extra-terrestrial. The chance to study their blood could definitely help us determine how to fight them."

The Rear Admiral nodded in slow thought. "Thank you all for your time. I want you all to go back to work, and I want you talking with DARPA. I want to know what of our existing arsenal we should bring to bear against these things." He rose to his feet, then added, "Doctor Pivarti, please stay behind for a moment."

After the others had left, he turned his attention back to Pivarti. "Less than an hour after Enki's televised interview, you were on the news giving reactions and commentary. How did that happen so quickly?"

She gave him a slight smile. "I called the network and volunteered."

"And from the first," he said slowly, "you've spoken with certainty, not speculation. Trying to project confidence?"

"No. I *have* confidence."

"Explain."

151

"These things are not new to me, Admiral Bridges. I have been aware of them for some time and studying them as best I was able. Quietly, until now, as scientific reputations can be very fragile. I still find myself feeling a bit reticent, or I would have said more in the meeting. Had you not asked to speak with me, I would have approached you and requested a private conversation."

His heartbeat quickened. "Do you have some ideas about how to fight these things?"

She smiled, reaching into her coat pocket. "Better than ideas, Rear Admiral. I have prototypes." She pulled a bullet from her pocket and handed it to Bridges.

When he took it he felt...something. A warmth, an energy. It felt almost alive.

Finally, someone with answers. "Come with me, Doctor Pivarti. I think I have a great deal of work for you."

The two exited the room as the Rear Admiral began to bark orders to collect all the Ichor they could recover.

Chapter 13

The Problem with Omnipotence

When Ryan woke up, he was still outside his nanoverse's staging area, Athena looking at him through the glass with a raised eyebrow. She motioned him to come in. *Of course. If she comes out, the plants will eat her.* Ryan worked his way back to his feet and entered the way he had exited. "I didn't think I'd pass out in my own nanoverse," he grumbled to Athena.

"You're still Nascent. Expect it to keep happening." Athena was failing to suppress a grin.

"You thought that was funny!" Ryan accused.

Athena shook her head. "No. I more thought it was sad." She paused for a second, and then nodded. "And yes, I did want to laugh at you."

Ryan grumbled wordlessly and headed back to the console. After considering all the buttons, he hit one that said "Time Sync."

In an instant, they were back among the field of stars. Ryan had to shake his head to reorient himself. "That was abrupt."

"Omnipotence doesn't guarantee seamless transitions." Athena regarded him, "Nor, apparently, does it prevent slamming face first into your own staging area."

Ryan took the high road and ignored the second comment. "Why do we need to fly there, but can just bounce back out?"

"Because you thought that's how it should work, on some level. We are in your nanoverse, Ryan. Your rules. Now. Tell me what happened."

Ryan began to recount the story, leaving no details out. Athena took a chair and listened patiently as he did. "...so then I gave them a book of science," Ryan finished up, not for the first time wishing he was being met with

Crystal's endless exuberance as opposed to Athena's vaguely judgmental silence. *I'm looking forward to telling this story to Crystal.*

"Science? Which branch? There are multiple types of science, after all." Athena sounded...well, sarcastic, but maybe it was an amused sarcasm, not directed at him. *Or maybe that's just wishful thinking.* As much as Athena was ragging on him, at least she was answering questions. He appreciated that, so much he found himself warming up to the sarcastic goddess. *Is there a goddess of snark?* Either way, he liked her. Kinda. She was difficult to handle and had zero patience but spending a day in his nanoverse had given him some perspective on things. Ryan had decided that, in the grand scheme of things sarcastic and answered questions was about equal with friendly and told him to roll with it.

"Yeah, I know, but the book I pulled out - since I had to will it into existence - I just specified 'all the science they need to advance their culture to the modern era as quickly as possible.' Figured that would cover the basics."

Athena tilted her head, considering. "A circuitous route, I think, but given how time flows...but why not just *will* them to have advanced technology?"

Ryan grinned, glad to have an answer. "I thought about that, but anything I willed into existence wouldn't be any different from whatever we have in the core universe, right? This way, I could get some unique weapons, something no one's ever thought of before."

That got an actual, unmistakable turning upwards of the lips from Athena. "Clever. Did you change any physical laws while you were there?"

"No?"

"Good. That means whatever they make should still work here." Athena leaned over his shoulder and pointed at one of the icons.

"I thought so." Ryan pressed the icon Athena had indicated, and in the middle of the staging area a three-dimensional model of the Earth appeared, almost as tall as Ryan. He walked over to inspect it. "Hey, Athena, why do

Enki and his lot care what happens to Earth? Or, for that matter, why do *we?*"

Ryan was paying attention to Athena, and noticed the slight tensing of her neck muscles, the way her knuckles turned a shade whiter. *What the hell about that set her off?* "How do you mean?" she asked.

"Well, I mean," Ryan found himself choosing his words carefully, "I care because I've only been a god for like a week. So I've got people out there who care about me and stuff, and who I care about. But the rest of you are thousands of years old, right?" He shrugged. "I figured you would get callous after a while."

The tension faded as quickly as it had arrived. *Did she think I was some kind of sociopath that didn't care?* It was the only thing that made sense to Ryan, but he decided not to press the issue as Athena nodded and said, "Ah. I assume you mean aside from not wanting to watch an entire world die?"

Ryan was circling the globe now. *My god, it's everything.* Overall, it was every bit as impressive as seeing the Graphid home world from space. In some ways, less, since it was just an image. In other ways, however, it was even more imposing. He could see places he knew, places he'd been, places he'd wanted to go. He could trace the line of the Mississippi to Saint Louis and could see the collection of buildings that proved he was right. He wondered if he could actually see his apartment if he zoomed in somehow. He was sure he would. After all, it was the entire world laid out for him.

He would have expected seeing the world like this to make him feel more like a god, but instead, he found it humbling. He'd spent most of his life a small spec on that sphere. "Yeah, pretty much. I mean, we're in real time now. Every Graphid I met is probably already long dead. That star will probably die out before I turn forty. So isn't everyone used to it by now?"

Athena sighed. "Tell me, Eschaton...Ryan. When you were in that world, how did you feel?"

"Me? I felt great, powerful. I could just make a book full of knowledge and pop 'reading 101' into someone's head. I could have done it for everyone, if I wanted. I made myself invulnerable and could fly! It was like...like playing a video game with all the cheat codes on."

She gave him a nod. It wasn't that she agreed with him. She was just acknowledging he had said things and she had understood them. Ryan was getting the feeling he was going to Learn a Lesson. "Yes. And no Hunger afterwards, which means you didn't expend any effort, yes?"

"Oh, absolutely. I still fainted, but that's just my brain adapting to apotheosis, right?"

"Indeed." She walked over to him, and leaned forward, her eyes unblinking. "Now imagine spending a hundred years there. Omnipotent, unaging, and able to do everything you want."

"Okay, that's easy." He met her eyes, his brow furrowing. "So...what's the problem?"

"Tell me, what do you imagine yourself doing?" Her voice was calm, measured, relaxed, and lacking her usual sardonic edge.

"Doing?" The furrow grew deeper, a tiny canyon between his eyes. "I mean...making things?"

"After a hundred years?" She tilted her head again, and for a moment Ryan was absurdly reminded of a confused dog spotting a cat for the first time. "What would be left to make?"

"Uh..." He trailed off, realizing he couldn't think of anything. Not just after a hundred years, but after ten or less. He'd conjure a castle, and probably a dragon because he liked dragons, and maybe put the castle in space. Maybe he'd make replicas of his favorite fictional worlds, or alien species...but none of it seemed like it would take that long.

"Now, imagine yourself in a hundred years here. What do you see yourself doing, assuming the sun doesn't explode?"

He leaned back a bit from her gaze. He turned instead back to the model of the Earth. For the first time, he noticed tiny red and blue dots kept appearing on it and vanishing, with the occasional yellow dot with them. It was a quick process, clustered mostly around cities. "I mean, that one's easy. I'm rebuilding the world or building a new one if everyone died. Or helping. Maybe exploring, seeing what's around now that everything's changed. Or maybe, I dunno, Crystal and I and you and whoever, we take a break, bounce around the universe and meet some aliens."

"Does that sound like fun in your nanoverse?" He looked at her again, drawn away from the blinking dots on the globe, and shrugged.

"I mean, sure. But..." Again, he trailed off, struggling to find words.

"But not as interesting as setting foot on Mars? Or rebuilding civilization? Or meeting aliens in *this* universe?"

He shook his head, and she nodded, one of those ghost smiles creeping onto her lips. "The trap of omnipotence. When you can do everything, why bother doing anything? Life is struggle, it is challenge. The idea of retreating to fantasy lands we have complete control over may be appealing, but a thousand worlds built by a whim can't hold a candle to a single house built by your hands."

After a moment, it was Ryan's turn to nod, the motion slow and deliberate as he pondered every word. "So that's why we're fighting over the fate of the Earth? Because we'd be bored otherwise?"

Athena thought that over, chewing his words for a bit before swallowing them. "No, not exactly. Because without struggle, we'd have no reason, no purpose. Earth gives us purpose."

Ryan frowned. "I still don't buy it."

"I really don't think this should need explaining," Athena said.

"Look, I care because I have people out there. My sister. My friends. But...why do you? I mean, you've seen more people die than I've even met, probably. You're like three thousand years old!"

"Older than that," Athena clarified, and sighed. "And that's exactly why I care, Ryan. I have millennia of reminders of how fragile human life is, how precious it is. If you're not a monster, you won't lose your ability to bond with them and enjoy their company and yes, grieve for them when they pass."

It was Ryan's turn to sigh. *Does she not get it? Or am I crazy?* "Don't you get callous to it after a while? I mean, we have entire nanoverses full of people that die every second. We crush nanoverses to kill each other. And even then, people die all the time. How do you...keep caring?"

Athena was silent at first. She wasn't looking at Ryan, but off into the distance. "It used to be rare," she finally said.

Ryan's eyebrows furrowed at the segue. "What did?"

"Destroying nanoverses," Athena explained, her voice as distant as her gaze. "It used to be the limiting factor between us. If you want to kill a god, you have to be okay with snuffing out billions and billions of sentient lives too. Lives with hopes and dreams and...and everything. It was an almost unthinkable act, one that was reserved only for if a god was so dangerous, so mad, that it was..." she groped for the word for a moment. "We used to call it the Great Kindness, when we did it. The logic was that if a god had become so awful as to deserve that fate, those enumerable billions of people were likely trapped in an eternal torment anyway. I never bought it. I've never destroyed a nanoverse. It seemed too monstrous."

Ryan nodded, a small gesture to avoid disturbing Athena. She was in a mood, and he didn't want to break it. "What changed?"

"It wasn't any one thing. It just sort of happened, over time. More and more gods forgot about the billions of people within, instead focusing on the fact that they wanted to destroy their opponent – permanently. We stopped seeing it as an act that was rarely justified. Focused on the idea that within the nanoverse, pretty much every being alive would have died from old age before the collapse finished, so we weren't really killing anyone, were we?" She chuckled, a hollow, bitter sound that made Ryan shiver. "It's still not common. We're not all sociopaths. But...fine, you're right. It does get hard. Nanoverses are tools, but they're still full of people. Humans are still people, but they don't last long."

"Then…how do you manage to still care?"

Another long silence followed, so long Ryan almost asked again before Athena spoke. "I never forget what it was like to feel powerless. I don't let myself. The moment I do, I'll become like some of the others. As long as you hold on to that, you should be fine." She glanced sideways at Ryan. "Of course, with how little you know, you're probably going to die before that ever becomes a concern."

Moment over, apparently. Ryan forced a grin in response. "Bet you fifty bucks I don't die before the world ends."

Athena rolled her eyes. "If you lose, I'll never be able to collect that debt."

"Yeah, but what do you need fifty bucks for anyway?" Ryan responded.

"You do realize that if you end the world, money will have no more value?" Athena asked, quirking her eyebrow again.

"Well…" Ryan shrugged. "Good incentive to keep things intact when I do, right?"

"Fine," Athena turned back to the globe that was dominating the room, done with the conversation.

Ryan turned with her to look at the globe watching as it spun in a lazy rotation, clouds whirling across the simulated sky. "So...what's this do?"

"It's a Zoisphere. A living globe. You can use it to manipulate weather across the world."

Ryan closed his mouth and swallowed. "So I could, what, make a hurricane and throw it at DC right now?"

"It's not as precise as being directly on location and sending down thunderbolts or forming hurricanes, but yes." She raised an eyebrow. "You've heard stories of gods, in their wrath, sending great storms to throw ships off course or destroy cities, yes? But when you've been on the ground, could you imagine manipulating that much power?"

He shook his head, remembering the effort of holding back the tornado before Enki interrupted.

"So this gives you an alternative. Much less precise, slower to work. For example, if you wanted to, as you put it, 'make a hurricane and throw it at DC', you'd have to start it a way out as a tropical storm and feed it till it grew into what you wanted."

Ryan chuckled slightly, drawing a curious look from Athena. "Just...the way the conversation went. 'Here is why having unlimited power is boring. Now check out this cool globe that lets you control weather across the world!'"

Athena chuckled faintly. "I see the humor there," she said, and again – wonder upon wonder - Ryan earned a non-sarcastic smile. It faded almost the instant she noticed Ryan noticing it. *What, worried I'll think you're less of a hardass if I see you smile too much? Not going to happen.*

"So what are the little dots then?"

"Red is a death, blue is a birth. Yellow is a manifestation of a god's power." She glanced at Ryan's eyes, and answered the question he was about to ask before he could give it voice. "I'm not surprised Ishtar didn't show this to you sooner, at least in this case. If your divine sight was not strong enough, it would have shattered your mind."

"Divine sight?"

Athena sighed. "Ishtar didn't even give you the proper terminology for that? Of course she didn't. Divine sight - how you see the underpinnings of reality, how you know what you're looking at to manipulate."

"Oh." He sighed. "I'm really looking forward to getting to the point where my mind breaking isn't a risk. So this is how Enki was tracking us the first time around?"

"Yes. Yellow is normally rare, so if he just went to each one, he'd eventually find you." She shrugged. "Once you both sent out your little letters, I imagine the manifestations of divine power became far more frequent as gods started looking to see what was going on. Being able to see where they manifest isn't a very useful thing, unless you're looking for a concentration of gods."

Ryan watched for a moment, the eternal cycle of life and death playing out as pretty little dots across the globe. The weight of it began to set in, and he wanted to sit down...when something got his attention. A massive yellow dot was slowly fading. In its wake, red dots were appearing with increasing speed, dozens, spreading out from a central point like a ripple in a pond, but these waves were human lives being snuffed out. "What's going on in Texas?"

She focused her gaze there. "We have to go. Something terrible is happening."

They both ran through the doorway to Crystal's staging area, and Athena went over to the controls and began pushing the touchscreen. Apparently, she could read whatever language that was.

"Think it's Enki?" Ryan asked, bouncing on the balls of his feet in anticipation.

"Absolutely. And for whatever purpose, he's killing hundreds. Thankfully, we're not far - in fact, the door has just been placed."

Ryan turned to rush out of it, Athena vaulting over the staging area to follow him. They opened the door and stepped out into the street, just in time to watch a tall, gaunt, eyeless mummy, half wrapped in tattered cloth, pull the heart out of a man's chest. The streets around this mummy were devoid of life but littered with the dead. Ryan had to fight back a wave of nausea at the sight. He'd never imagined anything like this.

"Oh, hells." Athena whispered, drawing a sword out of thin air.

The mummy turned to them and let out a low, echoing scream.

Chapter 14

Athena swung her sword at the mummy, altering the blade's velocity seamlessly as she did. The sword sliced through the desiccated corpse's skull at around Mach 3, sending the top of its head rocketing into the sky while the rest of its body collapsed from the blow.

The sonic boom cut through the cacophony of screams.

"Oh, Athena...why? Why not silent?" Ryan began reaching into his own nanoverse for a weapon.

"I beg your pardon?" She glanced over her shoulder at him, and with her sword still flung out and her hair whipping in the wind, she looked like she was posing for a fantasy book cover, only instead of some elaborate outfit she was wearing comfortable jeans and a practical t-shirt.

"Noise! Haven't you ever watched a zombie movie?" Ryan didn't waste any time admiring the power stance, tugging the weapon he had grabbed on to and pulling it slowly out. *Feels heavier.*

Athena furrowed her brow. "No, and I fail to see the relevance. Hollywood often incorrectly displays such things."

"Damnit." Ryan glanced down the street. "Rule one of a zombie apocalypse-

"-Mummy." Athena interjected.

Ryan shook away the correction and continued, "Mummy apocalypse then. Loud noises draw the horde."

Ryan's response was cut short by the sound of dozens upon dozens of approaching footsteps.

Athena watched the horde, and a flicker of fear crossed those impassive eyes. "Ah."

More than a flicker of fear crossed Ryan's brain. It was an entire horde of fear, and it pounded through his brain like the rushing horde on the street. "Athena! What's the difference between zombies and mummies?" Ryan's voice nearly cracked as terror began to settle in.

"You have to remove the head *and* stab them through the heart or they'll reform." Ryan noticed the mummy Athena had felled was trying to rise, clawing frantically towards the gods. With a contemptuous flick, she brought her sword down on the corpse before her to demonstrate. The creature went rigid as the sword impaled it, and then let out a dusty sigh as it collapsed. "And mummies have supernatural powers. And aren't slow. And hate gods that didn't create them."

Ryan and Athena had been standing in an empty street, but figures were filing in. Granger, Texas was a fairly small town near Austin, and this street was a row of one and two-story shops with minimal alley space - just a couple on either side of the street, a block to the north and a block to the south. Ryan noted with mounting horror that there were people in the shops, some armed with guns - *God bless Texas,* he couldn't help but think - while others huddled behind the ones who were armed.

A couple of the gunmen were pointing their weapons at Ryan. *Oh, right. I'm the Antichrist.* At least they weren't firing at him. Yet.

The mummies began to charge, many of them hunched over on all fours. Others were standing, wielding staves or strangely curved swords or axes that looked like pendulums blades from a video game trap.

Ryan took his eyes off the approaching doom to glance at his own weapon. It was...a sword. He felt a surge of disappointment. *I guess I didn't give them enough time to make it out of the Iron Age.* But then his divine sight kicked in, and noticed that the equations surrounding the sword were incredibly complex. He couldn't get enough focus to figure out what they were for, though - not in the time a bunch of undead would need to close the gap.

He and Athena moved back to back. "What's that dust cloud behind them?" Ryan asked, not looking over his shoulder.

"It's more of them, still in a discorporate form. They'll try to fill our lungs while the others attack." When Ryan squinted, he could see vaguely humanoid shapes making up the cloud.

"Good thing we don't need to breathe, then."

"Yes. Up until they become solid in your lungs. Messy way to die."

Ryan clamped his mouth shut and wished for nose plugs. *You don't need to breathe, Ryan. Try and just exhale the whole time.*

"Charge!" Athena shouted, running to meet the horde head on, and, screaming in a mixture of anger and complete terror, Ryan did the same.

He swung the sword as soon as he was close enough. As he did, the mass shifted to the leading edge without dulling the blade. It wasn't part of his power, but something inherent in the sword. As soon as it was through the mummy's neck, the mass shifted to the other side, and Ryan was able to stop his wild swing in much less distance than normal. He brought it back, with the shifting mass adding acceleration, and buried it in the mummy's side, right into the creature's heart.

Another opponent was leaping through the air, though, and Ryan didn't know if he could pull the sword out in time, but the sword's blade went almost completely liquid, flowing like mercury until it had to solidify again to puncture his foe. The angle was awkward, and Ryan was sure he'd miss the heart, but the sword adjusted itself slightly in his grip to make sure it hit where it needed to.

What the hell just happened? Ryan wasn't sure, but he wasn't complaining, instead whirling to strike at another mummy. Again, as he swung the blade began to shimmer and flow, and Ryan felt his swing pulled towards just an inch - enough where it met the mummy's neck. Ryan flinched as bone and desiccated flesh flew from the point of impact.

There wasn't time to figure it out. There was too much going on. Ryan began to let the minor adjustments the sword made compensate for a lower energy style on his part, conserving as much strength as he could. The dust cloud closed around him, and he started a long, forced exhale to try to keep it out. Visibility dropped, to the point where he could only see the nearest foes, but that was enough to hold them at bay.

Loud bangs erupted from between Athena and himself, and Ryan had to hope the gunmen were shooting at the actual threats. *Hell, at this point, I'm fine with them blind firing into the dust. At least the odds are better they'll hit a mummy than me.*

Ryan looked out over the horde of approaching mummies. It was a sea of necrotized flesh, easily a hundred. Maybe more. Ryan took a moment to wipe sweat from his brow before it could stream down into his eyes. *How do we fight this many?*

A shout came from behind him and he could only hope that Athena's cry had been elation and not pain. He'd find out soon enough. They were driving him back, leaving him no option but to back away or be surrounded and sliced to ribbons. Soon he'd either find himself back-to-back with Athena again, or back-to-face with Athena's side of the battle, and if it was the latter he'd be cut to pieces.

Fortunately, when he felt something at his back, it wasn't a mummy trying to tear open his skull, but Athena, watching the horde approaching from behind him. *Great. We might die, but at least we'll go out looking like something from an action movie.* They paused in their assault, and the dust began to disperse a bit to form more mummies in the back lines.

"Hey, how's it going over there?" Ryan couldn't help but resist a chance to banter in the breather they were being given. It helped distract him from the way his legs were starting to shake with the exertion and kept his mind off how many mummies remained.

It was a nice distraction from how utterly hopeless things felt.

"Oh, it's fine. I've always wanted to fight the mummies of lost Ys in the middle of a Texas summer."

Ryan had to glance over at her. "Was that...was that a joke?"

He thought he saw a glimmer in her eye for a moment, but then focused back on the horde. "Why aren't they attacking?" Athena asked.

"You complaining?" But it did bother Ryan too. The way they stood there, eerily still, even as some of the shooters put bullets in them was even more unnatural than the walking dead already were. *They should at least try to deal with the shooters.*

"Yes. An opponent doing something unexpected is always bad."

"Always? What about-" He stopped when, at that moment, they both felt it. A change in probabilities, a twisting of the equations.

Behind the two hordes of mummies, rising over the sound of intermittent gunfire, a buzzing began. Low at first, but rapidly getting louder and harsher.

Ryan swallowed hard as he saw a dozen giant insects. They were immense, the size of a small car, with dragonfly wings and wicked stingers on arched tails. Their faces, though, were the most unsettling. They looked like human faces, although they lacked any kind of expression. Among the crowd Ryan saw a face he recognized - the man whose heart they had watched get torn out earlier.

"Okay, never mind." He raised his sword, wondering how they were going to survive these things. "Something unexpected? Always bad."

The new monsters began to swarm them.

"Athena! Can you hold off the flying scorpion man face things? I have an idea." Ryan's voice was a quarter octave higher than usual, and he took a deep calming breath after the words were out of his mouth.

"Manticores." There was an edge to her voice too, although nowhere near as pronounced as the note in Ryan's.

"What?" Up to a half octave higher.

"They're called manticores."

"Oh, good. Now that we have the terminology sorted out, can you hold them off?" Thankfully, his voice didn't go any higher this time.

"Yes. Do whatever you're doing quickly." She drew her blade, and Ryan tossed her the one he'd been using. She caught it without turning, an offhand grab that Ryan envied.

"But you-" The manticores were getting closer. Time was drawing short. "Alright, go." Ryan started manipulating the equations with all the speed he could manage, knowing every second he waited was one that could result in both of their deaths. As he completed each twist of the numbers, he started changing variables governing electron dispersion and static buildup.

Athena nodded, and first took her sword and threw it. She manipulated her own variables. Ryan couldn't follow what she was doing – the math looked *wrong* to him. The end result was apparent, however - the sword began to orbit him, creating a whirling shield around his body as he moved.

Then the manticores were on her. As Ryan continued his manipulation, he got a chance to see her fight for the first time as an ally, when he wasn't distracted by the fact that Athena was trying to kill him and Crystal.

One of the manticores struck at her with a bladed tail, and instead of dodging or parrying she caught it in her free hand and buried the mercurial blade right behind the stinger. Then, when the beast tried to tug the tail away, she let herself be taken with it so she could sever the stinger and use the momentum to propel herself up to another of the monsters.

This manticore she met feet first, her heels digging into the human eyes on the face. It screeched, and she kicked off to come back down on the first one, the sword lodging itself in its skull. *It's so different than Crystal.* Crystal fought with grace and elegance. Watching her move was like watching a dancer in some complicated ballet, winding and twirling. Athena, on the other hand, fought like someone just out to win. She was precise and powerful, and moved with efficiency, no movement that wasn't strictly necessary.

Ryan was so impressed, he almost couldn't tell that she was still hopelessly outnumbered. But the mummies were moving back in, and that impressive stunt had only killed one of the manticores. *I have to finish this.* As soon as Athena went down, he'd be dead. Some of the mummies were even trying to advance on him, although so far those that got too close to the orbiting sword were faring as well as blades of grass trying to slip past a lawnmower.

Another round of gunfire erupted from the stores. Ryan caught a glimpse of someone. An older woman, looking like someone's kindly grandmother, but instead of fresh-baked cookies she had fistfuls of hot lead. The mummies, in their hatred of divine beings, had continued to ignore the ordinary humans nearby, but bullets still proved to be inconvenient for the attacking horde. *That's right, need to make sure I don't kill the civilians in the process.* Fortunately, for what he had planned, they should be fine.

First move - give Athena a better chance against the manticores. Their primary advantage was flight, so he needed to take that away. He could increase gravity on each of them, but with no idea how strong they were, he could waste time under doing it, and it would have to be one at a time.

Instead, he assigned direction to every molecule of the air surrounding the entire group, creating a single burst of wind that sucked all the air out from around them. Although the monsters were unnatural and biologically impossible, they still had to obey the laws of physics to a degree, and wings don't work so well without air to push against. The sudden vacuum turned off all sound in the area and brought the manticores crashing to the Earth.

Athena gave him curt nod of approval. Now that the manticores couldn't fly, they could only approach her one at a time, and as a bonus, Ryan didn't have to worry about them flying over the orbiting sword.

Second move was to end the fight. While Athena continued to brute-force her way through her attackers - Ryan almost winced in sympathy as she drove a flying knee into one of the manticores' faces, then reached up and impaled it on its own flailing stinger - Ryan continued to manipulate electron fields and static charges.

There are some phenomena that are poorly understood by science. Even after acing physics, Ryan didn't have a grasp of how these equations worked, but it didn't matter - he reached out and manipulated them, and an instinctive knowledge of what he wanted guided his hand.

It worked. The hair on the back of his arms stood up as orbs of ball lightning began to streak out of the spinning blade. Each one dove unerringly towards the first target it could find, with the exception of Athena, who Ryan had grounded to keep her clear of the charges. As soon as they met their targets, be it manticore or mummy or evil sentient dust cloud, they exploded, filling the vacuum with a gas that reeked of sulfur and a ball of blue light. If there had been air in here, the thunderclaps would have been deafening, but instead the entire barrage played out in eerie silence.

Of course, his Hungers wouldn't allow something as extravagant as slowing time. He was spent. Ryan fell to one knee, his vision darkening. He held onto consciousness long enough to cut off the flow of current before it could reach the civilians nearby, and then - with a resigned sigh as the expected took over - passed out.

***

Bast took a sip from her martini, her green dress shimmering in the sunlight. Moloch swirled his glass of whiskey, before taking another drink, letting the amber liquid run between his yellowed teeth. His suit was already starting to look worn and frayed, as if just being in contact with his flesh was enough to cause the garment wear and tear. Their seats were overlooking the battlefield. Athena was dealing with the last of the mummies of Ys, and the Eschaton was unconscious.

"We could go into the fight now," Bast said, although her voice lacked strength and conviction. "Athena will be exhausted, and with the Eschaton passed out…"

Moloch regarded her. "I don't get the impression, my dear, that you're particularly interested in doing so."

Bast shook her head. "Enki only wanted the Eschaton distracted. That has been accomplished. I'm not feeling particularly inclined to take extra steps when he treats us like his slaves. Especially not since I completed my task and want my damn reward. You?"

Moloch shook his head. "I Hunger too much from my exertions today. Although you could help me fill some of that Hunger and then perhaps…" He couldn't finish, letting out a dusty cough at the disgusted look on Bast's face.

"We'd have to be far more desperate than this, Moloch. And really, hunger? You did that all with sacrificial power. Someday, you'll tell me why you refuse to use the powers of your nanoverse."

"Unlikely," was Moloch's only retort.

Bast glanced down again. "The Eschaton is proving more dangerous than we expected. Athena, Ishtar - we knew they would be difficult prey. But this one is…"

"Clever." Moloch finished for her. "He's clever, my dear. I think we need to begin to make preparations."

"Preparations? What for?"

Moloch watched Athena decapitate the final mummy. People began to pour out of the shops around them. Some still had their guns raised, but others were holding their hands in the air. "For if Enki fails in his quest. I do not want to get dragged down with him, and I assume you feel the same?"

Bast nodded. "A fair point. And for now?"

"For now, we report our failure to Enki, deal with his wrath, and then prepare for our next move. We're survivors, you and I. And I think we'll find others who are interested in survival as well."

She grinned. "Then take care of your Hungers. I'll deal with the brute. He still has information we need, and I'm going to try to get him talking." She turned on her heels, and headed to the door that lead to her nanoverse. Moloch did the same.

They both suspected that they shared a thought, and they both would have been right. Enki wasn't the only one they were willing to throw under the bus if it meant their own survival. Each one would happily sacrifice the other.

But for now, they were still allies, and could only hope the trigger-happy Texans would finish what they had started.

Chapter 15

The Reverend and the Goddess

Reverend Jeremy Howard did not expect to end his day crouched behind a counter in a convenience store, clutching a shotgun. It had started out a fairly normal day. His wife was out of town visiting her sister in Dallas - *and thank you, merciful God, for that* - so he'd woken up and gone to his office to work on Sunday's sermon.

Church attendance was at all-time high, something he was grateful for. He just wished it was for a different reason. But with the "Church of Adversity" promoting Satanism and claiming Hellfire was now something to be desired, with this 'Enki' on the television claiming to be a pagan god trying to fight the Antichrist, people were scared. After the big fight yesterday between the alleged Antichrist and some of these pagan gods, it would likely be even more packed this coming Sunday. People were scared and confused. Scientists hadn't been able to give answers, so people were returning to faith.

I believe there will be an Antichrist, the Reverend had written. *The Good Book promises us that such things are ahead. That dark times will come. But I do not believe this man is the Antichrist. The Rapture is not upon us, and the End of Times has not yet arrived. It is not for me to know when it will happen, but the Bible lays out a road map for what to expect. Those signs are not present. What we are faced with is a crisis of faith. "I am the Lord, your god, and Thou shalt have no other gods before me." A commandment so important that the good Lord put it very first on his list. In recent times, in modern times, people have not been putting other gods first. They've been putting themselves first, denying the power of the Lord.*

Now we have beings that claim to be gods. These are not part of the End Times. This is a test of faith. Can

*we maintain our belief in a god that is ephemeral, that
makes himself known in subtle ways, when there are men
and women running around with powers ancient man
attributed to the gods?*

I believe we can. I know I can. But...

He'd trailed off. There was a commotion outside.
Gunfire. Screaming. He'd run to the window.

For a moment, he thought this *was* the End Times.
The dead had risen from their graves and were hunting the
living.

He'd gone out to join the chaos, hoping to provide
some order. A move that was, perhaps, born of hubris. Of
pride in his status as a Community Leader. He'd
accomplished nothing but adding another body to the sea
of humanity, not until someone had shoved a shotgun into
his hand.

The bible said "Thou shalt not kill," but as far as the
Reverend was concerned, if the good Lord had a problem
with the destruction of the living dead, He would have
made sure that was clear.

In the chaos, a man with a clear voice and righteous
determination had been ignored. A man with a clear voice,
righteous determination, and a shotgun commanded
respect. He'd managed to get a group of people into Jodi's
convenience store, and there they'd holed up as the dead
swarmed around them. Then the supposed Antichrist had
arrived, with Athena in tow.

The Reverend was not ashamed to admit that his
conviction that these weren't the End Times had faltered. It
seemed, for a moment, that these two were at the center
of the chaos, perhaps even the ones behind it.

The duo had dispelled that fear by attacking the
monsters that swarmed Granger.

Now the battle was over, and the man Enki called
the Antichrist had fallen. Athena was the only one standing.

"We should shoot her," Billy muttered beside the
Reverend.

"Billy! They saved our lives." Billy had been a
member of Reverend Howard's congregation since he had

just been a wee lad, and the Reverend had never seen such an evil gleam in his eyes.

"The devil has power to take a pleasing shape," Billy said, "it says so in the damn bible."

The Reverend took a deep breath. "Don't call it the 'damn' Bible, Billy. And that wasn't from the Bible. Shakespeare was a master of wordplay, but he did not write anything that is found in the Bible, nor was he a theologian," the Reverend countered. "This is not about their shape, it's about their action."

Silas popped up. "How can we trust even that? Maybe they're just gonna try and give us the Mark of the Beast as soon as we step out."

"Then we will refuse it." Reverend Howard did not see the point to arguing about the Antichrist part right now.

"Or," Jodie said, rising from behind the cash register, "we could just let them go. Enough people have died, Reverend. Why not just wait for them to leave?"

"Because," the Reverend said, finally getting to his feet, "they have saved our lives. The least we could do is thank them."

Billy spit on the floor. "I don't trust them."

Nor do I, the Reverend thought. The fact remained that whatever they were, they claimed to be gods. A title that belonged to one being, and one being alone. That made them suspect. "Then keep your gun up, Billy. But don't you dare pull that trigger, not unless there's a good reason."

And with that, the conversation was over. They stepped out of the convenience store, guns at the ready.

Athena rolled her eyes and lifted her hands in the air, dropping Ryan's sword, as the armed men and women approached her. *Fantastic weapon. I must see if Ryan will allow me to keep that one.* The sword she had put in orbit around Ryan had buried itself in the ground after he'd fallen. Athena knew that these bouts of unconsciousness were a normal part of being a Nascent, but they were so frequent. She didn't recall her own nascency being so full of fainting spells.

"I've laid aside my arms and yet you still point weapons at me. If you intend to fire, I'd prefer you get to it." A bluff. Bullets could still kill a god or goddess, although it would take a great deal. When a god used a weapon, like when Bast had shot Týr - and that thought was enough for Athena to clench her hands into fists before she could fight it back - they put a portion of their power into it. Mortals did not have that ability, but their bullets would hurt, and enough would provide the force needed to do her serious injury by striking somewhere vulnerable. Still, humans were at their most dangerous when they were panicked and acting out of that fear. Given time to talk and think, they tended towards something resembling rationality.

And you're out of power, Athena thought, hoping it didn't show on her face. *You're just a woman right now, as far as bullets are concerned.* Her Hungers were scrabbling at the back of her mind, and she did her best to put them aside. *Have to keep it together or this ends badly.*

"You just saved our lives," the Reverend said, lowering his gun. "I figure I could give you the benefit of the doubt there."

Athena started to relax when Billy spoke up, his gun not wavering. "I heard on the news that one there is the Antichrist. I say we put a bullet in him to be safe."

Her heart sped up. She could recover from death. Ryan would not. "He did most of the hard work in saving your lives." Not entirely true, but what these people needed to believe right now.

"Yeah. Or that's what you want us to think. But we got dead walking the Earth, and that's biblical right there.'" Athena took it as a good sign that they were still talking, even though he - and several others - still were angry and frightened.

"Dumbass," Silas interjected, glaring at him. "There's no Bible verse that says that. Don't you ever read it?"

"Can we stop arguing about the damn Bible?" Jodi said, her gun still trained on Athena, although she glanced over at the Reverend. "Sorry for the language, Reverend. But fact is, these two fought against the zombies, but that doesn't make them friends. Now that we're out here, if he's the Antichrist, we do the world a favor by ending him and anyone who works with him."

"May I speak?" asked Athena, keeping her hands raised. She was careful to keep her tone neutral, since it kept the sarcasm she was feeling from creeping into her voice. When no one objected, she continued. "I never had the pleasure of meeting your Christ. He didn't come to Greece. But his disciples did. Good men, for the most part," she said, glossing over several uncomfortable truths in the process. *Give them what they want to hear,* "and I never once opposed their attempts to convert my people."

"Oh yeah?" Jodie looked interested, at least. "Why not?"

"Because I don't care about being worshipped. Most of us don't. There are a few who did - Zeus, Odin, Quetzalcoatl, Enki - but I have no desire for worshippers."

"Why not?" Her eyes were narrowing, as were a couple others. "Y'all call yourself gods, right? Doesn't that mean you want to be worshipped?"

Athena shook her head. "It's a limitation of language. When we first became public, we were called gods because we were beings with power beyond normal comprehension. There's still no other good word for it in your language. Superhuman might cover it, but that conjures images of men and women in colorful costumes which isn't really what we do. I don't intend on running around in a skintight costume."

Silas took a moment to look her up and down, and leered. "Maybe you should think about it."

Pig. Athena didn't rise to the bait. She lowered her hands, and while the guns tensed, no one shot. "If I meant you harm, I had ample time to do horrible things. Instead, I'm talking. Shouldn't that earn me some credit?"

"Lower your guns," said the Reverend, his voice calm but loud. Projected. *He knows how to speak to crowds.* "I don't see an Antichrist here, and I don't see gods. Just a couple of people with the power to help, who did the right thing."

"Reverend! We've already got those Satanists runnin' around, now we got false gods, don't you think that means we're lookin' at the end times?"

"Billy," the Reverend said, his voice calm and authoritative, "these may be dark times, but until the good Lord sees fit to Rapture up the faithful, I think any claims to Armageddon are premature."

"Your Reverend speaks well, and truly. I have read your Revelations, and it's quite clear what will happen when it is time for the end of the world." Athena didn't even blink at the lie. In a sense, Ryan was their Antichrist, the man who would end the world. But only in a sense.

One by one the scared gunmen started lowering their weapons. Athena found it easier to relax after each one. "Might I take my friend and go? He needs to recover from our battle...and I have a feeling the next battle is not far away."

The Reverend nodded, and since no one looked interested in arguing with him, she did just that, talking as she scooped Ryan up. "If any of the mummies remain, you must destroy both head and heart. Else they will simply reform."

"Sounds good to me. Billy, Silas, Jodie. Spread the word to others and if any cops are still alive and kicking, make sure they know. National Guard or Army will probably be showing up soon, we gotta convince them of that anyway. Anything we should know about the - what'd you call them? Manticores?"

Athena hoisted Ryan over her shoulder. "Shoot them until they stop moving, and then keep shooting until it ceases to amuse you. They are hard to keep dead. If you can get ahold of their stingers, dip your bullets in their venom. It will kill them instantly. Don't let it get on your skin if you value your life..."

"Noted. Thank you, ma'am, for your help." The reverend gave her a broad smile. *You're not a goddess,* he thought. *But whatever you are, or whatever you claim to be, you're on His side. Even if you don't know it.*

She nodded in appreciation, glad to at least get some gratitude, and carried Ryan back to the doorway they had left open. Once inside, Ishtar's staging area created a bed for him, and she laid Ryan next to Ishtar's corpse. *I suppose I should start calling her Crystal, as he does. I wonder why the affectation?*

She stared at Ryan for a moment. The man who would end the world. He looked so...tiny, like this. He didn't have a commanding presence, but he did have *a* presence. Seeing him laid out like this after watching him destroy an army of mummies really drove home how fragile he was in his Nascent state. *I will keep you safe, Eschaton, and we will find a way to end this world without you becoming what those ignorant brutes fear you to be.*

She just wished she had some idea how she would keep either of those promises.

Chapter 16

Ryan woke up with his head pounding. *Pushed it too far.* Athena was standing close to the bed, swinging his sword. It sang in her hands, each strike humming through the air as she removed limbs and heads from straw training dummies.

He took a moment to just watch. Her motions were still full of the brute force she had used earlier, a raw power that years of video games and movies had caused Ryan to associate with the masculine. She didn't flip about, and there was no waifishness to her movements, none of the delicate grace that was given to action heroines or even that he had seen in Crystal. Seeing a woman rip into target dummies with a savagery that in no way matched her features, all with a near emotionless face...it was so enthralling, it took him a moment to realize they weren't in the silver planetarium of Crystal's nanoverse.

The sky above them was still swirling galaxies and stars, but it was much brighter than Crystal's - although not quite as bright as his own. Instead of a row of touchscreens, it had marble tablets with inscriptions that shifted and flowed like something organic. The floor was likewise marble, although with some carpeting in spots, and around the edge were pillars that held up arches. The whole thing, fittingly, brought to mind a Greek ruin.

"You moved us," Ryan whispered, not wanting to interrupt her destructive dance.

"Yes." Athena impaled the final dummy as she spoke, dragging Ryan's sword up to cut it in half before continuing. "Spending so much time using Ishtar's nanoverse was feeling invasive. She's still in there, but that archway," she pointed with the sword, "leads there now."

Ryan sat up, his movements gentle to account for his still throbbing headache. "Makes sense. How're you liking the sword?"

"It's a remarkable weapon. I think I figured out how it works," Athena studied the blade for another moment "Feel up to using your divine sight to confirm my theory?"

"Sure, what am I looking for?"

"Programmable matter. I think the people of your nanoverse figured it out."

Ryan took a deep breath and opened his divine sight. The equations that swirled around the blade were incredibly complex, and it took him a moment to figure them out. "Yeah, hole in one. Programmable matter with micro cameras. It's a...it's a smartsword."

Athena held up the blade and smiled at it. "I don't suppose you'd mind me keeping it? Assuming you can pull another from your nanoverse, of course." She gave it another few swings.

"Sure, if you'll answer a question for me." She raised an eyebrow, encouraging him to continue. "Why the swords? Bast used a gun, but pretty much everyone else has fought with swords - and I think I was subconsciously imitating that when I pulled mine out."

Athena walked over to one of the pillars and hung the sword on it. Looking around Ryan realized the pillars all had weapons hanging from them. Swords and guns and axes and pikes and other, more exotic implements.

"As Socrates was fond of doing, I'd like to answer your question by asking you some. How do you see your power?"

"Uh...I'm adjusting equations. Changing variables, sort of...hacking reality, I guess?"

She gave him a smile. An actual, genuine smile. "And your nanoverse, it obeys those same laws, yes?"

"Of course. You said it obeys the laws of reality unless we change them, right?"

"I did, although that was imprecise." She sat down on a stool that rose from the floor near the bed. "It would be more accurate to say it obeys the laws of reality as you understand them."

"Okay, so what's the difference?" He had to admit, he enjoyed getting answers, even in this roundabout way, more than being told to roll with it. *Although, in Crystal's defense, I'm probably further along than I was then - if she'd told me, it might have broken my brain.*

"I was born in Greece, millennia ago. I was twenty-three when I got my nanoverse. How much do you know about the classic elements?"

"That's earth, air, fire, and water, right?"

She nodded. "And Aether, the less famous one. It was believed that all matter was made of those five elements in varying ratios. Since that was what I believed, those are the rules my nanoverse abided by for millennia, before I could adapt it to keep up with modern understanding. Now, why do you think I would have had to rely on swords, shields, and other simple weapons?"

Ryan thought for a moment, chewing his cheek as he did so. "Because...that's not how reality works, so the advanced weapons didn't work in the core universe?"

A genuine smile again. It almost would have been patronizing, a teacher giving an exceptionally bright student a rare moment of approval, but something in it was just soft enough to not feel like that. "Exactly. Now? I could pull out guns and other, advanced weapons, but...well; they say you can't teach an old dog new tricks. It works equally well if you swap the first and last letter of dog."

A moment passed before Ryan got the comment, then he started to chuckle. Not because the joke was all that funny, but because it was the first straight up joke he thought he'd ever heard from the normally dour goddess. After a couple moments he got his laughter under control and asked, "So Bast just decided that she'd be an exception to the rule?"

Athena nodded. "Which, following our earlier line of reasoning, does make sense." Ryan's mouth hung slightly open as he tried to figure out where she was going. *Please don't make me ask you what you mean.* "She was associated with cats, after all."

That got another round of 'it's a lot funnier coming from you' laughter out of Ryan. "Okay, you got me there."

Athena's smile hadn't wavered. It was nice to see her looking something other than vaguely annoyed or frustrated, and it was a relief to see a smile that wasn't sarcastic. "I do have good news for you, Ryan. Ishtar's body is beginning to warm again. She's started her rebirth cycle."

"Oh thank God." He paused, realizing that was a bit of an odd turn of phrase given what he *was* now, but rolled with it. "No offense, of course. I'll be glad to have her back, is all." Ryan didn't admit, out loud at least, that he'd also had doubts that she'd come back. He'd believed Athena when she'd told him, but...he still hadn't internalized the idea that death wasn't always permanent.

"None taken. When she does revive, you should talk to her without my presence - after all, when she died, I was still an adversary."

Ryan nodded. "Makes sense. In the meantime...Enki's still an ongoing problem. We should be doing something. With all those marks on the Zoisphere in Granger..." Ryan shuddered. "How many people died?"

Athena shook her head, the smile vanishing from her face. "Dozens, at least. More likely hundreds. Maybe even more. Just to draw us out. I agree we need to deal with Enki before he kills more, especially since they now know it will draw us out, but..." Athena sighed. "But we do not know where they are, or what they want. We have limited options to strike at them."

"I think we do have an option there. We go back on the news, only you do most of the talking. Given that you were part of his original team, you talking about how awful he is might actually carry some weight."

Athena shook her head. "I see where you're going with this, Ryan, but I don't believe it's our best course of action. That will provoke him into another fight, in the middle of a civilian population. We'll be putting dozens of people at risk, especially now that he's proven willing to allow innocents to be slaughtered to further his cause. No, we need something more definite, something more decisive. And we lack the intelligence to do it. She stood up. "Let's go into the core universe. You have Hungers to fill, and perhaps we'll learn something."

Ryan felt his stomach agree with the idea as he climbed out of the bed and followed her to the door. The street they walked out on wasn't one Ryan recognized, but that hardly mattered. As always, his phone started buzzing with notifications as soon as he hit a cell tower, and he pulled it out to check it as they walked - making a mental note to charge it while they were in the core world.

Without even thinking about it, Ryan opened his email. Part of his brain though it was an odd choice - he had over twelve thousand notifications now, and there was unlikely to be anything interesting or useful there, but it was open, and he was scrolling through it. In fact, now that he thought about it, he'd already turned off his notifications, hadn't he? Back the first time he and Crystal returned to the core world from Cipher Nullity.

As odd as these intrusive thoughts were, he still found himself opening an email.

Ryan,

We should talk. I think we can help each other out a great deal. Or, rather, my boss and you can help each other. Especially with this whole 'antichrist' mess you've gotten into. Give me a call, and let's talk about what we can do for each other.

Amy Preston

Heresiarch

Church of Adversity

It was followed by a phone number. "Church of Adversity...I've heard of that," Ryan muttered. *Yeah, it's been in the news lately.*

Athena was still walking. "Ryan? Are you coming?"

It was like the words lifted a fog on his mind. Ryan nearly threw his phone across the street. Someone, or some*thing*, had made him open and read that email. If whoever, or whatever, had done that had meant him real harm, they could have made him walk into traffic, not open an email.

Holy crap, what was that? Ryan knew his voice was shaking when he finally spoke. "Athena? What kind of power could make me open an email?"

Athena glanced over her shoulder and frowned. "That's not something that normally happens. Why?"

Ryan held up the phone to show her the email. "I think we have something we need to do first."

***

Rear Admiral Dale Bridges was getting tired of being one step behind these things. By the time he was able to touch down in Texas, the Antichrist and Athena were long gone.

They'd left a trail of bodies behind.

"Reverend Howard," Bridges said to the only witness he considered worth his personal attention, "please, walk me through what happened."

Bridges listened attentively, glad to have a witness who wouldn't bother with science fiction mumbo-jumbo, who would stick to what had actually happened: demons slaughtering innocent people.

Except that wasn't the Reverend's story. Bridges listened as the Reverend recounted how the undead had come from nowhere, how they had swarmed the town. How the Antichrist and Athena had fought to defend the town.

Despite the sweltering Texas heat, Bridges felt cold. *They've managed to deceive a man of God.*

"Did you consider it could be a false flag operation?" he asked the Reverend. "This sounds like it could be a deliberate attempt to gain people's trust."

"Can't say that I considered that," the Reverend replied, scratching his chin. "And if it was, it was a stupid one, to be honest. They both were in danger. We almost shot Athena's head off in the aftermath. Ryan was unconscious on the ground."

"And you really think bullets would have worked against them?" Bridges demanded. Progress on the new rounds was going slowly, and Bridges was itching to have weapons to use against these things.

"Don't know, and quite frankly, I'm glad we didn't find out." The Reverend studied Bridges for a moment. "They're good people, Rear Admiral."

Bridges had no desire to berate a man of God, no matter how wrong he was. "I hope you're right about that," he said. "Thanks for your time."

You won't be right, of course, Bridges thought as Reverend Howard walked away. *You've been deceived by the Antichrist. It's not a judgement on you, Reverend. They don't call the devil the Father of Lies for nothing. But I won't be taken in. I will stop you, Ryan Smith, and those that follow you.*

Then I can deal with these other "gods".

Chapter 17

"Mailbox!" Athena called, just in time for Ryan to avoid a collision.

"Thanks," he said, swerving around the obstacle and then looking back to his phone.

"Lamppost!" she called a minute later.

"Thanks," Ryan said again, with another course correction.

"Extreme rudeness!"

"Huh?" Ryan stopped dead on the sidewalk, looking at Athena in bewilderment.

"Actually, you've already run into that one. I find this modern habit of blissfully ignoring the world around you extremely irritating."

Ryan signed. "Athena. Correct me if I'm wrong, but didn't you say that you had no idea what the Church of Adversity really is?"

"Yes."

"And didn't you say that we should try to find out as much as we could before this meeting?"

"Yes."

"And didn't you also say that we should have the meeting as soon as possible?"

"What is your point?"

"My point is that if we're going to do all of that at once, then you're going to have to deal with me being a little bit rude."

Athena frowned. "Well, then, how much longer will you need to find the answers we want?"

Ryan took a moment to savor his small victory, and then admitted, "I think I've pretty much got it."

"Well, then?"

Ryan's grin grew to a broad smile. The walking and researching had done wonders to disperse the fear he'd felt from the freaky email. Plus, the chance to be the one who knew something for once was immensely gratifying.

"They're kind of like New Wave Satanists," he said.

Athena gave him a patient look.

"Right. So a couple years ago, the Church of Adversity popped up, with their Heresiarch Amy Preston. She claimed that Lucifer had abdicated his throne to some mortal named Arthur. That Hell was under new management. Their whole thesis is that you should enjoy life, and you'll get to go to Hell."

Athena furrowed her eyebrows. "And people think that's a good thing?"

Ryan shrugged. "Like I said, Hell's under new management. Apparently, he's retooled the entire place to basically be an amusement park mixed with a club mixed with...well, pretty much everything that can be fun. If you wind up in Hell, the only way you're getting eternal torment is if you actually did awful things. According to the Heresiarch, a bunch of people were going there that didn't deserve it. People who'd committed minor sins that still barred them from the pearly gates. Premarital sex, minor thefts, things like that which shouldn't get you eternal torment. So now it gets you an awesome party, and the real sins – murder, rape, genocide, the actual awful stuff – are given the real eternal torment."

"And who is this Arthur?" Athena seemed genuinely curious.

"Some random guy who worked at a restaurant, got hit by a car. Apparently, he got to be King of Hell because he was next in line. Nothing special about him, he just picked up the winning lotto ticket." Ryan frowned for a moment. "I can kinda relate to that, I guess."

Athena motioned for him to continue.

"Well, I'm not the Eschaton because there's anything special about me, right? I'm just the poor asshole that found the last nanoverse. Only instead of getting to be King of Hell, I get to be...the guy who ends the world."

"Ah. I see." Athena's interest had waned.

"It's an interesting countermovement that's gaining popularity. Nega Christians. Instead of being saved by grace – which they claim can actually get you perks, like wealth or health or something like that, you sell your soul. Go to Hell instead of Heaven. Of course, I don't believe in any of it."

Athena's interest returned. "Any of what?"

"Heaven, Hell, angels, demons, all that."

"Oh." Athena frowned. "Well, you should. They're very real."

Ryan stopped dead in his tracks. "I'm sorry, come again?"

"Heaven and Hell are real, Ryan. Most afterlives are." Athena furrowed her eyebrows. "Wait. So you've accepted that you're a god now, and you know you read that email because some force outside your control made you read it, but you're struggling with the afterlife?"

"I mean...that means humans have a soul, right?"

"Of course they do. Why do you think some gods can draw power from human sacrifice? A soul is an incredible source of divine power. That's part of how your nanoverse grants you power, Ryan – it's full of souls."

Ryan felt himself turn pale. "Wait, so I'm...what, destroying souls when I use my nanoverse?"

"Why do you go to the worst possible scenario? No, Ryan, you don't harm them. You just take a tiny bit of power, but it has billions. And souls have to go somewhere. In our universe, they get powered by their own beliefs. If you believe in Heaven or Hell, that's where you go. Hades? That's where you go. If you believe in reincarnation? You'll do it. That's why Underworld gods work differently than the rest of us."

"They do what?" Ryan was already missing being the one who had the answers. *Just for one hour. I couldn't have kept the damn feeling for one hour.*

Athena had her best 'I'm being very patient with how little you know' voice on. "Underworld gods don't have nanoverses. They have afterlives. They draw power from the souls of the dead within. Instead of squeezing their nanoverse for power, they sit on their thrones."

Ryan had so many questions, but tried to limit himself. "So...what, is Satan real? Is he going to be coming for Amy? *For us?*"

Athena shook her head. "No." Ryan breathed a sigh of relief that was cut short with Athena's next sentence. "Oh, no, he's very real, but I doubt he'll be our problem. Angels, even Fallen ones, operate under more rules than we do. Less free will. And he's busy - there's a civil war in hell right now. I'm assuming this Arthur is behind it. I just didn't know the details." Athena resumed walking, leaving Ryan to catch up once he'd picked his jaw back up off the floor.

"So, this whole thing...we're actually dealing with someone with real power here?"

"Oh, absolutely. As if the email trick wasn't giving it away." Athena said, her voice growing a shade grim. "On top of having power drawn from the souls of Hell, Arthur likely has the same gifts Lucifer did. Angels are in a different class than us, Ryan. Fighting them isn't suicide, but they don't get tired, they don't have Hungers, and they manipulate reality like we do. Unlike us, however, it's instinctive for them. No thought required."

Ryan took a deep breath. "Okay, that sounds bad, but-"

"*And,*" Athena continued, "on top of that, fallen angels – which Arthur must have the power of – can make deals with mortals to bring wishes true in exchange for their souls. Within limits. Oh, and he would command all of Hell's demons."

"*Demons?*"

"Demons are too much? That's where you draw the line?"

Ryan sighed. "Kinda, yeah. I mean, everything else so far was fitting together. Gods and nanoverse and-"

"And Curators? Where did they fit in?" Athena tilted her head.

"I...okay, I have no idea."

Athena nodded. "There's much more to the universe than you know, Ryan. Once you think you know how it works, assume you're about to find out how wrong you are."

And, leaving Ryan with that thought to chew on, she walked into the building, Ryan on her heels.

The main office for Amy Preston, Heresiarch of the Church of Adversity, wasn't what Ryan expected. To be fair, it was Ryan's first time going to any entity's church since all this had started. For that matter, he hadn't been inside even a Christian church since he and Isabel had buried their parents. He didn't have much to base his expectations on. Still, if he had tried to imagine the office of the High Priestess of Hell, he would have imagined something grand and decadent, probably filled with attractive and half naked young people engaging in depraved acts.

He did not imagine Suite 113 of a fairly nice and upscale office building, with a neat little sign informing you of the occupant's name and title.

They were greeted by a receptionist, a perky blonde young man with a name tag that read "Cam." Cam stood up to shake their hands. "Athena and Ryan, right? So sorry to have to ask you to wait for a moment, the Heresiarch is on a call with the Governor of Alabama right now. Can I get you anything? Food, drink, anything at all?"

Ryan almost shook his head, but his stomach chose that moment to remind him he still had pending hungers that remain unfulfilled. "Sure," he said, "I'll have whatever you have."

Cam gave him an enigmatic smile. "Oh, I understand. But tell me, what do you *really* want? If you could have anything right now, what would it be?"

Ryan thought for a moment. Why not play along and see where Cam was taking this? "I'd love a Philly cheesesteak."

"One moment." Cam blinked and vanished in a cloud of yellow smoke. Ryan recoiled in shock and at the sudden disappearance, glancing over at Athena. At least her eyes were wide too. "Was he - was that a demon?" Ryan asked.

"Must have been." Athena looked around for a moment, as if expecting Cam to reappear behind her.

Oh crap oh crap did I just sell my soul for a Philly Cheesesteak? "Did he turn invisible?" Ryan asked.

Athena shook her head. "Seeing through invisibility is easy. No, it appears he teleported."

"Teleported? But where did he -"

Before the word "go" could leave Ryan's lips, the smell of sulfur faded, and Cam reappeared. He bowed his head slightly and sprayed some air freshener before offering Ryan the most delicious looking cheesesteak sandwich he had ever seen. "Straight from the kitchens below."

Concerned, Ryan took a moment to look at the sandwich with his divine sight. The equations surrounding it told him it was exactly what it looked like. Cam, on the other hand, was not exactly human. *You just watched him bounce to Hell and back, is that a surprise?* "Did I just sell my soul for a sandwich?" Ryan asked, his heart still pounding.

Cam laughed. "Oh, no. This one is on the house. We can do small things *gratis.*" He paused and shrugged. "Plus, why would we want to buy your soul? You're an immortal, so it would be ages until we could claim it."

Ryan shuddered at the thought, but the smell was too good. Unable to resist, Ryan took the sandwich from Cam's hand, took a bite, and let his taste buds take a trip into the wonders of a Hell-made cheesesteak.

Athena studied Cam a moment longer as Ryan took another bite of the best cheesesteak sandwich on the planet. "Cam. Short for Cambion, I take it?" she asked.

He chuckled, that overly friendly chuckle usually reserved for managers, politicians, and used car salesmen. "They don't call you the goddess of wisdom for nothing, do they? Yes, I'm a Cambion, and since our true names make us very vulnerable, I just go by my type."

"Whaff a Cambion?" Ryan asked, the words distorted by the lump of sandwich.

"We're the result of a human-demon hybridization. Most of us have succubi or incubi for parents - my dad was an incubus, mom was a normal mortal." He smiled widely as Ryan polished off his food. "Amy just let me know she's wrapping up. This way, please?"

He led the two of them back behind the reception area and opened the door to Amy's personal office. She still had a phone to her ear, and held up an apologetic "one moment" finger. Her phone voice was chipper and friendly. "Look, the fact of the matter is you're impugning on our religious freedom. I'd prefer to resolve this without getting the law involved, Governor, but if you don't drop this ban I'm going to take the entire ACLU, turn it sideways, and shove it up your ass so far you'll vomit lawyers." She paused, letting the man on the other end scream for a bit. "I tried being polite, and that didn't work. This is me starting to get impolite. But insult me like that again and I'll take it personally, and you won't like how I resolve personal conflicts. Remove the ban by Monday or legal action is coming." She hung up the phone without waiting for a response. "So, so sorry. Some people seem to think that because our religion is new, we don't get the same protections as others."

She offered a hand to Athena, then Ryan. Same order as Cam. Ryan had to wonder if they were deliberately acknowledging seniority with the handshakes. While shaking Ryan's hand, she continued. "If you decide you want to start building a religion around yourself, we'll be happy to share our experience cutting through the red tape. Please, have a seat."

They both did so, Ryan finding the woman's energy infectious. *You also found her email infectious.* With that thought her good nature took on a more sinister undercurrent, the charisma she exuded suddenly seemed dark and unnerving. She was only about five feet tall with short, curly hair - again, not what Ryan expected from someone running what was basically Hell's Church on Earth. He returned her smile after trying to make sure he was reacting of his own free will. *Be careful, Ryan. There is a demon in the waiting room, and the woman across from you is comfortable with demons and, worse, politicians. Don't underestimate her.* "You'd help a competitor?"

"We'll help anyone who needs help. It won't be free, of course - we don't do anything for free - but I think you'll find our prices are reasonable." She glanced at Athena. "That goes for you too, of course, although you're already more established, so you won't have all the same hurdles."

Athena just nodded. "I do not desire worshippers," she said after a moment. Her tone was cautious. Ryan had figured Athena would be as suspicious of Amy as he should be, and it was good to see he'd been right. *And hey, she's the knowledgeable one, if she's suspicious, there must be something to worry about.* Then again, she'd been suspicious of him all those...had it only been two days ago? Without the need for sleep, or the need to eat or drink or really anything that tied you to your biological clock, *and* constantly hopping between universes, Ryan was rapidly losing any sense of time in the normal sense.

Amy met the dour response without flinching. "Fair enough. Although you might want to talk to Hades at some point - worshippers might start working in all of your favor again in the near future."

Athena's eyes narrowed. "Hades is locked away in the depths of his realm, only able to travel to Purgatory and back, same as most other Underworld deities."

"For now." Amy's eyes sparkled, but she chose not to elaborate. "Of course, you all can use your nanoverses to hop where ever you want to go, even into an afterlife or seven, right?"

Ryan looked to Athena, who nodded.

"Good, because that's what I wanted to talk about. How we can help each other." Amy leaned forward. "My boss isn't happy with the way things work downstairs. He doesn't like that you get tortured for eternity for things like 'promiscuity' and 'lying too much' or other such nonsense. He's changed Hell for the better - it's a party down there, unless you're the kind of sinner who really deserves torment - murderers, rapists, child molesters, the people that no one cares about getting eternal suffering. You both should come visit at some point." She smiled, and unlike Cam, the smile did reach her eyes, causing them to sparkle.

"Perhaps," Athena said. When she glanced at Ryan, he could only shrug. *Visit hell? Visit **hell**? No way. Even if what she's saying is true...it's **hell**.*

Amy nodded like she had expected the noncommittal answer. "Look, guys, I'm not going to bullshit you and say I'm on your side. But you want to stop Enki from doing whatever shady shit he's pulling, and we want to stop Heaven from turning Hell back into a billions-served torture chamber. We like the idea of stopping Enki, and I imagine you two like the idea of not seeing billions tortured for minor infractions?"

Ryan pursed his lips but nodded. "Why do you care about stopping Enki, though? I mean, it's so far been a 'he said, she said' in the media, right?"

"Oh, totally." Amy grinned. "But we know he's lying about one thing, by claiming you're the Antichrist. So if he's caught in one lie, no reason to believe he's doing anything other than trying to feed us a complete line of bullshit. Even if that wasn't enough, Arthur doesn't like people trying to blame stuff on Hell. Bad for image management."

After a moment's thought, both Ryan and Athena's heads moved in agreement. *It makes sense. It's a nice, straightforward, clear cut answer. But the fact that it's coming from someone who works for Hell...*Ryan was still reeling from the idea that Heaven and Hell were real. That some normal dude was in charge of it. That all that happened because Satan needed a holiday and abdicated his throne. He found himself bluescreening again, and Athena had to pick up the conversation.

"So, what, exactly, does Arthur offer us? And what does he want in return?"

"Straight to business, then." Amy leaned forward again, pressing the tips of her fingers together. "For starters, we can help you with your little 'Antichrist' problem. Publicly announce you are in no way affiliated with us, that your actions speak for you and you alone. With a subtle push to get people to take it seriously."

"You mean some kind of mind control?" Ryan didn't realize how sharp the question was until it came out of his mouth, but he couldn't help but remember his overwhelming need to check that email.

"Nothing so crass, just a general feeling that the statement can be trusted. And I'm sorry about that trick with the email but needed to make sure it didn't get lost in the shuffle." Amy tensed slightly at his tone, like a tiger preparing to pounce. Ryan checked himself. *This woman put some kind of spell on your email, Ryan, one that made you read it.*

He suddenly realized exactly how far out of his depth he was, and he'd already been thrown into the deep end at the start of all this. For all Ryan knew Amy could squash him like a bug. *Let's not find out how strong she is, okay? Or, for that matter, her boss.* Ryan went forward in a more level tone, "No harm, no foul. And there's more? You did say for starters."

She nodded. "We know about that little trick Moloch pulled in Texas. We're terminating our relationship with him - that's not part of a deal, that's just because he's a prick."

Ryan blinked. "You had a relationship with Moloch?"

Amy shook her head. "The old management did. He would take out people Lucifer didn't like. In exchange, Lucifer would pass him intel on something Moloch wanted to watch. Sorry that we don't know what. But we're terminating it regardless - he never dealt with us, and he's a prick." Even Athena gave a faint smile at that. "But we want to help even the odds for you next time you go up against him. Arthur's willing to commit a full legion of demons to your cause - completely obedient to the three of you until Enki is defeated once and for all, at which point they'll return to hell immediately."

Ryan let out a low whistle. While he couldn't be sure what exactly a legion of demons was capable of, it certainly sounded impressive - and the look on Athena's face confirmed that.

"A fairly large offer," Athena said, glancing at Ryan. "But what does he want in return?"

"It's actually fairly low cost to you, though I'll admit it involves a fair bit of trust. Like I said earlier, Arthur is trying to make Hell a better place. Heaven? Not a huge fan of that. We have a plan to win, but it involves busting the Underworld deities out of their prisons. Since you all have nanoverses and can jump around like that, he wants you all to break them free."

"He wants us to help him win a war against Heaven?" Athena sounded thoughtful, and Ryan had to scratch his chin. Normally he'd think it would be a terrible thing to do, but...well, they were going to end the world fairly soon, and when your To Do list included beat an evil god, wait for your friend to come back from the dead, and *end the world*, adding something like 'help Hell against Heaven' felt pretty minor at the end of the day. *On the other hand...*Ryan had read Faust in college. He'd seen both version of *Bedazzled.* It was pretty much impossible to grow up in the West and *not* know how bad deals with the devil went. He looked at Athena, whose frown matched his own thoughts.

"I'm a bit worried about cutting a deal with the Devil," Ryan said. "Usually, that ends badly for everyone but your side."

"You're thinking of old management, remember? Arthur doesn't like trapping people in complex legal bullshit." Amy's smile widened. "Oh, sure, we make sure the deal ends up being as much to our benefit as possible. I mean, we're still kinda human. But if we start trapping people like that, we'll end up as despised as the old guy was."

Ryan scratched his chin again. "Then again, that's what you would say if you wanted me to believe you."

Amy sighed, leaning forward on her desk. "Ryan. That line of logic means you can't trust a single thing I say. The facts of the matter are this: you are outmatched. You need backup. We have a plan, but it requires that we have divine aid to accomplish it. We need you. It's the very definition of a mutually beneficial relationship. No tricks, no web of lies, no misdirection. We both want something the other one has. We're dealing in good faith."

Ryan glanced at Athena, whose frown had deepened. "What do you know that we don't, Heresiarch? Why do we need an army?"

Amy smiled. "I was going to save this for later, but no reason to hold back. Because Moloch didn't throw his best army at you in Granger. He's got something nastier in his back pocket. It's not going to be an even fight, god against god. It's going to be god against god backed by monsters."

"What's this army?" Athena asked, her eyes narrow.

"Don't know, sadly." Amy shrugged. "My boss is working on it, but a lot of paperwork got lost." She looked between them. "Athena. Ryan. I'm dealing as honestly as possible here. You need our help. We need yours. This shouldn't be complicated.

It wouldn't be if you weren't in league with Hell, Ryan thought. He glanced at Athena, who gave him a slight nod. *Guess it's time to roll the dice.* "Deal." Ryan sounded every bit as sure as he felt, which wasn't half as sure as he wished he was.

"My favorite word." Amy offered a hand, and they shook on it. She handed him a case. "Here's a rune to summon and banish the legion when you're ready. We'll be releasing press statements within the hour. And when it's time to hold up your end, Arthur will give you a call. Which reminds me - in the case is also a set of soul-powered runeforged phones. They work across dimensions, and Arthur's really pushing getting everyone on these so we supernatural types can stay in touch better."

"I'll try it out," said Ryan. *Once I'm sure it's not just some fancy way for your boss to spy on everyone.*

"Great. Now, and please don't think I'm being rude here, but I do have a call coming about getting on TV to debate some evangelist asshole. If you can, you should check it out - it's going to be legendary."

They said their goodbyes and headed out of the office.

"I think that went well," Ryan commented to Athena, who still looked thoughtful.

"We shall see. I think, at least, we did not get the raw end of the deal. Now, then - we really must see to our Hungers, yes?"

Ryan couldn't argue that point, not with how he'd devoured the sandwich like he hadn't eaten in weeks. Also, he noted the "our" this time - *I must not have been passed out as long as I thought, otherwise she would have taken care of the Hungers already.* "Any good ideas for how to take care of the Social need quickly?" At the look Athena gave him, he winced. "I didn't mean-"

"I know." Her eyes slightly sparkled with mischief, and Ryan noticed that now that they were alone, her voice was getting some inflection back. "We're going to go dancing instead. We'll need to change first to blend in, follow me."

He fell in behind her, wondering why they weren't headed back to her nanoverse to change and where, exactly, she was going.

Chapter 18

How the Divine Unwind

Athena was, much to his surprise, taking Ryan shopping. The store was the sort of up-scale location that Ryan had seen in TV shows and movies but never been in before - he thought that, technically speaking, it was a boutique, but he couldn't be sure.

Athena approached shopping with the same ruthless efficiency she used in battle, and Ryan - and the poor woman helping them - found themselves drawn along with her like leaves floating on whitewater rapids. He was poked and prodded and measured, and by the time it was over, Ryan wasn't sure what he had bought, what Athena had bought, or how they'd paid for it. The clerk, for her part, was sure of those things, and was trying to figure how to cash the Roman denarii the strange woman had given her as a tip. She'd faint a couple days later when she found out they appraised at almost 10,000 dollars.

After shopping they had gone back towards the nanoverse. While they were walking, Ryan turned to Athena. "Why didn't we just pull clothes out of our nanoverses, anyway? Was there a point to buying them?"

Athena made a face. "It would be tacky, especially where we're going."

"And where are we going, exactly?"

This smile actually reached Athena's eyes. "To dance." She'd not been willing to offer any further explanation.

Back in Athena's nanoverse, they changed as the nanoverse traveled to their mysterious destination. "It might be little while to travel," Athena had said from behind the curtain. "We're going a bit of a long way."

"That's fine," Ryan responded, working on the clothes. "I'm still figuring out what I'm putting on myself."

An exaggeration, but only by half. It was a suit and vest and button-down shirt and tie thing. Prior to this Ryan had the same relationship with suits that cats had with a vacuum cleaner - they were fine when they were in the closet not bothering anyone, but the moment they got anywhere near him it was time to panic.

He put the whole ensemble on like it might bite him at any moment, but once he was dressed (after using a bit of twisting of the equations that govern how things tangle to make the tie knot itself perfectly) and looking in a mirror, he had to admit it was a good look. Part of it wasn't the clothes, but that thing Crystal had mentioned, where he was becoming an idealized version of himself. He'd lost fat and gained muscle, and the outfit did a good job of accentuating that. Beyond that, though, there was something just classy about the suit-and-vest look. *Heh. Me, classy.* He barely recognized himself. Not that he had been ugly before, but just...ordinary.

Then Athena came out from behind her curtain, and he was distracted by the shock how she looked. She looked like...well, she looked nothing like the Athena he'd seen before. She'd traded her usual, functional clothing for a classic "little black dress," one that flared out a bit after her waist as opposed to hugging her hips and legs. *Even dressed up, she's thought of mobility,* the analytical part of his brain commented. Her hair, instead of the usual ponytail, was down and loose.

Overall, the effect made her look like a completely different person. Then she scowled at his silence. *Ah, there's the Athena I know.* He realized he should say something and went with the tried and true "You look amazing."

She gave one of those ghostly smiles in response. "You look presentable." She winked to take the sting out of the comment. "Shall we?"

Ryan offered his arm, and she took it. They stepped out the doorway and once again, Ryan found himself needing to collect his jaw.

It was a "club" in the same way a tiger was a cat. Both were technically correct but one was a gross understatement. The first thing he noticed was the ceiling - they were directly under Crab Nebula, close enough where it looked like something out of a photo. Multifaceted lenses dotted the roof to capture and reflect the light from the nebula into rainbow rays that spotted the dance floor. Those rays drew Ryan's eyes away from the splendor above him and to the splendor below. Three sides of the outer edge were lined with a bar, its surface silver and gold with dozens of bartenders flitting about behind it. The stools at the bar were mostly unoccupied.

When his eyes moved to the dancers, they needed a moment to process, giving his ears a chance to take over. The music wasn't exactly like anything Ryan had heard before, a mixture of deep club rhythms with a delicate, ethereal melody running above it. His eyes began registering what they were seeing as soon as his ears had picked up the beat, as if having the rhythm added in understanding. The floor was full of dancing beings. There was a man with the wings of a dragonfly, dancing with a woman with pale skin and fangs. Near them a man with the legs of a goat was locked in an intense gaze with a man covered in a serpent's scales. Another woman floated to the ceiling in a graceful leap, all four of her arms spread out in a ballerina's pose and was caught by a man with three faces. All across the floor, a writhing mass of beautiful beings moved in tune with the music.

Athena glanced over and took a moment to enjoy his stupefied gaze. "Welcome to Empyrean Provocation. Where those with powers beyond mere mortals come to let their hair down."

"Wow."

"Indeed. So, Ryan Smith, dance or drinks first?"

"Drinks," he said, without a moment's thought. "Definitely drink."

"Well, you have my arm. Lead on."

"Athena? Oh my goodness, I didn't think you'd be showing your face here anytime soon!"

Ryan didn't immediately look over to the speaker, instead glancing at Athena. Her lips were a tight white line, and her hands twitched for an instant. She turned to face the speaker, and Ryan turned with her. The speaker was a Japanese woman, who was regarding Athena with a grin full of mischief.

Athena spoke. "Uzeme. I guess I shouldn't be surprised to find you here. Do you ever leave?"

"Of course I do. There's plenty to do on Earth still. Not that you'd know that – I didn't think you understood the concept of 'fun.' And this? Did you bring a mortal?" Before Athena could answer, Uzeme peered a bit harder at Ryan. "Oh, no, my mistake. It's the newest god. The one there's so much fuss about."

Athena motioned to Uzeme. "Ryan, Ame-no-Uzeme. She goes by Uzeme. Uzeme, Ryan Smith."

Every other time Ryan had met a fellow god had been with a purpose or panic. He suddenly realized he had no idea how to interact with deities beyond those two instances. *When in doubt, be polite.* He offered a slight, awkward bow towards Uzeme. "Charmed."

Uzeme held up her hand to her mouth, a gesture that did nothing to actually contain her mirth. "I appreciate the attempt," she said, and offered her hand. Ryan shook it, wondering how badly he had just embarrassed himself. "At least you attempt manners. Why don't you join us?" Uzeme glanced at Athena. "You too."

Ryan looked at Athena, who gave him a slight shrug. "Sure," Ryan said. *If nothing else, it'll be nice to see what gods do when things aren't desperate. We're here to socialize, after all.*

Uzeme lead them back to a table where a few more beings, that at least looked human, were sitting. "Everyone, I found the 'Eschaton'." Ryan could practically hear the air quotes around the word. "Everyone, meet Ryan. Ryan, meet Svarog, Brigid, and Brahma." She pointed to each of the gods in turn.

Svarog was a huge man, bearded and built like a truck, with an easygoing smile. Brigid was pale with bright red hair, and her smile was much more reserved than Svarog's. Meanwhile, Brahma – an Indian man – stood up to shake Ryan's hand. "It's good to finally meet you," he said, making eye contact, "after everything we've been hearing."

"Thanks," Ryan said as Uzeme brushed past him to her seat.

"Oh," Uzeme added, "I also found Athena."

Athena rolled her eyes.

"Thanks," Ryan said as Braham offered him a chair. "It's nice to meet you all."

"Believe me, Ryan," said Svarog, "It is much nicer to be meeting you. First new blood we've had in…when was the last one?"

"The 1800's, I think," Brigid said after a pause for thought. "I was beginning to think there were no more nanoverses to find."

"Well, good thing there was," Ryan said, trying to force himself to be at ease. On the other hand…he'd heard of some of these people. Brahma was a big deal in Hinduism, Ryan was sure of that. Uzeme was a major deal, or at least well-known deal, in Shintoism. *Then again, Athena is a big deal in Greek mythology. You'd heard of Bast before, too.*

Somehow, this was more nerve wracking when they weren't trying to kill him.

"For your sake, absolutely," Brigid said, and furrowed her eyebrows. "Or did you mean something different?"

"I mean, otherwise the world would have already ended, right?" After the words were out of Ryan's mouth, he saw Athena wince.

The four new gods shared a look. The silence was broken by Svarog bursting into laughter. "Ahh, come now friends! We should not judge him too harshly. He is still Nascent, and Ishtar has been filling his head with nonsense since he found his nanoverse."

"She goes by-" Ryan started to say, but he was interrupted by Uzeme.

"Of course, that doesn't excuse everyone who falls for her nonsense. Does it, Pallas Athena?"

Athena sighed. "Uzeme. It's real, I'm sure of it. Enki sa-"

Here Brahma was one to interrupt, although he held up a hand as opposed to just talking over Athena. "Begging your pardon, Athena, but we are talking about Enki here, yes? I hate to resort to an ad hominin so early in the conversation, but Enki is stark raving mad, is he not?"

"Oh, he absolutely is," Athena said, and Ryan noticed how tight her knuckles were getting on the table. "But he-"

Uzeme interrupted again, turning to Ryan. "Ryan, darling, you're Nascent so you can't be expected to know these things. But you've fallen in with a bad crowd. Ishtar has managed to piss off pretty much every god and goddess she's met by being a self-important bitch. Enki is a madman. Moloch is just...I mean, you've met Moloch." She shrugged as if that explained everything, although Ryan didn't think it did. "Bast has been obsessed with finding a legendary artifact she claims Ra possessed, but Ra has been dead for a millennium and a half and none of the rest of her pantheon has been able to find it. And Athena, well, she was cast out of-"

Athena returned Uzeme's habit of interruption. "Uzeme." The single word cracked in the air like a whip. "If you finish that sentence, I will break the peace of this place and make sure you have to regenerate from only a head."

"Now, now, no need for that," Svarog said. "No one is actually going to violate the sanctity here."

"As I was saying-" Uzeme began, but Brigid stepped in.

"Uzeme, please. Can we at least let her finish a sentence?"

"Why? It's absolute madness!"

"Because," Brahma said, "some of us remember what manners are. And I very much would like to hear how Enki convinced Athena, who was once known as 'the Wise,' of such madness."

At the reminder of her old title, Athena's face went from sour to bitter. Ryan didn't think Brahma had meant it as an insult, but Athena had clearly taken it as one. "I believed Enki that Ishtar was trying to use Ryan to end the world. The first nanoverse found in centuries, doesn't that seem significant? Perhaps it did hold some special power."

Svarog laughed. "Every nanoverse is the same, Athena. Tiny in your pocket, big when you walk in, and full of stars and people. There's no 'special power'."

"I'm not certain," Athena said. "The Titans existed. Beings that weren't quite mortal, weren't quite monster, weren't quite gods. There are archangels who have no need for a nanoverse. The underworld gods. All this strangeness, and we cannot accept that there may be an Eschaton?"

"I'd like better evidence than the word of Ishtar and Enki, Athena," Brigid said. "We've all had end-time myths we've told our people, to teach them or warn them of one thing or another. That doesn't mean the world is actually going to end."

"What about Prophecy?" Ryan said, looking around. "I mean, I know I can't do it yet, I'm Nascent, but I have a button for it in my staging area."

For some reason, that got a chortle out of everyone, and even got Athena to smirk. Ryan frowned. "No, seriously, why not?"

"You'll understand when you try it," Brahma said with a smile, and Ryan got the impression he was trying his hardest not to be condescending. "But in short, prophecy will fill your head with vague images that are highly symbolic. You almost never know what they mean until after it's passed, and sometimes you never do. It was a good trick back in the day, when – if you were wrong – it wouldn't spread far or fast. Now though? It's pretty much useless."

Ryan sighed. "Damn. I was actually looking forward to being able to see the future."

"We all do, dear." Brigid says, shooting a sidelong glance at Athena. "You didn't warn him it didn't work like that?"

Athena gave a small shrug. "I didn't know it was important to him. Otherwise I would have."

"So, then, we are back where we started," said Svarog, leaning over towards Athena. "How did that American astronomer put it? 'Extraordinary claims require extraordinary proof?' Right now we have no proof, Athena."

"Enki was desperate to stop Ishtar, so much so that he betrayed us to do it." Athena's frown showed that she found that argument as weak as it sounded.

"And again, Athena, Enki is *crazy*," Uzeme said with a dismissive flip of her hand. "If he was desperate to seize the world's cheese supply, would you assume that meant there was some cosmological significance to it?"

"Ishtar's argument hinges on Ryan being able to end the world. If he can't, if she's lying, then what does it matter?'

Here Brigid's cool demeanor cracked. "You were on the damn news, Athena! The entire world saw you, all of you. We've enjoyed centuries of laying low, and now we're out in the open."

"Uh," Ryan raised a finger to get attention, "Why does it matter if you're known or not? You can all shapechange, right? Who cares if people know the gods are real?"

Brahma shook his head. "Faith is important, Ryan Smith. That's why we've remained hidden for so long. When we take too active a role in things, humans rely more and more on us to do things for them. By staying in the shadows, and helping where we can, humans can only have faith in us. Not knowledge, faith. Faith is strength. It breeds a desire to improve, to develop, to grow. To live. Knowledge of the divine? Weakness, apathy. Why struggle for answers when you can ask a god?"

"Yeah, but it's different now." Ryan said, looking around the table. "I mean, people aren't just going to blindly follow you."

"Won't they?" Brahma asked. "My faith has over a billion followers across the globe. Billion. I help them where I can, but if I reveal myself to them? Some won't believe, others will. They will fight each other."

"That is the other reason, Ryan," Svarog said. "Too many wars fought over whose gods were strongest, whose gods were real, and whose gods were best. Even with us retreating it still happened, but it became less. At least with us out of the fight, divine powers are not being thrown around."

Ryan shook his head. "But you all could do so much good and could have done so much good! I mean, the Holocaust? You could have stopped it."

The gods shared an uncomfortable silence. "We are not omnipotent, Ryan," Brigid said finally. "Tell me, since becoming a god, how much more aware are you of the tragedies that still plague the world?"

"I..." Ryan frowned and sighed. "I guess not any more aware than I was before."

Uzeme spoke up, and, for the first time since Ryan had met her, seemed to be sincere. "We were fighting, Ryan, during that war. Fighting each other. I had quite the battle with Dianmu in China, believe me. But our focus was too narrow, and we missed the bigger horror until it was too late. And that is the third reason why we hide. We are fallible. We make mistakes. We back the wrong side, we miss things we shouldn't. And with our power, we could dictate the fate of the world. So we let humanity guide itself." She shot Athena a sidelong glance. "Otherwise, we could end up supporting a madman."

Athena shook her head. "This is different. If Ishtar is right..."

"If," Brahma said firmly. "If she is, then we need proof. And then we can decide what we should do about it."

"Týr is dead," Athena said softly. "Bast killed him. If nothing else, that demands justice."

Uzeme shrugged. "Did you see her do it? Did you witness the destruction of his nanoverse?"

"Of course not," Athena snapped.

"Then why should we believe that Bast would go that far? Isn't it more likely that she is merely storing it somewhere, so he resurrects in a cell and remain there until this fight is over?"

"Hey, question for the table," Ryan asked before Athena could boil over, although his own tone was about as sarcastic as he ever got. "Out of curiosity, if Athena told you all it was raining outside, would you believe her, or would you need to check?"

The other gods all stared at him, Athena looking most shocked of all.

"I can get not believing me," Ryan continued. "I'm the dumb new guy who believes Ishtar, who apparently you all have beef with. But fine, whatever, I'm the moron who believes her. But Athena? You yourself said she was called the Wise. Enki is crazy, sure. But Athena? Does she seem crazy to you?"

"You don't know what you're talking about, boy," Svarog said in a low tone, all sense of humor gone, but Ryan wasn't done.

"You're right, I don't. I don't know shit from sandwiches right now. But she," he gestured to Athena, "she does know exactly what she's talking about. Whatever happened to the benefit of the doubt? Or are you all just so wrapped up in your own little pledge of inaction that you will take any reason to avoid doing anything?"

Brahma held up a hand for silence. Somehow, the man's calm insistence with just a gesture was more effective than Svarog's warning tone. "We will act in this, Ryan. If there is proof that you do have the ability to end the world, I assure you, we will act." Ryan didn't like the warning note in his tone. "But without proof, we will not start a theomachy in the modern world. Thousands or millions could die. For all we know, starting such a war is exactly how Ishtar intends to end the world. So for now, we will watch. We will wait. But…" He caught Ryan's gaze, and underneath the calm look Ryan could see a fire burning. "I assure you, if needs be, we will act."

Ryan glanced at Athena, who gave him a small shrug. "I guess we're done here, Ryan," she said, standing up.

They started to walk away, but then Athena turned to face the group. "Oh, and one more thing?" She gestured to Ryan. "I've only really known him a couple days. I don't particularly like him, if I'm being honest."

"Thanks," Ryan muttered.

"But right now, I'll take him over all of the old way. He may be naive, new, easily manipulated, and kind of dense, but he's trying to do *something*. We've let far too many horrors happen because of our insistence that our reasons to hide are good enough."

"You don't get to decide that for all of us, Athena," Uzeme snapped.

"Well, apparently, I did." Athena turned around. "Come on Ryan."

Ryan followed her away from the gaggle of gods and over to the bar. "I don't know if I should thank you or be asking for an apology," Ryan said.

"Well, I'm a goddess. It's my prerogative to be mysterious." She gave him a small smile. "Besides, I did that for your sake. It's always better to be underestimated. Don't worry, Ryan. I only meant half of what I said about you there."

Ryan blinked. "Which half?"

But Athena was waving to the bartender, and Ryan maneuvered around the edge of the dance floor to get to the bar. The bartender was a woman with dark grey skin, six antennae emerging over each eyebrow and wide, dark eyes that glittered like obsidian. Her eyes widened and she exclaimed, "Athena! I haven't seen you since...was it the sixteenth century?"

Athena nodded. "It has been awhile, Candia. This is Ryan Smith, the newest god on Earth."

"Oooh, Ryan Smith. Very...interesting name you have there."

He grinned. "My name's boring as sin, which among gods I think makes it unique."

That at least got a good laugh out of the woman. As Candia calmed herself Athena added, "Candia is one of the Fae."

Candia nodded. "Not many of us left anymore, and most of our kingdom's been sunk till all we were left with was a wee island. Ended up needing to retreat to the Otherworld. Things got a bit too hot on Earth with you all stomping around."

Ryan was still reeling from meeting four different gods, so a Fae barely registered. "Yeah, I guess that...that make sense."

Athena ordered in Greek. Staring at the wall of alcohol, Ryan felt a bit overwhelmed. "Uh...what do you have on draft?"

Candia giggled. "Everything, take your pick."

"Uh...I'll have your best pale ale?"

The woman flitted away, back in a moment with the golden drink. He took a sip and had to admit it was the best he'd ever had. "So, about what happ-"

Athena cut him off. "Let's talk about literally anything else, alright?" She finished her drink, and ordered another as Ryan sipped his beer. "Besides, you should know that these drinks contain Ambrosia. It's one of the very few things in existence that can still get us drunk. No hangover, though, and it's not a toxin."

Ryan stared at his drink for half a moment before he downed it in a series of massive gulps. In what Ryan thought must be some kind of universal law across all bars in all reality, someone began to chant the ritualistic "Chug, chug, chug!" As soon as Ryan finished the beer, the Chug-chanter shifted to a shout of "wooooo!", as tradition mandates, then wandered back to their own group.

Ryan smiled at Athena. "So no matter what, I won't get sick, or die?"

"Precisely. And I like that you asked that after inhaling a drink with an unknown alcohol content."

"Well," he paused, thinking it through. "I'll be honest, Athena, this is the first time I've done something straight up fun since I became a god. Crystal and I were dealing with life-or-death the entire time, and even the fun things we did were about training - like the mud fight on Mars - or about..." *But that was about filling Hunger and nothing else. Have I really not had a real break?* Technically this was about filling Hunger too, but it felt...different. He coughed, thinking he should have asked how strong that ale was.

"You seem very fond of her."

Athena's voice startled Ryan out of his reflection, "I mean, yeah. But not like...you know?"

She nodded. "I do. So finish that drink," Ryan wasn't sure when the second ale had arrived, but he took it with a smile, "and let's dance."

"Okay. But I should warn you, I don't know how to dance."

Athena's lips turned up slightly. "You also didn't know how to wield a sword, yes? I think you'll find you can do just fine."

He downed the drink, just slowly enough this time to avoid summoning the chug-chanter. "Well...let's see how I do."

Athena pulled him on to the dance floor, and like with his swordplay, he didn't let himself think too much. Instead, he just let the beat of the music become the pulse of battle and let himself flow with it. That seemed to be what Athena was doing, and her movements still had that power to them, that raw primal energy she unleashed on the battlefield, but now they were tempered by a grace that he found absolutely enchanting.

Ryan was only half aware of what his own body was doing with the music. It felt every bit as arrhythmic and awkward as it always did. It probably was. At least Athena didn't seem to mind. He could hear Crystal's advice. *Roll with it, love.*

So he did, letting the music flow through him and Athena. He danced like the end of the world wasn't looming over his head, he danced like there wasn't a small cabal of gods out for his head, and he danced like he knew what he was doing.

Which, of course, he didn't, but for once that didn't seem to matter.

Chapter 19

Hijinks Ensue

Crystal gasped for air as life returned. Huge gulps, like emerging from deep under water. Her lungs burned with the need, and with each gasp the burning sensation began to fade. *Can't move.* She tried, but her limbs weren't responding. Only her mouth and lungs, sucking in as much air as they could hold. Despite Crystal's age, the primal fear of suffocation had not faded. Again, and again, and yet again she took frantic breaths that made her head pound and spin.

She flopped to the floor as her muscles started to respond in a series of spasmodic, uncoordinated jerks. A fresh wave of panic set in that she would suffocate now that her face was on the floor. A few more gasps reassured her that wasn't going to happen.

Panic began to fade. She had more pressing concerns. Her mouth was dry, drier than the Sahara at noon, drier than the dust of Mars. Her stomach wasn't growling, it was roaring, a hunger so tight and painful she started to curl into a ball to clutch at her gut in agony. *No. Fill it.* The small part of her rational brain that still functioned demanded she uncurl, that she seek food and water before madness consumed her.

It took an effort to get her limbs to respond with anything other than twitches. She finally made it to her hands and knees, gasping at the effort. A low groan escaped her lips. *Food. Water. Need.* Crawling wasn't a conscious decision. It was just the best she could manage at the moment. Inch by inch, she dragged herself over to where the refrigerator was hidden in the floor.

Her staging area sensed her desire and the refrigerator rose from the ground. She nearly tore it off its hinges. Inside was a jug of ice cold water and a cold cut sandwich labeled in all caps "ONLY EMERGENCIES." It contained as much meat and cheese as she could fit between two slices of bread and still reasonably call it sandwich.

Crystal gulped the water straight from the jug, wanting to sigh in relief as it passed her throat. She only didn't because that would mean she had to stop drinking, something she didn't do until the jug was empty. She ate the sandwich with a similar frenzy, in a manner not unlike a piranha attacking a cow. She tore huge chunks out of the poor food, barely masticating her prey before she moved onto the next bite. Neither drink or food was enough to do more than take the Hunger from brutal need to strong craving, but at least that was an improvement.

Then she wrapped her arms around herself and started to weep. It wasn't sadness, but a loneliness so intense it burned like grief. A desperate need for human contact welled up within her. Something, anything. A touch, a word, a caress, even a strike would be welcome right now. Anything to make her feel something other than all alone in the universe.

"M-music," she managed to choke out. Her nanoverse responded, and Beethoven's Moonlight Sonata began to float through the empty staging area.

By the time the song had finished, she'd gotten her tears under control, and managed to stop hugging herself. Her first real, rational thought came to her.

Dying is the worst.

She forced her brain onto a more useful topic. *Why the bloody hell am I even coming back to life?* In a normal conflict between gods, it was considered over when one side died, and no effort was made to destroy or corrupt the nanoverse. Enki was playing by his own rules, though, and

Ryan. Oh bloody hell, what happened to Ryan?

She forced herself to stumble over to a chair and sat down to think.

She was back in her nanoverse, which meant Ryan had survived Bast somehow. No other god would have been able to find her door and take her back here. *Means there's a chance he's still alive, yeah?* Which was good because that meant there was some hope of saving the damn world from being incinerated by a solar supernova. *But he's not here, so he could have died while you were dead. Which means everything is bloody ruined.*

It would also be sad if Ryan was dead too, but that was an incidental concern compared to the entire world.

She contemplated that for a moment. If he was dead...maybe there was a chance another Eschaton could be found and made ready in time. Maybe. And maybe she could reprise her role of Eschaton - Crystal Ends the World Part Deux: Revenge of the Eschaton - but that also had no guarantee of working. *It won't happen, Crystal, you know that. Last nanoverse of the era. It has to be Ryan.* She couldn't think about that. It was too much. *Ryan has to be alive. He bloody has to.*

Reassuring herself that the universe wouldn't shag her that badly without at least buying dinner and - *oh damnit, do not think about shagging right now when all you've had is music to deal with that stupid Hunger* - she poked her head out of her door to see where Ryan had left her.

Her head pulled back like she had stuck it on a hot stove, and she slammed the door. *Athena. Oh you bloody bitch. Okay, Crystal, think - hard.*

She hadn't let on, but it had hurt when Athena sided with Enki against her. Things had gone badly between them at the end, to the tune of a hundred years of warfare and the death of an entire empire, but they had been close thousands of years ago. Which also meant Athena knew how Crystal thought. Maybe Ryan was dead, and Athena had saved her out of some old sentimentality. Maybe he was her prisoner, and Athena had just locked Crystal's doorway in place, so she'd have to go through the Greek goddess to get out - until Crystal could walk out the front door, she couldn't open a doorway anywhere in the core universe. *Maybe she's holding him in her actual nanoverse, where she's all-powerful. It wouldn't be the first bloody time someone pulled that trick.*

Baseless speculation was leading to panic, and Crystal had to get it under control. If Ryan was alive,

Athena would know where he was. Crystal could take the risk of trying to walk out of Athena's nanoverse. *No.* Better to wait for Athena to come back and take her out then when she was alone. Get information on Ryan's fate. If he was alive, rescue him. If he was dead...*bloody hell, Ryan, you better not be dead.*

Crystal grabbed everything she could to fill her Hungers. Bottles of water and granola bars and a few books. Those gathered, she went back through the door, into Athena's nanoverse staging area, and took up a position behind one of the pillars Athena was so fond of. She pulled down the sword hanging over her head and settled in to wait, keeping her ears open as she tried to fill as many Hungers as she could before Athena returned.

Don't fret, love. I'm going to save you, soon as I get Athena to tell me where you are.

***

The dancing went on for hours, broken up by more drinking, and at the end both of them were flush from exertion and alcohol. They started stumbling back towards Athena's door, doing that unique drunken lean where both parties tried their level best to pretend they were supporting the other one and not at all relying on support themselves.

Ryan realized something odd. His need for Company was full - the dancing had been a great way to take care of that - but he had felt full a good three hours ago, and still hadn't wanted to stop. *There's an emotional...thingy. Like a...like an extra part. A gear. No. A component.*

"Wha?" Athena asked, and Ryan had to wonder how much he had said out loud.

"I was just thinking. With...my brain." He poked a finger to his temple to make sure Athena got the point. She giggled, and Ryan's mouth fell open. Athena, actually giggling! This was surely a sign the world was coming to an end! Ryan's face fixed itself into a half-witted grin.

"And what were you, were you thinking?" She smiled at him, and that smile obliterated any hope of rational thought.

"I was thinking...words. Yes. I forgot." They both stared at each other a moment, then burst out laughing outside Athena's door.

"Well, in that case...I don't know where I was going with that." Athena fumbled at the knob. The first couple tries, her hand slipped off. After that, she got it to turn, first one way, then the other. Then, and only then, did she remember she needed to push as well. One more try to both push and turn, and the door swung open. "Let's...let's go in. Oh hell, I'm drunk."

Ryan stumbled before going in, which was unfortunate, because it meant Crystal knew that Athena wasn't alone. She didn't know it was him, however - just that Athena was inebriated and therefore vulnerable.

Athena shouted in surprise when she found herself pressed to the ground, someone on top of her, a sword - Ryan's liquid silver sword - pressed to her throat. "Don't say a damn word. Just tell me - where is Ryan?"

The Greek goddess took a moment to try and focus on her attacker. "How...how can I tell you if I'm not 'posed to say anything?"

"Bloody hell, you're pissed off your gourd. Are we in Empyrean Provocation?"

"Mmmhmmm. Ishtar? Is that you?"

Crystal sighed, lessening the pressure on Athena's throat. Intimidation wouldn't work, and Athena wasn't a threat to anyone right now. "Athena, love. Is Ryan alive?"

Athena's face contorted with the effort not to laugh. "I'm sorry, I'm sorry, it's not...you're worried. Yes." Athena's laughter became real. "Ryan, come in and convince Ish...Crystal-tar I'm not the bad guy anymore?"

Ryan stumbled in, his eyes focusing on Crystal on Athena, his sword in Crystal's hand and pressed to Athena's throat. "Oh nooooo! Crystal, don't hurt heeer!" He ran for them, but tripped over his own feet.

When he rolled over, Crystal was standing, her hands on her hips, her face somewhere between horror and trying not to die from choking to death on her own laughter. "Okay. I'll be honest, I didn't anticipate this being what I came back to, yeah? So...will someone tell me what the bloody hell is going on?"

Before they did, Athena and Ryan had to get over another round of laughter at her indignation.

***

"Okay, I think I got it." Getting Athena and Ryan to drunkenly spill the story had taken long enough that they were starting to sober up, and Ryan noted that Crystal was rubbing her temples. *Frustrated with us? Or side effect of coming back from the dead?* "One thing I still don't get, yeah? How did Moloch know you were going to be in Granger?"

"Maybe you should-"

"Ryan, love, if you say I should roll with it one more time I'm going to beat you with your own bloody shoe." She grinned, to take the sting out of the retort. "But seriously, loves, you only went there because you happened to see it. No way he could have predicted that."

Ryan shrugged, but Athena furrowed her brow. Watching her try to concentrate while still intoxicated had not stopped being funny yet, and Ryan covered his mouth, so his laughter wouldn't distract her. "I think...I don't think he was planning on us being there. I think we got lucky - he was turning the dead into Manticores. I think he wanted to throw those at us." She held her hand up, and Ryan grabbed her another mug of coffee.

Crystal nodded, her face a model of sobriety. "Okay, that makes sense. And you two are sure this Arthur chap's on the up-and-up?"

Ryan took this one. "No, not really. But since the world is going to end soon anyway, would it really matter if he wasn't?"

That got a laugh out of both his companions, though Athena's was a second behind Crystal's. "Fair enough, love. So what's the next move?"

"We go on...on TV. Once I'm sober. I call Enki mean things on TV, his ego gets hurt, and he does something stupid we can..." He paused to belch, then turned pink and put a hand over his mouth. "That we can take advantage of," he muttered into the hand. He looked up at Crystal with watery eyes. "He killed a town, Crystal. So many...so many bodies. He has to be stopped. We have to...we have to stop him."

"A good idea. But, if you don't mind me suggesting a slight change?"

Ryan nodded, and Athena motioned for her to go on.

"Well, I'm thinking we take it a step further, yeah? We don't just tick him off and see what he does; we bloody well call him out. Give him a time and a place and tell him to meet us there for a big old dust-up over this whole thing."

"You really think he'll fall for that?" Athena asked.

"I don't really see a way he can avoid it. He made this big deal about how he's gonna save the world from us, yeah? Well, between that and his pride, if we say 'we're willing to settle this if you've got the guts...'"

"...He'll pretty much have to," Ryan finished, nodding. He was nodding a lot this conversation, which was probably not good for his impending hangover. *Oh, wait, no, I don't get hangovers anymore.*

"Bingo," Crystal grinned. "Then we just have to make sure we win."

"And...Do you have a plan for that?"

"Nope!" Crystal's voice was cheery, but the cheer seemed like it had been stretched on a rack for a few days. "But once you two are sober and I've gotten my post-death hungers all taken care of, I'm sure we'll come up with something."

"Sounds like a plan." Athena muttered, laying her head back. "Being sober would be a wonderful thing right about now."

"I bet. And I hate to do this while you're still drunk, love, but there are a couple things that maybe you and I should clear the air on?" That strain again, nearly at its breaking point.

"You never were one for patience, Ishtar," Athena muttered, sitting up.

"It's Crystal now, Minerva." Ryan noted the edge to her voice, and slid further away from the two women, trying to clear his head as the lizard part of his brain started warning him of impending danger.

"I don't go by-" Athena clamped her jaw shut, realizing how stupid the protest would sound. "Fine, Crystal. What do you want to 'clear the air' about?"

"Why'd you join Enki?"

The question seemed innocent enough to Ryan, but the way Athena's eyes flared indicated there were layers he was missing. "Isn't that obvious? You two were going to end the world, and I didn't know about this sun exploding thing." Athena's eyes narrowed. "Or maybe that isn't the question you really wanted to ask. Maybe you meant something else."

Crystal opened her mouth, and then took a deep breath. "No, love, you're right. It's just that, well, we hadn't spoken since..."

Athena clearly had her own sharp retort but bit it back as well. "I know." She sighed.

For a moment they both looked just so sad. Ryan wanted to speak up, but without knowing the history...as if he had spoken out loud, they both looked at him.

"I was there during Athena's Roman years."

Athena nodded. "And we were...close."

"But then we had a...falling out?" Crystal glanced at Athena, who gave her a slight smile at the term.

"An ugly one," Athena amended.

Ryan swallowed, but had to ask. "What...what happened? Not to cause it, no need to rehash bad blood, but what made it so ugly?"

They looked at each other for a moment, and Crystal shrugged. "How good is your Roman history, love?"

"Uh...fair?"

"Heard of the Punic Wars?" Athena asked, "Rome vs. Carthage? Salting the Earth at the end?"

"Yeah, I'm familiar." They both looked at him for a moment to let that sink in. "Wait...that was because of you two having a *falling out?*"

Crystal winced, "Well...not entirely, yeah?"

Athena grimaced, "But it was a factor. Sort of the spark that lit the powder keg."

"And then kept throwing oil on the bloody fire," Crystal said, looking over at Athena.

Ryan sat back, needing to process that. The two women, meanwhile, were looking at each other.

"You know, love, you *were* Minerva back then."

Athena thought for a moment over the comment, and then replied, clearly choosing her words with care, "And you were Ishtar."

"So maybe we can just say Athena and Crystal don't have a history, yeah? Minerva and Ishtar did, but they're both gone."

Athena nodded with exaggerated care. "I'm not exactly sober, but that still sounds like a good idea."

"Great." They both relaxed. "So why don't you two sleep off the booze, and I'll head out there and get my dance on till I don't have any more Hunger, yeah?"

They could only nod at that. "Lovely. Enjoy!" Crystal bounced out of the staging area, and for a moment they got to enjoy the sound of music wafting back in.

Ryan flopped back as soon as she was gone. "I thought you two were going to...to have a fight."

"We got most of the fight out of our systems a few centuries ago." She leaned over and looked at Ryan. "What, worried you'd get caught in the crossfire?"

Ryan laughed. "Goddamn right I was. I'm half drunk, you're three-quarters drunk, and Crystal was half-mad with hunger. I didn't see that...going well for me."

Athena chuckled. "You're a wiser man than you seem, Ryan Smith. I'm glad it's all out in the open and dealt with."

"Agreed."

"When we get up, you should check on your nanoverse. We all should check on ours, really. Make sure they haven't gone to a mess while we were gone."

Ryan shuddered at the thought. "Fair. In the meantime...I guess we should sleep?"

For a long moment, she held his eyes. "Yeah, I guess we should. Rest well, Ryan." She rolled over, her chair forming into a bed.

Ryan sat there for a moment, then opened a door to his own staging area. A bed formed for him, and he flopped into it with a sigh. He was asleep before he could even form another thought.

Chapter 20

Unforeseen Consequences

After a night of drinking so much that he'd been tripping over his own feet, Ryan expected to wake up feeling like he'd slept in a sweaty gym sock that was being tossed in a cement mixer. For an instant, he almost managed to give himself a psychosomatic hangover, but divine biology was good for things besides not needing to breathe on Mars, and once the moment passed he realized that he felt fine.

He got out of bed and paused to look around his staging area. It had changed some since he was last here. The panel of touchscreens had morphed into classic, Hollywood style floating holograms, which made him grin - he'd wanted them to look like that. A chest-high wall also encircled the entire platform, which reduced the feeling that he was standing on the edge of reality and could fall off at any time.

Finally, and most importantly, a gentle hum filled the air, punctuated by the occasional beep. On some level he knew those sounds did and meant nothing, but compared to the semi-eerie silence of Crystal and Athena's nanoverses, it was a welcome addition.

He poked his head through the door into Crystal's nanoverse. She was splayed across a chair with the complete lack of dignity usually reserved for sleeping cats that had fit into an impossibly small container.

The stars and galaxies drew his eyes. He hadn't really looked at them in the past couple of days and now he noted that they were heading more and more strongly towards red and darker yellows. *I'll ask her about it when she gets up.* Instead of waking her, he moved with every bit of caution he could muster.

Athena was awake, inhaling coffee. Not in the figurative sense of drinking it quickly, but actually just sitting there, cup in hand, breathing in the steam. "Good morning," he said quietly, closing the door to Crystal's nanoverse.

The look Athena gave him was borderline friendly, although full of the fuzz that clings to some brains as they wake. "Crystal still asleep?"

"Yup. Though I think I saw her shift as I closed the door, so she might be up soon."

"Noted." She finally took a drink of the coffee. "Headed to your nanoverse then?"

"Think I'll wait for Crystal to wake up. You?"

Athena nodded. "I haven't been in almost ten thousand years their time, so I'm probably forgotten. Will need to take a bit of time to establish myself as their goddess."

"So, wait. If you weren't in your nanoverse, and you weren't keeping up with the core world, what were you doing."

Athena smiled. "There are other worlds with sentient beings, Ryan. I spent much of my time out among them, away from everything else."

Ryan's eyes widened. "Well, color me jealous as hell. After this is all done, maybe you could show me around out there."

Athena shrugged. "Maybe."

"I'll take maybe." Ryan smiled at her. "Hey, speaking of our nanoverses, I was wondering about something. I know worshippers don't get us anything over here, but in our nanoverses?"

Another sip of coffee. "Some argue that it does, that you can get more power out of a devoted nanoverse, but others argue we just *want* them to worship us, that it's a Hunger we gods have."

That made sense to Ryan. *Might be worth keeping up with, just in case it gives me an edge.* The door to Crystal's nanoverse opened and she walked in, her hair what she'd likely call a "right bloody mess," yawning. "Oh, good, caught you two before you scampered off to your 'verses."

They focused their attention on her. "Something on your mind?" Athena asked.

Crystal nodded. "Didja see the state my bloody nanoverse got into while I was dead? Half the stars burned out, even some of the red dwarves, cosmic microwave dropped to .3 k. I'm going to be dealing with bloody iron star formation soon - I'm not going to bother going into mine. Just going to run it to the ground and do a Big Crunch after we kick Enki's arse."

Athena gave Crystal a look that just said *this is a perfectly sensible line of reasoning and not a bunch of science fiction gibberish*. Ryan followed the astronomy part but had no idea why it mattered. "What's all that mean?"

"Oh, a problem you don't have to worry about for a good ten thousand years, or more. My nanoverse is dying; same way the core universe would eventually if it wasn't for the cycle of ending worlds to keep stars burning, yeah? So I'm going to wait for life to go extinct and collapse it all into a singularity. It'll force it to go through a Big Crunch followed by a Big Bang. Total reset, start fresh." Crystal grinned. "I've done it more than a few times, love."

"What happens if you don't?"

"Entropy takes over, love. Galaxies fall apart, and you're left with a bunch of dead stars, brown dwarfs, free floating planets, and black holes. Then those start to decay or vanish due to quantum tunneling, and then...heat death." Crystal grimaced at the thought. "It's the only other way for a god to die for real, yeah? Let their nanoverse undergo heat death. Some of us just get tired of living and go somewhere quiet to let their nanoverse die."

Thinking about a universe like that, dead and lifeless and cold, made Ryan shiver. Athena and Crystal gave him sympathetic looks, and Athena brought the topic back to its original point. "When you do a Big Crunch, though, you go through something like a Nascent period again. Not the fainting spells, but it's a bigger strain to use your powers, and during that time your death could be permanent, same as where you are now. Something you best want to save for when things are calm."

"Gotcha," Ryan said, both glad for the information and sorry he had asked. Crystal seemed to pick up on his mood, and Ryan was reminded of how much he'd missed having her around.

"Since I can't do much about that now," Crystal said, "I'll keep myself busy while you two tend to your nanoverses. Gonna do some recon, see if we can't find a nice safe place to have our battle with Enki without getting a bunch of civilians caught in the crossfire, yeah?"

Agreeing that was the best choice, Athena and Ryan headed off to their nanoverses. While passing through Crystal's to get back to his, Ryan did his best not to look at those red, dying galaxies.

***

Ryan dropped into his nanoverse and pulled up the holographic display. He took a few moments to enjoy moving about the universe by flicking at the holograms.

One display in particular drew his attention, the one that showed intelligent species. He pulled it over into view and expanded it. "Graphids are still there," he muttered to himself, "wonder what happened to the other two?"

Could be anything, Ryan reasoned. Asteroid strike, gamma ray burst, global ice age, global warming - the number of ways an entire species without space flight could die was extensive.

Besides, there were so many *more.* Ryan flicked through the list, noting them one by one. Here was a species that lived on a world that orbited a red dwarf. They had no eyes and were covered in fur that looked like armor. There was a species on a gas giant that looked like enormous jellyfish. Apparently, they were using metal they syphoned from the air. Another species were plants that burrowed roots into the brains of unintelligent animals and rode them like meat suits.

Okay, that one's less wonderful and just gross.

As enticing as meeting a whole new alien species would be, he was more interested in seeing how the

Graphids had progressed. He dropped into realspace and set a course for their home world.

A small part of his brain noted this was the first time he'd done anything major without support. Sure, Athena hadn't been with him when he met the Graphids the first time, but she'd been back in the staging area, so if anything went wrong-

That part of his brain was interrupted as he got close to the Graphid home world, his mouth quite literally hanging open as he looked.

The planet was circled by series of platforms of dark metal, large enough to qualified as a ring and far enough out to be in geostationary orbit. Similarly massive structures, the size of small moons, sat at the Lagrange Points. Vessels travelled back and forth, and when he focused on them, he could tell they were full of members of dozens of species.

A particular ship that drew Ryan's attention was painted black and glowed with red lights so bright they cast shadows on nearby planets. From the edge of the ring jutted huge spires that stretched for hundreds of feet and looked like horrid spines.

It looks like a rebel ship should be running from it, Ryan mused. *Like something out of the evil empire's wet dreams.*

A quick scan told him no such ship existed, but his control panel informed him he was being hailed.

When the holographic screen appeared, Ryan's eyes widened further. The man had the telltale grey skin and the stocky build of a Graphid, but too many features Ryan didn't recognize. A glowing red eye with a metal iris that dilated as he peered at Ryan. Wires running from his forehead to his shoulders, which jutted back unnaturally like they had metallic wings. Ryan hit a button on his screen to scan the man. Genetically, he was a Graphid, but so many cybernetic augmentations had been jammed into his flesh, Ryan could barely see the original species. The cyborg Graphid glared at the screen, his telescoping eyes narrowing. "I am Daasti, Captain of the Fearmonger. You are violating Imperial Graphid Space - state your name and your designation or be disintegrated."

Some perverse anger rose up from a pool Ryan didn't know he had. Days and days of being hounded by Enki, lectured by Crystal and Athena - and now someone whose entire life depended on his existence was giving him threats?

"I don't have a designation. My name's Ryan Smith, and I'm your god, you totalitarian dipshit." *I'm a good guy. This some messed up crap going on. This isn't what I meant! It's...it's wrong.*

"Heretic!" Daasti screamed at the camera, his veins literally bulging with rage. "You will be purged in the true name of Ryan Smith for daring to claim to be our Lord and God! In the Name of Our Emperor, Ryan's Son and Heir of his Chosen, open fire!"

The name of my what now? One of the larger ships turned to face him. It looked like the talon of some bird of prey, and the claws rotated to show a lens in the center. It was facing directly at Ryan.

Seeing the incandescent energy building up in the center of the lens, Ryan felt his heart begin to pound. Apparently the Graphids had mastered fusion, and the harnessed power of a star was unleashed in a beam of white-hot plasma, an entire solar flare's worth of energy lashed and bound into a single beam and expelled with enough force to scour a planet clean.

His body screamed in terror, but his brain clenched its teeth in rage. *They* dare *fire at me?* With a flick of his hand, he stopped the beam, midway in space between the two ships. He glanced at the screen and saw Daasti's eyes begin to roll with fear. "Are you paying attention, Captain? Because you won't survive a repeat performance."

Daasti's head jerked up and down.

Ryan clenched his fingers, moving them towards a fist but stopping while there was a small gap between fingers and palm. At the same time, outside, the billions upon billions of watts of energy rolled into a cylinder less than a mile across. Making sure Daasti was watching, Ryan held his hand to his mouth and blew through the gap.

Outside, all that power, enough to purge an entire planet of heretics, simply winked out of existence.

"My God!" Daasti exclaimed.

"Told you." For a moment, that perverse anger rose again, and Ryan considered waving his hand to erase Daasti's entire warship. But the rational part of his brain, the part that was still reeling from what he had done, tackled that rage to the ground and choked it out before he could wipe out thousands of lives for the sake of a slight. *I need to get a handle on my temper. This is my mess. I need to clean it up.*

Daasti stared at him, too terrified to speak. Ryan leaned back against the console, letting his grin widen.

"So, Emperor, huh? I think he and I should have a talk."

***

The throne room of the Emperor, Ryan's Son and Heir of his Chosen, was one of the Emperor's favorite places in the entire station. It was the seat of his power. The vaulted ceiling was nearly a hundred feet over the heads of any who ventured within, and when they approached him the petitioners had to walk nearly twice that length to reach his throne. The throne itself was thrice as tall as the tallest Graphid, and the walls were adorned with the skulls of species who had dared to oppose his power.

"Your worship," said this petitioner, one of his Admirals bowing low before him. The Emperor couldn't remember his name. They all looked the same with their faces pressed against the floor. "I have received word from the Fearmonger. Daasti says that they have fired their main plasma cannon."

"So a world was eradicated." The Emperor shrugged. "What of it? My empire is full of worlds."

"Nothing was eradicated, your worship. May I show you?"

The Emperor gave him a magnanimous nod. "Of course." A video began to play in the air between him. An exchange between Daasti and some lowly heretic claiming to be Ryan incarnate. *Utter nonsense.* Ryan was a myth, a fable, a drug used to placate the masses by claiming that there had been some mystical origin to their science, some grand purpose to their weaponsmithing, that-

The plasma beam stopped in empty space, and after some more taunting from Ryan, vanished. The Emperor's jaw fell open. "Ryan's name," he whispered.

"Is it truly him, your worship?"

Sweat began to bead the Emperor's forehead, and he was never gladder that the Admiral could not look at him. The Admiral was a Freemind, and only the reeducated could gaze upon the Emperor in all his glory. *Although I suppose I'll have to make an exception.* Whoever, whatever this being was, it had powers the Emperor had never imagined. "So it would seem," he said, careful to keep any wavering out of his voice. "Send word to Daasti. I cannot wait to meet our god."

Of all the lies the Emperor had told his subjects over the years, that one may have been the largest.

***

Ryan was strongly considering turning this throne room pink just to prove a point as he turned to face the Emperor, his "son". "So, you're the Emperor around here, huh?"

Ryan, in his jeans and blue t-shirt, looked hilariously out of place here. The room was surrounded by men and women who looked like they were cut from the same cloth as Daasti, armed with fancy looking rifles and those mercurial swords. *Need to pull one out to keep for myself when I hit the core world again.*

He had a feeling that after he was done here, they'd vanish before he'd have much time to make use of them.

At the head of the room, on a platform that scuttled on spider legs, sat the Emperor, his alleged son. The sight of him was nothing short of revolting. His skin had been pierced by dozens of augmentations, many of which were gold and silver and, as far as Ryan could determine, purely decorative. The skin at the edges of those implants was beginning to rot, giving him a half-undead look. His legs were shriveled and warped from disuse - a cable connected the back of his skull to the platform, letting him control it mentally. His eyes were huge and lidless, with tiny implants occasionally spraying them with moisturizing water.

"We are, your Divinity." Those wide, unblinking eyes were focused on Ryan, and his blistered tongue slipped out to moisten his lips between words. The voice was...well, if you could imagine a teapot with a particularly phlegmatic cough trying to speak, you had the Emperor's voice. "And we would ask of you - why have you returned after so much time? The Book of Science is nearly a hundred millennia old, Father."

"Okay, don't - yeah. Don't ever call me that again. I don't have any kids." The soldiers at the side twitched at the blasphemy, but...well, can God blaspheme?

"Perhaps you didn't know," the Emperor said. "When you gave us the Book of Science, and lay with Saphyn, you begat my ancestor. Your seed-"

Ryan interrupted with a retching noise. "Yeah, don't...that goes right up there with calling me father. I don't want to hear you say that word again. Saphyn and I never got together. The only thing I gave her was knowledge, and we definitely were horizontal when it happened. Moving on, now that we've cleared that up..." Ryan stuck his hands in his back pockets, tearing his gaze from the monstrosity of flesh on the throne. He knew he was jumping topics, but the last thing he wanted was to let the Emperor ramble on any more. "A hundred thousand years? Man, time does fly when you're running around fighting a war with an evil god."

Ryan snapped his fingers, creating a chair for himself. A nice comfy office chair, which he experimentally rolled a short distance across the floor. "Well, your highness, I swung by to see what you were making of the gifts I left you a hundred thousand years ago." Ryan still felt the anger seething below the surface. More than he expected, but he figured it was at least partly justified. *They turned everything I had in mind into some perverse mockery of what I wanted.* So he spun around to face the Emperor.

Those lips were parted by blistered tongue again. "Well, your Divinity, we...created weapons, as you ordered. And then spread your worship across the cosmos! This entire Galaxy now bows to you."

"Mmmmmhmmm. And the weapons, I'll admit, you got those right. But what did you do those who didn't worship me?" He smiled as he asked the question, trying to put the mass on the throne at ease. *Set him up, Ryan. Set him up and knock his pudgy ass down.*

"We purged them, your Divinity. Over seventeen entire species have been eradicated - in your name, of course." That tongue, which was just getting grosser every time Ryan saw it, flicked out over his lips. "And others, like the soldiers here, were reeducated."

Ryan was silent for a long time. Seventeen entire species, wiped out in his name. "Wow. You're serious?"

"Of course, your Divinity."

Ryan rolled his chair over to Daasti. "You were reeducated?"

"Yes. I had not seen the wisdom in following you, but now your light fills me!"

Ryan looked at the man, then back at the Emperor. "My light fills him."

"Yes, your Divinity. So, mmm, if I may ask...what do you think of your Empire?"

"Eh. One second." He held up a finger to silence the Emperor. "My light fills you?"

"Your Divinity, I-" the Emperor began.

Ryan snapped his fingers, and the Emperor's mouth stopped emitting noise.

"Now, Daasti. When you say my light fills you, what do you mean by that?"

"I was lost. I rebelled against the Emperor. I sought to unmake all of Your work. I called you an evil god, a god of death. But now your light fills me!"

"Mmmhmm." Ryan looked at Daasti with his divine sight. A part of Daasti's brain had lit up as he said, 'your light fills me'. Ryan asked, "And what do you think of my light?"

The same spot activated. "It is wonderous to be filled by your glory!" *There's a chip. In his brain. They put a chip in his damn brain.*

"Wonderful. You all have a real thing about filling, don't you?" Apparently, the chip didn't know how to handle that. *Probably for the best.* Ryan rolled the chair across the room, motioning some of the standing re-educated soldiers out of his way. He got to a window, which gave him a great view of ships coming in and out. He took a moment to study the devices they were using - it appeared they'd found a way to create stable wormholes.

He could feel the Emperor's expectant look on his back. "Honestly, Emperor? You *really* want to know what I think of *my* Empire?" Ryan snapped his fingers again, allowing the Emperor to speak.

"Of course, your Divinity."

Ryan nodded, still not looking back at that pulsating mass. "I think you have a kingdom of rot, a dystopia of pus. I think you have created the most disgusting mockery of all that is right and good with science, and once I'm done dismantling it to its component pieces the only echoes of your legacy will be a cautionary tale on how one should never pervert reason like this."

The Emperor's disgusting little voice piped up here, "Your Divinity, I mu-"

Ryan whirled to face the Emperor, his voice amplified so that every single person on this massive moon of a vessel could hear it. "I AM NOT FINISHED."

He enjoyed watching the Emperor quake. He kept his voice amplified so that everyone on the ship would hear every word. "You have the nerve, the absolute nerve, to claim to be of my blood, to commit horrors in my name, and then you ask me what I think of it?"

The Emperor's wide eyes widened further. "You told us to build weapons!"

Ryan stopped, taking a deep breath. "You're right. I did. My mistake." *I have to do something.* This Empire was awful. The fact that something like this had been created in his name disgusted him. The fact that he'd done it to get himself weapons appalled him. *I condemned these people to thousand's of years of torment just so I could have a cool sword. I have to think before I just fly off the handle.* Ryan took a deep breath. This Empire maintained its control, as far as Ryan could tell, through two main venues: the wormhole network, and the reeducated. If he broke that control, it would give the pending rebellions a chance to flare up, to establish something better. It would mean years of war, but things could improve afterwards.

Ryan nodded to himself. *Time to take away their toys.*

Ryan snapped his fingers. The Emperor flinched. The soldiers flinched. When they realized they were still intact, they looked at him, until the Emperor worked up the courage to move his disgusting little meat hole. "What did you do?"

"Oh, that? I just fixed a little loophole in physics you were exploiting. No more wormholes. Apparently, you all can't be trusted with faster than light travel, so I'm taking it away until you prove you can behave."

The huge eyes bulged further. *"What did you do?"*

Ryan tilted his head to the side, eyebrows going up. "In what way was that unclear?"

"That will unmake the Empire! Without the wormholes, how will we control the slaves!? The network that keeps the re-educated in check - it will collapse!!" The phlegmatic teapot was shrieking now.

Ryan gave him a thumbs up and a broad grin. "Look who's paying attention."

"The Empire will collapse! The greatest civilization in history will be in ruins!"

That was it, enough to propel Ryan out of his chair, to his feet and into the air, where he floated, crossing his arms across his chest - half divine wrath, half disapproving father. "I am aware, you tiny, pathetic man. I'm deliberately collapsing this empire, because there is nothing great about it. And while I'm at it -" He snapped his fingers again, and the Emperor screamed.

"What did you do!? Oh Ryan's Holy Name, what have you done?!"

Ryan ignored the irony of having his own name taken in vain against him, instead focusing on the question. "As a friend of mine is fond of doing, let me answer your question with a question." Ryan turned to Daasti. "Hey, Daasti! What do you think about the Empire?"

Daasti took a few ragged breaths and said something quietly.

"Sorry, Daasti, couldn't quite make that out."

Daasti looked up at him, and Ryan was taken aback by the hatred he saw. He'd gotten hate in his life, and even more since becoming a god, but Enki's rage was a candle being tossed into the sun compared to the hate Daasti directed at him.

"I said. I had. A family."

Daasti charged at Ryan, the silver sword springing to his hand. There were about a thousand ways Ryan could stop him, but instead, he just did the invulnerability trick he'd tried when he first arrived in his nanoverse, then floated down to the ground so Daasti could wail on him for a moment. Around the room, other re-educated eyes, seeing with the clarity that comes from free will for the first time in years, turned towards Ryan.

After a few moments, Daasti was panting, and Ryan put a hand on his shoulder. "I'm sorry. I didn't mean for any of this to happen. But I'm going to make it right. For starters, I've restored your free will, all of you."

Without looking, Ryan raised a hand. The Emperor, who was trying to scuttle away, floated into the air. "Really, *son*? I broke your hold over every re-educated in the galaxy with a snap of my fingers, and that was right after I *literally rewrote the laws of physics.* And your response was to sneak off?"

He looked at the formerly reeducated and moved the Emperor over to them. "I'll let you do what you see fit with this. Daasti, can I talk to you a bit longer?"

Eyes still burning with hate, Daasti rose to his feet. "You are a monster god, a war god. What do you *want* with me?"

Ryan took a deep breath, looking out the window. "I...man, you have no idea how crappy I feel about this. I just wanted to accelerate technology, but I didn't think about providing any kind of ethical framework for it. You hate me, I get that - this is all my fault."

Daasti regarded Ryan as Ryan stared at the Empire. "So, what? I'm supposed to feel pity for you? You're Ryan. You're *God.*" That ugly rage welled up in Ryan, and he focused his attention on Daasti. To his credit, the man who had seen him wink a planet destroying plasma beam out of existence didn't flinch. "Go ahead, if you're going to," Daasti said, not breaking Ryan's gaze. "Annihilate me. At least I'll die free."

Damn, Ryan, you're glaring at him *now too? He just pointed out you're the worst kind of absentee dad and you're going to get pissed at him? This place is messing with your head, fix it and get out.* But that ugly feeling remained as he stared at Daasti. Ryan narrowed his eyes. *Think, Ryan. You just threw this galaxy into chaos.* Something would need to happen to make things better here. Otherwise the civil wars Ryan just created would never end. These people had been controlled for years. They'd need a guiding hand.

Who better than someone who knows how monstrous the Empire really is?

"No, Daasti. I'm not going to annihilate you. I'm going to do something much worse." Ryan reached out and put a hand on Daasti's forehead. In a series of clattering clanks, every augmentation fell out of him, bouncing on the floor. Daasti stood there, as natural as the day he was born. "I'm going to make you a savior."

Daasti shuddered and, if not for Ryan's hand on his elbow, would have fallen. "What did you...what happened?"

"I just made you into a demigod. You're a good man, Daasti." Ryan wasn't sure of that, but he was hoping. Ryan knew he made a mistake with these people before and trusting Daasti with this kind of power was a huge gamble. *This time, I won't just leave it be and hope for the best.* "You're full of rage, and with a hate for this Empire and this twisted version of what I want people to believe, but you're a good man." *At least, you better be.*

Ryan looked out over the Empire again, where ships were lining up in front of the no-longer functional wormholes, a traffic jam of war machines in the space between worlds. "I don't believe people need religion to have morals. But I found a primitive culture and accelerated their technology without doing the same to their philosophy. I created a monster. You have the power now to slay that beast."

Daasti stared at his hands. "So, what, you're going to leave again?"

"Yup." Ryan gave Daasti a smile, and began to feel that hatred, that rage, fade away. "Between you and me - I have no idea what I'm doing. You can't possibly screw it up worse than I did. But don't let it go to your head. I'll be back, and if you turn out to be just another Emperor - well, then I'll have to fix things myself."

"It's too much for one man alone, Ryan."

"Oh, I figured. That's why you can share the power. Pick carefully, and good luck."

And with that, Ryan was back in his staging area. He felt sick, and weak. *What the* hell *is happening to me?* Knowing only that he had to get out of here, he dropped out of realspace and began the journey back to the Core.

I really, really hope Crystal doesn't expect me to roll with this.

Chapter 21

Deluge

Ryan stumbled out into Crystal's nanoverse. She glanced away from her globe and over at him. "Bloody hell, what happened to you?"

"I was hoping you could tell me." A chair appeared for Ryan, and he sank into it. "I was in my nanoverse, and while I was there, I found out my followers had made...I don't know. An evil empire? I guess that's the best term."

Crystal walked over and called a chair to sit across from him. "Let me guess. You got there and you started feeling angry, imperious, cocky - went a bit 'Bow before me, worms!' on them?"

Ryan gulped and nodded. "Yeah." For a moment it felt like old times, when Crystal had first picked him up - what felt like a lifetime ago - and had first explained to him what a nanoverse meant. That moment of comfort, of familiarity, was enough - and with no hesitation, the entire story of what had transpired came rolling out, his breath getting ragged with fear as he described the way he was acting. "So what the hell happened to me, Crystal?" he finished, almost shouting, but not at her. "Why did I turn into that guy?"

She paused to let him catch his breath and gave him a grin to try and defuse his panic. "I'm guessing you'll try to sock me if I tell you to roll with it, love?"

Ryan's eyes narrowed and he felt his fingers clench, but the response was so absurd it got a much-needed laugh out of him. "It had crossed my mind."

"Right. Well, I told you your mood influences your nanoverse, yeah? Goes both ways - your personality, especially when over there, is shaped by what people believe you are." She patted his knee and gave him a reassuring smile.

Relief flooded Ryan for a moment, but before it had time to settle in it was tackled to the ground by its total opposite in blind panic. "Wait, what you do mean especially when over there? What about over here?"

She smiled. "And that, love, is why you should always go back and check on your nanoverse every couple of weeks at least. It takes a while to start impacting you in the core world, but it can." She frowned. "I wonder if that's what happened to Enki?"

"Come again?"

Crystal got up and walked back to the globe. "Want a story to distract you, love?"

Ryan settled into the chair. "Hell yes, I could use a distraction."

Crystal gave him a small smile. "You sure? I'm warning you, it's not a happy one, yeah?"

"Please."

She moved her hand, spinning the globe a bit, as she started to speak "So back in the day, when you lot were first figuring out this civilization thing and the first round of deities were fading away, sick of life and letting their nanoverses die, a man of a hunter-gatherer tribe - it's been so long I've forgotten the tribe's name, not that it matters - found a nanoverse."

Ryan settled in to listen.

"This newfound god, on the short list of human gods at the time...oooh, but that man was a bloody clever bugger. So clever he ended up - after a couple thousand years - helping found the first really urban spot of humanity, good old Sumer, and the five cities that made it up. He was worshipped, like all the older gods were, but he wasn't all that interested in being worshipped, at least, not at first." Her voice trailed off for a moment, and Ryan let her vision drift for time before prompting her.

"What happened?"

His voice seemed to startle her, and Crystal ran her hand through her hair. "Back then I pretended like I had just found my nanoverse, same as that clever bugger and his friends - the first pantheon with a city. And let me tell you, love, it was something else. Watching humans figure out language and pottery and weapons and culture - it's not like watching it happen in a nanoverse, where you see it happen in millennia long spurts. It's different seeing it happen in real time."

Crystal shook her head, like she was trying to clear something away - perhaps the moisture in her eyes. "But with civilization comes war, sure as rain makes mud. And for the first time, Enki, god of craft, god of intelligence-"

Ryan couldn't help himself. "God of intelligence? *Enki?*"

"Oi, do I interrupt you?"

"All the time."

She chuckled at that. "Fair enough, love. Yes, Enki, who was associated back then with being a clever boy and making stuff. Can I continue?" She didn't wait for Ryan's nod. "Where was I? Oh, yeah. For the first time, Enki found the limits of his power. Lamashtu - that's who we were up against - she created a whole bunch of monsters and just threw them at us. We were losing, so badly that Enki only saw one way to deal with the mess, only one way to win."

"What was it?"

"The Deluge. The seven of us - the Seven Gods who Decree they called us - flooded the whole damn valley. Drowned all the monsters and the people, because Enki figured we could always get more people, but Lamashtu would need too long to get more monsters."

"That's..." Ryan swallowed, thinking through the logic there. "That's horrible."

Crystal nodded. "So imagine how bad Lamashtu's monsters had to be, yeah? If I was going to sign off on that, they had to be pretty nasty."

Ryan decided he didn't want to think to think too hard about how bad they must have been, instead nodding in agreement.

"And it worked, Enki's plan, even though it boiled down to 'if we can't save it, we'll decide how it ends.'"

Ryan coughed. "Isn't that what we're doing?"

Crystal shook her head. "We're going to find a way to save everyone, that's the thing. Back then, we just wanted to...to save what we could. It worked, to a degree.

It wiped out Lamashtu's monsters and left us with enough people to rebuild. But he wasn't the same after that, not really. Spent lots of time in his nanoverse, sure there was a way he could have done it better. He brought me there once." Her voice was low, and she focused more intensely on the globe in front of her.

"What was it like?"

***

The streets of Isin were full of corpses.

Ishtar fought the urge to look away. *You killed these people,* she reminded herself. She and Enki and Anu and - all of them. Granted, the alternative had been to let Lamashtu kill every single person in the valley. But...*Is this all you are? A mass murderer? The lesser evil?*

It had been years since the Deluge. Most of the corpses had rotted down to skeletons, and those that hadn't had been mummified by the sun and heat. Ishtar glanced up to see the predominant inhabitants of Isin: crows. Their population had grown in the aftermath of the Deluge, although it was now thinning as the carrion decreased. One of the birds was regarding her with a hungry eye. *Will you die? Will I be able to eat you?*

Ishtar reached out and twisted reality. The screech of an eagle pierced the air, and with it the crows scattered. They were clever animals and did not want to be around when predators arrived.

None of the surviving people had dared to come back to the city. To find them, Ishtar had to travel to the wilderness, searching for the remnants of this once-great civilization. She wanted to see the people before meeting Enki. *And if he's bothered by my tardiness, I'm sure he'll find me.*

Eventually, she found a small cluster of tents. Human eyes peered out, but quickly ducked back inside at the sight of Ishtar, the goddess of war and fertility, one of the Seven.

"I don't come to harm you," she said, reaching to her back and pulling around the basket. "I've brought bread, and seeds to regrow the fields."

"Leave us alone!" someone shouted. "You've done enough to our people!"

Ishtar winced. It was hard to hear those words, to know the truth of them.

"What, did you expect gratitude?" said a voice from behind her.

Ishtar glanced over to the speaker. Enki, the First among the Seven, was striding out of his nanoverse. He was a regal sight. His hair was meticulously groomed, his beard kept perfectly trimmed. He wore only a skirt, as the men often did, and his torso glistened in the sunlight.

Ishtar didn't understand why the male torso was less enticing to humans than the female, but in this heat, she envied Enki the privilege of being able to walk around bare-chested. *Humans are so weirdly prude.* "Not gratitude, Enki," she said, shaking her head. "But I figured they'd at least allow me to help."

"Something about humanity you've never understood, Ishtar: the importance of pride. Accepting aid from the people responsible for the suffering? Better to starve." Ishtar searched Enki's eyes as he spoke and saw the haunted look to them. Enki had been worshipped as a god of intelligence, knowledge, and crafting. *How much did it hurt, old friend, to become a destroyer?*

"They'll come around, Enki," Ishtar said, quietly. "If not this generation, then the one after, or the one after that."

Enki's lips pressed into a line, and he gave her a curt nod. "Maybe. I don't care if they do, honestly."

Liar. In all the time she had known him, Enki had cared more deeply than any god of even Ishtar's age about what happened to the people that worshipped him. It was one of his more admirable qualities, and part of why Ishtar had trusted him with the truth of her origins. "Then what do you care about?"

"About making sure it never happens again. Never again will we have to purge a country to save it."

Ah. That, at least, sounded like the Enki she had known. "You know I want the same thing."

Enki gave her a searching look. "Is that how you did it, Ishtar? With oceans of water?"

For the second time that day, Ishtar fought the urge to look away from something that made her uncomfortable. "No. I purged the world with the oceans of fire that lie beneath the land."

From his face, Ishtar had put more venom in those words than she intended. "I...I had to ask," he said

Ishtar sighed. "I understand needing to know. Maybe later, I'll tell you the full story." *If I can even remember it. A million years is a long time.* Ishtar had been vague about how long in the past her epoch had been. It made things simpler. "Is this why you called me, to ask that question?"

Enki shook his head. "I figured something out. Come with me, Ishtar. I want to show you something." He motioned back towards his staging area.

Ishtar put down her basket of bread and grain before following. As she entered his nanoverse, she glanced back to see curious eyes looking at it. *Maybe they'll take it. I hope they do.*

Enki's staging area was a flat stone room with a single altar that functioned as his control panel. He walked over to it and began to trace the cuneiform lettering. "Thinking of taking us fully into your nanoverse, Enki?"

He gave her an intense look, and Ishtar's heart skipped a beat. There was something in that gaze she'd missed out in the core, a glint that set her teeth on edge. Suddenly she was wondering if entering his staging area was the wisest idea. *Don't be absurd. This is Enki we're talking about. He won't hurt you.*

"Just for a bit. Do you mind?"

Ishtar shook her head, although part of her wanted to object. She fought those objections down.

They dropped into his realspace, and Enki began piloting by tracing his fingers along the control panel's engravings. "I've spent a lot of time in here lately," he said, "thinking. About how we could have done better."

"We did everything we could," Ishtar said, frowning as the system they were approaching loomed ever closer.

It looked...familiar. *It's our solar system,* she realized with a start.

"Did we, though?" Enki asked, shaking his head. "I don't think we did, Ishtar. And I can prove it."

They arrived near Earth. It was Earth, Ishtar was sure of it. She'd seen it from the moon enough times to know that blue and green sphere. "Enki...what are you doing?"

"I know we can't create nanoverses in our own. So I did the next best thing. I call them godstones. They make the people in here into gods, same as we are except without the personal universe."

Ishtar walked over to the edge so Enki couldn't see her face. *This is wrong.* Recreating Earth? Making fake nanoverses? It was...abhorrent. "Why?" she asked.

"Let me show you."

They flew down to a copy of Sumeria. Ishtar knew these cities, knew these fields, knew these *people.* He hadn't just recreated Earth, he'd copied everything that had once existed in the core world, people and all.

Lamashtu's monsters were swarming the people of this world. A recreation of Ishtar's second greatest failure. Horrible creatures out of nightmare, crawling out of fissures Lamashtu opened in the Earth.

Ishtar wanted to be sick. She wanted to scream. Instead, she whirled on Enki. "Stop this, Enki. Stop this right now! It's sick. People are *dying.*"

Enki shook his head. "Shh. Look. Watch."

As Ishtar did, she saw another Ishtar engage the beasts. *Endless Void, he even got my movements right.* Her double danced among them, a storm of steel and thunder. They clawed at her, creatures of smoke and talon. As Ishtar watched, one of them even raked her Nanoverse duplicate across the back, and Ishtar's own hand involuntarily went up to where she'd received the same wound.

"They're us, Ishtar." Enki said in her ear, almost startling her into jumping. "I recreated everything perfectly. This world is going to be flooded soon, as they almost always are."

Ishtar shuddered at the thought. Thousands of lives, snuffed out, and Enki didn't care. Something else about what he said nagged at her, but she couldn't quite place it. "Enki...why? Why torment them like this? For that matter, why torment *yourself* like this?"

If Enki saw the horror of what he was doing, it didn't show on his face. "I've added a small variant. What did you call it? Chaos theory. They are exactly like us, but they still have free will. So sometimes they choose differently. Anu holds the bridge across the Tigris because he brought Enlil, putting aside that damnable grudge. You and I go together to the nests hidden in Ur, instead of Utu and me. Different variations each time."

As horrified as she was, Ishtar had to admit it was a damn effective learning tool, if you were willing to cast aside any shred of decency and morality. *Which, apparently, Enki is.* "And what changed?"

"Nothing. Every single time we lost. No matter what we did, this world lost to Lamashtu until they wiped the land clean with some disaster. Tornadoes, flooding, earthquakes. Something to deter the Mother of Monsters, seal her back below the earth."

"Then why show me?" Ishtar asked, nearly shouting. "You now have proof that we did the right thing, that we-" Finally the earlier thought sunk in, and Ishtar stopped to stare at Enki with an open mouth. "*This world?*" she asked, her heart pounding. "Enki, what have you done?"

Instead of answering, Enki ran his hands over the control panel, and they flew to the next solar system. The next exact same solar system. It was Earth, all over again. The flew down on another River Valley, another Sumeria, where Anu was being torn apart by Lamashtu's horrors. "On this world that wandering storyteller, Anansi, joined us. We still lost." Again his fingers ran through the cuneiform, and again they moved to another solar system, another Sumeria. Ishtar watched in horror as Enki's head was bitten off. "Here the Aesir responded to our call for aid. We still lost." Yet again he brought them to another world. "Here all of us save you committed suicide so you could make us into monsters to fight her monsters. We still lost."

Ishtar was speechless as world after world flashed by. A world where they had unleashed the caged Titans, who promptly had joined Lamashtu. A world where they had found Lamashtu the moment she emerged, before she could marshal her power. A world where they never flooded, and Lamashtu's monsters consumed the remainder of humanity. On and on and on. Every time Ishtar watched one of the Seven die before they moved on to the next one. A million Earths, orbiting a million suns, with a million river valleys being invaded by a million Lamashtus and defended by seven million Gods that Decree. The same situation, playing over and over again, each world resetting as soon as they flooded the valley.

"Enough!" Ishtar finally screamed, tears streaming down her face. "Enki, what is the point of this. Why are you showing me this...this abomination you created?"

"One more world, Ishtar. One more world and I promise it will be clear."

They flew to the next Earth, Ishtar shaking with horror at everything Enki had done.

On this world, Enki's double was fighting Lamashtu directly. Ishtar shuddered at seeing her again. Standing three times as tall as a building, Lamashtu's chitinous body sat atop a bed of tentacles. Individual arms ended in stingers that lashed out at Enki, who was...blocking them? None of them had been able to do that. Ishtar's eyes narrowed. Enki wasn't just blocking them. Enki was *winning.* The monsters lay broken and dead around the battlefield, and the people were cheering!

"How?" Ishtar managed to choke out. Then she saw it. Around this Enki's neck, a string of beads. What Enki had called godstones, the things that stood in for nanoverses.

Nanoverse Enki wore *seven*.

"With seven stones, they can hold off Lamashtu. Fight her directly. Had more power than even Lamashtu could muster. With seven nanoverses, I could have done the same thing. Don't you see, Ishtar? With that much power, I could make sure we never failed again. With the power of enough nanoverses, I could even prevent the end you came to warn us about. I could abolish death itself!"

"Enki..." Ishtar took a deep breath. "Enki, it's impossible. Nanoverses cannot be shared."

"I'll find a way," Enki said, and here Ishtar fully saw what she feared in those eyes, the gleam she'd only glimpsed earlier.

Enki, her first friend among humanity, the first human she'd ever trusted, the man who had become the first of the new gods, had gone mad.

"Did the others give this Enki their godstones willingly?"

Enki shook his head. "He had to slay them and claim them. I don't want it to be like that for us, Ishtar. We can be different. You and the others don't need to die." Ishtar could finish the thought for him though, see what he wasn't saying. *But you will if you refuse.* Enki held out his hand. "Give me your nanoverse, Ishtar. If you do, the others will follow."

Ishtar's mind raced. "Not here, Enki." The other god frowned, and Ishtar continued before he did something rash. "You're omnipotent here. The others will never believe I gave it willingly. We have to return to the core world. There I can give it to you with no doubt I did so of my own free will. The others won't question that."

Enki stared at her for a long moment, then nodded. "Of course. We can't have that. But you will?"

Ishtar gave him a smile she hoped did not look forced. "Of course, Enki. It's the only way."

***

"Of course as soon as we were back in the sodding core, I blasted him with everything I had and ran. Found the others. I helped them get away, and then I kept running. It was the beginning of the Dynastic period for Sumer, when it became more secular, since the gods had apparently murdered each other or vanished. I lost track of him for centuries afterwards, and then we ran into each other in the Crusades. He didn't know I was still alive, tried to kill me again. I had to rabbit, and don't see him again until he popped up trying to kill you."

Ryan sat in silence. After collecting her thoughts a bit more, Crystal took a deep breath, shifting her shoulders as ifto get rid of a weight. "Anyway, I think spending so much time in his nanoverse while replaying the whole thing is part of what drove him so mental. So take it as a cautionary tale, love. Your nanoverse isn't your playground, and it can warp you if you let it. Go every couple weeks - anywhere from ten thousand to a couple hundred thousand years local time, depending on how time flowed that period - make sure you prune the dead branches and plant some good soil - but otherwise leave it alone."

"Yeah, will do." He watched her take a few more deep breaths. "The story helped. But are you okay?"

She gave him a smile that came nowhere near her eyes. "Of course I am! Just some old wounds, that's all - they'll fade right quick."

Ryan considered pressing her, but Athena chose that moment to return from her nanoverse journey. Or maybe she'd been back and waiting for the story to end - Ryan could see her doing that.

"How'd things go?" Athena asked, looking at Ryan.

"Ugh. Apparently giving primitive people a bunch of advanced science with no context turns them into assholes, and them being assholes makes you one too." He rolled his eyes.

"I thought that was a possible outcome of your actions. Did you deal with it?"

"Yeah. Why didn't you warn me when I gave them the book?"

Athena looked at Crystal, who gave her a supportive shrug, then back to Ryan. "Some lessons are better learned through experience."

Ryan stared at her. "Athena, what the hell? It was a lesson?"

Athena nodded.

"That's...that's messed up. A lesson learned through experience for me came at the cost of millennia of horror! Hundreds of thousands years of suffering, created because you didn't give me a heads up! We could have stopped that."

Athena shook her head. "Suffering happens, Ryan. A general cannot spend her time worrying about every individual soldier in her army."

"Army?" Ryan recoiled. "Athena, these are real people! They have lives and hopes and dreams! It's *wrong* to just let them suffer like that."

"I suppose," Athena said, but it lacked conviction. Ryan shook his head. He couldn't take the argument any further, or he'd be screaming at Athena. She took it as an opportunity to move on and turned to Crystal. "Any luck with a location for our battle with Enki?"

"Oh yes. Think this is our best bet." She pointed to a spot in the ocean north of Canada, in that huge chunk of islands that made up much of the northern part of the country. "Graham island. About two kilometers across in both directions, home to zero people. Big enough for a proper dust up, yeah? But no innocents in the crossfire."

Athena nodded. "That sounds optimal. So I guess there's naught else to do but prepare our challenge."

Both Ryan and Crystal voiced agreement. "I think it should be me," said Ryan, "to give the challenge, I mean. I think he hates me most, so if I'm the one to call him out, he's likely to respond."

"That also sounds optimal. So, what do you need?"

"Nothing we can get here. Give me a couple hours to draft the message, and then let's give Gail a call."

Ryan headed back into his nanoverse, giving Athena and Crystal time to catch up, and sat down to figure out how to best convince Enki to RSVP to a War.

Chapter 22

Wargames

Enki's staging area was carved from bones, hundreds of leg bones laid together to form a platform, and his command console was composed of skulls that were carved with runes. *And yet he wants to claim heroism,* Bast thought. *He's every bit as gauche as Moloch. And these are your allies.* "Bast! Moloch! So good of you to show up. How's the Eschaton, hmm?" Enki's smile was wide, but Bast noted the way the veins in his forehead bulged, and the red discoloration to his skin.

Bast growled, wondering if she would have to draw weapons. Here in Enki's staging area, they were still on equal footing, but if he dropped it into his nanoverse...*I won't allow that.* She took a moment to observe the layout in case it came down to a fight, to get ready to get between Enki and his control runes. Realizing Enki was going to stare at her expectantly until she gave him what she wanted, she spat out an answer. "He was distracted."

"Gosh gee whiz, Bast, you don't say? You and Moloch, you unleashed an entire army of mummies, and you couldn't kill one little-"

"Enough, Enki." To Bast's surprise, it was Moloch who interrupted the brute. He clenched his rotten teeth with such force Bast had to wonder if they'd snap out of his head. Then he continued. "He arrived before they had a chance to create a city of Manticores for me, else he would have been slain. And the new King of Hell has severed ties with me. We need an advantage, so spare me your recriminations and offer something useful."

"Getting real sick of your shit, Moloch," Enki growled, the fake cheer dropping at meteoric speeds. "I expect some damn initiative from you two. He was *unconscious.*

Athena was completely *drained.* You could have killed them in without breaking a sweat. Why the hell didn't you?"

"We were supposed to distract him. You're holding out, Enki. We want our payment, and we-"

Enki cut her off with a snarl. "I'll give you your shit, Bast, but I'll do it on my own time. Especially since, now, I got some actual work done."

Enki turned and waved, the galaxies moving around them. For a moment, Bast thought they were dropping into his nanoverse, but then realized Enki was showing them an image.

The view resolved on a fleet of ships. Thousands, if not hundreds of thousands. As Bast narrowed her eyes, she could see glimmers even further in the distance - similarly sized fleets. Warships, fighters, cruisers, solar cannons, destroyers - every imaginable type of spaceship. "Impressive, Enki," she commented, glancing at the obscenely proud god. "Impressive, but useless. What point is there to making such an armada in your nanoverse?"

"Maybe if you'd wait a bit, Bast, you'd see. Watch and shut the hell up."

Once this is done, I will kill you. The thought wasn't a threat or a promise, just a realization. Moloch, at least, showed her the respect due to a fellow deity. Enki had gone too far, long ago, and she wouldn't suffer the indignity indefinitely. For now, however, they needed him, so she shut her mouth and watched.

In front of the vessels space began to warp and twist, forming what looked like wormholes - but they were wrong, a fundamental unnaturalness to them that caused the hair on the back of her neck to stand to attention like soldiers. She saw Moloch's eyes widen - he felt it too.

"What abomination is this, Enki?" she asked, feeling sick looking at those gaping holes in reality.

"Oh, just the culmination of five thousand years of work; and that's core world time..." His grin widened as the ships flew through. "Just an invasion."

Moloch spoke here, his normally hoarse voice now carrying a slight tremble. *Is that fear, Moloch? Do you feel it too?* "Invasion of where?"

Enki pulled out a pair of small black orbs. Nanoverses. Only they weren't separate anymore, instead looking like a pair of cells halfway through mitosis. "I finally did it. You two wanted to destroy Týr's nanoverse - I decided conquest was a better option. Two nanoverses are under my domain now."

Bast's heart pounded, and Moloch's face froze. "It's impossible!" she blurted out - not because she didn't believe what her eyes and divine senses were telling her, but out of some desperate hope that denial would undo the truth.

"No, Bast. It's very, very possible. And you both are going to, right here right now, get down on your faces in full on supplication, or I'll kill you and add your nanoverses to my collection." He let them stand there dumbfounded for a few seconds, basking in their expressions, but then those beady eyes narrowed. "Right. Now."

Bast did, and out of the corner of her eye she saw Moloch doing the same. They prostrated themselves the way their worshippers once had before them.

"That's it, right there. That's how it should be. So here's the plan - keep your head down, Moloch, I didn't give you permission to move - we're going to kill Athena, Ishtar, and the Eschaton. I'm going to merge their nanoverses into mine. I'll *be* the Eschaton then. And then, once that's done, we give everyone an option - join or die. If you two haven't pissed me off between now and then, you'll get to stay on the 'join' side. If you have...well, there's always room for more. You may rise and speak now."

Bast did, trying to unclench her jaw as she stood. Moloch, also, seemed to have schooled his expression. "There's still the little matter of our price, Enki." Bast saw his face, saw the veins of rage return, and amended herself before his temper could spiral out at her, "Lord Enki." That, at least, seemed to mollify him.

"Not to worry, Bast. I'll make sure you know where to find what you're looking for if things go to shit in the last fight. I don't know why you want it so badly, but I don't give a shit anymore, because you're my bitch now, and you'll tell me when it's important, right?"

Moloch's nod was a slow motion, while Bast couldn't even manage that, instead baring her teeth in what she hoped was a grin of agreement.

Enki turned his attention to Moloch, as if the nod reminded Enki that Moloch still existed. "Aww, poor little baby-killer. Don't worry Moloch, we're going to wreck that little whore's day so hard she'll be nothing other than an example of why you don't mess with me. We good?"

"Yes," Moloch hissed between rotten teeth, "we are good."

"Good. Now get out of my sight, and make sure you come when called. Go. And find the Eschaton while you're at it!"

They both did, and when they were out of his nanoverse they shared a moment born of pain and humiliation.

Enki had to die. The only things more important than that - the only reasons not to cast their lot with the Eschaton and his guiding goddesses - were getting their promised prizes. *What's that term? Sunk cost Fallacy. But this is important. You can endure a bit longer, Bast.* Moloch's face said the same, and they shared a nod.

"Well, my dear, that was unexpected. Any suggestions how we might find the Eschaton now? I doubt our....no, I can't keep up the pretense when he is not present. I can't imagine that self-important heap of sentient offal will tolerate a delay."

Bast reached into her pocket, which was buzzing. She'd set up some alerts on her phone - guns weren't the only way she embraced modernity. After reading the screen, she showed the headline to Moloch.

Ryan Smith to Enki - "Let's End This." Underneath the headline was a picture of Ryan, and a brief blurb, "Ryan Smith, the alleged Antichrist, has issued a challenge to Enki, calling him out for a final confrontation."

"Should we tell him?"

Moloch thought for a moment. "I need a few hours before I can endure his arrogance again. You?"

"Same. But at least we won't have to wait long."

Soon. They'd both have what they wanted, Ishtar, Athena, and the Eschaton would be unmade - and then, before he could claim their nanoverses, so would Enki.

Chapter 23

Ryan's first impression of Graham island was grey. The sky was grey, the rocks were grey from the smallest pebbles to the largest boulder. Ryan shivered as the cold air hit him. It was a habit - he didn't actually feel uncomfortable, but the air was cold and his body was telling him it was time to shiver. Given that some of the patches between the rocks were filled with ice, his body might have a point. *C'mon, Ryan, it's easier than not breathing.*

Ryan peered up at the clouds hung low over the island as he forced himself to stop shivering. *Maybe we can use the cloud cover to our advantage?* Ryan wasn't sure how best to do so, but there probably wasn't much that could be done there. *Still, should ask Athena or Crystal. If nothing else, at least it sets the mood well.* Ryan shook his head to stop his woolgathering and looked around.

Crystal was already there, standing by her doorway. It clashed with the barren landscape, a single door resting upright in the middle of a field of rocks where no structure had ever stood. Not that his own door looked any less out of place. Crystal was moving her hands and arms while staring at the open air near the shore with an intensity that surprised Ryan. His divine sight informed him of the dozens of equations she was weaving together, equations that governed fluid dynamics and airflow and moved gravity in wild and weird webs.

He saw a few specs flying through the equations. Ants. Apparently in their quest for food, most of an ant colony (awoken from hibernation by the temperature changes Crystal's equations were causing) had wandered across the path of an area of reversed gravity strong enough to rip them off the ground. For a moment, Ryan felt a great deal of empathy for those poor little bastards. They were just going about their business, doing ant things and living ant lives, and all of a sudden forces they couldn't comprehend ripped them up and tossed them about.

"Hey," Ryan said, rubbing his hands together.

She smiled without looking at him, not wanting to take her eyes off her equations. "You can't be cold, love. We had a mud fight on Mars, being cold right now is just your brain thinking it's supposed to be. How'd the challenge go?"

Blushing at the reminder, he tried to ignore the cold, hoping he could override his brain soon. "Well enough. I imagine Enki will be rushing out here for a showdown as soon as he sees it, if we have him pegged right." He twisted an equation of his own, pulling the ant colony out of the gravity web. "Where's Athena?"

"I sent her out for some needed things. Food, drinks, all of that. If the fight ends up being more of a battle, we'll need to be ready for a chance to rest and eat up, yeah?" She twisted a few more equations, each number being chosen with deliberate care, her breathing coming heavier as she did. "And even if it doesn't, I'm going to be Hungry after I finish this."

"Makes sense." He squinted harder at the equations. "Okay, I know you're building some kind of...gravity matrix, I guess? But I can't tell what it does."

Crystal's smile widened. "Give me a moment and I'll show you." She did a few final adjustments, then stretched. "Whew. Be a dear and turn the rock there, there, and there molten, would you? Keep melting it till I tell you to stop."

Bemused, Ryan did as she asked, changing the temperatures to over two thousand degrees. As soon as he did, the molten rock got pulled upwards and began flowing along the gravity channels. "Keep the heat up, love!" she said, sitting back on a rock to catch her breath. "That's about four hours of math right there."

Like how falling dominoes form a portrait, the molten rock quickly took shape. Soon a small castle, complete with a wall and battlements, stood at the end of the island.

Ryan let out a low whistle as Crystal dismissed all but the gravity equations, causing the molten rock to cool as quickly as the arctic air. "Okay, you have got to show me how to do that," Ryan said.

Crystal gave him a thumbs up. "Took me about seven thousand years to master that trick, love, so it'll have to be after this is all done."

"You sure? I could ask Enki to hold off for a few millennia." For the moment, at least, he was warm from the heat radiating off the conjured castle.

Athena chose that moment to return, giving Crystal a knowing grin as she stepped out of her doorway. "Already showing off, Crystal?" Ryan noticed there was a half second hesitation before saying the name - Athena seemed to be struggling a bit more with remembering not to call Crystal Ishtar than she did with not calling him Eschaton. "Had to do your instant castle trick?"

"If you had ever mastered it, love, you know damn well you'd do it every chance you got."

"Granted." Athena hefted a duffle bag - one that looked far heavier than snacks could possibly account for. "I've finished my task. With a bit extra."

"I was wondering why it took you that long to nip off to the corner store," Crystal said, walking over. Athena just handed her a box of cupcakes, which Crystal snatched greedily.

"What else did you get?" Ryan asked, knowing it would be a little while before Crystal had the presence of mind to care.

Instead of answering, Athena unzipped the bag. The top layer was food and bottles of drinks, some alcoholic and some not, as well as playing cards, books, and games. The bottom layer - swords, knives, guns, and bullets. More than enough for the three of them.

"Woah. Why the arsenal?" Ryan asked. Crystal didn't even glance up, currently in baked chocolate heaven.

"During long fights, you might find your weaponry options from your nanoverse change. Best to have some options from the core world if weapons get dropped or broken."

Ryan sat down. "I guess that makes sense." He glanced at the guns, then at the still-cooling castle. "So, this is really it, huh?"

"I should bloody well hope so. Otherwise we just went through a lot of effort for no reason."

Athena nodded. "We issued a challenge, with a location. Enki has to know we'll prepare the island for a battle, and with Moloch on his side Enki will have an army of some conjured horror or another. We, courtesy of the King of Hell, will have an army of demons.

They lapsed into silence for a few minutes. "Hey, since we've got a moment, I've got a question - if we become gods by finding nanoverses, is Zeus actually your father?"

That got a ghost of a smile out of Athena and an actual laugh out of Crystal, who was paying more attention than Ryan had realized. "No, he wasn't. In old times, humans often presumed familial relationships between gods, and we rarely cared enough to correct them. In those times, people would have likely assumed the three of us were siblings, since we all look to be about the same age." She glanced at Crystal, who was still chuckling, and rolled her eyes. "It's part of why so many tales exist of supposedly related gods being...intimate."

"Ah," was all Ryan could say. He had to fight back his own laughter, while turning slightly red at the thought. Athena quirked an eyebrow, then glanced at Crystal. He saw the realization on her face, but not the reaction - if she cared at all, she didn't show it.

"Okay, I'm good enough," said Crystal, standing up and getting her last few chuckles under control. "Ryan, since the deal was with you, be a dear and call up our demon legion. Athena, can you still do that lensing trick? Might be good to know if Enki is here yet."

Athena nodded and began weaving reality. Ryan watched - he'd never really gotten a chance to see Athena work. Every other fight, it had been mostly a melee. There was still math there, but the equations didn't make sense, looking more like random gibberish math written on a board for a movie that wanted a character to look smart.

Guess it's because she's working with elements. Ryan stood up, and raised his arms, focusing on calling up the Legion of Hell. Crystal watched him expectantly. For about thirty seconds he stood there as Athena did her equations. "Uh. So, funny story. The Heresiarch? Didn't exactly tell me how to call up the Legion, and I don't know how to work the weird phone she gave me."

"Oh dear. Well, maybe just...call?"

"Yeah, sure." Ryan rubbed his hands together and threw them out again. "King of Hell! I, Ryan Smith, call upon the Legion thou hast promised! Send them forth!" Silence followed. Crystal coughed, and Athena stopped her mathematics to look at him with a concerned frown.

"Thou hast promised?" Crystal asked, and he could all but hear the smirk in her voice.

Ryan felt himself blush again - not from Crystal's teasing, but from the look Athena was giving him. "It felt right, I guess?"

"Well, maybe you should try aga-"

A pillar of black stone erupted out of the ground, causing them both to jump back. It rose, jutting through stone and ice like the devil's fingertips. Athena dropped to a crouch, drawing her sword, and Ryan stumbled backwards, frantically trying to grab onto the equations to be ready for an attack.

As he did, lightning struck the pillar, a bolt of unnaturally red electricity that defied the natural order of lightning to ignore the castle and instead strike its target. Ryan had to blink to clear his eyes from the flash of light, his heart racing. *C'mon, what the hell is going on?*

His vision cleared just in time to watch as the pillar split down the middle and the two halves began to slide apart. Athena was backing up, and Ryan did the same, readying a bolt of lightning to try and throw at...at whatever was happening. A field of crimson energy formed between the split halves until it was a portal almost twenty feet long.

Demons began to emerge. *Did they have to make such a dramatic entrance?* Ryan thought as his heartbeat slowly returned to normal. The host of fiends were fairly uniform, their skin dark red or deep blue. Each one was well muscled, with large, goat like horns, and tails that ended in little arrowheads. They wore armor of some black metal and carried a variety of weapons; Ryan spotted swords, halberds, and bows.

As they marched forward, the portal drifted away to deposit more, until nearly five hundred soldier demons stood on the rocky island. One of them stepped forward. His armor was more ornate than the others, and he was one of the ten Ryan could see with large, bat-like wings emerging from his back. He bowed to Ryan, and the Legion followed. "Sir. I am Ashtaroth, and my legion and I are ready to serve at your command."

"Oh. Awesome. Uh, you may rise?" They did and looked at him like they were expecting orders. Ryan glanced at Athena and Crystal. Athena had gone back to manipulating equations, and Crystal was grinning.

"Maybe," she said, tapping her finger on her chin like she was deep in thought, "they would like to man the castle and the battlements, yeah?"

Ryan turned to Ashtaroth. "Take your soldiers and man the castle and the battlements. And treat any order given to you by these two as if it came from me."

If Ashtaroth found the exchange amusing, he didn't indicate it, just bowed and began barking orders. The Legion headed out to take their places. From what Ryan could see, it was ten groups of fifty, each one commanded by one of the winged demons. The groups seemed to be segregated by weapon types, with the two archer groups taking the best vantage points.

"Thanks for the save," he muttered to Crystal, who gave him a pat on the shoulder.

"Love, Athena and I were war goddesses, remember? Don't stress about what to do with the army, we've got that covered." Ryan nodded with relief, glad he didn't have to figure out how to command an army of demons.

"Got it," Athena said, drawing their attention to a spot in the air. Ryan saw what she had done - by making solid spots of air and playing with refraction values, she'd created a spot where you could stand and see various sections of the island magnified. "It won't last long," she said, pointing to a spot in the air, "but they're here."

When they stood shoulder-to-shoulder with her, they could see what she saw - Enki, Bast, and Moloch standing on the opposite side of the island. Bast was lounging on a rock, loading her pistols. Enki's back was to the lens as he worked on some twist to reality, a complex one. Moloch was weaving equations, and it looked to Ryan like he was working with actual mathematics. *It's Athena's lensing trick* he realized. *Huh, I can see Moloch's math.* Ryan didn't waste too much time pondering that as Moloch pointed to a spot in the air, and with a chill, Ryan realized they were looking at each other through these lenses.

Enki turned around, grinning and speaking.

"Should we attack now?" Ryan asked. "Before they have backup?"

Athena and Crystal both shook their heads. "They could have their own backup by the time we get there," Athena said.

Crystal gave a murmur of agreement. "We only get one shot at this, love. They're undefended right now, and I know Enki doesn't know how - wait, what?" Hearing her confusion, Ryan focused his attention back on the lens. Molten rock was rising out of the ground, twisting and shaping itself much like Crystal's had - but on a larger scale, and far quicker, the molten stone flowing like water instead of gravy.

"No way," said Crystal, frowning. "No way he did the work that fast. It took me four hours to do the equations - no way is he powerful enough to do that much twisting that quickly!"

"Crystal, what's that mean?"

But Crystal didn't answer right away, still staring in growing shock and fear. Athena spoke for her, after a hard swallow. "It means Enki is far more powerful than he's let on."

At that moment, Enki looked straight up into the lens. Moving with the slow deliberation of one who wants to make absolutely sure you don't miss what's happening, he raised his middle finger, giving enough time to be certain they got a good look at the extended digit. Then, with a twisted grin, he snapped his fingers and caused the lens to shatter.

"He wanted us to see," Crystal muttered. "He wanted us to know how absolutely screwed we are. Which means this has to be new power...somehow, he's gotten stronger."

Ryan let out a long breath. "Look, it doesn't matter. Just means we...we have to out think him! He didn't magically get smarter, right?" They nodded.

"Okay, so..." It was his turn to trail off. "You guys hear that?"

It took a bit, but then they heard it too - the thrumming of helicopters blades. Four of them came into view, each one white and emblazoned with different logos. Of news stations. Ryan groaned.

"There's going to be press here? Why the hell?"

Athena let out a humorless chuckle. "We should have thought of this. Humans have always loved the spectacle of gods at war - that certainly didn't change in the era of twenty-four-hour news cycles."

Ryan rubbed his eyes as Crystal let out a curse. "And we practically invited them," he muttered.

"Oh yes," said Athena. "The whole world is going to watch the first Theomachy in almost a thousand years."

"Anything we can do about that?" Ryan asked, knowing the answer was no - not without trying to forcibly remove them.

Crystal collected herself, and shrugged, "Only thing left to do is give them a show they'll never forget, yeah?"

Ryan and Athena both nodded, and with a growing feeling of dread, they headed into the castle to prepare for war.

***

The sun seeped through the clouds in patches, pockmarking the island with spots that managed to be less dreary than the rest of the landscape. Ryan stood atop the castle. After Athena's lens had been shattered, they'd decided to rely on less detectable means of gathering intel and had gotten a pair of binoculars.

Enki's castle was visible to the naked eye, standing nearly twice as tall as Crystal's - she'd muttered something about overcompensation. Whatever monsters Moloch had summoned were humanoid, though even with the binoculars none of them had been able to make out enough to figure out what kind of humanoids.

"Any movement?" Athena's voice at his side startled a slight jump out of him - he'd been too engrossed in staring at the castle, like he'd manage to peer through those walls somehow, to notice his surroundings.

"Mostly milling about, setting up defenses."

Athena frowned at that. "I believe we have a problem," she said as she bit her lip in thought. "Right now neither side has any incentive to attack the other - we both have fortified positions, and the aggressor would therefore be at a disadvantage. Both sides gain the most from trying to wait out the patience of the other."

Ryan turned it over in his head and realized she was right. "Any idea how to break the stalemate?" he asked, hoping she could give him something to work with.

Athena shook her head. "Normally I'd try throwing some of our power at them, but I believe - until we know the source of his power - it's best we simply wait to defend against his effort to do the same."

Much as he wished he could, Ryan couldn't find a hole in that logic. They had to be reactionary right now, and with Enki not taking any action to react to, they really only had the option of waiting. "We stick to the plan then. After all, it's the first time we've had one that wasn't just 'find them and have a big fight'."

Athena nodded. The island had been prepared for their battle before the challenge was issued - they'd only waited on the castle to create the appearance they were just arriving.

Explosive charges were hidden throughout to give them detonations they could trigger with minimal power. Pits had been dug, filled with spikes, and then carefully hidden. Caches of food, weapons, and supplies were hidden in case they got stranded. Athena had created several alcoves where troops could hide for ambush. Graham Island had become a death trap and only they knew where everything was. Enki's newfound powers would make the fight harder, but they at least had home field advantage - or something like it.

"There's got to be something else we can do," he muttered, as much to himself as to Athena.

"Well...I suppose we could risk trying to provoke an action out of him somehow. Step off the battlements, make a probing attack. But those carry their own risks."

Ryan nodded glumly, chewing it over with the intensity of a dog with a particularly large chunk of peanut butter. "Wait. No, I think I've got it."

Athena raised an eyebrow, but Ryan was already twisting the laws governing echoes. "Get ready, and tell Crystal and Ashtaroth to do the same. Enki's about to throw something big our way." Athena nodded and headed down the stairs.

Once he was done, Ryan spoke carefully, calmly. *Tick him off, Ryan, and make sure you don't sound desperate.* "Hey, Enki, what's the hold up?"

The response was immediate, the same twisting Ryan had done to get the message to Enki but amplified even further - so much so it was less of a voice Ryan heard, but a physical force pressing down on him. "I'm looking forward to you finally being dead, you little shit."

Ryan laughed, with more amusement than he felt. "Big talk, Enki, but so far you're not doing well. Our first fight I was still brand new to this, you sucker punched us, and you still lost. Second fight, you ran and hid like a bitch for the whole thing and let your lackeys clean it up. This time? I don't like your odds."

Ryan could almost see Enki, the veins bulging out of his face and his mean little eyes narrowing to hateful specs. "You think I can't end you? Have you been paying attention to anything that's happened since I got here?"

"Yeah, I have," Ryan retorted, and he realized Crystal had given him the barb that would force Enki to action. "And I know why you're holding back. You just realized that since no one on our side needs to breathe, you won't have drowning everyone as a fallback when you start losing. I mean, that's what you do, right?"

Enki blew apart the equation Ryan had set up to allow the echo to carry. Ryan grasped for the binoculars and pulled them up, waiting to see what Enki was going to do about his taunt. On top of the battlements, he could see the stocky man manipulating the fundamental forces of the universe. *Okay, good, you got him ticked off enough to attack, now what's he doing...oh god I know that math.*

No time to think. Ryan leapt from the top of the castle, lowering the gravitational constant on himself so he'd hit the ground gently.

And not a moment too soon. Enki sent, in half the time Týr had needed, a bolt of pure sunlight lancing out of the sky. It blew the clouds away in a ring, punched through the entire castle from top to bottom, and bored into the Earth beneath it. Crystal and Athena were already changing the rules governing heat transfer to keep the damage localized, but it had been a close strike.

From Enki's side came a horn, and the sound of movement. Ryan ran over to Crystal and Athena, nervous sweat beading his brow where it froze into a frost crown. "I think I managed to get him to come our way!"

They both gaped at him, then at the castle. Thankfully the beam hadn't destroyed the walls, just punched a hole from roof to floor. "What the bloody hell did you do?" Crystal looked aghast.

"I taunted him. He's such a sensitive soul, apparently. And he's coming our way."

Needing no further motivation, the two women leapt to the top of the wall, and Ryan followed, putting the binoculars back to his eyes. Enki's army was on the march, with Enki and Bast at the head. He didn't see Moloch, but given Moloch's modus operandi so far, he was likely staying in the castle and watching. Ryan waited and watched until he could start making out more detail on the soldiers, then handed the binoculars to Crystal. "Any idea what he has with them?" They looked fairly human, clad in armor and carrying medieval weapons, but Ryan could now see they had two golden irises in each overly large eye, and what he'd first thought were fur coverings on their arms and legs were now clearly their actual fur.

She focused for a moment and then swore. "They're varcolaci."

Athena muttered a curse as well.

"What's a varcolac?" Ryan asked, squinting - like that would help. But there were some habits that didn't die easy, and one of them were absolutely futile gestures like thinking that narrowing your eyes would magnify your sight somehow.

"Bloody Romanian monsters," Crystal said, sweeping the binoculars over the group. "Worst parts of vampires and werewolves rolled together into one nice little ball of hate."

Ryan glanced at the army of demons that were readying bows. "How do they stack up against our troops?"

"No idea," she said, handing the binoculars to Athena. "Never heard of varcolaci and demons fighting. Any ideas, love?"

Athena took a minute or two to study the forces herself. "I think Enki's looking for you, Ryan. Whatever you said must have really struck a nerve."

"I reminded him of how he had to use the nuclear option against his own people."

Crystal let out a low whistle and Athena replied, "That would explain it. Given how powerful he is, we need to devote our attention to countering him. Bast...Bast can wait, let the demons keep her busy."

Then Enki launched himself at them, flying the length of the island far ahead of his army.

Headed straight for Ryan.

Ryan began tweaking equations as Enki approached, his heart pounding. He reached into his nanoverse, pulling out the strongest weapon he could find to meet the charging deity.

He pulled out a pointed stick. His eyes came off Enki so he could gape at it, realizing as he did that the stick wasn't even all that pointy – it just ended in a vague suggestion of a point. The kind of stick parents would tell their kids not to run while holding, but not worry about enough to get up and try and take it from them.

Oh, come on!

It was the worst possible time to realize he'd forgotten to get a replacement sword from his nanoverse.

Enki was almost on top of him, and Ryan raised the stick with every bit of defiance he could muster.

Chapter 24

To Ryan's complete and utter lack of surprise, Enki completely ignored the stick. Instead, one of those massive hands came down and grabbed Ryan by the face. He felt something in his neck wrench - probably from the force of having his face clutched by two-hundred and fifty pounds of enraged deity travelling at over a hundred miles per hour.

He heard Athena or Crystal - the combination of hand covering his face and sudden increase in velocity made it hard to tell which - shout his name. Ryan reached up to scrabble at Enki's arm, but he might as well have been trying to tear down a tree with his bare hands. Enki changed course, and Ryan winced as his neck strained at the whiplash. *If he keeps this up he's going to break your neck.* Ryan renewed his attacks on Enki's arm, beating it with his fists. He felt like a small child trying to punch a gorilla. *If I can get in and hit him somewhere weaker than his goddamn arm, I'll have a shot at breaking free.*

He attempted that, swinging wildly, but those long arms were too much. Ryan couldn't manage to get his fists close enough to Enki to land a blow. Switching tactics, Ryan tried to focus on some way to use his powers to break the hold, but the crushing grip was a distraction he couldn't push past, and the lack of vision meant all his divine sight could see were the equations governing Enki's grip on his face.

A sudden pain stopped all attempts at rational escape. Enki had slammed the back of Ryan's head into the ground, and planning went out the window as spikes of red hot pain flashed across his vision. Part of Ryan was aware that Enki hadn't just planted him in the dirt, though.

Instead he maintained their flight as he dragged the back of Ryan's skull through stone and ice and dirt.

Overwhelming panic kicked in. If Ryan didn't get out of this soon, he was acutely aware that his skull would shatter from the repeated impacts.

Thinking through the pain and fear was near impossible, so instinct had to take over. Ryan kicked upwards. To his relief, he felt his foot impact something. Whatever it was, the blow had enough power to get Enki's grip to loosen. For a wonderful moment, Ryan's vision was freed of sweaty palm, and the blissful sight of the gray Canadian sky filled his vision - but then that was obscured by Enki's leering visage. A pair of massive hands closed around Ryan's throat.

"I'm going to tear your head off, you little shitstain."

"Aghrk!" Ryan retorted, displaying the same rapier wit that had gotten him into this mess in the first place.

"Not so clever now, are you, huh?" The veins in Enki's head were bulging, his eyes were bloodshot, and his spit was literally spraying Ryan's face as he screamed. "What's the matter, you little *bitch*?"

"Gaaark," Ryan explained, which did not satisfy Enki. Ryan's vision started swimming as Enki's hands got tighter. *Wait, I don't need to breathe. Why am I blacking out?* It was an unimportant riddle at the moment, and the throbbing in his skull didn't provide an answer beyond a reminder that figuring out why was less important than figuring out how to stop it.

"And the best part? The absolutely best part?" Enki leaned in ever closer, and for one mad moment Ryan considered kissing him, seeing if the threat to Enki's masculinity would be enough to get him to toss Ryan away. Much to Ryan's combined joy and regret, Enki didn't get quite close enough to make that a viable option.

"Caaghwr," was the best response Ryan could muster. He was kicking at Enki, digging his nails into those massive forearms, but whatever had empowered Enki so much was also protecting him from Ryan's increasingly feeble blows.

"I saw you pull that stick out of your nanoverse. Once I'm done killing you, it's going to be a complete joke to take over. Your people have *nothing* that could stop me." Enki bared his teeth, the smile a cat might give a cornered mouse. "Got any more clever comebacks? Anymore witty little barbs?"

Ryan didn't bother making a noise, seeing that the triple-threat of "aghrk, gaaark, caaghwr" had thus far not impressed. Instead his mind was racing as he tried to find the energy to struggle harder. Ryan stopped trying to attack Enki directly, reaching around him for something he could grab onto. A weapon. Maybe a rock or a shard of ice or…

…or that damned stick. His fingers closed around it, and it didn't take any great tactical genius to figure out exactly what he should do with it.

There are some habits that, no matter how long you were not truly mortal, you never could break. You would still get goosebumps in the cold, you would still sneeze if your nose was irritated, and no matter what, you would clutch at the injury if a piece of wood - even if it was only slightly pointed - got rammed into your eye.

Enki's hands flew off Ryan's throat and grasped at his eye. Red liquid began to flow through those meaty digits when the pointed stick fell out. While the stab did have the effect of getting Enki to stop choking him, Ryan's vision didn't clear fast enough to take advantage of the injury. Instead, Enki backhanded him, sending him airborne and bouncing across the rocks and ice of Graham Island.

Okay, this buys you time to OH GOD! Ryan rolled at the last second as Enki's feet abruptly occupied the space where his head as been a moment before. "You're dead, Eschaton!" Enki screamed, stomping again as Ryan rolled frantically. "Do you hear me!?" Each stomp cracked stone and ice, sending tremors through the ground. Ryan tried not to think about what they would do to his skull. Instead, a twist of Ryan's wrist changed a simple equation, and the friction of the stone Enki was using to support his non-stomping foot vanished. Enki joined him on the ground.

Ryan didn't bother trying to get up, not with Enki close enough to again wrap his hand around Ryan's neck again. Instead of trying to get away, Ryan rolled on top of Enki, driving the slightly pointed wood down towards Enki's remaining good eye. Enki's hands came up, catching Ryan's wrists, but now gravity was on Ryan's side, and he bore down as hard as he could.

For an eternity, the two of them were locked in that pose, Ryan using every bit of leverage and weight he could muster to drive the stick towards Enki's eye, and Enki bringing all his strength to bear on stopping him. Then, slowly, inch by agonizing inch, the stick started moving - upwards, away from Enki.

No. No no no. Ryan tried to find some more strength, and Enki saw the panic in Ryan's eyes, saw the fear growing...and he grinned. At the end of the day, Enki was stronger than Ryan, by just enough where this struggle was going to be a loss.

"You see it too, huh?" Enki's voice was low, intense. "You know you can't win. As soon as I push this away, you die."

Ryan's muscles were already strained to their limit. He wanted desperately to bring more to bear, to find the strength in him somehow - but it didn't exist. He didn't know if he had it him to even manage to twist an equation, but he was certain that if he could, it would not be enough to make a difference.

Then, out of the corner of his eye, he spotted them. Ants. Maybe they were the same ants he'd saved from the lava earlier, or maybe they were a different colony disturbed by the battle taking place on their home. They were marching towards them, a single file line hunting for food.

As the stick slipped more, Ryan made a twist with the last of his strength. A tiny, minor change. But the ants responded to it, and soon were marching up Enki's face - and towards the pheromones now coming from Enki's eye.

The first ant to crawl onto Enki's eyeball was distraction enough. Enki's strength slipped. Not enough for Ryan to blind him, but enough for him to shatter the wooden stick against Enki's forehead, drawing a shallow cut in the process. Enki's massive hands, freed from trying to fight against the stick, came up and he clapped Ryan's skull, with enough force to set his entire head ringing, and then he grabbed Ryan by the ear and flung him back towards the castle.

Ryan hit the wall with his back, hard enough to crack the stone. As he tumbled down, sliding towards unconsciousness from the injuries, he could only hope Athena and Crystal were faring better.

And that they'd get to him before Enki finished the job.

✳✳✳

"Ryan!" Crystal shouted as Enki's hand enveloped Ryan's face. Enki flew off with Ryan, circling back towards his own castle. Athena glanced at her, then back at the oncoming army.

"Go!" Athena said to Crystal, "I'll hold them here!"

Crystal gave a single curt nod and took off running after the flying pair, swinging her path wide to move around the varcolac army.

Sending Crystal was a tactical decision, Athena told herself. *She is older and more experienced - both in general and in terms of knowing how to deal with Enki.* She almost convinced herself of that - but then she saw Bast again and felt her teeth clench. *You did not send Crystal to assist Ryan because you want to make sure that evil bitch dies. You have a war to fight.*

Athena hated the modern concept of war. Soldiers on either side with weapons that could kill for miles, robots being commanded by people half a continent away, planes that could be miles away before their targets had even died. It was messy and indiscriminate and, she admitted to herself, she was bad at it. She respected modern soldiers – they faced weapons that would have made the most disciplined troops of the ancient world cower in terror - but the last time Athena had participated in a war, the biggest military advancement was Byzantine fire.

Athena sneered at the memory of the uses that had been put to. *I'm glad I destroyed the records of its creation.*

Ares was the one who reveled in the death and destruction of war. Athena had always been more at home in the elegant beauty of tactics, the individual honors soldiers could earn, and outsmarting your adversary.

A war between gods, a proper theomachy? This was her home. It was her place to lead the troops.

And you want to make sure that evil bitch dies.

She surveyed the island through the binoculars. Graham Island had been chosen, in part, because its terrain offered plenty of chances for one side to gain the upper hand, but no spots where either side could have gained an unbeatable edge. Ridges, hills, a frozen river, and patches of ice a mile or two across. All of these she could use.

Then again, so could Bast. The woman was leading the varcolaci army out from their castle. Athena clenched her fists. *Easy, Athena. Calm. War is not won with passion and rage. Do not fall victim to it.* Easier said than done, but she knew that she had to put aside her hatred for now. Anger was like the Greek fire – if not used carefully, it would consume the wielder and anyone near her, friend or foe.

"Get your troops ready to move out, but await my command," Athena murmured to Ashtaroth. "Leave a detachment of archers. Have the others sheath their swords and draw spear and shield." The sword was a fine weapon for solo combat, in Athena's opinion. It also was a liability on the battlefield. Swords inspired soldiers to seek individual glory. Swords were meant to be used when order had fallen apart and organization had failed.

He frowned. "Ma'am, begging your pardon, but if they mean an assault – we are behind the walls right now. We hold an advantage."

Athena shook her head. "I know little of varcolaci, but one thing I do know is that they are expert climbers. The castle is a fall back point if we are losing on the field."

Ashtaroth nodded. "As you wish."

Athena watched while the demon barked orders. Bast's troops carried no weapons but now that Athena could see them better, she saw they had little need. They were huge, easily a head taller than Athena, and while they looked mostly human their hands ended in long, straight claws. Right now, they seemed to be prepared for literal hand-to-hand combat. A plan began to form. *What I wouldn't give for cavalry right now.* Their forces were roughly equal in numbers, and all infantry on both sides. Some good, solid horses could turn the tide of battle.

Might as well wish for elephants.

Athena took a deep breath. It was time to do something, time to move.

It was time to go to war again.

***

The demons were waiting for her, arranged as she had ordered. "Form a single column, five deep."

For a moment, Athena considered giving them an inspiring speech, but these were *demons.* They didn't need inspiration, they needed spilled blood.

Well, I can certainly give them that.

"Behind me. You know the plan! Stick to it and victory is assured. Now - Charge!"

Athena raised her sword and led the assault, twisting reality as she did. She formed a cone of air in front of her, an artificial shockwave that moved with her footsteps. Behind her she heard the sound of hundreds of demonic hooves, all of them straining to keep pace with her stride.

Bast's army of varcolaci stopped. The beast-men began to howl like wolves, a battle cry that cut deep through Athena's logic and reason and reached straight into the part of her brain that, thousands of years ago, had still just been human and had known that sound meant death was coming. Bast was shouting orders to them, but over the din of Athena's demons it was impossible to make out what she was saying. It didn't matter. Right now all that mattered was the charge.

Ashtaroth was beside her. As they closed in on the battle, the polite, quiet, obedient demon she'd known up until then began to fade away. His eyes burned with hellfire, and his face was contorted in a savage grin. He met the varcolaci roars with a scream of his own, and it sounded like the screams of the damned. Other demons picked up the sound, until the island was filled with both the howls of wolves and demonic screeching.

The varcolaci began to bunch up. Athena did not give her demons the order to break ranks, to form up into a unified line. Instead they were a spearhead, aimed directly at the center of the varcolaci mass.

Bast was smirking. *She thinks I've lost my edge, that I'm committing my troops to a suicide run.*

Bast would have been right, if Athena's plan had been a head on charge. Those kind of tactics were the things born of Hollywood. The grand melee looked great on film, but in reality, it just meant chaos. Real warfare depended on strategy, tactics, and discipline.

"Archers!" Athena shouted. Those demons, roughly half her army, stopped moving, and began to redeploy to open fire. "Volley!"

Demonic arrows arched into the air in single mass. They trailed black smoke behind them, and they struck the varcolaci like a mass of swarming bees.

Athena saw them hit, saw the enemy stumble to their knees - and then saw them get up. As she watched, one of the varcolaci pulled an arrow out of his flesh. Another had one punched through his eye and he left it there. Bast gave the order to charge, and the surge of monsters ran to meet the army of demons.

Every pounding footstep brought Athena closer, and just before she reached the front of the varcolaci army, she dropped her twist. The air she had bunched in front of her slammed into the varcolaci, even bowling some over.

At the same time, she and her army vanished.

"No!" Bast screamed, realizing too late what had happened.

One hundred yards to the east of the dropped illusion, the actual thrust of demons, with Athena still at its head, rushed forward. Athena's column pushed around the Varcolaci flank. At the same time, the archers threw down their bows to meet the foe with blades drawn. The varcolaci started to wheel to face Athena's forces.

Then she snapped her fingers and the ground erupted under the enemy's feet.

The combination of explosions and a broken formation meant the varcolaci were already falling into disarray, and her troops' spearhead formation allowed Athena to push past the monsters and face her real target.

Demons and monsters both could kill gods. But if only one side had a god, that side would hold the real advantage.

Athena charged straight for Bast, who raised her pistols in defiance. Shots rang out. Athena dodged to the side, zig-zagging erratically, making herself a harder target. Then they were in melee. Athena's sword flashed down, but Bast blocked it with her right pistol, bringing the left in an arc towards Athena's face. A quick flick of Athena's sword and the left-hand pistol's shot went wild, but that gave Bast a chance to bring the right one back in line for a shot...

Athena knew she couldn't make a mistake here. If she could deflect every shot for just a bit, Bast would have to reload. But if she missed even one, it would be the end of her.

Steel rang against steel, each time just a fraction of a second before the report of gunfire. Athena's ears started to ring from the sound even when there was no clash of metal, but she pushed that aside, ignoring everything but Bast's eyes and guns, until, finally - *click*.

The moment the guns clicked empty, Athena brought her sword in towards Bast's neck. The other woman jerked her head back and tossed the guns aside. Now she was on the defensive, dodging and weaving between Athena's blows.

"If I didn't know better, Athena, I'd think you'd taken me stabbing you in the back and shooting your boyfriend in head personally." Despite being forced back with every strike, Bast was grinning. "But then again, you don't have feelings, do you?"

Athena didn't rise to the bait, instead keeping her assault up. But Bast had the reflexes to back up her cat-like reputation, and Athena found herself menacing only air with each blow.

Stars of Olympus, she's fast! Athena spun around as Bast landed behind her, her sword out for a wide strike. Bast leaned back under the blow, springing up to fire two rounds at Athena. It was an effort to roll away before Bast could pull the triggers, and one of the bullets grazed Athena's cheek. She winced at the pain but was too wrapped up in the movement to even flinch.

Instead, Athena continued the roll, coming up on Bast's side. Athena lashed out with her blade in a quick thrust, but Bast was already moving, jumping over the blade with an easy grace, high enough that Athena couldn't redirect the sword. The next two bullets almost struck home. Athena had been too off balance to dodge - if Bast had opted for something less showy than a backflip, she might have managed to put some rounds into Athena.

This won't just be settled with flesh and steel, Athena realized, and she twisted her hand, trying to impede Bast's movements - but the other woman was able to focus entirely on her protection, and she countered, undoing the changes to reality as quickly as Athena wove them. Their fight had taken them out of the bulk of the army. Bast flipped away, getting enough clear space to reach into her nanoverse and pull out a sword of her own.

To her side, in the corner of her eye, Athena could see a pair of Varcolaci that had leapt over the demons' lines tear into one of her soldiers. Ashtaroth was suddenly there in a flash of hellfire, slicing into the enemy. *Ignore it, Athena. You have your own battle.*

Now the ringing returned as Bast began to parry Athena's blows, and Athena had to return the favor. They were evenly matched in this - at least, as long as Bast kept backing away. *Eventually you'll run out of space. Eventually I will get you.*

"You didn't even flinch when I shot him in the head. Barely even blinked when his brains splattered across the street. Did he really mean nothing to you? Or are you just a sociopath?"

"Shut. Up." Athena hated letting even that slip, but the woman's barbs were beginning to land.

"Oh, you can speak! Lovely." Bast brought her sword down in an overhead blow that Athena deflected, giving her an opening to kick Bast in the gut and - for a moment - silence her. Athena tried to take advantage of the blow but Bast was already twisting away.

"Were you lovers? You two had been travelling together for so long, and-" whatever Bast was about to say was cut off by a grunt of pain as Athena landed a blow, slicing a six-inch furrow in Bast's bicep.

Bast again flipped away to get more distance between them, her free hand going over to injury to stem the red flow. She hissed in pain. "I'm glad you slipped past the varcolaci," Bast said, ducking under another blow. Her eyes flashed in a combination of anger and pain. "Makes this personal. This is between you and me."

Athena didn't care. She'd drawn first blood, Bast had dropped her guard, and she readied herself to finally land a killing blow...

Before Athena could bring the sword down, the ground erupted beneath her feet. Athena was thrown backwards, landing on the stony ground hard enough to send a jolt of agony through her back. Athena did her best to push down the pain and roll away from the source of the disturbance as a massive serpent came out into the open. Its scales were pale green, and its two clawed hands were large enough to wrap around Athena in a single grab. *No, no no no. Please don't let that thing be what I think it is.* It was a lindworm, that much Athena was sure of. What terrified her wasn't the ferocity of the beast or the threat it posed - both of which she knew were considerable - but what it might mean.

The serpent hissed in fury as Athena scrambled to her feet, which felt suddenly heavy with dread.

"Well," said Bast, her grin returning, "between you and me and Týr. Say hi to Athena, Týr!"

Athena's heart dropped. *Týr...* The lindworm was all was left of him. Athena had known she'd lost him, but...but this was proof. Ever since the Empyrean Provocation, a small part of her had hoped that Uzeme was right. That Týr had been allowed to resurrect and was being held captive, that she could show up after this was all done and free him. They'd have a good laugh about it.

But now that the Lindworm was here, Athena had proof that would never happen. She'd never see Týr again. All that was left was this monster that was a defilement of everything Týr had ever cared about.

The lindworm reared back and opened its jaws. For a moment, grief held Athena in place as she watched it prepare to unleash whatever substance it could muster. Unlike dragons, lindworms did not breathe fire - instead, it spat a line of acid at Athena. *Move it, soldier!* Athena snapped at herself. *The living still rely on you.* The thought almost came too late - she had to scramble in a rush out of the way, diving behind a boulder large enough to shield her as the acid splashed where she had just been standing.

"Aww, I think he missed you," Bast taunted, reaching into her nanoverse to pull out a fresh pistol. Athena was glad to see that the injured arm hung limply at Bast's side - she must have cut the muscle badly. Just not enough to get Bast to cease her endless prattle. "Since you're about to die, any last words you want to say to your ex?"

Athena could smell and hear the rock dissolving under the acidic spray of the Lindworm that had been Týr.

"No," Athena said, loudly enough for Bast to hear. "My *friend* is dead. I have nothing to say to the abomination that was spawned from him."

"Pity, that. Oh well," Athena could hear Bast cocking the pistol, "guess it's time for you to die, then."

***

"Go!" Athena said, much to Crystal's relief. "I'll hold them here!"

She didn't waste any time, giving Athena only a quick nod and bolting off after Ryan. *Athena can hold her own against Bast. As strong as Enki is, he'll bloody kill Ryan if I don't get there.*

For a moment, Crystal considered taking off flying after Enki. The act of flying was fairly simple for anyone who'd finished apotheosis - once your brain wrapped itself around the fact that you could fly, it was easy to figure out how to do so, but it was a massive drain of power - one that Enki could apparently afford. *Or he's gone absolutely mad.* She dearly hoped for the latter - if he wasn't as strong as he seemed, he'd burn himself out before he could do too much harm.

If she wanted to, flying fast enough to catch up to them in time to save Ryan's life would be easy. However, she wouldn't have anywhere near the strength to pull off the rescue when she got there. *Just have to hope Ryan can hold on.*

She had to swing wide to avoid the varcolaci, but a few of them broke off from the main army to follow. "Oh come off it!" she shouted over her shoulder. "I don't want to deal with you wankers!"

Unfortunately, it would take more than the most British insult she knew to discourage her attackers. Annoyed, she reached into her nanoverse for weaponry. *And it won't be a bloody stick. Poor bastard.* She drew out a pair of short swords and kept running, waiting for the swifter monsters to catch up to her.

After a few seconds, the first one did, leaping into the air with an animalistic snarl. Crystal leapt to the side as it landed, swinging her sword. It bit into the varcolac's neck, and Crystal found herself down a foe. As much as the quick victory elated her, it also stopped her forward momentum, allowing the other four to close the gap between them.

"Come on, then, loves. Who wants to die next?" She grinned, hiding the pounding she felt in her chest. The delay was taking too long, she wouldn't get to Ryan in time...

As the varcolaci closed back in, she realized the problem was time. She didn't have enough of it, not with Ryan facing off against Enki. Varcolaci were not things to trifle with - she'd seen them tear apart gods before. If she took too long, by the time she dealt with them Ryan would be dead. As much as she wanted to save her energy, she had to burn some power. *Even then, it might not be enough.*

Then the time for fear had passed.

She ducked under a narrow strike from a varcolac sword. Instead of dodging back into the waiting strike of another, she pushed forward, tackling the varcolac. Her momentum caught it off guard, and they went tumbling to the dirt. Crystal raised her sword to bring it down on her opponent's head, but the other varcolaci were ready. A sword sliced across her back. Crystal hissed in pain and rolled off the one she had tackled. Her foot lashed out in a kick, a blow that shattered something in the thing's leg. She got a howl of pain for her effort, which made her grin savagely.

Unfortunately, that kick meant she was still on the ground when the other one dove in. Crystal brought her blade up to parry the overhand blow. They stood there for a moment, Varcolaci sword bearing down on her face. She could feel herself bleeding into the ground. *No.* Crystal began to push back, as hard as she could. "I am not some...petty mortal prey..." she hissed.

The uninjured Varcolaci came around the side and lashed out at Crystal's wrists. At the same time, she kicked up at the one over her, sending it flying back. The newest strike still managed to bite into her arms, but she moved away enough that it was a shallow slice.

Her blade still almost slipped from her fingers. She held onto it and leapt away from her attackers, forcing them to charge her again.

Oh damnit, the third one's already back up. Whatever she had done to it, it had healed before she could do anything more. *Not enough time. Time's the problem.* She smiled at her opponents as she realized that it also could be the solution and twisted an equation.

Time dilation was a nasty side effect of trying to travel close to the speed of light. The closer you got, the slower time passed for an outside observer. If you got close to the speed of light, the rate of time got close to zero. Crystal took that equation in a small area surrounding the varcolaci and removed the speed of light, replacing the blistering pace of 299,792,458 m/s with a much more sedate 1 cm/year.

The result? Each varcolac froze in place, unable to move even an inch. If they were gods, they could have undone the effect in a matter of seconds - a temporary inconvenience at worst. Since they were not, however, they would remain frozen until the edit she made was corrected.

I...am really bloody glad that worked, she thought, though she didn't take any time to admire her handiwork. Her back was bleeding from the shallow cut, her wrists were aching from their own slice, and Ryan was still in danger. She took off again, headed towards where she had seen Enki and Ryan impact the ground.

As she drew closer, she heard the most beautiful sound that ever could have reached her ears - Enki letting out a bellow of pain. Ryan was still alive and still in the fight. Unfortunately, before she could get much further she saw Ryan's limp body go airborne, where it impacted the wall of Enki's castle with enough force to crack the stones before Ryan collapsed to the ground.

She saw Enki take to the air to follow Ryan. *Screw it.* At this point, it wouldn't matter how weak she was - now speed was the only thing that mattered. She took off, changing the direction and strength gravity pulled her to variables she could alter at her whim. Her swords were held before her, and she silently begged the universe for Enki to be caught unaware, so she could just impale him and be done with it.

The universe heard her plea and decided that she could just sod off. Enki twisted out of the way at the last second, and while Crystal was able to get a good slice off, it didn't have anywhere near the stopping power she had hoped for.

"Well well well, Ishtar! So glad you could join us! Was worried no one was going to get to see me tear the Eschaton to little pieces."

Crystal arrested her flight, zeroing out gravity's pull so she could float across from Enki. "Come off it, love, you're better than these lame taunts."

Enki snarled. It had an interesting effect on his face, with one eye fully gouged out. *Guess I know why he screamed now, yeah?* "I am not the villain here, *Ishtar*," he spat, infusing her name with more venom than she'd ever heard from him. "I'm going to *save* the world from you! I'm the goddamn hero!"

"You damn idiot! If you kill Ryan, the bloody sun explodes. There won't be a world to save!" Crystal knew they were both stalling for time. She was hoping Ryan would get up to turn this into a two on one. Enki was probably hoping she'd wear herself out with the mid-air banter.

The snarl that had crossed Enki's face earlier turned into a smile. "You don't know a thing, not a single thing. You could have been a part of it, Ishtar. You didn't have to work with the Eschaton." His voice was almost soft.

"No, Enki. I can't watch the world burn." She glanced down. Ryan was wasn't moving, and she was going to wear herself out. Stalling wasn't an option anymore.

"You wouldn't have to. I figured out a way to merge nanoverses. Ishtar, I did it! I can save *everyone.* Once I've merged enough nanoverses, we won't need an Eschaton. I can hold back the sun!"

For a moment Crystal was Ishtar again, back in Enki's staging area, Enki's hand outstretched asking for her nanoverse. She saw in his eyes that same madness and the same hope she had seen then.

"No, Enki, you can't. You never could."

"Don't you see?" Enki bellowed. "I'm thrashing this little punk. I'll tear you apart. I can merge nanoverses, I have the power I need."

"That's not what I meant, Enki." Crystal took a deep breath and readied her sword. "Your plan only works if you slaughter enough people. It always had that flaw, the one flaw you couldn't see. Týr is dead. Your merger kills gods. Probably the people in the nanoverse, too. No matter what, your plan is just another Deluge."

Enki howled in rage, and Crystal hurled herself at him, bringing her sword around in a wide arc aimed at Enki's neck.

She expected him to dodge, or maybe even pull something out of his own nanoverse and parry. She didn't expect him to just raise his hand, catching the blade like it was plastic. A thin line of blood came from his fist, but it was obvious that it didn't bite his skin as deeply as it needed to.

"Dumb move, bitch," he growled, bringing his hand up in what would be a devastating blow, but Crystal was already moving away, dropping to the ground. *No point to meeting him in the air anymore, he holds the edge there. How did he get so bloody strong?* In the distance, she heard something let out a horrible roar. *Athena!*

No time to worry about her. Enki slammed into the ground feet first, only inches away from crushing Crystal. She was able to dance out of the way, but the impact still left a crater where she had stood. "You lost! Just admit it and *die* already!" He threw out his hand towards her, sending a gale of wind hurtling her way. She stuck her sword into an ice patch and held on.

Enki's windstorm struck her with the force of a tornado. She felt her fingers start to slip on the hilt and thrust her other hand forward to get a better grip. It was a short sword, meant to be wielded with one hand. It didn't offer much room to grab it. She clutched at the cross guard, letting the blade bite into her fingers a bit. The wind stripped up rocks and sent them hurtling at her. One struck Crystal on the shoulder, another on the forehead. Each blow almost broke her hold on the sword, but she managed to stay safely anchored.

Although the sword anchored her, it opened her up to a new attack. With his hand still outstretched to buffet

her with wind, Enki brought down his other hand, and a
bolt of lightning leapt from the clouds to strike her. Crystal
gritted her teeth as lightning coursed through her and into
the ground through the sword. He brought down his hand
again, and another bolt struck her. She heard someone
screaming. She knew it was her.

"Just. Die!" This time the lightning didn't vanish
immediately, but struck and continued to pulse energy.
She could smell her skin burning, feel lines of agony racing
through every inch of her body. The small part of her brain
that wasn't consumed with pain offered up one small
thought.

This can't be how it ends!

Crystal clenched her fists. She had come so close, so
goddamn close. A million of years of waiting. A million
years of fighting and holding on to some shred of sanity. A
million years, all to get up to the finish line. The end in
sight. The Eschaton was found, the end was coming. *I was
going to do better! I wasn't going to let it happen again!*

And now she was going to die under Enki's lightning.
Crystal tried to force her legs to respond, tried to push her
way to her feet. Something, anything. Some way to fight
back. But Enki's assault was relentless. The electricity
didn't let up, and as it coursed through her body her
muscles would not respond.

Already she could feel the skin on her hands and feet
start to char. Crystal screamed, a sound of agony and rage
and despair. She had come so close. This *couldn't* be how it
ended.

She was still screaming when the lightning stopped.
She was momentarily deafened as thunder rumbled around
her. She blinked her eyes, barely able to see. Enki stared
at his arm. Or what was left of it. It ended at the elbow in a
charred stump. Shock wore off, and Enki howled in pain.
Clutching at the stump, Enki leapt into the air again. Not to
attack, this time, but retreating into his castle.

Crystal glanced over her shoulder. Ryan had risen
slightly off the ground, his own arm outstretched. By the
equations that were dissipating, it looked like he'd pulled all

the heat from the lightning to a single point, centered on Enki's elbow.

Bless you, Ryan.

"We need to..." she gasped, her mouth full of copper. "We need to follow. We have...to finish him."

Ryan shook his head and said two words. "Moloch. Athena."

Crystal's brain, still reeling from lightning, took a moment to process what he meant. If they went into the castle after Enki, they'd have to face Moloch at the peak of his strength. And if she was still alive, they had to save Athena. She nodded and slowly, achingly, they both rose to their feet and began to limp back.

Chapter 25

The rock sheltering Athena had adopted the structural integrity of a wooden statue of swiss cheese. The lindworm lunged at her again, and what remained of the boulder shattered. Athena dove to the side, barely missing becoming the lindworm's lunch. Snarling at its escaping prey, the monster reared up again.

Athena reached down, grabbing a block of ice out of the ground, and with a quick twist shaped it into a shield. The acid splashed against the improvised barrier. She was still forced to hop back - the shield was as large as she could make it, a proper hoplon shield, but it still left her legs exposed. Athena clenched her teeth as droplets of acid splashed against her legs.

The shield was already breaking down from the acid. Athena had to pull more water from the air to and hold it together, thicken it, strengthen it. Bast fired a few rounds. The shield cracked under the bullets, but they didn't punch through. *If they circle me, I'm done for,* Athena thought, leaping back to make sure that didn't happen.

The sword in her hand had never felt more useless. If she couldn't get close, she couldn't counter attack. If she couldn't attack, she'd eventually be worn down. There was no denying that. *I need better protection.*

Athena twisted reality again, wrapping herself in a vortex of wind. It barely came up in time - Bast had gotten to the side and opened fire. The vortex couldn't deflect bullets, but it could redirect them enough. None of the shots landed on Athena as they buzzed by like furious hornets.

Athena used the same vortex to push herself into the air. Not true flight, that would be a waste of power, but enough to get her over the Lindworm's acid spray, enough to get her mobile so she could fight back. She angled her shield to meet the lindworm's attack as it rose towards her. The acid was blocked and she let the force of the spray carry her a bit higher in the air. Bast took the opportunity to fire a couple shots, but Athena was able to twist out of the way again.

"Damn, Athena, you really don't know when you've lost," Bast said, reloading her pistols. "I mean, really, at this point - how long do you think you can dodge?" Athena had to roll as she hit the ground, the Lindworm already spraying another green line her way. "Another ten minutes? Fifteen? Either way you're dead as soon as you slip up."

Bast fired a couple more rounds. One of them tugged on Athena's sleeve, the other sent a few strands of hair falling. *Too close.* Bast was right, to a point. Athena couldn't attack right now, could only dodge and weave. Eventually she would slip up, and then she would die. Bast would crush her nanoverse, and that would be the end.

Assuming I don't have a plan. Which, thankfully, I do.

She let another leap take her airborne, but pausing to pat herself on the back had been a mistake. The shield didn't come up quite in time for the next blast of acid, some of it splashing over the edge and onto her shoulders. She let out a hiss of pain, hearing her own flesh sizzle under the spray, but maintained her course. *Almost there...*

Bast raised her guns to fire again. The pain from the acid slowed Athena, and she felt one of the bullets graze her arm. Any closer and it would have punched a hole in her. She fumbled with the leap and found herself landing in a heap at Bast's feet. *Damnit,* Athena thought as Bast started raising the guns. "Finally," Bast said with a triumphant smile.

Athena brought down her sword with every ounce of speed she could muster, driving it through Bast's foot and pinning her to the ground. "Agreed." As Bast hissed in pain, Athena counted *one-one thousand* and rolled again, a final twist fusing sword and stone.

Bast's eyes widened and she threw out her hand. She hissed in pain as some of the lindworm's acid spray splashed over the meager wind she conjured.

Athena took a deep breath in the momentary respite. *Used up so much power I'm starting to need to breathe.*

"You stupid shitty dragon! Stop trying to spray her and just bite her in half!" Bast screamed. The lindworm, obedient to her will, stopped the spray of acid and began to slither across the ground towards Athena.

Athena rose to meet it, pulling a new sword out of her nanoverse. The weight surprised her for a moment - they had new blades made from depleted uranium. She made a mental note to check back on them after the battle, but at the moment she was thankful for the added heft, even though it made the cut in her arm and acid burn on her shoulder groan in greater pain.

The lindworm reared up like a cobra, then lunged down with jaws spread wide. She met the bite with the heavy blade, drawing a line of blood from the roof of its mouth. It reared back, hissing in agony, and then blinked at her with a comically confused expression. Every instinct it had told it to avoid another bite, but its mistress had commanded it to bite.

Athena took advantage of the lindworm's confusion to slice a chunk out of its scaled hide. More of the bright red blood spilled out, steam rising from the heat in the winter air. Pain from the dual cuts seemed to bring the lindworm clarity - it had been forbidden from using the acid, but not from clawing at Athena, which seemed far safer to its reptilian brain.

Athena tried to parry the lindworm's strikes, but the weight of the sword worked against her - she couldn't move it quite fast enough to block both blows, and the Lindworm batted her away. She hit a rock hard and felt a rib crack.

Get up, Athena. Get up or you're dead.

The lindworm saw it too, and raced across the ground towards her, ready to finally take its meal. Athena held up her sword in a final act of defiance. Just as the lindworm was rearing back for the final bite, an invisible hand slammed it to the ground with enough force to crack the stone below. Athena raised her arm to protect her eyes from the shards of rock flying away from the impact. The lindworm thrashed under the invisible bonds.

Athena glanced around, afraid to hope, and let out a shout of excitement. She regretted it as soon as she did, punctuating the shout with a groan of pain from the broken rib. Still, seeing Crystal and Ryan standing there was a relief she had needed. They were both injured and leaning on each other for support, but their hands were outstretched - each one had massively increased gravity on a part of the beast, pinning it in place.

"Are you *serious?!*" Bast shouted, nearly shrieking in pain and rage. "Enki didn't manage to kill even *one of you?!*"

"So it would seem," Athena said, rising. She blocked out the pain as best she could. Crystal and Ryan both looked ready to pass out from the effort of saving her, which meant she had to keep Bast focused on her while they kept the lindworm pinned.

Bast was reaching into her nanoverse, and Athena hurled the depleted uranium sword at her. It stuck in her good leg and drug her to the ground. Athena kept stalking towards her.

"Athena...we need to get back..." Ryan gasped out.

Athena shook her head. "Not yet, Ryan." Athena held out her hand, and the lighter sword that had been impaled into Bast's foot came flying out, eliciting another groan of pain from Bast. Athena caught it and bent over Bast, who grimaced and spat as Athena loomed closer.

"Get it over with, Athena. I killed your man, you kill me, right?"

Athena, again, shook her head. "You get to fight another day, Bast. If you send the lindworm and varcolaci back. Call them off, and I'll spare you for now."

Bast studied Athena's face and sighed. "Fine." She reached into her nanoverse - causing Athena to tense up - and slowly pulled out a horn. She sounded it, and the sound was repeated by the varcolaci army ahead. "Hey, you stupid lizard!" Bast shouted, after the sound of the horn died down. "Back to the castle, now."

Crystal and Ryan released the gravity bonds, and it slithered back to where it came from.

"Okay, Athena, I guess we'll meet - URK!"

Athena's blade came down, driving through Bast's gut and spine. "And now," she whispered through gritted teeth, her face inches from Bast's. Blood was starting to pour from the other woman's mouth, "I've shown you the same faith you showed me." Bast tried to say something, some retort, but she could only let out a wet rattle before she died.

Ryan and Crystal said nothing. Athena patted Bast's pockets and swore. "Her nanoverse...she must have thrown it away when you showed up. We have to get it back! We have to..." She saw the look on her companions' faces. Ryan was barely standing, his face a swollen mess. Crystal was covered in lightning burns and her clothing was half melted to her body. For that matter, Athena had acid burns, a bullet wound, and broken ribs.

None of them were in any shape to head into the ocean right now. Athena sighed. "Let's...let's get back."

"Good call, love." Crystal's speech was slurred. "After all, we've got round two tomorrow, yeah?"

Athena could only nod, feeling the exhaustion settle into her bones.

***

By the time they got back to the castle, night had begun to fall. The already overcast sky was rapidly growing darker, and the moon was just a vague spot of illumination behind the clouds. All of their Hungers were screaming for attention, at least for Ryan and Crystal. Athena, in spite of her broken rib, was in the best shape of the three, so she diverted from the group to talk to Astaroth while the other two went to find food.

"How did the rest of the battle go?"

Astaroth, his armor dented in places but his skin unbroken, sighed a heavy, weary sigh. "To paraphrase a scholar from your homeland, too many such victories and we'll be undone. We can't put the varcolaci down permanently, ma'am. The bastards die, but their souls stay in their bodies and heal up. We've tried the classics - silver, salt, garlic - but we haven't found their allergen yet."

Athena pursed her lips into a thin white line. "And your demons?"

Astaroth's neck tightened with frustration. "The varcolaci are not angels or god, so they can't permanently kill us, but it'll take a full month for any of my legion that falls up here to reform back in the pit. If the battle comes down to us and them, they'll win through attrition. It would help to have a goddess in the fight"

Athena brushed aside the note of reproach in his voice. *I had more important matters to deal with.* Instead, she chewed on her lip, and then nodded. "It won't come down to that. As long as you can keep the varcolaci busy so we can focus on their gods, we will."

"And we'll do that for as long as we can, but you need to understand," Ashtaroth made sure he had Athena's gaze before continuing, "we will eventually be worn down to the point where we cannot keep the fight going."

"Understood." She handed Ashtaroth the depleted uranium sword. "Try this, perhaps they'll be weak to it."

He accepted the sword with gratitude, and Athena went to find her companions.

***

As Athena broke off to talk to Ashtaroth, Crystal and Ryan found their way to Crystal's staging area. In there, they dove into the sandwich storage. They took some back to the castle and were eating in silence when Athena found them. Crystal motioned to an untouched sandwich when Athena walked in. "For you, love. You still like tuna, yes?"

Athena answered by grabbing the sandwich and taking a large bite. Ryan looked at her and gave a weak smile. "I'm guessing no good news from the demons?"

"They can't permanently kill the varcolaci, and they heal faster than the demons. Our forces will be overwhelmed in time."

"So that's a no. At least we're ahead some, right? With Bast out of the picture, I mean."

Crystal smiled sourly. "Oh," she said, "there's no doubt we're in a bloody better spot than we were before. But Ryan, you haven't told Athena the best sodding part yet, yeah?"

Athena looked at him expectantly. "Enki's found a way to use multiple nanoverses. He's drawing power from both his and Týr's."

They watched as Athena clenched both teeth and fingers. "That's impossible," Athena hissed. "How?"

"I don't know. But he let it slip when we were fighting. Or figured he was going to kill me so it didn't matter."

"But the two of you were able to fight against him, so the three of us should be able to best him..." Athena trailed off when she saw that Crystal was shaking her head.

"The problem there, love, is we didn't really hold our own. We got in some sucker punches, sure, and Ryan did take his arm and eye, but both times we got bloody lucky or caught him off guard." Ryan noticed for the first time the burn marks the lightning had left on Crystal's arms. They looked like trees with thick trunks that started near her shoulders and a spider web of branches that arced towards her hands.

Athena threw up her hands in frustration, startling Ryan. "Then what do you suggest we do? Lay down and accept our fate?"

"You know I didn't mean that, Athena. Bloody hell, I'm just saying we should stay realistic about things? We need a solid plan or we might as well just give up!"

"Okay," Ryan said, cutting off the argument before it could develop too much further. They both turned to look at him, and he continued. "Let's whiteboard this. We need to figure out how to beat Enki after his...I dunno, double apotheosis? Dubpotheosis, let's call it that."

"No, let's never call it that." Athena said. Crystal nodded in agreement, but they both smiled to lessen the sting of that stupid name. "And what do you mean, whiteboard?"

"Something I heard about somewhere," Ryan said. "We put down every idea, no matter how stupid it is, or insane, or impossible. Everything goes up, and then we try to wheedle it down to the best plan."

Crystal and Athena shared a look, and Crystal shrugged. "I've heard worse ideas."

Ryan reached into his nanoverse to grab some paper. *I wonder if this just vanished off some poor scribe's desk. At least whatever they're doing, they still use paper.* "Okay, so for starters: drop a nuke on Enki." Ryan wrote it down.

"Yeah, love, that's not going to happen," Crystal said, leaning in.

"Well, we still write it down. But why not?"

Athena went ahead. "First of all, we'd be caught in the blast radius. I can't speak for Crystal, but I'm not overly fond of being in a nuclear explosion."

Crystal nodded agreement.

"Secondly, and more importantly, no one god could create that much power. We can't cheat reality like that - we have to put as much power into it as we get out. The effort would kill us."

Ryan sighed. "Fair."

"And I don't think we can say 'no god,' anymore." Crystal said, tapping her fingers on the table. "I think Enki could at this point."

"I suppose two gods working in tandem could manage it..." Athena said with a frown.

Crystal shook her head. "Not what I mean, love. Sure, they could. But Enki wouldn't even need to push himself." Crystal frowned right, then lit up as an idea occurred to her. "Ooh," she said, "Anything goes? We could feed him to some bloody piranhas." Both Ryan and Athena looked at her. "What? You said no matter how stupid? Piranhas are stupid, but I'd feel pretty good about it if we could make it work."

Athena chuckled as Ryan dutifully wrote it down.

"But seriously," Crystal said, "what about a gravity inversion, like what Ryan pulled before? This time with all three of us doing it. If we can launch him far enough into space, his Hungers might get him before he gets back to Earth."

Ryan wrote it down, then chewed on the end of his pen as Athena tapped her chin.

"We don't know how long it takes before his Hungers are a problem," Athena finally said. "If we're trying to wear him down to the point where he'll suffocate, it's likely that he'll last far longer than us. That being said, it might be viable to try wearing him down enough to weaken him. Hit and run, focus on physical attacks and conserve our power, force him to burn as much as possible."

"Possible," Crystal said as Ryan nodded.

"I think we might want some kind of home run move once we get him worn down," Ryan added. "Something to hit him with once he's down to, well, at least our level. Can we, I dunno, break him apart at the molecular level?"

Crystal shook her head. "It's really hard to make changes to another gods form. I think it might even still be hard for Enki, since he didn't try it. Otherwise the fight would have been over when he got you, love."

Ryan shuddered at the thought.

"If we could, it'd be easier to turn him into a cabbage," Athena said.

"That's the most random thing you've ever said," Ryan said. "Why a cabbage?"

"I loathe cabbage. I'm not going to defile the good name of a carrot or Brussel sprout by turning him into one."

Ryan's forehead furrowed. "Brussel sprouts have a good name? They're the vilest of all the vegetables, we should turn Enki into one of those! He'd fit right in."

"Just because you hold on to your childhood bad taste doesn't mean we all do."

Crystal cleared her throat to interrupt. "As much as I love the idea of turning Enki into a vegetable, loves, we should probably focus on something more realistic."

"So...make him into a fruit?" Ryan shot Crystal a grin.

"Nah. Too sweet for him."

Ryan jotted down "Vegetable plan".

"What about flooding?" Athena asked. It was Ryan and Crystal's turn to stare at Athena, who raised a hand to hold off their objections. "Think about how he reacted to you even mentioning it, Ryan. It's possible that a flood will cause him to panic, react stupidly, make mistakes. If we waterproof the castle, we can stay submerged and then hit him when he's disoriented and panicking."

"Seems like a huge bloody risk. If he doesn't panic, we've just disadvantaged both sides equally, and he's still as powerful as he was."

"Still writing it down," Ryan said, "Because it's something we should think about."

Crystal nodded. "Also, Athena, I do like the idea of attacking Enki's psychology. If we can exploit his weak points there, we're fighting him on the one field where we have the advantage. As bloody powerful as he is, we're smarter than him, and nothing he's done suggests he's *more* emotionally stable after gaining phenomenal powers."

"About that, though," Ryan said as he added the words 'psychological warfare' to the list. "Can we be sure we'll outsmart him? I mean, wasn't he really smart back in your time, Crystal?"

"Not the way you're thinking. Enki was considered a god of intelligence and crafting, but he was always a linear thinker, never the most creative type. Back when the wheel was the biggest technological advancement, being inventive wasn't nearly as important as being able to implement things. Enki doesn't come up with new ideas, for the most part. He makes other people's ideas happen."

"Gotcha. Well, if we're trying to outsmart him," Ryan cast a glance at Athena for her reaction, "we could put ourselves in a wooden horse."

"Oh, goody," Athena said dryly, "a Trojan Horse joke. I can assure you that, in the last three thousand years, those haven't gotten even slightly stale."

"That's good," Ryan responded. "I'll be sure to make more of them then."

Crystal sighed. "We're not making progress here. This is a good idea, Ryan, but I'm calling a break right now. We're all too close to this. We still need to mentally heal and get ready for tomorrow. I suggest we go into our nanoverses, take some time to think, and meet back up after we have a bit of S and S, yeah?"

Athena nodded, although Ryan looked perplexed. "S and S?"

"It's like R and R, but instead of Rest and Relaxation, it's Sleep and Social."

"Ah. Sounds like a plan then." He frowned. "Plus, I really want to find out why the hell I got a stick for a weapon."

Chapter 26

Paradise

The first impression Ryan got when stepping onto the former Throneworld of the Emperor was how overwhelmingly clean it all was. He had to shield his eyes for a moment to let them adjust to the gleam. The streets were made of polished marble that seemed to bear no trace of dirt left by people walking on it. The buildings were gold and silver, skyscrapers that truly earned the name - some looked like they might reach out of the atmosphere. The vehicles emitted no gases Ryan could see, and under his divine sight it was confirmed they were only letting out water vapor. The people were dressed in a thousand different colors.

It immediately put the hair on the back of Ryan's neck up. *There's got to be some trick. Daasti's turned into a damn Tyrant. I wish I could get someone to show me around.*

A pair of individuals approached him, both wearing uniforms of red and silver with badges that marked them as law enforcement. He didn't recognize their species - green skinned and humanoid, but with compound eyes and long antenna. "First time on world, traveler?" one of them asked.

"First time in a very long time," Ryan said, putting on a grin for them. *I didn't actually come down to the world last time, so it's been what, two hundred thousand years? Less? More?*

"Well, let us show you around," the other said. Now that his eyes had adjusted, Ryan could see they had distinctive ripples of lighter green across their faces.

"I mean, sure, but shouldn't you two have more important things to do?"

They both laughed. "I've been a Lawbringer for thirty cycles, traveler, and had exactly one crime in that time period. I think we can spare an afternoon." The speaker offered his hand. "Rello, and my podmate, Callo."

Ryan blinked. *That can't be right. Cops that only have a crime every three decades?* "I'm…" *Let's not start off with "I'm god" this time?* "Nayr." Flipping his first name backwards was the best he could come up with.

"Well, Nayr, how about it? Guided tour by two bored Lawbringers?"

"It can't be just that you're bored," Ryan said with a frown. "I mean, is this what you do? Walk up to new people and offer them tours?"

The two shared a look, and Ryan could sense confusion in the wavering of their antennas. *Why would they be confused? Is it…*He remembered his thoughts upon arriving. *Oh crap, I made them approach me and offer. No wonder they seem so confused.*

Ryan considered sending them away, then realized that doing so would only further their confusion. "You sure you won't get in trouble?" Ryan asked.

Rello relaxed. "Oh, absolutely."

"Well, in that case, lead on." *I bet you're part of Daasti's secret police anyway. Go ahead, throw a black bag over my head. I dare you.*

Rello and Callo did not seem interested in trying to haul him off. Instead, they were serious about giving him a tour of the city, helping him into their vehicle. Callo leaned over to push a button. Before Ryan's eyes, the roof and sides became completely transparent. Callo pointed to one of the buildings as they started to drive. "Over there is the Hall of Companions, where the Hundred Companions, led by Daasti, oversee the Republic."

Ryan grunted. He had to admit it was an impressive building, a tower that expanded at the top to a series of gleaming glass pods that overlooked the city. "Is that where you Lawbringers work?"

They both laughed. "No," Rello said, "although every Lawbringer hopes to one day join the Companions."

Callo snorted. "Speak for yourself, Rello. It would be just as boring as being a Lawbringer, only you'd have to go into space. Spare me that."

"At least the pay would be better, right?" Ryan asked, trying to join in the conversation.

Instead of laughing, the two Lawbringers shared a look. "Son," Rello asked, "is someone demanding you work for wages?"

"What?"

"Because if someone was forcing you into a monetary system," Callo said, "you're safe here. You can tell us."

"No, I..." Ryan frowned, trying to keep up with the conversation. "No one's forcing me into a monetary system."

They glanced at each other. "If you're sure," Rello said. "You...you're from the Edge, aren't you?"

"Of course," Ryan said, hoping he caught the meaning right. As the vehicle kept moving, they wound a corner to reveal even more gleaming buildings. "Just some ignorant Edge tourist."

"You shouldn't talk about yourself like that," Callo said. "Edge schools are just as good as those on Throne, and forced monetary systems are just as illegal there." Callo's antenna waggled in agitation. "You were told being forced to work for a living is illegal, right? Your basic income should cover your needs - you are getting it right?"

Ryan took a deep breath. "Of course. I just...I have some more expensive tastes. I just like working for extra money to buy fancy things."

The two Lawbringers finally relaxed. "Oh, of course." Rello said. "Sorry. You just...you heard what happened out on the Edge in Corvip, right?"

Ryan shook his head.

"Oh Ryan," Callo said. For a moment Ryan's heart skipped at his name. *Relax, Ryan. You're still a religious figure here, right?* "It was terrible. The people were being lied to, their basic income seized. They were forced to work if they wanted to survive, not just as a way to earn luxuries."

"Terrible, terrible business," Rello said. "It was just, when you mentioned wages right away..."

Ryan forced another grin. "Of course. But, if I was on a world like that, would they ever allow me to leave? I mean, if I was running an illegal wage-stealing corporation, I wouldn't."

"That's...quite the devious mind you have there, son." Callo said, the antenna waving becoming more intense. "What business are you in?"

Holy crap they're sincere. They're really all on some kind of weird system where they get money just so...so they don't have to worry about starving? Ryan frowned at how logical it sounded when you put it that way. *Also would explain the lack of homeless.* Ryan hadn't seen a single one.

"I'm a...freelancer. Only work when I have something I'm looking towards, y'know? A little bit of this, a little bit of that. Just finished a full year stint as an artist to fund my trip here."

That got Callo to finally relax. "You're an artist! That's wonderful. Do you have any paintings for sale?"

I do now. Ryan willed a folio into existence in his bag, full of replications of the works of Van Gogh. Artist wasn't the best decision - Ryan couldn't paint his way out of a paper bag - but it was the first thing he'd thought of that omnipotence would make easy to fake. "Sure," he said, showing Callo.

Callo ended up buying Starry Nite for a thousand credits. Ryan had no idea how much money it was, but Callo seemed happy with his purchase. Ryan was ready to let them go. He wanted to explore more on his own. "Hey, question. Where does someone go to find a party around here?"

***

Five days later, Ryan walked into the Hall of Companions and teleported himself to Daasti's office. Daasti barely restrained a startled jump at the sudden interruption. Ryan, for his part, was surprised by Daasti's appearance. He could see lines of the man he had made into a demigod, but it was a faint echo. Daasti had filled out over the centuries, the relatively thin man had grown muscular and his dark hair gone grey.

"Heya, Daasti. Long time no talk."

"Ryan." He gave a perfunctory, reluctant bow. If Ryan didn't know better, he'd say Daasti seemed nervous. *Then again, Ryan, do you know better? Do you really? You met the guy once.* "I was wondering if you'd stop by while you were here. We've been watching you for the last couple of days."

Ryan shrugged. "I wasn't exactly hiding." He'd changed his clothes to match the style he'd seen exploring the world. However, when he'd seen the cameras he hadn't bothered altering his face.

"No, you weren't. Two Lawbringers showed you around, you spent time at a club, and since then you've been wandering. Like you were surprised by what you saw." Daasti frowned, not just with his mouth but with his entire face, a downward curl that reached his eye and forehead.

Ryan expected a question to follow that frown, but nothing did. "Everything alright with that?"

"Of course it's alright," Daasti said, smoothing his face. "You're God, after all. You can do whatever you want."

Ryan watched him for a moment. The stiffness of Daasti's posture, the way his hands were clenched into fists at his side..."Something bothering you, Daasti? Please, be honest."

"You sure you want that?"

"Of course I do."

Daasti took a deep breath. "Alright. If you decide to strike me down for this, just...you asked for the truth." Before Ryan could respond, Daasti continued. "I think you're here to destroy us. I think you're furious we've gotten rid of weapons, that we took away your toys. I think you're ready to break apart our Republic because of that. And I know I can't stop you, I know you're more powerful than I can imagine, but you will have to kill every single Companion if you try." Daasti raised his head a bit to make sure he was meeting Ryan's gaze. "The rest of the Republic may still worship you, but I remember what you are. A War God. A Death God. And a God of Tyrants."

Ryan took a deep breath. "And freeing you when I was here last didn't earn me any credit?"

"Freeing me from a system you created. I don't think you're soulless, Ryan. I think you just want things from us."

Ryan winced at the accusation. *Holy crap, he thinks I'm the Dark One. This is that part of the fantasy novel, the prologue, where the Dark Evil God destroys the perfect civilization that comes before the Chosen One's time.* "I swear to you, Daasti, I'm not going to undo what you built here. I'm not even mad at you." That last part was a lie, but Ryan wanted Daasti at ease.

It seemed to work, some. "Then, may I ask you a question?" Ryan nodded. "Why spend almost a week among us, pretending to be mortal?"

"My power is almost unlimited, but not completely, and I never claimed omniscience." Ryan smiled, "Besides, there's a big difference between watching from on high and walking among the actual people."

Daasti jerked his head up and down, accepting that. "And what did you think of what we've done since you were last here?"

"It's a paradise." Ryan didn't see any point in dissembling. "I'm not seeing anyone hungry, any sign of oppression, and crime seems to be almost nonexistent."

"It's rare," Daasti said, relaxing a bit. "But not unheard of. With no poverty, no hunger, no *want,* there's no motive for most people to commit crimes."

That matched what Ryan had seen, too. "And then there's the fact that you've gotten rid of all weapons."

Daasti nodded. "And found harmless ways to replace tools that could be weaponized - knives and spades and the like." He smiled. "Even those gripped by madness or rage find it hard to actually kill someone with their bare hands. Some people get creative - break sticks to points, tie chunks of metal or stone to them - but that's a High Crime. All weapons are."

Ryan did his best to keep his face blank. "There's a problem there, though."

Now the tension, and Daasti's full face frown, returned. "You said you wouldn't. You literally just did. I should have known better - it was your first commandment. 'Here is the book of Science - thou shalt use it to make weapons in My name, and thou shalt wage war with those tools'." Daasti spat. "We destroyed all records of *that* in the holy text."

Ryan winced. "Not actually what I said. I didn't command war. I didn't want that."

"You commanded weapons and didn't want war?" Daasti sounded incredulous.

"Well, when you put it that way, it sounds pretty dumb." Ryan forced a smile. "But I have a war I'm still fighting. Against Enki."

Daasti blinked. "Enki is *real*? I thought he was some fairy tale, used to frighten children."

Ryan chuckled, trying to contain his rising fury, an echo of that dark hate he'd felt last time he was here - an urge to wipe Daasti out, to just cleanse this entire civilization and start again. They were *ants,* and this entire galaxy was an ant farm that was questioning why it should have clear sides not realizing *it was the entire reason they existed.* Like the ants he'd sent into Enki's eye - they were tools at his disposal, nothing more. "Oh, no, he's very real. Kicked my ass not long ago, in fact, in part because I fought him with a damn stick."

"I can see that going poorly." From Daasti's expression, he wouldn't have minded watching that fight. "And why is that something we need to worry about?" Daasti's voice was calm, level, but it made Ryan's eyes widen like he had been slapped.

"I'm sorry, what?" Shock was giving way to anger faster than Ryan could process.

Daasti replied, "You've been here twice. Once you set things into motion to turn it into a hellhole, the second time you eliminated the need for yourself. So why should we care about your war with Enki when we have a paradise?"

Ryan stared at him, his mouth hanging open. Then he felt himself starting to laugh. "Oh damn, I didn't mention it, did I? Or if I did, it got lost through the ages."

Daasti's eyes narrowed. "Care to share the joke?"

Ryan nodded, needing a moment to calm his laughter. "If Enki wins, he'll destroy the universe. Or take it over."

Daasti stared at him. "I don't believe you."

Ryan shrugged. "I don't care if you believe me, because it's the truth. He'll destroy the entire universe," Ryan didn't feel the need to explain the nanoverse was just one of many - it would only confuse the discussion, and Daasti wouldn't care. "He has the power to do it - if I'm dead. As long as I'm alive, he can't. But I can't keep him at bay if the best weapon I have to pull on is a damn sharpened stick."

"Why not just make your own then?" Daasti's eyes narrowed.

"It doesn't work that way, Daasti. I have rules I have to follow, same as anyone else."

"So...what? We created a perfect society, and now we need to tear it apart or the universe will be destroyed?"

Ryan opened his mouth, closed it. *These people have suffered enough.* The idea of destroying what he had seen was sickening. They'd built a galaxy without want or need or war. As badly as Ryan needed weapons, these people had a right to their peace. "No, Daasti. I've screwed up your society enough by trying to meddle with it. I'm going to go to another galaxy, create new life. The lightspeed cap should prevent them from ever bothering you, and I'm going to limit your divine powers to prevent you from jumping to another galaxy."

Daasti nearly slumped with relief. "We can provide our scientific research, so they can-"

"No, I learned my lesson there. I'm going to be a bit more careful this time. Just give them enough to master agriculture so I don't have to wait millions of years for them to figure that out."

"Makes sense, Ryan. And...what about us?"

Ryan smiled. "I'll swing by every so often, say hi, make sure you and the One Hundred Companions don't turn into a bunch of dickholes. But as long as you don't, I'll let you do your thing."

Daasti returned the smile. "I can live with that."

"I hope so, Daasti. Good luck."

"Same to you, God."

Ryan, grinning at that, vanished.

Chapter 27

"So, how'd it go this time?" Athena had beaten Ryan back from the nanoverses, although Crystal was still off. Ryan figured that was appropriate - Crystal had easily been the worst injured of the three of them, and she would need the most time to heal. He checked his phone, knowing he was stalling. It still showed 10:40 PM, one minute after he'd left. When you factored in the fact that he'd had to walk from his nanoverse into the castle to find Athena, he'd only been gone a matter of seconds in the core world.

"You know, I've just realized I haven't plugged this thing in, not once since everything started, but I've still got a full charge." If Athena was bothered by his attempt to change the topic, it didn't show on her face. "At first, I figured it was because I was hopping realities, barely using it, and time was flowing weird. I didn't really respond to any messages or make many phone calls because, well, I was worried about losing the battery. At least, that's what I told myself."

Athena leaned on the battlement, looking at him. She still had her usual sardonic grin, but now, after so much time, Ryan found something oddly warm in it. It wasn't a stone wall like he had originally thought. "We could die tomorrow. For real."

She nodded, "You're not used to that by now?"

"Nope," Ryan said. "You know, before all this, I had a life." She raised an eyebrow, inviting him to continue. "I mean, it wasn't much of one. Only had a couple friends, really, and my sister." He paused to think and felt himself grinning. "And like five hundred friends on Facebook, people I never talked to except online. There needs to be a term for 'person you're connected to through social media who has status updates you randomly Like.'"

"And you haven't spoken to them since this all happened?"

He shook his head. "I mean, they've texted or called. Or sent me messages. I've been on the news as a god or the Antichrist, and now they're watching me fight for my life on a remote Canadian island, and I haven't even spoken to them. And if I die...well, that'll be that."

Athena's half-smile didn't expand, but it somehow came closer to reaching her eyes. "Well, are you going to reach out to them?" Although the tone was a question, Ryan got the feeling she knew the answer.

"Not now. I guess I'll use that as something to live for. Does that seem stupid?"

"No." The smile faded slightly as she spoke, but the light stayed in her eyes. "I've been with many people as they realized tomorrow could be their last. Most of them think of regrets, of missed opportunities, but if given the option to address those, they focus on the here and now. For that matter, I did too."

"Did?" Ryan asked.

Athena shrugged. "I'm thousands of years old, Ryan. If I spent too much time dwelling on regrets, I'd never get anything done."

Ryan nodded, but found he didn't have any words to add. They stood in silence for a little while, staring at the stars. This far north, the Aurora Borealis was clearly visible, green and blue lines dancing like serpentine lovers writhing across the sky.

"They'd created a utopia," Ryan said, breaking the silence.

"You sound almost sad," Athena murmured.

"No, just...I wish I could let the entire nanoverse be that way. No weapons, no wars. Just good people doing good, y'know?"

Athena gave a sound that might have been agreement. "So what did you do about it?"

"I let them keep their utopia. I just went elsewhere and created some places where it wouldn't happen. On one world I put two different groups of the same species on different continents, and gave them similar but different commandments and languages. Different skin colors. That's been enough for humans to war for all of history, I figured. On another world I put three different species with no commandments, no sign of my presence. On a third world I made one species nocturnal, the other diurnal." He shrugged. "I figure if any of those worlds finds a time of peace, the other two won't. And they're all only a couple light years apart, so if they all find peace, they'll probably do it just in time to start warring with each other."

Athena waited for a moment, to make sure he was finished. "And you feel like a monster for doing so?"

"I need them to fight, Athena. I almost died because of the peace, and if I had the world would have gotten blown up when the sun went nova."

Athena let out a small laugh. "You're a good man, Ryan Smith."

He looked at her, his forehead furrowing. "I'm sorry, but what?"

A full, genuine smile crossed her face. "You're not unique, you know. Most gods, when they find out that weapons come from their nanoverse, go into it and demand weapons. With similar results. My first dystopia was a matriarchal one where men were lobotomized so they could be useful for reproduction and otherwise were basically well-trained pets." She laughed a bit, a rueful sound that was oddly flat in the cold night air. "I might have had some issues that crept into it. Just like your feeling that you were out of control in your life helped shaped a tyranny of absolute power. Absolute control."

Ryan shuddered at the thought. "But if that's the case, why were they able to create a utopia?"

"Because you still let them have free will, and now your subconscious was over correcting to the horrors you had made. Again, same as mine. I imagine it was the same for Crystal, Týr, Enki… even for Bast, too."

"But not Moloch?"

"Moloch is a legitimately disturbed man who used to literally eat children. I don't think he ever had anything redeeming in him."

Even if he had wanted to, which he didn't, Ryan couldn't find a flaw in her logic. "And you're saying I'm a good man because...?"

"You could have destroyed the utopia. You could have created a race with a thirst for blood or war. You could have made two races that felt a powerful aversion to each other's pheromones, so they'd never know peace. You could have commanded they war with each other, or even just repeated your first mistake and demanded weapons. But instead..." She reached out and put a hand on his shoulder. "Instead you allowed for free will, and just trusted that there are always enough people who will choose to be bastards. But you allowed for them to chose peace, if they can."

He didn't know what to say at first, and it took him a bit to find the only words that seemed to fit. "Seems pretty pessimistic of me, though."

She chuckled again, and this one wasn't flat in the night air, but was warm as it hit his ears, friendly and amused and bright. "Don't ever confuse cynicism with evil, Ryan. You can be a good cynic, and you can be an evil optimist." *And these are the lies we tell ourselves to get through the day, Ryan. You're not ready for the hard truth, that sometimes a general must let soldiers die to win the war. I hope you never have to face it.*

Ryan nodded, and did feel better. It didn't erase the fact that he could have created more utopias, more worlds of peace...but, if nothing else, it was a salve for his conscience.

"Thanks, Athena."

Ryan and Athena shared the silence for a bit, then she left. Ryan considered following her, but decided to stand there for a moment before catching up. The clouds had cleared, and he wanted to enjoy the stars before they were hidden again.

After all, it might be the last chance he had to see them.

In my nanoverse, I set people up to destroy themselves. Ryan shifted at the uncomfortable thought, trying to focus on the important detail. At least, it felt important. *There has to be some way to do that to Enki. After all, we're smarter than him. It's the one edge we have left.*

Ryan blinked. *There has to be a way...*

He ran down to find Athena. "Hey, Athena, if I made a fireball, would it burn me?"

Athena frowned. "Of course. We're still subject to physics."

Ryan's eyes lit up. "Get Crystal. I have a plan. The beginnings of a plan. I have like a third of a plan. Okay, I have an idea, but it's a good idea. I think."

Athena nodded. "Let's see what you've come up with."

***

Dawn broke sullenly through the thick clouds that still hung over Graham Island. The scars of battle still scored the landscape. They had a plan, true, and in theory it was a good plan. The reality was that the plan depended on their being right about two very major assumptions, and if either was wrong, they were probably all going to die.

Not just die, Ryan reminded himself. Worse than that - they'd have their nanoverses taken over by Enki while they were turned into horrible monsters by Moloch. *Which reminds me, we still have to deal with Týr the lindworm. Maybe we'll get lucky and Moloch will keep it nearby because he's spooked by Bast's death.*

They'd spent most of the night practicing, but they hadn't been able to push things too hard. Everything they were doing required a massive expenditure of energy, and while you could get the occasional fix for your hungers in your Nanoverse, like Crystal had explained, "You don't want to do it too bloody often, love. If you do, you'll end up like a rubber band pulled too far, yeah? Just...snap." So to conserve their strength, the practice had to be limited.

Astaroth and his demons stood at the ready to hold the varcolaci at bay again. The demonic steel didn't reflect much of the sullen sky - it was dull and matte, an effect reinforced now that it was battle scarred and dented. There was one version of the plan where the demons were the ones to finish the job - if all four gods died, Astaroth would

310

have to beat Moloch to their nanoverses. *Assuming we can trust him on that.*

Crystal and Athena had gone ahead to the battlefield to get things ready for Enki. Now, Crystal gave Ryan a thumbs up as they re-entered the castle. Ryan's job was to lead Enki there, to where the real fun would begin.

And that would have to be soon. He grabbed the binoculars and focused them. As he expected to see, Enki's forces were on the march. Although the bodies of demon's still littered the battlefield, the Varcolaci were at full force. The sound of their armor on the stones of Graham island echoed through the air. *We'll get torn apart if this drags on.*

Enki himself was floating again, just over the rest of his army. Ryan noted with some satisfaction that one of Enki's arms was metal, controlled by Enki's constantly changing its properties to move like a normal arm. *Stupid and vain,* Ryan thought. Maintaining flight would be hard enough, but keeping the arm lifelike? That had to be a drain he would notice even with his new power levels.

Or maybe not. How powerful is he?

Ryan pushed down the fear. *No matter what, he's powerful enough to defeat himself.*

Ryan reached down to twist the equations that governed how fast he could run. He checked before he did, making sure Enki couldn't see him. *No need to give the bastard new tricks.* Crystal and Athena joined him back on the wall.

"Everyone ready?" He asked them. They both nodded, and then they all turned back to the battlefield.

"If we don't make it out of this, love," Crystal said, "it's been nice to have met you."

"Same," said Athena. "And Crystal...it's good to be fighting at your side again."

Crystal gave Athena a small smile. "You too. Ready, Ryan?"

Ryan nodded. "Tell me when."

Athena watched the approaching army grow closer. "Now."

No hesitation. If today was going to be his last day alive, Ryan was determined to make sure he got to do *this* at least once. "Fire!" Ryan shouted, pointing towards the approaching army. Ryan shouting also served a tactical purpose - it made sure Enki knew where Ryan was.

Arrows streaked from their castle and bit into varcolaci flesh. Ryan watched as a few went down, and wished they wouldn't be getting up again. He didn't see what happened next, though.

He had Enki's full attention.

The other god flew at him for another face grab. *Knew it, you repetitive sonofabitch.* This time, Ryan rolled out of the way without too much effort, earning a curse from Enki. "What's wrong, big guy? Not in the mood for banter today?" Ryan said

As he taunted, Ryan began to run along the length of the wall with his newly enhanced speed. Of course, since he could fly, Enki was still right behind him, snarling through a smug grin. "That's right, Eschaton. Run away! Run for your life! I'm going to rip both your arms off."

Please don't let him catch me too soon, Ryan begged the universe. Ryan didn't look over his shoulder, instead crouching his head just a few inches. His instinct paid off when, moments later, one of those massive fists, the fleshy one, passed through the air where his head had been. He'd gone far enough now where he could leap off the wall and start heading towards the battleground. "Rip off my arms? C'mon, Enki, I blew yours off yesterday. At least be original in your threats."

The response was a wordless howl and a near-instant blast of sunlight, exactly like the one from yesterday, exactly like Týr's. Ryan felt a surge of validation - Enki couldn't modify the math, he had to throw it the same way Týr did. *He doesn't know how it works.* It confirmed what Crystal had said about him being a linear thinker and gave Ryan a shred of hope for this stupid, crazy plan.

At Ryan's current speed, combined with juking back and forth, Enki couldn't hit him. The sunbeam was just sound and fury and light. It cast Ryan's shadow into sharp relief in front of him, and he could feel the heat searing his back, but did nothing else.

"I'm going to atomize you! Completely disintegrate you! You can't run forever, you little bitch! All I need is to hit you once and you're a corpse." Enki's words were loud and hoarse and angry...and correct. If even one of Enki's attacks hit Ryan, it'd be over.

The good news was, the plan didn't call for him to run too much longer. One more rock to vault over and - there they were, Crystal and Athena. "Help!" Ryan mouthed.

They both twisted their hands the moment Enki came over the rock, each ripping at his flying modification. It worked - the dual assault caught him off guard, and once again he was plummeting back to Earth, at the mercy of that cruel mistress named Gravity.

He got up, dusting himself off, looking at the three of them. He chuckled, the single most hateful chuckle Ryan had ever heard in real life - a sound utterly devoid of mirth or kindness or warmth, a sadistic, ugly sound. If a wildfire could laugh, it would make this sound.

"So, this is where we are. The Eschaton, the Whore, and the Coward. The three of you against me. The last hero with the balls to stand up to you. I'm going to kill you all, and I'm going to save the world."

"You're delusional," Ryan said flatly. "You're not the hero, and you're not going to win."

Enki grinned broadly. "We'll see. Come at me. Let's end this."

So they charged for the fate of the world.

Chapter 28

In a single motion Enki dodged under Crystal's sword, grabbed Athena's wrist with one hand - Ryan thought he could hear an audible crack when he did - and brought his other fist up into Ryan's gut. As Ryan doubled over and went airborne, stars flashing in front of his eyes, Enki's leg swept out to catch Crystal in the hip, sending her flying to the side. Swinging around, he tossed Athena away with an easy grace.

Enki stood there for a moment, guffawing in what now seemed to be genuine amusement. "Too right, too damn right. Three on one, and I'm going to whip all your asses."

Ryan rose to his feet unsteadily. Crystal's own rise favored her right side, the left hip obviously injured, and Athena held her wrist against her stomach. *I did hear a crack, he snapped it. Five seconds into the fight, and already Athena has a broken wrist.* Panic rose in his throat again, a serpent trying to crawl its way out of his belly. He clamped his teeth to keep from screaming. *She doesn't need that wrist for the plan, Ryan. Calm the hell down, the plan requires Enki to be stronger than you all.*

At least Enki was waiting for them to come to him, rather than pressing the attack. They had to attack him again, keep him off balance - if they jumped to the endgame too soon, he'd be suspicious.

Suspicion seemed to be the last thing on Enki's mind. If anything, he seemed to be having *fun.* He was grinning, a sick joy flashing through his eyes.

Let's see if we can't spoil playtime. Instead of charging as a group again, they began to spread out, taking spots around Enki. Enki stood at the center of the circle, cracking his neck, waiting for them to move.

One at a time this time. Athena went first, keeping the injured hand pressed against her chest. She leapt up in a kick, one that Enki blocked with a thick arm.

Before Enki could counterattack, Athena pushed off that solid limb and sent herself flying back in an arc - right in time for Crystal to come in, her sword strike low and aimed at Enki's kidney. He brought a hand around and punched the blade on the flat, cracking the metal. Like Athena, Crystal sprung away before Enki could counterattack.

While they had attacked, Ryan had reached into his nanoverse to pull out a weapon. To his relief, he found himself holding a sword - not a fancy one like the one that he'd had from his nanoverse in Texas-*oh goddamnit I could have grabbed that from Athena's staging area*-but a simple steel blade. A second after Crystal moved, he did the same, and leapt into to the air for a high strike.

Enki moved again with that inhuman speed, rolling away from Ryan's blow. Ryan sprung back, and it was Athena's turn again.

Like they had discussed, the three off them rotated their attacks, dancing in and out. Athena dashed in with a quick blow to the back of Enki's head as he was facing Ryan. As soon as he whirled to face her, Crystal danced in with a quick cut to his side. Enki hissed, more in frustration than pain as he turned again - this time towards Ryan, anticipating an attack from that direction. Athena charged in again. When Enki turned to face her, Ryan moved in, managing a stab into his leg. None of their blows seemed to have much impact on Enki, but at least he wasn't landing any more of his own strikes. The veins on Enki's neck and face were beginning to bulge, his irritation growing at the stinging wasps biting at him.

"Enough!" Enki shouted, and a torrent of wind sent the three of them flying back. They began picking themselves up off of the ground with all the speed they could manage, and once again Ryan felt the fear, the terror, rising. *He can do wind, none of us did that trick, the plan-* Ryan bit the panic back down. *Of course he can manipulate wind. That was the first thing you ever saw him do, force the tornado down against Crystal. The plan's still solid.*

Enki had started ranting at them, and in the momentary panic Ryan had missed part of the rant. "-pathetic! Just realize you lost, lay down, and *die already.*"

I think he said that some other time. He's running out of things to scream at us. Ryan gave Athena a nod.

Athena shouted, drawing Enki's attention, "We will never surrender to you, Enki. Not so long as we draw breath." Now that she had Enki's attention with a rather cliché taunt, she twisted, forming a pair of gauntlets around her hands.

Making your own weapons was only worth the effort if you needed a particular composition - in this case an alloy of titanium and uranium-238 for most of the gauntlets, besides the palms. Athena nearly staggered from the effort of creating them but stayed on her feet. *At least we gave her the gauntlets,* Ryan reflected, *hopefully it'll help brace that wrist.*

Enki watched her form the gauntlets and answered her taunt with a sneer before charging. On the defensive, she was able to duck under his grabbing hands and land a boxer's quick one-two punch against Enki's ribcage - wincing at the pain as she landed the blows. Ryan let out a breath of relief when he saw that the gauntlets worked - the added mass meant even with his enhanced strength, Enki felt the blows, and grunted as they landed. He jumped back, looking comically surprised to have felt that.

Then Enki grinned widely. With apparently absolutely zero effort, he formed a pair of his own gauntlets - identical to Athena's. Ryan checked, peering with his divine sight, and felt a surge of relief - they were exact replicas, although he'd merged the gauntlet on his metal arm into the artificial appendage.

"You know why we won't surrender, Enki?" Ryan shouted. *C'mon, Enki. I'm over here. Focus on me.* It worked, and Enki turned his head towards Ryan, his beady eyes glaring.

"Is it just because you're too stupid to know better?" But Enki wasn't waiting for an answer, he was charging in. Ryan desperately threw up the barrier.

The barrier was a work of art, in Ryan's increasingly-not-so-humble opinion. It compressed a field of air around Ryan, forming a foot-wide field where the pressure became astronomically high - six times more intense than the pressure at the core of the Earth. Enki's blow slammed into it, and a shockwave erupted from the spot where the two met.

Enki slammed his fists against the barrier a few more times, his face turning red. He started to snarl with each blow. However, even with the added mass of the gauntlets, he didn't come close to breaking through it. Not that Ryan could maintain something of this magnitude for long. Like flight, keeping this air pressure barrier in place was a constant drain, and as soon as Ryan dropped it Enki would turn him into paste.

But the plan was contingent on the fact that Ryan wasn't fighting alone. Athena and Crystal moved in and managed to land a couple solid hits before Enki slammed his hands together, creating a pressure barrier of his own - an exact replica of Ryan's, and one he could maintain much longer than Ryan could.

"Nope!" Crystal chimed in, getting Enki's attention by continuing the earlier conversation. "It's because you're just too sodding ugly to be seen surrendering to, yeah? Just humiliating." While she spoke, Crystal created her own weapon, a sword with a unique, wavy design. The blade itself was sharpened ceramic.

Enki saw her create the sword and at the same time proved he hadn't gotten so stupid he couldn't see the basic pattern forming. Instead of charging Crystal, he whirled around to angle his charge towards Athena - who was now helpless against him. Athena managed to slip away from the first blow by mere inches. The second punch grazed her side and sent her tumbling back. Enki laughed as he seized the opportunity, leaping into the air to bring his fist down towards Athena's head. Athena barely managed to get the gauntlets up in time to block the blow. The sound of their gauntlets impacting rang through the air.

Athena's leg snapped. *Holy shit,* Ryan thought, *he hit her so hard the shockwave broke her leg*.

Can we really beat this?

Seeing his opportunity, Enki raised his fists again, but Crystal had caught up with him and slashed with the ceramic sword. It slid through the barrier like nothing was there and drew a line of bright red blood across Enki's back. He howled in pain and struck out with a backhand blow, striking Crystal across the face and sending her flying. She landed and didn't move.

She's fine, Ryan, she's fine. I hope.

Ryan watched Enki frown, and then a slow smile formed on the brute's lips. He'd figured out there was an exception into the barrier, one that allowed ceramics to slip through. *He knows how to kill me.*

Enki had an opening now, a chance to kill Athena. Ryan struck out, hard and fast with a twist to send a bolt of lightning Enki's way. The energy dissipated while trying to pass through the ultra-dense atmosphere of the pressure barrier, but it got Enki's attention. With Crystal unconscious he could stalk over towards Ryan as Ryan dropped to one knee from exhaustion.

"You know, Ryan," Enki said conversationally, "I'm so sick of you. I should have shot you in the goddamn head that first day. But now I'm going to fix that shit. Ishtar's unconscious, Athena can't walk. You're about to die, you annoying little shit. Any last words?"

Ryan tried to come up with some witty comeback, some action-movie one-liner that would prove his badassery - but at this point, it took every bit of energy Ryan could muster to maintain the barrier. All he could do was glare up at Enki, who was raising his hands. *Come on you bastard. Do it. Stop talking and stab me.*

"Too bad. Oh well." And with a twist, Enki formed a copy of the ceramic blade that Crystal had formed, the gauntlets wrapping around it - and as soon as his fists closed, Enki saw the curve of Ryan's mouth, saw the smile, and knew he had made a mistake.

Then Enki was engulfed in nuclear fire.

"It's called Californium-252," Ryan had said the night before. "It has the lowest critical mass of any isotope of any element."

Crystal nodded for him to go on, but Athena couldn't contain a sigh. "I know what some of those words mean."

"Sorry," Ryan said, unable to stop grinning, "Important version? You only need a little under three kilograms to make a nuclear explosion."

"We already covered that," Athena said with a frown. "We can't create a nuclear bomb. Too much power."

"Right, I get that," Ryan tapped his foot eagerly, "but what if we got Enki to assemble the Californium-252 for us?"

"How would we do that?" Athena's frown was starting to fade

"That's the part I don't know. Like I said, only thirty-two percent of a plan."

Athena sighed, but Crystal practically bounced in her chair. "We show him what to make. Have you all noticed what he's done since we started fighting him?"

"Uh...chains from the ground?"

"Moloch uses that one when he needs to escape." Crystal interjected with a motion for Ryan to continue.

"Okay," Ryan went on, "he fought your tornado, blasted you with lightning, threw me with wind, punched me a whole lot, raised a castle, and did Týr's solar death beam."

"Exactly!" Crystal stood up like that explained everything.

"Oh," Athena said, and Ryan noticed her eyes widening.

"Okay, you two got ahead of me. Bring it in for me?"

"The lightning bolt, the gusts of wind, those are common tricks. Everything special, everything unique? Love, he did that by copying some other god. He can use anyone's power, but he doesn't know how to adapt them, so he just copies them."

Ryan nodded excitedly. "Okay, now we're getting somewhere. But how do we use that?"

"Sword and gauntlets," Athena said, joining in the energy that was infusing the room. "How dense is Californium?"

"Pretty dense," Ryan said, "denser than lead, if I remember."

"Making our own weapons would normally be a stupid waste of power. But in this case, we show him how to make them, and we wait for him to blow himself up."

"Won't need to wait," Ryan responded. "As soon as he brings two halves a critical mass together, boom."

"Okay," Crystal said, frowning. "So we get him to make the sword and gauntlets, yeah? And then...what, we all die?"

Ryan needed a bit more searching to find the answer to that question. The internet was less forthcoming with what would be needed to contain a nuclear blast, since most research into surviving an explosion of that strength was about keeping the blast wave and heat and radiation out, not keeping the entire blast locked in.

"Well, this site says that you'd need pressure orders of magnitude greater than the Earth's core to hold it in place," he'd finally said, after an hour of searching.

"And you can trust everything you read on the internet, love?" Crystal's tone remained upbeat and teasing, but her brow furrowed. "I'm not exactly keen on getting nuked."

"Nor am I. Especially since you, Ryan, wouldn't come back. You're still Nascent. Enki would likely reform before we did, given his new strength," Athena added.

Ryan shrugged. "But it gives us the last piece of the puzzle! He'll make the gauntlets to show off to you, Athena. He'll mimic the barrier because it's a damn good barrier, and then we build in an exception...it's the only thing we have that's even remotely workable"

As Ryan watched now, the nuclear explosion expanded in a bubble of plasma and heat and radioactivity.

320

The high-pressure barrier bulged out, and for one horrified instant Ryan thought it would burst, that he'd done the math wrong or Enki hadn't made it strong enough, and he was about to find out first-hand what it felt like to be disintegrated by a nuke. *No no no.* Ryan threw out his hand like anything he could do would stop it.

Thankfully, the barrier held, and the explosion was reflected back in. It started to pulse there, the force ricocheting back and forth. *Almost...there,* Ryan thought. Without Enki maintaining it, it was easy to open a tiny hole in the top of the barrier, changing it from a nuclear bubble to nuclear rocket.

The effect was instant, and Ryan was thrown back as the bubble slammed into the ground. It shot down into the last part of the plan, a chasm they had dug before the battle had started. Ryan peered over the edge to see the sphere had already vanished into the darkness below, punching through the thin layer of rock and then again into the bedrock beneath that.

The island shook again as the last explosion went off, the barrier finally failing. *It worked,* Ryan thought, flopping onto the edge of the pit. *It actually worked.*

Athena's leg was broken. Crystal was unconscious. And now, next to the hole that marked Enki's radioactive tomb, Ryan's Hungers overtook him, and he fell asleep.

Chapter 29

Ryan woke up bit by bit, his consciousness piecing itself together as something shook him. He swatted his hand at the source, a pathetic blow that carried as much force behind it as the beating of a gnat's wings. "Five more minutes," he muttered, rolling over. The motion shifted the rocks that were stabbing into his back. They were now stabbing into his side instead, which wasn't much of an improvement. The pain forced his eye open.

Athena was looking down at him, her normally olive skin the sallow color of a dried corpse. Given her injuries, it was frankly amazing that she'd managed to crawl over here to wake Ryan up. "Get to your feet, Ryan Smith." Her words were hissed between teeth clenched in pain, and Ryan had to fight the urge to throw up when he saw the bone poking out of the skin of her leg.

"Athena." Ryan fought the exhaustion clawing at him. "Crystal?"

She nodded at the question. "I think she is alive. Ryan, you have to get Enki's nanoverse. We need to destroy it."

The statement was so ludicrous, Ryan felt a flash of annoyance. "We nuked him, Athena. I'm sure it's shattered into dust by now." He studied her face for a moment, saw the genuine concern that lurked beneath the pain, and felt himself grimace. "Right?"

"No." Athena was swaying where she stood, and it dawned on Ryan that he was not the only one clinging to alertness. "We have to take it into one of our nanoverses to destroy it. Where we're omnipotent. Nothing else will do it."

Ryan groaned in frustration. *We won,* he thought, knowing that it was stupid and childish, but he couldn't shake it. *We won. I'm supposed to be able to rest now.*

He looked again into Athena's eyes, and there he saw the response to his unvoiced complaint. *No, Ryan. We haven't won until the nanoverse is destroyed, until we can be certain he will not return.* He found himself nodding, both to agree with the thought and to prevent himself from dozing off. He rose to his feet, swaying drunkenly. He activated his divine sight, which was still working - he hadn't succumbed to his Hungers yet. "Keep an eye out. I'll go get it."

She gave him a weak thumbs-up, and Ryan walked to the edge of the pit that had swallowed Enki. It was a yawning abyss, far too deep for the faint light that managed to slip between the clouds to provide any illumination. He reached into his nanoverse, groping for a light source.

Thankfully, Daasti's utopia had plenty of light sources, and he pulled out a small orb. When Ryan activated it by giving it a solid squeeze, the light shone with the brightness of a high-end flashlight and the surface became sticky. He pressed it to his shirt, right over his heart, and when he pulled his hand away it stayed in place.

Without knowing how deep Enki's nuclear-powered descent had pushed him, calling rope out of his nanoverse could end up being far more effort than a simple twist. Ryan peered down into the chasm again. It was a yawning darkness, with only a single spec of glowing red coming from the heart of the pit, a single eye staring hatefully up at him. Ryan thought he had enough power left for what needed to be done. *Barely.*

He leapt in, twisting gravity to slow his descent. He didn't risk any changes to his direction - more twists meant more power, and already his Hungers were clamoring for attention. The light on his shirt glowed to try and counteract the darkness. It wasn't designed to illuminate an entire cavern, but it provided some vision in the inky blackness that surrounded him. The drifting was so gentle, it almost lulled him back to sleep.

Ryan smacked his thigh a few times, trying to force himself into alertness. *Finish this, Ryan. Finish this, damnit.* He was so weak that when he hit the cavern floor, even as slow as he was moving, he collapsed to the ground.

When he reached out to clamor towards that spot of red he'd seen before, he saw how withered his hand looked. His divine powers were fading. He was almost completely mortal. *If I lose power before I get the nanoverse, I'm dead.* It was a cold realization, but Enki's ultimate resting place would be red hot and radioactive still. Hot air was still pushing out of the hole, and it felt like sticking his face into an oven.

Don't think. Go. Push.

The red dot was a second pit, the one where Enki had buried himself. Ryan tumbled into it, slowing gravity again.

He emerged into a second cavern, this one a sphere of rock that still glowed from the heat and explosion.

Nuclear blasts were supposed to completely atomize matter caught at ground zero, but at Ryan's feet were slivers of blackened bone. Seeing them made him shiver in spite of the heat. *Enki was so strong it couldn't completely annihilate him.* That thought was logical, that thought was rational. Another one came immediately on its heels. *I killed him.*

In spite of everything, Ryan hadn't killed anyone until now. Mummies had been deanimated, manticores had been blasted, but an actual human life? Ryan still believed it was the only way. No matter what, Enki needed to die. it didn't change the fact that Ryan had helped killed someone who was guilty of believing he could save the world.

A hiss distracted him, reminded him his shoes were melting into the stone below. Ryan didn't have time to reflect right now. *Right. Nanoverse.*

He spotted the nanoverse laying among the radioactive stone. Or, to be more accurate, the nanoverses. To Ryan's eyes, the fusion looked less like cells dividing and more like one nanoverse was a cancerous mass growing out of the other. It reminded Ryan of photos of injures. They were sickening and appalling, but it was hard to look away. Something about it radiated a *wrongness* that made Ryan want to heave just from the sight of it. Ryan found himself wishing he could just leave the hideous thing down here, collapse the island on top of it and let tons of rock and seawater shut it away from the world.

Because that works so well in the movies, Ryan reminded himself as he bent down to grab it. If there was one thing Hollywood had taught Ryan, it was that leaving something dark and terrible buried beneath the Earth was a good way to make sure it became some future generation's problem. *And since you're immortal now, it would probably be your problem then, too.*

His fingers were still inches from it. He couldn't make himself touch it. Instead, Ryan pulled off what was left of his shirt and wrapped it around the nanoverse. He had to spend a bit more power to prevent the cloth from bursting into flames. *Stupid waste.*

As he stood there, a horrible fear swept over Ryan. *He'd burned too much power, he was mortal now. The hole above him had closed. There was no way out. He could feel the radiation seeping into his body, feel it causing his cells to break down. He tried to twist equations to open the rocks, to escape this prison, but his hands were swollen from the decay and his mind was sluggish.*

He got close, almost managed to force a gap open, but then Enki's bones rose up and stabbed into his calves. Ryan let out a howl of pain and dropped to his knees and suddenly he knew, he was certain that he would die here. He would die here, and his body would become as diseased and cancerous as that horrible twin nanoverse.

Stop it stop it stop it!

Ryan managed to get ahold of the panic and shove it back into his mind. He'd done it. He had it. The diseased nanoverse safely secured in his pocket, Ryan looked up to make sure he was standing under the hole that led to the surface. That confirmed, he reversed gravity's pull and just let himself float up and out of the radioactive cave.

He looked back as he ascended. Beneath them he saw the bone shards, the final pieces of evidence that Enki had once walked this world. They seemed, to Ryan's exhausted eyes, to twitch as their owner's nanoverse was taken away. It was almost as if they realized their last chance of ever being whole again was vanishing.

Then again, maybe they didn't. After all, they were just bones. The man they had belonged to was dead. When Ryan passed into sunlight again, the light globe attached to his chest dimmed back to flashlight levels. He felt a hand grab his ankle and tug him away from the pit, and once he was clear he let gravity return to normal, dumping him unceremoniously near Athena.

The cold air was immensely welcome after the oppressive heat below.

She gave him a questioning look, and he nodded, holding up the charred remains of his shirt that held that cancerous nanoverse. "Right here," he croaked.

A sigh of genuine relief escaped Athena's lips. "Good. The varcolaci withdrew while you were down there - passed right by us. I think Moloch is cutting his losses."

"I'm fine with him being a problem for another day. You?" He did his best to give her a confident smile, but the overwhelming desire to sleep tugged at him again.

Athena gestured to her leg, which was now splinted. "We fought enough for this day, I think," she managed to get out around the pain. Ryan thought of that bone jutting through the skin and then of the shards of Enki's bones left in the pit below.

"Yeah...I think we did enough for one day." The voice startled both of them. Ryan glanced over to see Crystal had made her way over to them. Her face was twisted with pain, although she attempted to keep a grin plastered across it.

"You okay?" Ryan asked, knowing the question was stupid but unable to help himself.

Crystal gave him a dismissive gesture. "I think that last blow broke my sodding hip. You look half dead, love, and Athena..." She pursed her lips. "Athena, you look three quarters of the way there. I don't want to know how bad I look. Let's...let's get back to the castle, yeah?"

Ryan opened his mouth to agree, but his body had enough. His Hungers were dominant, and right now Sleep was winning over all the others. He raised his fist to hit himself in the leg again, try to keep himself awake, but Athena reached out to grab the limb. "Rest, Ryan. We're safe."

Or at least, that's what Ryan thought she said. The word after "we're" had faded rapidly into darkness, and Ryan fell asleep.

***

As he slept, the nightmare vision from earlier repeated itself. Rising from the caverns, bone spears stabbing his legs, falling back into darkness. Alertness came to him like a tsunami wave crashing onto a lightless city, forcing him out of sleep and dousing him with a cold sweat. For a moment he thought it was just another symptom of the radiation poisoning, that he was still in that nuclear tomb. He reached up in a blind panic, expecting to see the swollen, bleeding limbs he had in the dream. Instead, he saw his normal arms and hands silhouetted against the galaxies of his nanoverse.

As his heart slowed down, he realized his stomach was demanding his attention and his throat was painfully dry. He was in his staging area. *Did I get myself here? Did someone let me in?*

Either way, he stumbled over to where he kept food and drink. Even though he knew it had just been a nightmare, he was still shaking as he took care of his Hungers. He considered just heading into his nanoverse fully right then and there, so he could destroy Enki's twin nanoverses. Instead, he got out of bed and walked towards his doorway, hoping to find Athena or Crystal awake.

He found both, the two of them in deep conversation at a table. Crystal was slumped back in her chair, looking half alert. Athena was still splinted, and had her arm and leg resting at awkward angles. Ryan smiled to see that both of them looked much better than when he had last seen them, the color returned to their faces and their movements much more animated. He noticed that Ashtaroth stood nearby, and instead of interrupting the goddesses' conversation, Ryan walked over to the demon. "Hey Ashtaroth. How long was I out?"

The demon didn't answer right away, instead glancing out a nearby window. "Pretty much all day. Crystal said you burned yourself pretty hard on top of a healthy dose of radiation and we shouldn't worry."

Ryan shuddered involuntarily at the realization that the radiation could have killed him and had really poisoned him. "Any sign of the enemy?" he asked, wanting to focus on anything else.

"No. We sent out scouts earlier today - they report the castle abandoned, with no sign of varcolac, lindworm, or Moloch." Ashtaroth smiled, a grim expression on the demon's face. "We also couldn't find Bast's body. But Enki is defeated, yes?"

Ryan could only nod.

"Then our half of the contract is filled," Astaroth said. "Do you still have the device Amy gave you?"

Ryan nodded.

"Good. My King will contact you with that when it's time to fulfill your half."

"I'll be ready. And - thanks. I know it was just a deal, but we couldn't have done it without you."

"You're welcome. I'll look forward to being able to say the same. Good luck." With that, he turned to collect what remained of his legion.

By their tone, Athena and Crystal's conversation was winding down. Ryan made his way over to them, pulling out the diseased dual nanoverse and putting it on the table in front of them.

The look they gave the tainted mass told Ryan they found it as repellent as he did. "So, this is why Enki was so strong."

Athena reached out to touch it, but pulled her hand back before actually reaching it. "It's...abominable."

Crystal nodded in agreement. "We should break it soon. Make sure Enki doesn't reform before we do, yeah?"

Athena and Ryan both voiced their agreement. "I'll do it," said Ryan, even though he didn't want to touch it again, "but I'll need one of you to tell me what to do."

The other two looked at him, but Ryan shook his head. "It was my idea, to nuke Enki. If someone has to end the life of every person in that horrible thing, it should be me." *I'll bear that burden.* The thought made it even worse.

After the other two thought for a few seconds, Crystal spoke up. "I'll just take care of it, love." She smiled at Ryan. "This thing is bloody horrible, but it's also unique. Best someone with more experience does it, yeah?" She grimaced. "Besides, I've done it before. You shouldn't have to ever deal with that guilt, love."

A part of him felt guilty at how quickly he agreed, but the whole process - both touching that foul thing and the idea of snuffing out that many lives, repulsed him so much that he was more than happy to pawn that duty off to anyone who would take it. By the look in her eyes, Athena felt much the same way.

Crystal reached into her nanoverse, pulling out of a pair of tongs. "No time like the present then, yeah? We can talk next steps once I'm done." When neither of her companions objected, she took the nanoverse up in the tongs and headed towards her doorway.

***

Once she was back in her staging area, Crystal called up a pillar to put the nanoverse on so she didn't have to carry it. *I'll be glad to be done with the damn thing.* Even though she hadn't touched it, she felt a desire to wash her hands after carrying it even that short distance.

Instead, she headed over to her console and dropped the staging area into her nanoverse's real space, finding herself in orbit around one of the dwarf stars that made up the majority of her nanoverse's remaining stellar mass. This particular star was on its way to burning out completely, and it barely provided any illumination - just a dull red glow. Too much longer and it wouldn't have enough mass to keep fusion running. The planets around it, which had once sustained life, were all now cold wastelands.

Life was gone from her nanoverse.

You're stalling, love, she chided herself. But to

destroy that blasphemy, she'd have to touch it, and Crystal found herself wanting to do literally anything else. She knew she had to, knew that if she didn't Enki would come back from the dead and all that effort would be for nothing...but there was such an air of wrongness around the thing that she didn't really think she could be blamed for wanting to avoid it.

Before she could dwell on it any longer, she strode over to the pillar and grabbed it. The surface felt slick and oily, and Crystal gagged and dropped it.

Come on, Crystal, you can do this. Her skin was still crawling from the sensation. Taking a deep breath, she reached out for it again. As soon as her fingers touched it, she started to heave. If she'd had anything in her stomach, she would have emptied it right there. As it was, she found herself gasping and retching.

She hadn't picked the nanoverse up, but was maintaining her grip on it. *Don't...don't let go.* She didn't think it was worth the time to try and acclimate to it. *This thing is so strong...I'm omnipotent, and I can barely hold it.*

Crystal tried not to think about what someone smarter than Enki would have been able to accomplish with it. *Time to end this.* She teleported herself out of her staging area, to the other side of the dying star, and then begun to squeeze Enki's nanoverses between her hands. She was shaking and fighting her stomach's attempt to escape through her esophagus. It was the same gesture she would use to draw power out of her own nanoverse, but instead of compressing under her grip it was rock solid. She kept applying pressure, feeling it begin to crack under her hands, the fractures spreading across the cancerous nanoverse with an agonizingly slow speed.

Her physical strength was about as relevant for her task as the color of her eyes. What mattered was her power, her near omnipotence. The same strength she would use to send her entire nanoverse spiraling into a Big Crunch also allowed her to shatter a foreign reality once it was within her domain. But that omnipotence wasn't complete, it was still "only" near omnipotence, so shattering two realities at once required actual effort and time on her part.

It was a relief to see the cracks begin to spread across the surface of the twin nanoverses. Now that she was sure she *could* destroy it, she found herself wondering what this looked like from the inside. Did giant rifts appear in the sky, forming slowly over thousands of years? Or did it happen in an instant - the universe going from normal to fracturing like stained glass before shattering into infinite shards?

It was a useless question. If she ever got the chance to see for herself, it would mean she was about to die. With a final push of effort, she felt the twin nanoverses crumble to dust.

The nearby star, the dying red dwarf, flared to life at the exact moment the corrupt nanoverse died. It started to glow as brightly as it had in its prime, but the light wasn't normal red or even yellow - instead it shone a deep, unnatural green color, like a sickly emerald.

Oh yeah, I'm definitely doing a bloody Crunch now. What the sodding hell was that? That green hue was already fading, and Crystal was relieved to see it die away, but after that weird side effect she thought the best option would be to wipe the whole nanoverse clean and start fresh. *It's wrong. As wrong as that damn nanoverse. I'm so glad there's no more life here so I can wipe the slate clean.* Not trusting it, she didn't take her eyes off the fading verdant star as she started to set a Big Crunch into motion.

Maybe if she had, she would have noticed the same color had spread to every other star in her nanoverse.

Chapter 30

Aftermath

Crystal had been gone for a handful of seconds when she walked back out of her nanoverse. She had a haunted look to her eyes and was shaking slightly. Ryan and Athena had barely had enough time to feel relief the dual nanoverse was gone. Crystal didn't seem to share in their relief. Her omnipresent smile was drawn and didn't quite reach her eyes.

"Are you alright?" Athena asked, and Ryan was glad to know she saw it too.

Crystal shrugged. "I just snuffed out two nanoverses worth of life and started the Big Crunch on my own, love. I'd have to be a sodding psychopath to be perfectly alright, yeah?"

"Fair enough," Ryan said, his eyes drifting to Athena. By her frown, she wasn't fully buying Crystal's explanation either. "As long as you're sure."

The nod she gave them was a bit too eager as she changed the subject. "We've got a lot of work to do still, loves, so I figured this was the last chance I'd get to do the Crunch for a bit. After all, we still need to find a loophole in this whole 'end the world' business."

"Right." It had been so long since he last worried about the impending apocalypse that the reminder was like a bucket of cold water being splashed across his face. He shook his head. "I'll be honest; I have absolutely no good ideas about how to do that."

Athena perked up at that, and for a moment Ryan dared to hope she would have some miracle cure. Instead she asked, "Well, we can work with bad ideas, perhaps improve them."

"Sorry, I'm out of those too. I'm guessing you two

are in the same boat?" Their looks told him everything he needed to know, and he let out a deep sigh as Crystal took back her vacated chair. "Guess that would be too easy. Crystal, how long do we have?"

"Hate to have to say this, love, but no way to know for sure. We'll know when it's close - the sun will start pulsing - but that could be in a matter of weeks or a matter of years." She shook her head, a clearing gesture, and her smile slowly became more natural. "And best part is, Moloch and Bast are still out there, and hells only know what those two wankers are up to."

Athena's lips tightened into thin white lines. "I actually think I can top that."

A groan escaped Ryan's mouth, and she looked at him, a glimmer of sympathy behind her eyes. Crystal just regarded him curiously as he slumped in his chair saying, "We won. We should be celebrating! Going back to that bar and getting hammered or something."

"I know." Athena regarded him steadily, "and I think we should after we're done. But it is important to debrief after a victory, while the details are still fresh."

He looked over at Crystal, but she was nodding in agreement with Athena. He let out another breath of air. "Okay, hit me." The punch Athena landed on his shoulder had no force behind it, and the gesture got an appreciative laugh out of Ryan.

"Glad to see you haven't forgotten how to be amused. Unfortunately, the worse news?" Ryan motioned for her to go on; putting his nose in the air and every ounce of royal arrogance into the gesture he could manage. It got a snort from Crystal and the ghost of a grin from Athena, though that vanished pretty much the instant she began to speak.

"I don't think Enki taught the others how to merge nanoverses. He was too power hungry for that. But I do think that we have to assume Bast and Moloch both know how. Worst case scenario has to take priority over what we hope happened."

Ryan wanted to slam his head into the table, but instead leaned forward and rested his face in his palms.

"Christ, Athena, you weren't kidding when you said you could make it worse."

"I know."

Crystal spoke up, "But she's right, love. It's a bloody shame that we have to worry about it, but we've got to find out what they're up to."

"Can't we have Nabu send the other gods messages?" The silence that followed lasted long enough for him to pull his head out of his hands. Both Crystal and Athena were giving him nearly identical patient looks. Beyond patient, really. The expression was the exact same for both of them, a face that said *We understand why you're not thinking clearly right now, but you'll feel better if you figure out why that's a terrible idea without us needing to spell it out for you.*

It was a very specific expression, but once you've gotten that face, you'll recognize it anywhere.

After he had time to think, he caught up with them, and was glad to have figured it out for himself. "You're worried about other gods knowing it's possible."

"Bingo," Crystal said, leaning forward slightly. "Even if they don't know *how*, they might figure it out if they know it's not a waste to *try*."

"So if we can't warn them, what do we do?" Ryan did his best to keep the despair out of his voice. This whole thing was starting to feel increasingly hopeless.

"Well, we kill two birds with one stone." Both Athena and Ryan looked at Crystal, and the smile made her eyes gleam. "We tell them it's time to get off their arses and get to work. We head out and find them, be they on Earth or in their own realms. We hit up Asgard, Olympus, Kunlun, Tir na Nog, Mictlan, Penglai, Takama-ga-hara - all of them, every bloody one." She actually stood up in her excitement.

"We tell them it's the End of the World, and they sat out round one, but round two won't give them a chance for that. They're going to have to take a side because you don't get to just sit on your thumbs when it's the Apocalypse, yeah? And then, once they sign on, we ask them for help in finding a way to do it that doesn't require six billion deaths. One of them is going to have an idea or know where we can look for one."

Ryan felt the tension begin to ease. He didn't know what half those places where or how to get there, but at least it was a proactive step. Athena nodded in a more measured, calmer agreement. "So...party first, then we head to recruit?" Ryan asked.

"Sounds like a plan to me. Athena, you in?" Athena voiced her agreement and Crystal continued. "Great. Come on, loves! First round's on me." She practically skipped towards her nanoverse, and Ryan rose to follow. Athena put a hand on his arm as he did, and he looked at her.

"You sense it too. Something's off about her."

Ryan flicked his eyes towards Crystal's doorway, confirming it was already closed. "Yeah, I do. Any ideas why?"

Athena didn't actually say no, but her eyes spoke volumes. "I suggest we keep a careful eye on her."

"I'm not too worried about it. After all, if it was really important, Crystal would tell us, right?" He watched Athena closely, and felt his confidence drain away. "Right?"

"I don't think it's worth risking."

"Fair enough." Ryan sighed, then shook his head to clear it and gave Athena a grin that was only slightly forced. "But not tonight, Athena," he said, pulling her to her feet, "tonight we drink and dance and celebrate winning, okay?"

That got a genuine smile out of her. "I think that's an excellent plan." Ryan offered her his arm, and she slid hers through with a wink.

They headed towards his nanoverse, not worrying about anything other than how to enjoy the night as best they could.

Epilogue

Getting the civilian news helicopters to leave the area had been easier than anyone could have expected. In Rear Admiral Dale Bridges' experience, reporters valued getting "the scoop" over their own safety to the point of insanity. In this one case, however, telling them this had become a joint USA-Canada operation to contain the threat from these alleged "gods" had gotten them to clear the area with a previously unseen haste. They'd seemed almost relieved to have a reason to comply.

At least we weren't too late this time. With the island being uninhabited, the Rear Admiral had decided to hold back. As far as he was concerned, everyone would be better off if these two groups punched each other to death on some godforsaken island.

For their part, these gods didn't seem to even notice the change to military helicopters and drones. Didn't seem to be aware of the massive force that had gathered in the water and air and on nearby islands. *Or maybe they did,* he thought. *Maybe they did and just didn't think we were relevant.*

Dale shook his head. *And to think I was starting to doubt.* After talking to the Reverend, after watching how the Antichrist had fought, he'd begun to wonder if maybe the Reverend had a point. Maybe this man wasn't the actual Antichrist. The man the "Church of Adversity" claimed to worship made more sense.

Then he'd watched as Ryan had summoned an army of demons to fight by his side. *I never should have questioned. This man is the Antichrist, and the others are some kind of demon.* Maybe there was some war in hell, the way the Church of Adversity claimed. Maybe Enki and his ilk worked for one side, and Ryan for the other.

It didn't matter. What he was sure of was that they were not gods, and that they had to be stopped. They had to be sent back to the pit they had spawned from.

To ensure he could effectively contain the battle, he'd been given command of a whole new breed of aircraft carrier. It was a Hive Class carrier that carried no pilots but swarms of drones. The vessel was so advanced, so experimental that it had no official name, just DARPA-17.

Beyond the drones, the ship's three nuclear reactors could generate a plasma field that was the closest thing to a science fiction force field the real world was likely to get before the End Times, and the drones had been equipped with both missiles and experimental Directed Energy Weapons. The Admiral had spent the entire battle hoping the so-called gods would spill out into the ocean, that he would be authorized to find out if his faith could slay demons when backed by the greatest weaponry the United States of America had developed.

It had not, and now his men were joining the Canadians in scouring the island to find out more about what had happened. This was part of the joint operation. Canada was a military power, stronger than most people gave them credit for. However, in the face of unholy war breaking out on their soil, they'd turned to their neighbors and asked if maybe they had anything up their sleeve that would possibly help against the unknown. Like the neighbor knocking on your door, asking if you could spare a cup of sugar and a three-billion-dollar piece of military hardware.

The USA had been happy to oblige, sending two Nimitz class carriers and the one operational DARPA-17. They'd done so with a smile on their face because there would be a time after the battle when cleanup had to happen, when the dust settled, and the good old US of A intended to seize every asset they could to prepare for war against a foe they barely understood.

"Sir?" The Admiral was startled out of his reverie by

the younger man's voice. "Some of the Marines have returned. They have something." Bridges dismissed the man and headed to see what they had recovered from the battlefield.

The spoils were in two boxes that had previously carried equipment. This pleased Admiral Bridges, because it meant the Canadians didn't know they'd recovered these. The smaller box of the two contained a small black stone, perfectly round, about the size of a golf ball. It was warm to the touch, and looking closer Bridges could see stars in it, like it was a hole into space.

In the other box was the body of the young woman who had claimed to be the Egyptian goddess Bast. Bridges remembered her being pretty enough on the news, but this was a frostbitten corpse, one with dried blood caking her foot and abdomen. He frowned at the sight, noticing one oddity.

"What are those?" He pointed at her wrists.

One of the Marines stepped forward and saluted. "Sir. They are zip-ties, sir."

The Admiral's frown deepened. "I'm sure there's a good reason you restrained a dead women, Captain..."

"Evans, Sir. Roger Evans. And yessir. The dead woman has a pulse, sir, but no other signs of life."

After already deepening once, the Admiral's frown seemed like it surely had reached its limit, yet at this news it extended further. "I see." He looked at the half-frozen body again, the half-frozen body that was clearly not breathing but apparently still had a beating heart, and shuddered. "Seal it up. We'll let the eggheads deal with it." *I hope this is what the doctor needs to complete her work.*

"Yessir."

The Admiral turned to head back to the bridge. It was time to take the DARPA-17 back to American waters with this precious cargo. Let the Canadians have whatever scraps remained on the island where so-called gods used nuclear weapons against each other - something told Rear Admiral Bridges that they already had the greatest prize.

Next time these demons claiming to be gods go to war, he thought, feeling a sensation of certainty sweep over him, *they'll find we mere mortals won't just stand by the sidelines.*

We'll show them that we cannot be ignored.

Acknowledgements

This book is the culmination of a year of writing at a breakneck speed. Even with that, I never could have done it without the support from several people. First of all credit must be given to Laura Beamer, my dearest friend and long-suffering editor, who has put up with months of going over my prose and showing me how to make it sing, and that's after years of helping me through my learning process of becoming a writer. She's done an incredible job of keeping me on track and reigned in, and without her this book would not be nearly as good.

Second of all some particular reddit users are owed particular thanks. Funique has been providing me a ton of line edits on the first draft, taking a huge burden of dealing with my typos off my editor. SilverPheonix41 has been a huge aid in making sure the table of contents for the reddit is up to date and accurate, which is great because I'm terrible at keeping track. Ecstaticandinsatiate was an immense help in lettering the cover art, and Inorai had been amazing for me to bounce ideas off of, and have listened to me gripe about how *hard* writing can be more times than I can count.

Third, I have to acknowledge my amazing cover artist, Iris Hopp. You can find more of her work at http://www.irishopp.com. She did a fantastic job with my cover and navigating my fumbling attempts to describe what I wanted.

Finally, and very importantly, there are my Patrons over on Patreon, who have been instrumental in keeping me motivated. I love all my fans, and you all are great for keeping me on task and reassuring me that I don't suck nearly as much as I fear I do.

$1:Ari Plessner, Andrew Marino, Steve Meckman, Youri, Ashlyn Jacobs, Brad Massett, Justin Brady, Stefan Heimersheim, Thomas Howard, José, Scott Andre, Melissa S. Caitlyn T Nummerdor, James Paik, Luis M, Jacob, John, Matt Barnes, C, Blake Haulbrook, Andrew Wasson, Reese Delgrande, Ben Lagar, Rob, Varun Malik, Nathaniel

Wardwell, Matthew Nicolas, Zackary Hoyt, Callum Watson, Nathan Monfils, Jared Clark, Jarred Hull, Meg Momohara, Michael Abdoo, Tyler Morgan, Bob, Edward, Kasper Laitinen, Koen Watcher, Rosella Gugliotta, Iris Hartshorn, Brandon Shafran, Adam Kdonain, Shelby Lanie.

$3: Anne Janina Patolla, Caleb Rheam, Nicolai Groves, Jonathan Kirk Kuerschner II, Markus Hamann, Shalth, Raphael Hammerli, Pierre Lucchini, Kim Roy, Micah Kroeze, Corin, Mat Carington-Mackenzie, Morgan Whiterabbit, Carlos Dominguez, Randomdrawing, Richard LaBrecque, Andrew Frey, Ethan Fesmire, J L, Todd Whaley, Ace, Tanner Robert Muro, Jodie Francis, SirGregor, Sam Lacey, Michael Paul, L Yaniv, Daniel Enrique Serna Guevara, Kaeli McAlister, John Hollingsworth, Daniel Rocker, Jacob Palmer, Kai Ove Lynvær, Hurkan Asmaci, Boop, Eugene Lorman, Colton Ranstrom, dapinkone, Cameron Paulsen, Merlin, Diane Tam, Brittany Shane, Rajin Shahriar, Ivan Stroganov, Adam Bolton, Isabella Huges, Tsogt Oliver ENKHBAYASGALAN, Ryan Deckard, Mikel Ward, Nick Clifford, Eric Spain, Ryan Diaz, Matt Willis, Pierce Boucher, Sinkleir, Mortiz Naujoks, Holly Keast, Billy Kwong, Anton Espholm, Lars Hoekseme, Anthony Guy, AbsolutePotato, Jono Chadwell, Steven Hall, Dallas Nelson, Guilbaud, Mikal Waage Gismervi, Suzanne McNeil, Matt Clury, John Reed, Darin Stockman, Craig M, Luke Peavy, Neel Trivedi, Dan Cowell, Aaron Fryer, Will Kenerson, David Kay, Linus J. Holm, Francesco Barbera, Janis Svilans, Daniel Kauppi (Kissaget), Maya, Krista Knight, Cosmo Knox, Bart Smeets, Thanatos Lin, Derrik Tran, Aleksander Høgh, Noel Toh, Kara Miller, Emilie Hørdum Valente, Justine Lipe, nicolas j nosek, Emtasticbombastic, Chris On, Paul Thomson, Trevor Bisson, Chris Franklin, Fabian Seidlmeier, Tim Schmidt, kattattak, Mikail Khan, Travis Lovelady, Dodoni, Rajeev Iyer, Timothy Halpenny, Allante, Zack Griffin

$10: Dennis van der Slik, Kyle Bernzen, Bryce, Austin Reynolds, William Piper, Siri Oaklander, Justin Steel, Ivan Smirnov, Noah Nelson

$20: James Primmer, O$I, Dakota Jordan, Ryan McPherson, Stefan Oshinski, Micah McFadden, Spencer, Dorian Snyder, Rachel, Issac Pebble.

More of the author's work can be found at http://www.smallworlds.blog in first draft form, and the author's website can be found at alexraizman.com

Front cover art by Iris Hopp

ISBN: 9781983249402
Imprint: Independently published

29881675R00208

Printed in Great
Britain
by Amazon